Tristopolis Chasm

JOHN MEANEY

Nulapeiron Press

ISBN-13: 978-1-8381217-4-7

BOOKS BY JOHN MEANEY

Paul Reynolds series
On The Brink

Case books (Case & Kat)
Destructor Function
Strategy Pattern
Concurrent Execution

Josh Cumberland series
Edge
Point

Donal Riordan (Tristopolis) series
Bone Song
Dark Blood (UK title) Black Blood (US title)
Tristopolis Requiem
Tristopolis Howling
Tristopolis Revenge
Tristopolis Chasm

Pilots universe
Absorption (Ragnarok 1)
Transmission (Ragnarok 2)
Resonance (Ragnarok 3)
Paradox (Nulapeiron 1)
Context (Nulapeiron 2)
Resolution (Nulapeiron 3)
To Hold Infinity

Standalone
New Jerusalem
Whisper of Disks (short story collection)

PRAISE FOR JOHN MEANEY

"A brilliant, inventive writer." *The Times*

"A spectacular writer. He makes SF seem all fresh and new again." Robert J. Sawyer, Hugo Award-winning author

"Cumberland leaps off the page, a trained killer whose anger and grief at his daughter's condition is brilliantly portrayed; the depiction of his simmering rage, barely held in check, and how he channels it, provides a masterclass in characterisation." *The Guardian*, reviewing Edge (Josh Cumberland book 1)

"What starts off as a simple missing persons enquiry develops into a full-blown coup against a fascist state... Set in a Britain extrapolated from today's violent streets, yet still highly recognisable, Edge is the first in what will hopefully be a long running series." *Total Sci-Fi*, reviewing Edge (Josh Cumberland book 1)

"Within five pages...I was completely hooked... the perfect blend of action and science fiction... I can only hope that there will be more." *The Eloquent Page*, reviewing Point (Josh Cumberland book 2)

"I absolutely don't want to live in the world [Meaney] has created. I didn't want to in Edge (the first book in the series) and I most certainly don't want to now. I do, however, want to read about it. It's relentless and gripping, with a brilliant balance between the personal and the political." *BiblioBuffet*, reviewing Point (Josh Cumberland book 2)

"Absorption is the best hard science fiction I've read this year, well written, exciting, mysterious, full of interesting characters and ideas..." *The Times*, reviewing Absorption (Ragnarok book 1)

"...the world building is phenomenal and the pace as chapters switch from time zones is just right, keeping the tension levels up. The female characters are particularly strong and literally jump off the page, particularly the WWII code breaker Gavriela. The novel is also steeped in historical accuracy and authenticity." *Terror-Tree.co.uk*, reviewing Transmission (Ragnarok book 2)

"Resonance is a book driven by big ambitions. Meaney has penned a story that aims to be epic beyond even the level of Dune or similarly famed series. Furthermore, the amount of research that has gone into the book adds a surprising degree of credibility..." *Starburst Magazine*, reviewing Resonance (Ragnarok book 3)

"Meaney's creepy death-haunted world lingers in the mind long after the book is closed... a smart and spooky read." *The Times*, reviewing Bone Song (Donal Riordan book 1)

DEDICATION

To my bro, Colm

vi

ONE

There were better things to do with a loaded Magnus than use it as a paperweight, but Donal was fed up with filling in his accounts, and putting the pistol on top of the vellum sheets made some kind of statement about his mood. Not exactly a welcome sign for visitors.

And he could in fact hear footsteps in the hallway outside: three sets heading this way, and maybe another three further behind, still ascending the stairs.

Pebbled glass filled the upper half of his office door, the metallic crimson lettering of *Riordan Investigations ULC* showing in reverse image. To Donal's left, the window overlooked a busy street, and the honking of horns nine storeys below would have been audible even to a redblood.

Maybe someone had parked in the reserved spaces in front of the building. Someone who didn't care about annoying taxi or delivery drivers.

Someone who needed to hire a PI, perhaps.

I do need new clients.

The accounts were taking time to fill in because he hated paperwork. There hadn't been that many payments to record.

But new clients, when they turned up at his office, usually arrived alone.

Donal shrugged his shoulders and tilted his head from side to side, then settled with his hands palms-down on the desktop, right hand close to the Magnus. He could tell by the sensation at his throat that his tie remained knotted okay.

Everything to professional standards.

Silver runes newly inscribed by Ingrid Johannsdóttir on the inside of the door glimmered softly, then faded. That told him only what he knew already: his approaching visitors carried weapons but with no immediate intent to use them.

Something else: the runes also hinted at the use of hex, either defensively or as hex-impregnated rounds; and with luck that meant a rich nervous client with professional bodyguards.

No knock, but the door opened.

"Hello," said Donal.

Two stone men in business suits walked in, stopped, and looked around. One of the petrimorphs pointed at the Magnus on Donal's desk. The other continued to scan the office.

"Please put your firearm away," said the one who was pointing.

The other gestured towards the window. "Defensive runes outside."

"Yes," said the first. "Good."

Back in the day, Donal had travelled on a troop transport across the Penumbral Sea, along with a detachment of petrimorph infantry. By the standards of those guys, these two were downright chatty.

"Let me guess." Donal kept his hands in place. "Rich boss, has a job for me."

"Yes," answered the petrimorphs in unison.

"Alright."

Still sitting, Donal pushed the Magnus into the shoulder holster beneath his left armpit, inside his jacket. Leaving his jacket unbuttoned, he leaned back in his chair.

He called out: "I'm decent, honey."

The lumpy-faced man who entered looked unamused. "Wise guy."

"Happy to help," answered Donal. "You the boss?"

Wide lapels, broad pinstripe, heavy fabric on the suit, a pale deathblossom in his left lapel. A shiny wormsilk tie, silver as a switchblade, and thumbnail-sized human skulls for cufflinks, except they looked like carved knucklebones, not actual shrunken heads.

"What do you think?"

Donal thought this was the kind of guy who'd look good on the other side of a cell door or cuffed to a table in one of the interrogation rooms in Police HQ on Avenue of the Basilisks.

But Tristopolis PD was no longer Donal's employer, and clients weren't exactly clamouring to get in.

He said: "I think that auditions go both ways. Your boss has a job for me, and you want to check me out. Fair enough. But I'm picky about the jobs I take on."

So far the best payers had been two insurance companies. They'd given Donal multiple assignments during the ten months he'd been in business.

In his more cynical moments, he thought maybe crooks abounded everywhere, corporate offices included, and some just acted more politely than others. But the companies who hired Donal performed the function they were supposed to, as far as he could tell. Bureaucratic callousness happened by accident, not design.

He hoped he wasn't fooling himself.

"Picky." The lumpy-faced man looked around the office. "I can tell."

Maybe the guy felt nervous beneath the cruel persona. Or maybe he didn't.

"My name is Donal Riordan." He stayed sitting and kept his hands in place. "What's yours?"

"Axelson."

In his redblood days, Donal might have blinked. "You work for Talon."

Axelson was nicknamed the Axe because the underworld lacked poetic originality, or because anything else would prove unnecessary: the moniker said it all.

On the other hand, Konrad Talon – Axelson's boss – had no need for intimidating labels. People's hearts tended to beat faster if they heard his name.

Unless they led ordinary lives so insulated from criminal wrongdoing that they would recognise no name from those parts of society: the kind of person who might walk past a crime without seeing what was happening.

Some people lived that way. Maybe even most of them.

"Is the boss here with you?" said Donal.

"You think Mr Talon would come to a dump like this?"

"Far too classy."

That could refer to either Talon or the office. Axelson's eyes slowly closed and opened. Perhaps he understood the ambiguity; perhaps he didn't.

"It's a sensitive job." Axelson's voice rasped as he spoke.

He seemed to mean what he said.

Donal glanced with deliberation from one petrimorph to the other. They stood like statues dressed in suits that fitted better than Donal's. Axelson gave the tiniest of nods.

Whatever was going on, it was sensitive enough not to talk about here, in front of street soldiers. No matter how well they dressed.

A problem, therefore, that couldn't be solved by ruthlessness and violence. For those things, Talon didn't need outside talent.

It occurred to Donal that the other members of the party had taken up positions in the hallway outside. Guarding Axelson?

Or just a show of force for Donal's sake?

"I won't surrender my weapon," said Donal. "Or submit to a blindfold. None of that stuff."

"You'll do what—" Axelson paused. "Alright, Riordan. You got it."

It told Donal something, but he wasn't sure what, exactly.

"Is this a family matter?" Donal was stabbing a guess.

"I… Sure."

Axelson had been going to say he didn't want to discuss it here, or that his boss would fill in the details, something like that. Donal nodded.

"I'll go along with you," he said. "No guarantees, but I'll hear your boss out. Good enough?"

"Awkward guys, I don't like." Axelson's lips thinned. "But yes-sir, no-sir ain't gonna get this job done."

"Hades, Axelson. Is that the nicest thing you've said to anybody?"

"Or maybe this ain't gonna work out after all."

"But maybe it will." Still seated, Donal slowly buttoned his jacket. Just one button, but enough to hamper a quick draw. "Sign of faith, okay?"

After a moment, Axelson gave a twitch of the mouth.

"You ain't failed the audition," he said. "But you ain't passed it yet."

Donal held back from making a smart remark. Zombie self control.

"Likewise," he said.

Perhaps that sounded a bit smart, but Axelson looked satisfied. "Let's go."

Donal stood up and followed Axelson out, while the petrimorph pair fell into step behind him. In the hallway, all three lookouts turned and headed towards the fossilised ebony stairs.

Footsteps clattered.

Am I making a mistake?

You never knew. Maybe this would prove to be an easy job.

Street soldiers taking him to some unspecified location: what could go wrong?

Around halfway down, on the fourth-floor landing, a pale wraith extruded her head and shoulders from the wall, took in the sight of Donal's companions, and slipped back inside the stonework without a word.

Wonderful.

Just another day at the office.

TWO

As always, the outdoor world looked darker and felt cooler than indoors. Two black chitin-covered saloons were waiting at the kerb, facing against the traffic. A purple taxi was pulling away further along the street.

It splashed quicksilver from a puddle onto a startled woman who almost gave vent to shrill invective, then stopped when she caught sight of the men surrounding Donal.

Maybe they were the reason the taxi had taken off so fast.

Do they know something I don't?

He hadn't read the news because he'd come in early, before Darkly Dave opened his newsstand around the corner. Maybe something had happened.

And maybe I'm slipping.

Movement, high up at the edge of his visual field. Against the backdrop of the dark, always-purple sky, a municipal scanbat slowly glided, following the line of the street.

Tartarus Stillway at its dingy best.

"Not afraid to be seen?" Donal gestured upward with his chin.

"With a lowlife like you?" said Axelson. "My reputation can take it."

"Thanatos." Maybe the Axe was smarter than Donal had thought.

One of Axelson's men – standard human with stone implants for eyes: a sniper – held open the rear door of the lead saloon car.

"Alright," said Donal.

And slid inside, moving across on the seat, expecting Axelson or the guy holding the door to follow him in. Instead, the door swung shut with a click.

"Lovely day for it," he added, addressing the driver up front and the wide-shouldered man sitting next to her, riding shotgun.

The driver turned to reveal blasted eye sockets, black and red tissue forming concave pits. She smiled with long, not-quite-pointed teeth.

"Yes-s-s," she said.

"I'm honoured," Donal told her, and meant it. "Thank you for driving me."

She held herself still.

Perhaps, before her eyes were ruined and burnt away, she might have blinked.

After a moment she turned back to face the front, twisted the bone key in the steering column, and caused the engine to growl into life.

Donal could feel the strong vibration through the seat beneath him, sensing the heaviness of the chitin-armoured saloon and the power of its engine.

If Talon could employ a senior witch or female mage as a driver – the distinction wasn't always clear – then he might be more formidable than Donal had thought.

Even more formidable.

He knew only one other person able to see normally despite the absence of actual eyes: his sort-of-friend, Mage Lamis. And Lamis was a senior mage, although considered something of a renegade by the powers-that-be at Mordanto and elsewhere.

Beside the woman at the steering-wheel – Donal made up his mind provisionally: witch, not mage – a big guy sat shotgun. Immense shoulders, thick neck to match, and a shiny pale-blue shaven scalp.

Inside each earlobe, a speck of emerald fire blazed. Living fire, tiny but alive.

And captive.

Donal had never seen anything like them.

Also, something had been bothering him about the car itself, and now it occurred to him: no driver's mirror, no wing mirrors outside.

Maybe this witch could see in all directions without needing to turn her head, but could this car really be designed or customised for her use alone?

Just what kind of workforce did Talon employ?

There was a pause in the oncoming traffic and the witch slipped the car into gear and crossed the lane and slid into the flow of cars on the opposite side of the street. It was smoothly done. Only a single abbreviated toot on a car horn signalled an objection.

The other saloon, with Axelson on board – Donal twisted in his seat to look back – took up position immediately behind.

Reflections from yellow-lit windows slid across that car's windscreen, making it hard to see inside. Donal turned to face front once more.

It bothered him a little that five men had accompanied Axelson, a tight squeeze for one saloon car – in Fortinium they'd call it a sedan – and he suspected that one or two of the men had remained behind.

If they were hoping to burgle his office, they were likely to meet disappointment. Breaking the defences wouldn't prove easy, and the contents of his filing cabinet hardly justified the trouble.

He wondered if he ought to feel afraid.

Soon enough they were speeding along a busy corkscrew tunnel in Knottingham Twistway, lit by caged flamewraiths and echoing with the sounds of engines, of tyres on tarmac.

Something about the motion caused Donal's eyelids to droop and his chin to lower, and he hadn't expected to relax but the car's warmth enveloped him like a soft, thick blanket and tension flowed down through his body and into nothingness because all was well and this felt fine and he could let his worries go.

Ease and stillness welcomed him.

And then he woke up.

Not from a natural nap.

Sleep trance, and I didn't even realise.

The car had come to a stop inside a shadowy space punctuated with dark, carved pillars and softly glowing flamesprites. This could be anywhere: some old temple or just an underground parking garage in one of the city's baroque, centuries-old buildings.

"Time to get out," said the witch.

The front passenger seat was empty. The big man stood outside, near one of the dark pillars, staring into the shadows.

Donal inhaled, then answered: "Yes. Thank you."

The witch at the wheel nodded.

She could have made him wake up feeling dreadful – he took it for granted that she had put him under for the duration of the ride – but if anything he felt refreshed and energised.

This witch had done him a favour.

He pushed down the polished-bone door handle, opened the door, and slid out of the car.

Words came from nowhere. "Mr Riordan. How good of you to come."

It sounded like a child's idea of how a crime boss talked. The voice, artificially deepened, had come from empty air, maybe nine feet in front of him.

Not Talon.

What the Hades is going on?

He took a step forwards.

And fell into total darkness… that lasted only a moment.

Blueness, a sapphire-blue brilliance, surrounded him like ice-cold fire, blazing bright enough to blind, or so it seemed; but Donal's eyes felt fine while his sense of balance flipped around and around: enough to nauseate a redblood but not him, not these days, and besides he'd travelled like this before.

Mage portal.
The brilliance winked out, and he was standing somewhere else.
"Impossible," he said.
Soft girlish laughter sounded.

THREE

"My name is Susan," said the creature. "And Konrad Talon is my father."

"Alright," said Donal.

Her white-skinned face shone palely, but she wasn't a zombie.

Those heart-shaped features sat inside a foot-thick cowl of slug-like flesh within an outer shell of speckled chitin: the inches-wide gap between her human face and the chitin's edge revealed the soft gelatinous flesh within, trimmed with a soft pulsating layer of orange in a shade that Donal thought looked pretty.

"Was that your voice I heard just now," he added, "when I got out of the car?"

She sighed, did the creature known as Susan Talon. "No one must know my father is missing, Mr Riordan. There'd be so much trouble if that happened. So yes, I disguised my voice when I cast it through the portal."

Her robe looked thick and soft: black and burgundy velvet, edged with a brocade whose golden threads caught reflected flamesprite light. It was cut especially for her, with three sleeves on either side, for her arms looked standard human apart from the fact that she had six of them.

She sat in a kind of curved throne and Donal wasn't sure she could stand up straight, but if she did, she would reach maybe thirteen feet in height. Her robe covered what might have been her feet or tail.

"And there's no one ready and suitable to inherit the family business?" Donal pitched his voice softly, despite the unkind words.

"I'm not naïve, Mr Riordan, but it's not my father's organisation or even his legitimate enterprises that interest me. I want my father back, and if his organisation gets dissolved overnight, I really don't care."

The air felt a little chilly against Donal's skin, which meant that to a redblood this place would feel icy.

But when he looked around, the wood-and-bone panelled walls suggested cosiness, despite the impressive size of the room: maybe two-thirds the volume of his and Mel's boxing gym, in the deconsecrated temple that they owned.

Here, bookcases against the walls contained volumes with crinkled spines indicating they'd actually been read. A credenza stood parallel to a long couch and seemed to act as a desk. Charts and intricate carved-bone slide-rules and compasses and other calculating instruments covered the credenza's upper surface, along with a framed blue-and-white photograph.

No windows in any of the walls, of course. He'd known that immediately. Closed doors led to five adjoining rooms, or seemed to: one door in each wall.

Gothic, and most likely subterranean.

Donal liked it.

"The thing is," added Susan Talon, shifting her immense slug-come-varicoloured-beetle body in her chair, "my father's competitors would move in with guns blazing, and I'm sure you know that."

If they knew Talon Senior was missing, she meant.

Donal shook his head, but not in disagreement. "I need to ask you something. How old are you, exactly?"

Her body type conformed to no configuration that Donal had ever encountered.

"I'm fourteen years old, Mr Riordan, but my tutors rate me as a final-year undergraduate academically, and my friends in Dad's staff say my psychological maturity matches my learning level."

She had none of those friends or tutors here with her, or anyone beside the flamesprites hovering near the ceiling. They cast a soft orange light, incongruously warm-looking, given the coolness of the air.

He'd thought earlier that her voice, projected from empty air in the parking garage, came from a young person trying to sound old. Yet in many ways she seemed the inverse: far more mature than a standard human of her age.

"I hear you have a wife and young son," she added. "A family."

Donal nodded. He and Mel hadn't actually married yet, but Finbar was five months old and the most precious part of their private universe.

All good reasons not to cross the line into working for an underworld family.

But she called him Dad.

After referring to "my father's organisation" for sure, but her voice hadn't sounded cold when talking about him at any point.

"If I take this on," he said, "you'll be my client, Miss Talon."

"Well naturally, Mr Riordan. I hardly expected you to work for free." She gave a tiny, half-sad smile within her slug-flesh cowl beneath the chitinous shell. "I know the daily rate you charge Xudiker Insurance, and I'm happy to pay double that amount."

"Alright," said Donal. "Thank you. But what I meant was, I'm working for you personally."

"Oh," she said. "Me, not my father."

Donal knew what Konrad Talon looked like now: he was the subject of the large blue-and-white photo standing in a carved bone frame atop the credenza-come-desk. If you didn't know better, you might mistake him for a successful businessman in an intellectually demanding field, one requiring scholarship and a modest manner as well as street smarts.

"It's not just an academic distinction," said Donal.

"I see." Susan twisted her huge form slightly to glance over at the photo portrait and then the charts atop the credenza-turned-desk. She turned back to Donal. "I rate academic achievement highly, but you weren't really using the word *academic* in a disparaging manner, were you, Mr Riordan?"

"No, ma'am, I wasn't."

Susan blinked and tilted her head, crinkling the soft flesh with pretty orange edging around her face. "And you're not making fun of me when you call me *ma'am* either, are you?"

"No, I am not."

The orange flamesprites' light shifted and made the shadows dance. Perhaps the sprites were responding to her mood.

"I thought I knew what to expect from you, Mr Riordan." Susan pitched her voice softly. "Maybe written reports, like textbooks, aren't good substitutes for firsthand experience."

Donal gestured with his chin towards one of the bookcases. "Don't discount the textbooks. I could spend weeks in here, reading all these. Months. And that's just the ones I might understand."

Susan giggled, and all six of her arms curled against her great torso. For a moment, she truly sounded like a schoolgirl, fourteen years old and only just beginning the transition towards adulthood.

It came to Donal that perhaps Konrad Talon, for all his tough dealings on the wrong side of the law, might be a good father, or at least did the best he could.

Whatever the background, Susan Talon had turned out alright.

Two-thirds of an hour later, Donal stepped out of blazing sapphire light and into the dark underground parking garage – that's all this place was: Susan had told him – where the same saloon car waited, currently empty.

The witch with the ruined eye sockets stood near a pillar, facing the big shaven-headed man with pale blue skin and living emerald ear studs.

Between them, above the witch's cupped hands, orange fire played and somehow supported – without burning – a floating bundle of what looked like shiny black twigs. Its part-structured, part-tangled shape looked like a cross between a raven's nest and some mathematical puzzle.

The big man reached with huge fingers and great care into the tangle of twigs, except they weren't really twigs but something else.

He withdrew a single pseudo-twig, turned it and appeared to read something on its surface – any words or symbols would have to be tiny – and gently reinserted the twig at a new position in the construct.

"Gotcha," he said, smiling at the witch.

"Maybe," she answered. "But we need to pick up the game later."

"I'm going to win."

"Not necessarily." She gestured and folded her hands around the floating construct, extinguishing the orange flames. Then she brought her hands together, and opened them.

Empty now. The game-puzzle-whatever no longer existed in the normal world.

Perhaps she'd tucked it away in some microdimensional pocket, in the compactified dimensions of crawlspace where wraiths felt at home.

I've been hanging around with witches and mages far too much.

Not to mention reading up on hex and all the rest: he'd been borrowing more non-fiction than fiction from Libraskull Library of late. Libraskull stood miles away from his nearest branch library, but its collection dwarfed most branches, even if it couldn't match the Tristopolitan Central—

"Puzzling out my puzzle, Mr Riordan?"

The witch was cutting into his thoughts and pretending to read them. Or actually reading them: he hadn't made his mind up regarding witches' potential for doing just that.

"If we're going to be working together," he said, "you can drop the mister and call me Riordan. Or Donal."

The parking garage echoed back his voice, just a little. The extended space felt empty, devoid of other vehicles as far as he could see, with only the witch, the big man and himself in here. But given the invisible portal and general circumstances, what else might he be missing?

"We *are* alone," said the witch. "So we can say what we need to say, and first things first. I'm Rilena, this is Balagron, and it's good to meet you, Donal."

Her eye sockets remained red and black and empty and ruined, but Donal looked into them steadily all the same. "Likewise. And, er, I've got to ask. You didn't create that portal, did you?"

He gestured back at the point in space he'd stepped out from. There was nothing to indicate the portal's presence, even now.

"Because I'm a mere witch?" said Rilena. "Just a girl?"

"Some women are mages, for Thanatos' sake. That's not what I—"

"Just teasing. Let's just say, I worked with the mage while he was building it, which allows me to reactivate it on demand."

If Donal had still been a redblood, he'd have blinked in surprise. "I didn't know that was possible."

"Witch-mage collaboration, or a reusable portal?"

"For Death's sake… Well, both. But mostly the reusable thing."

The big man, Balagron, shrugged his huge shoulders inside his suit jacket: an impressive sight. Even in Tristopolis, sprawling and lively and diverse, finding a tailor shop to outfit him had to pose a challenge.

"Talking about hex," said Balagron, "ain't gonna find the boss."

"Yeah…" Rilena turned her eyeless gaze back to Donal. "We guard and look after Susan. That's what we do. That's all we want to do."

"Alright…" Donal wanted her to go on.

"Mr Talon pays our wages, and me and Bal, we both have complicated pasts. But we don't get involved in Mr Talon's other business."

Balagron cleared his throat.

"Well, okay," Rilena went on. "Kind of peripherally, from time to time, kind of thing. We get involved a little bit. But mostly we're the good guys here."

Which begged an important strategic question.

"What about Axelson?" said Donal. "He knows Talon is gone, right?"

Axelson had made comments about the kind of person this job required. It implied he knew what the job entailed, even if no one had told him directly.

"Has to," said Rilena. "And I think he's doing his best to keep everything running and not let anyone know the boss has disappeared."

"But?"

"But he bought increased hex protection about three months back, and he was difficult enough to read before that. So I can't tell, truly, what he's thinking and what he's up to."

"Could he have made Talon disappear?" Donal had to press her on this.

"Maybe," she answered. "Maybe not. There's a lot of reasons for him not to."

"Either way, you think he might step into the breach, sort of thing?"

"You mean take over? Yes," said Rilena. "I think he could do that, if he thought it was best. If he could get away with it. The other bosses don't like him much, though."

Wonderful. As if thinking about one criminal organisation's internal conflicts didn't provide sufficient worry, now the greater background of the entire Tristopolitan underworld was coming into play.

Susan is my client.

A fourteen-year-old client, whose interests he would most definitely look out for.

"I must be mad," he said.

The big man, Balagron, gave a deep chuckle. The movement emphasised the massiveness of his chest.

"Welcome to the club, Riordan."

"Yeah. Is Balagron your first name or last? Or only?"

"Both. Look at my birth certificate, I'm Balagron Balagron, coz my folks got a sense of humour, like."

"Call him Donal, Bal." Rilena smiled in a way that felt genuine, although it was hard to tell for sure with those empty, blasted eye sockets. "We're going to be great friends."

"Thanatos help me," said Donal.

He wanted to say he worked alone, but he would in fact need their help; and he could work in a team if he had to, or he'd never have made it in the Army or TPD at all.

"So where shall we start?" added Donal, exactly as Rilena said: "Where do you want to start?"

Balagron shook his head, muscles bunching in his neck.

"This is going to go great," he said.

After a minute spent pacing around the pillars of the parking garage – up close, you could see intricate patterns, their knot-and-blade motif indicating the building was older than he'd thought – Donal stopped walking and jammed his hands in his pockets.

Maybe he ought to pray for a miracle.

A rush of memory: one of the schoolrooms, back in his orphanage days, had been used in the evenings for Mothers' Union meetings, when the old dears of the parish – or so he'd thought then: most of the women would have been middle-aged, if that – gathered with some of the Sisters of Thanatos who ran the place, and speed-mumbled their way through rosary prayers to St Helena of the Blade, the female equivalent of St Magnus of the Axe.

Or maybe the parish mothers had really gathered for the post-rosary sherry and cicada crackers and cups of helebore tea, and the chance for a chat away from home. Nothing more than that.

"Prayers won't help," said Rilena now.

Donal looked at her. "And what am I thinking right this second?"

"Picturing me without my clothes on, and no, goodness me, I couldn't possibly do that in front of Bal here."

Balagron said: "I could turn my back."

"Thanatos." Donal unbuttoned his jacket. "I could shoot you both. Or myself."

"Don't make promises you can't fulfil." Rilena smiled. "But we'll behave from now on, okay?"

"Speak for yourself." Balagron's deep voice rumbled.

Donal tried to let out a breath, realised his lungs were empty, and decided to keep them that way for a while. Zombies don't need a great deal of oxygen.

"Seriously," said Rilena. "Something Susan doesn't need to know the details about…"

"Tell me," said Donal.

"The boss sometimes meets, well, ladies of the darkness, if you know what I mean."

Balagron shook his head, causing the muscles of his neck to stand out like cables, looking half amused and half something else entirely.

"Sleazy assignations," said Donal. "Paid companionship."

"Since we're being polite about it," said Rilena, "then yes, exactly that. I used to drop him off in Kaldera Lane, back of the Cutsling Theatre, where he'd meet someone and go up to their room. Far away from here, so Susan would know nothing."

Also putting himself at risk, away from his normal protection.

Donal nodded. "Kaldera Lane. Lovely place."

Maybe that had been part of the thrill of it, for Talon: going alone into sleazy surroundings, with no one to guard him if things went wrong.

Balagron's voice rumbled as he spoke up. "Axelson's people tore the place apart. The entire street and most of the neighbourhood. No one knew anything, and he was kind of thorough."

"I can imagine," said Donal.

"Plus no one knows the phone number or the name of the escort agency," said Balagron. "The boss kept all that to himself."

So Balagron didn't consider himself one of Axelson's staff: a detail that might or might not prove relevant.

"All right," said Donal.

Getting hold of Talon's diary or address book, if he even kept such things, was clearly impossible. Without that, Donal had nothing.

Rilena's burned-out eye sockets looked unreadable. "I probably should have tried to find out who they were, the agency. But I never did."

Talon would have been displeased if she tried: understood. But it was a pity, all the same.

You start with the scene of the crime.

That was the general rule, but the problem was that Donal didn't have any particular resources around Kaldera Lane or the surrounding streets known locally as the Drab Zone. He never had, not even as a TPD detective lieutenant with an active network of informants.

Plus, if someone had snatched Talon there, they wouldn't be local: this had to be the work of professionals.

The place to look was somewhere else… but where, exactly?

It was going to take a while to get some traction on this case.

Finding a criminal because his little girl is worried.

Not the way he'd expected the day to turn out.

FOUR

Konrad Talon's cage occupied the centre of the seven-sided chamber.

All around it crackled purple fire, flames that could burn more than flesh, for he could feel their blazing resonance in his bones, and knew this for more than ordinary combustion.

He knew that for sure, not needing the obvious clues: the purple hue of flames that danced around him on a cold stone floor of bluish grey, with no fuel in sight.

Those warped pentagonal flagstones looked ordinary but weren't, because in the real world, the normal world, you can't stick five-equal-sided polygons together to form a surface with no gaps – you need hexagons or squares or triangles, whatever – but here, in the chamber where he'd been imprisoned, the pentagonal flagstones did exactly that.

"Rilena," he said. "You bitch."

It had to be her.

Betrayal from someone close was the only thing that could have bypassed his multi-layered defences and deposited him here, in a cage surrounded by purple flames the exact same colour as those he'd seen Rilena conjure up so many times.

And I trusted you to look after Susan.

He'd made mistakes in the past, including with Susan's mother. But putting a traitor in such a place of trust, exposing his own daughter to mortal risk: this was the worst mistake of all.

"You'll pay," he growled.

A thought to hang onto.

You'll pay with blood.

Assuming he escaped. For all he knew, he might not survive this day.

But while his captor or captors might kill him, might bring suffering upon him, they would not break him. No matter how strongly purple fire might burn outside his cage, they could not match the strength of the defensive runes burnt into his mind by Alej Kandroknar, that warped but oh, so powerful Surinese mage who'd enabled Konrad Talon's ascent to power.

An ascent washed in blood, but that was the nature of his world. Blood and secrets, and his secrets would remain safe, however much he suffered.

Susan. What about Susan?

That was the flaw, the weakness in his defence.

His plans, so carefully laid down and refined over the years – no underworld boss took long life and safety for granted – had included making sure his precious Susan would remain protected even if the worst happened.

Before he and Kandroknar parted company, no one could have made a move like this against him; but then, Kandroknar's own dark purposes had always remained unknowable: perhaps Susan would have been in more danger if Kandroknar had remained in place.

In the years since then, free of the mage's presence, running his organisation with only his own natural abilities and experience to call on, Talon had set robust processes in place, hiding Susan's existence as much as possible from the world, and erecting layered defences to protect her just in case.

But Rilena, along with Balagron, formed a core component of Susan's protection.

Betrayal.

Every passing moment brought increasing certainty that Rilena, that deadly but supposedly loyal witch, was the only possible traitor here. Someone had known where he would be, when he would be alone, and therefore vulnerable to being taken by surprise.

No one would be in a better position to do that than her.

I'll kill you, Rilena, with my own hands.

Then his thoughts of revenge blanked out, because something was happening at last.

Pale wraiths began to rise up from within the solid blue-grey stone of the floor.

Around his cage, the ring of purple fire expanded, opening up a greater gap between the flames and the sharp-edged bars that imprisoned him. In that gap, more and more wraiths ascended.

They manifested nothing like true faces, therefore no readable expressions; yet these wraiths – he counted: twenty-three so far – broadcast wave upon malevolent wave of hatred.

Of the need to make him suffer.

They began to extrude tendrils formed of crawlspace-dimensional matter brought into the ordinary world, and reached through the bars.

Reached for him, questing like blind worms or serpents searching for food.

For prey.

Coldness touched his flesh through his clothes.

No!

And slid inside him, cold and slick in ways he could never have imagined: around and through his internal organs, curling and winding.

Slithering.

Exploring.

Please, dear Thanatos…

A score of the things inside him.

More.

Don't let it end like this.

His mental defences would hold. They had to, for Susan's sake.

I can't…

More cold tendrils twisted through his intestines and heart, the tissues inside his body, and worse: a feeling of ice and slime where they passed through his bones, a kind of disgusting pain beyond anything he'd experienced before.

No. I will not break.

A greater mass of wriggling matter reached inside his core, teaching him that pain could slither and feel like ice and hurt even more than he had realised but he would *not* give in, he could not, he—

More tendrils entered him.

Even more.

I…

Finally he screamed.

FIVE

Donal entered the alleyway slowly, aware of its quiet isolation. The traffic hum was distant, and little enough light spilled from windows high up on the walls.

Overhead, the deep purple sky appeared darker than it was, almost black.

A couple of years back, he'd have felt more confident making this rendezvous, but his network of snitches had fallen dormant. His recent attempts to reactivate the net had fallen flat with a good fifty percent of his former informants.

All because he wasn't with the Department.

Other things had changed as well, but he needed to stop his thoughts wandering and focus on his dank surroundings.

Especially here, in the heart of Scrapeworthy Burough.

He'd taken his time scouting out the alleyway from the road that ran past, aware that in doing so, he might attract attention, but needing to do so all the same.

Here, white lizards were crawling over rusty, battered bins full of household refuse plus kitchen waste from a greasy spoon café whose back door was metal and rusted but solid-looking, most probably shielded with runes inside. Rotting scents hung in the still, cool air.

No sign of his informants.

Rajesh and Mary Fixtovax were brother and sister, cousins to Brian Fixtovax who still maintained the gun range at Avenue of the Basilisks. In the past, Raj and Mary had been among the most reliable of Donal's contacts.

Come on. Where are you?

Quicksilver puddles reflected patches of light from half-shuttered, half-curtained windows. No sign of anyone at ground level.

Earlier, while Rilena and Balagron waited in the car, he'd called Raj Fixtovax from a booth on Crisis Ave and Bloodway, needing almost to shout over the traffic, not to mention the restaurant kitchen clatter on Raj's end of the call.

There'd been a faint chill as a wraith passed nearby, and for a second Donal had considered changing the rendezvous, then dismissed that as paranoia when he could no longer sense the wraith's presence.

At the time, during that shouted conversation, Raj had seemed to need minimal cajoling to come here, and bring his sister Mary. Maybe just eagerness to get away from the kitchen.

So where is he?

Perhaps Raj hadn't been so keen, after all. Or maybe something bad had happened.

A scrape of not-quite-sound.

Followed by a whisper that might have been mental or acoustic: impossible to tell.

Softly and without fuss, Donal drew his Magnus and levelled it.

Not aiming at anything specific yet.

You won't need that comfort toy, lover.

Zombies gain conscious control over previously subconscious reactions: everyone knows that. But Donal blinked with surprise all the same.

"Gert… I mean, Aggie," he said. "Is that you?"

The wraith who drifted out of the wall on his left loomed large and seemed to sparkle inside. He knew her to be a freewraith, not indentured, who served the Tristopolis Police Department mostly because she wanted to.

Had served it throughout several generations of ordinary human life.

Would you like me to be someone else?

"I…" Donal looked down at the gun in his hand. "Bleeding Hades, Aggie. We're a long way from Avenue of the Basilisks."

He reholstered the Magnus but left his jacket unbuttoned, this time not for access but because he didn't need to button up formally in front of her, the wraith who had carried him up and down elevator shafts in Police HQ so many, many times across the years.

Mostly in her previous identity as Gertie, before merging with a detective freewraith called Xalia in order to save her from some kind of energy trap – as far as Donal understood the tale – thereby becoming a new individual called Aggie, which she claimed was short for Aggregate and probably was.

Gertie always had possessed a quirky sense of humour. Xalia, not so much.

Brian in the gun range told me you're asking about something… dangerous.

Donal stared at her billowing form as she hung above the alleyway floor, disconnected from the grime and quicksilver puddles. Peripherally, he noticed that all of the white lizards had grown quite still, staring up at Aggie as if fascinated.

"When did this happen?" he asked.

We talked two-thirds of an hour ago.

"I see."

And Donal did.

He imagined it: Raj claiming to be eager to meet here in this alley, then hanging up the kitchen phone in his restaurant, staring for a minute into space, then dialling his cousin Brian, and telling Brian exactly what Donal Riordan, former TPD detective lieutenant, wanted to talk about.

Which was that shady area of business that the newspapers – other than the *Tristopolitan Gazette*, which preferred more formal language, occasionally oblique in order to forestall libel action – referred to as the protection racket.

Every restaurant needed constant food and drink deliveries among other essential supplies, and preferred reassurance that no one was going to interfere with those deliveries. For Donal, that kind of unofficial arrangement formed a trail, a pathway into Talon's shady world.

Except Raj Fixtovax seemed to have informed Brian who then informed Aggie, which wasn't how this was supposed to work.

Aggie floated there in silence.

Not like her at all.

"So what's going on?" said Donal. "I get it that you're trying to warn me off. Or have I misunderstood?"

Oh, Donal Riordan. Always so impulsive.

"Not the way I see it. Come off it, Aggie. Why would you want to protect Talon's operation?"

Aggie's translucent, insubstantial form rose up some five feet in the air. She wriggled.

I really wouldn't, dear Donal.

"Then what's going on?"

I'm here to ask a favour.

"Normally I'd say… anything for you, sweetheart."

And normally I wouldn't dream of threatening my favourite human being.

"Excuse me?"

One of my favourites, anyway.

Aggie's translucent form rose a little higher still, and grew more transparent as she rotated more of her body mass out of the normal macroscopic dimensions.

Or mesoscopic… Scholars disagreed on terminology, depending on context. Donal had been reading all about it during the quiet hours when Mel and baby Finbar were asleep, and who the Hades cared?

The human mind wanders under stress, even after resurrection into zombiehood.

A chill spread across Donal's scalp and took hold of the back of his neck, in a way he'd almost forgotten, a throwback to his redblood days.

Maybe it was Gertie who'd been his friend, or seemed to. Maybe he should think of the Aggie personality as someone new.

And maybe I don't understand wraiths. At all.

A faint glow appeared within Aggie's floating form, a hint of silvery light.
You can't trust those men.

"Which men?"

They don't just want to see what you're up to.

"I have no idea what…" Donal let his voice trail off.

Scrapes of shoes soles on concrete, at the far end of the alleyway, out of sight behind buttresses on either side. They might have been there all along, but most likely they'd exited from a rear door of some business, hence the sound he'd heard.

I can smell their intention. They were following you, and they really want to kill you.

So Donal had attracted attention when scouting out the alleyway, or maybe someone had been following him for longer, in which case they were either very good indeed or had wraith help, because he'd seen nothing at all.

He drew his Magnus once more, feeling the weight of it as though for the first time. The world slowed down, or seemed to. His earlier confusion dropped away.

Reality became simpler.

I'm ready.

He felt his lips draw back in a predatorial smile, the kind that could often stop a fight before it happened, but not when professionals were about to make a hit.

Excuse me, lover. I need a moment.

Aggie swooped down, accelerating as she disappeared into the concrete alley floor like a human diving into water.

"Thanatos," muttered Donal.

His surroundings offered no real cover. The dustbins might conceal him, but if gunmen knew he was here and were targeting him, they could pin him down while drawing closer and then fire through the bins.

Fire escapes started high up, and with a series of leaps from on top of dustbins he might reach one of those escapes and swing himself up; or he could run back the way he'd come, trying to reach safety before bullets tore into him.

Maybe, but unlikely.

So option three it is.

He ran forwards, towards the danger.

Ran fast.

He sprinted hard on a single breath, fists low, Magnus in his right hand, body leaning forward, still accelerating as movement occurred and a figure burst out from behind the righthand buttress.

A second gunman stepped out calmly and a third exited low from cover, dropping down to one knee and also taking aim, and in that instant Donal knew that this was it and life had ended without a chance to see Finbar growing up, and all the years he'd planned to spend with Mel were gone forever.

He started to pull the trigger but far too late against three targets with all of them beginning to squeeze off their own lethal shots and then it didn't happen, none of it, in the way that seemed inevitable.

Aggie made the difference.

Smooth, her ascent out of solid ground.

I'd forgotten how bones sing when you pass through them.

She rose up *through* the gunmen's bodies before any of them could fire, catching one of them just peripherally, sliding straight through the torsos of the other two.

Two mouths opened as their breathing caught, paralysed and unable to scream.

The man she'd barely touched still stumbled, and when he managed to pull the trigger, his first round went wide. There would never be a second.

Donal fired, a triple tap.

Three flat crashes of sound and the gunman was down: an inanimate pile of matter. Just one more morsel of reactor fuel.

Aggie rose above the other two men, then extruded part of herself down into the one who was recovering fastest. His face darkened. A croaking sound burst out of him, and for a ninth of a second Donal almost felt pity.

She's squeezing his heart inside his chest.

The surviving man brought his gun up and runes glinted silver on the side of the barrel but far too late, even for a hex-enhanced weapon.

Donal fired.

Another crash of sound, and one more transformation of a living body into a bundle of bones and meat, able only to lie there until Energy Authority workers came to cart the dead thing away.

"How did they happen to be here?" Donal looked all around, checking for more danger, seeing nothing.

I don't know, lover.

Aggie billowed overhead, while the man whose heart she'd been squeezing fell to his knees with a crunch of bone against stone, then toppled forward and hit the alley floor with his face, and didn't move.

All three gunmen down.

Donal looked up at Aggie, seeing window lights through her insubstantial form. "If Raj rang you, I suppose he didn't want to come here at all."

So what's going on, dear Donal?

"That's what I want to find out, even though you're telling me to back off. Sweetheart."

He stared up at her, while she continued to billow in midair.

You can holster your weapon. Give it a rest before you need to pull it out again.

Donal shook his head. Gertie had never quite talked to him like this in the old days, but close enough: she was more or less the same wraith he'd always known.

He didn't reholster, though. Doing what other people tell you to do can become a habit.

Squatting down, he used his left hand to search the nearest of the bodies, and found a lizard-skin wallet. He flipped it open, and thumbed out a driver's licence.

The name, Larkinson, meant nothing to Donal, but he memorised the details all the same.

Then he did put away the Magnus, so he could search the other two corpses more quickly. The dead man with the rune-enhanced firearm carried a wad of banknotes but no ID. The last was called Filafr according to his driver's licence, a surname that Donal had never come across before.

None of this looked useful.

"Wonderful," he muttered. "You want to give me a clue as to who they are? Aggie?"

He looked up into empty air. Nothing to see besides the alleyway and darkness overhead and three dead gunmen at his feet: just another day in Tristopolis.

No sign of Aggie.

Really wonderful.

It felt as if he knew less now than when this whole thing started, and if things carried on this way, he'd be lucky to remember his own name.

Get a grip.

He stood up and looked around, lungs empty, aware of his steadily beating heart.

So I'm on my own.

Again.

Time to rethink his tactics.

SIX

Donal headed home.

I need to keep sharp.

A normal civilian would call the cops and tell them about three dead gunmen in an alleyway, but scene-of-crime diviners were good at their jobs, and might detect traces of Aggie if not Donal himself. He didn't want Aggie to get in trouble.

She might have tried to warn him off the Talon case, but she'd also saved his life.

The denizens of Scrapeworthy tended to abide by their own laws more than the ones written down on ancient vellum and stored in the deep, ancient vaults of Tristopolis and Fortinium. The Energy Authority collectors might not get a look in: the locals could have their own plans for three dead bodies.

Not to mention the gunmen's employer, who might send street soldiers to retrieve their dead comrades, to prevent both scene-of-crime diviners and forensic Bone Listeners learning things best kept hidden.

If Donal could have counted on that last possibility, he might have hung around to wait and see who turned up, but a lot could go wrong, the most likely being that his time was wasted while any traces left behind by Talon's kidnappers or killers grew ever less likely to be found.

He walked five blocks along Crisis Ave before flagging down a purple cab.

Zombies never quite switch off, but he let his awareness of the sidewalks and pedestrians and cars and shop windows – and the pterahide seat beneath him, the taxi's vibration, the hollowmint tang of the driver's hair tonic – fade as much as possible.

He needed to get a feel for whatever the Hades was going on.

The cab entered Danklyn Depths.

Something was happening in the background of the Talon case and he couldn't see it, not consciously, but maybe his subconscious could, deeper down than even he could access. Like a redblood seeking inspiration, he needed to occupy himself with something else while the deeper levels of his mind got to work.

This wasn't just passing time. Daily discipline, the need for physical training, was his greatest friend.

And I really need to hit something.

Soon they were into Lower Danklyn, a short drive along Hel Ave before swinging right and slowing down as Donal said: "Here will do."

He paid his florin and slid out, and waited until the purple cab drove on before walking down the narrow street to the dark mass of the deconsecrated temple he called home.

Mel wouldn't be inside. She and Finbar were due at the children's clinic for a checkup.

He entered by the side door beneath the *Mel's Gym* sign, and locked it behind him. He and Mel trusted a couple of the senior guys enough to leave the place in their care, but none were here right now.

Empty, as expected.

Across the gym stood the door leading to his and Mel's apartment, once the temple's presbytery or whatever it was called. He crossed the floor, footsteps giving off a faint echo, and opened the door.

In the short hallway stood his black-scaled motorcycle – still pretty new to him, though he wasn't the Triumphant's first owner – and which he hadn't ridden as often as he should.

Now, he laid a palm on its smooth fuel tank, next to its zinc spear-and-shield decal. "We'll go for a long ride soon."

The Triumphant purred, even though its engine hadn't come to life.

"Black Iron Forest," said Donal. "We'll blast through it. Really open up on those forest roads."

The purr deepened.

"Alright," said Donal. "Later."

Regretfully, he went to change into his ratty old workout gear, and patted the Triumphant once more on his way into the gym proper.

Time to get to work.

Bag work beckoned.

Zombies don't sleep, but normally he worked the heavy bags only during normal waking hours, because of the noise.

During the quiet hours, he could get away with jumping rope, provided he did it in the furthest corner where acoustics grew muffled; but normally he shadow boxed and worked push-ups and chin-ups and freehand squats and lunges, over and over while Mel and Finbar slept.

Or he ran along the quiet streets, for hours at a time. That always steadied

him.

Now, Donal began with bag work: hands untaped inside kimodo-leather bag gloves, working individual jabs and crosses at first, careful to start at distance in order to lunge in and out as well as circling sideways.

"Footwork is everything and hip twist is all the rest," his old coach used to say.

"And arms are just the delivery system," Donal often added when he taught beginners.

A zombie with no exercise habit can degenerate to a shuffling state that would kill a redblood; but the converse holds true for those with discipline: the response to exercise allows the buildup of extraordinary work capacity, far beyond redblood limits.

The joy of discipline, always his greatest and most loyal friend.

Ambidexterity was something Donal had always worked on, long before resurrection, and he switched stances now, every minute on the minute – according to his mental time sense – keeping the footwork going and the techniques sharp, focussing on skill.

No bright ideas rose up from his subconscious.

Doesn't matter.

He kept on working the bag.

Donal was seven rounds in and slamming in more power shots while mixing in some practical combos – elbow strikes and hammer fists included: rules for the street, not the heptagon – when an ice-cold draught flowed through the gym, followed by the sound of crackling flames.

A visitor, and not one who needed a door to enter by.

"I see you're still playing with the fisticuffs, my friend." A man's cultured voice.

Donal smiled as he turned, seeing pale features, blonde-white hair beyond shoulder length, and what he could only think of as theatrical garb.

Pale blue puffed sleeves protruded from a long burgundy vest-come-jerkin – it came with a wide black belt around the waist – above dark blue trousers without creases, and a pair of darker-than-burgundy hiking boots, pretty much the colour of wormberry fudge.

"Klaudius," said Donal. "Shouldn't you be on stage at the pantomime? Entertaining the children for the festive season?"

Not even remotely the right time of year for that. Or the right century for going around dressed like a pirate.

"You mean my stylish apparel?" Klaudius raised his palms, vapour clouds forming above them. "Fashion is so arbitrary, don't you think?"

Heptagons of lambent orange fire shone in his eyes. Twin irises of flame.

"Yeah, that's what they all say. Is everything okay down below?" Donal wasn't talking about this building's basement: it didn't have one.

"The denizens are behaving themselves, if that's what you mean."

Donal nodded. "Good."

Great caverns stretched beneath the minus two hundred and seventy-third floor of One, Avenue of the Basilisks. In the TPD's internal documents, the place was called just that: the Caverns, always capitalised, and those Caverns housed vast eldritch entities whose nature few people remotely understood, kept there by some treaty from the distant past and perhaps a lack of interest in the human world.

The greatest of potential threats, and on occasion restless.

Only two Guardians kept the peace down there, Klaudius and his sister Hellah, and while Donal had never visited those near-mythical Caverns in the depths of Police HQ, he knew exactly how the rest of humanity – and wraithkind and other citizen species – regarded the Guardians.

With absolute terror.

Klaudius's breath steamed. "Hellah's been in to see you and Mel and the baby, hasn't she?"

"A few times."

This was the first time that Klaudius had popped in unannounced, though he'd visited three times before, once alongside Hellah – on one of the rare occasions when the eldritch entities entered such a quiet state that both Guardians could leave the Caverns together.

For a while.

"That's good," said Klaudius. "She likes you, and your family."

"Well… Thanks."

Donal adored Hellah too, as much as she terrified everyone else.

His own lack of fear formed a mystery, one he wasn't tempted to unravel, and they'd become close friends in such a short time. Hellah's powerful nature made no difference.

Klaudius, in his deceptively foppish fashion, began to wander around the shadowy gym, noting the hanging bags.

Frost settled on each bag in turn as he passed it.

"My sister still teases me about the time you knocked me out."

Donal shook his head. "I can't imagine why."

A resurrected human dropping a Guardian: totally incongruous, barely imaginable, but the real surprise had been that anyone or anything could ensorcel Klaudius, for he hadn't been himself that day. If he had been, Donal would have stood no chance at all.

"And she loves the fact," said Klaudius, "that we don't scare you. Neither of us."

"Yeah." Donal tried to read the pale expression, but failed. "Hellah's the best, and you're not too bad."

"Ha." The icy vapour from Klaudius's breath contrasted with the orange flames of his irises.

Donal pulled off his bag gloves, and held them lightly in his left hand.

"You want a drink of some kind? I gave up on whiskey, but there's a bottle around here somewhere. Or helebore tea or coffee in the kitchen." Donal gestured towards the rune-decorated arch that led to the former presbytery, now his and Mel's and Finbar's family home.

Klaudius hooked his thumbs in his belt and shook his head. "I'd really like to, but not this time, okay?"

"Hades, pal. Is everything okay with you?"

"With me, of course everything's okay."

"Uh-huh." Donal walked across to a small folding table near the sparring heptagon, dropped the bag gloves on its surface, and turned back to Klaudius. "So does Hellah have a problem?"

Klaudius bit his lip, allowing a streamer of vapour to escape from his mouth. A normal human gesture of indecision, but from a Guardian, it seemed extraordinary.

"I really don't know. Look, Donal… How many times has she been to visit? I mean in the past five weeks."

"Er, nine times in total. Seven times when I was here, and twice when it was just Mel and Finbar. Unless Mel forgot to mention some other time, or Hellah turned up when the place was empty."

Since Guardians didn't need to travel by normal means, it was conceivable that Hellah could have popped into the gym directly from Avenue of the Basilisks, found no one here, and disappeared once more.

"She popped out seventeen times in that period." The flame irises brightened for a moment. "Saying she was off to the gym each time, which is supposed to mean visiting you guys here. And she stayed out for a good while on each occasion."

A normal redblood wouldn't keep count from sheer memory, but Donal was a blackblood resurrected man and Klaudius was a Guardian, and that made all the difference.

"Maybe she's started working out someplace," said Donal. "For real."

"Tell me one place where the gym-goers wouldn't flee screaming if my sister appeared."

"Hmm. Yeah."

"I suppose she could be paying a gym owner enough money to cover all the trouble, but I really don't think so."

It hadn't occurred to Donal that Guardians possessed or needed something so mundane as money. "Does the city pay you a salary, then?"

"Something like that." The corner of Klaudius's mouth turned up. "We're stinking rich, if we ever get round to actually using the funds we own."

Donal rubbed his face, not quite automatically: more like a conscious replay of a gesture from his redblood days.

"If she's keeping a secret from you," he said, "is that really a problem?"

"Not when you put it in those terms. *I* wasn't exactly truthful with *her* just now. She thinks I'm checking out Mordanto for any weird emissions, so I'll be swinging by there, before returning home."

That implied the Guardians kept tab on what leading-edge mages were up to, which raised some unexpected questions, but never mind: this was all about Hellah.

"Maybe," said Donal, "she's found herself a boyfriend."

"If anyone of our kind manifested nearby, I'd know."

"Right." Donal wasn't sure what to make of that. "And what if she found someone not, er, quite like you?"

Again the orange fiery irises brightened for a moment. "I rather thought she might be carrying on with you, my friend."

"Er…" Donal blinked, something he seemed to be doing more and more recently, despite his zombie self control. "I… What?"

They really were good friends, him and Hellah. An unexpected rapport had blossomed from their first meeting, so Klaudius's notion was logical.

Logical, but wrong.

"So you're not having an affair." Klaudius's voice dipped in what sounded like disappointment. "You and my sister."

"Sorry."

"If I ever had to end up with a human brother-in-law, you wouldn't be the worst thing that could happen to Hellah."

"Hades, pal."

"And if you were to follow her and find out what she's up to, you're probably the one human she wouldn't dream of obliterating. If she spotted you, I mean."

Donal gestured towards the spot where Klaudius had first appeared. "You and her, you can pop up anywhere. Even easier than mages can, far as I can tell. And if you're not going to do the job yourself, that's what you're going to need to tail her. A whole bunch of mages."

Klaudius shook his head.

Talk about out of my depth.

But if Hellah was in trouble…

"I don't know where to start," he told Klaudius. "Not yet."

"But you'll help."

"I will."

"How much do you charge per—"

"Nothing, pal."

Icy steam enveloped the lower part of Klaudius's face as he exhaled. "Sorry."

Donal pitched his voice more softly. "I might need funds to pay for mage assistance or something. If there are costs that are out of my league, you can pay them."

"Yeah. Be careful about working with mages, though."

"I've done it before. A couple of them are friends, pretty much."

"And if they confront my sister in the wrong circumstances, she'll turn them into toast. Or burnt crispy rashers, to render that metaphor more precisely isomorphic."

"Isomorphic. Right," said Donal. "You got any kind of sorcerous amulet or something that can be used to track her?"

Klaudius placed his hand on the nearest heavy bag, causing frost to coalesce and on the surface, and tilted his head. "If only it were that easy or mundane."

"Mundane. Yeah."

"Here." Klaudius dug inside a pocket of the jerkin that would have looked ridiculous on anybody else, and what he extracted looked a lot like an amulet to Donal's eyes: an amber ovoid with a slender chain attached.

"I thought you said…"

"It's a call crystal," said Klaudius. "Not the same thing at all."

"If you say so."

"Here, take it." Klaudius tossed the thing. "You can call me with it."

Donal snatched it from the air, having tracked its parabolic path precisely. "If Commissioner Sandarov needs to talk to you and Hellah, how does he do that? Like, do you actually have a telephone down there in the depths?"

"Just handwritten notes and a pneumatic tube. They tried installing telephones, years ago. The phones just kept screaming, because of the nerves in the phone lines. Plain wires don't work at all."

Donal had a vague idea that – usually – only main telephone cables needed nerves stripped from human bodies to form their functional cores.

"The telephone people," added Klaudius, "sent down teams of engineers and research witches a couple of times afterwards, trying to figure out a solution." He gave a minimal shoulder movement, not quite a shrug. "Unfortunately, one of the entities got a bit peckish, and one of the engineers stepped an inch over the protective line we'd created on the floor around her team, and after that, the phone company refused to send any more people down to visit."

"Oh," said Donal. "Was it just her, or did the whole team—"

Klaudius shook his head. "Not even a single usable bone or nerve left over from the lot of them. Maybe that makes it less ironic. I'm not too sure."

Donal shook his head, wondering how the Hades to even get started on tracking Hellah's movements, never mind the minor matter of his paid work: trying to track down the missing Konrad Talon, ferocious underworld crime boss but apparently decent father.

I was getting nowhere tracking Talon.

Daily training had always been mandatory, but the reason he'd come home at this particular time had been to mentally regroup, to work out his next moves on the Talon case.

"Different topic," he said, still thinking about Talon, and the way Aggie warned him off the case. "Is there anything unusual happening in the crawlspace dimensions, kind of thing? I mean something that would make an experienced police wraith act in an odd way."

"No. Would you like me to question this wraith?"

"Hades, no. I mean, no thanks."

Aggie was still a friend, wasn't she? Interrogation by a Guardian would put an end to that.

"Okay…" Klaudius looked hesitant.

Not an expression associated with Guardians, not normally.

"Hellah's back at HQ now, presumably," said Donal.

"Well, yes."

Not one of those rare occasions, then, when the denizens grew quiet enough to be left unattended.

I need to talk to Kelvin. Or Lamis.

Without mage help, he couldn't even get started on helping Hellah, plus on the Talon case, tracking down the missing crime boss might also benefit from sorcerous intervention.

"Alright," said Donal. "I've got another case on the go, but I'll work them both."

"Ah. It hadn't occurred to me—"

"Since you found me here training, that ain't surprising. It's normal for the job, though. The two at a time thing, I mean."

Not entirely true: as a detective lieutenant in the TPD, he'd often needed to work two or three cases at a time, but as a solo investigator these days, he'd grown used to working jobs sequentially. It was one of the things that he could do and regular cops couldn't: spend all his time on something, past the point where a normal investigation might be abandoned due to greater priorities elsewhere.

He would have to replace his daily rate with pro rata amounts to reflect actual time spent, when he prepared the final bill for Susan Talon. Assuming the case got that far.

Details. Trivial.

"If you say so, my friend." Klaudius exhaled more frosty air. "I don't know what else I can tell you, to get you started."

"I am going to need help. The way you transport yourself from place to place… Can you give me a lift to Mordanto?"

"Not if you want to get there alive."

"Oh… If I were a wraith, would you be able to do it?"

"Probably. But you're not."

"So it's a crawlspace dimensions thing."

Klaudius smiled while the icy vapour thickened in the air around him.

"You're pretty sharp. No wonder my sister likes you."

"Hades, Klaudius…"

Pillars of ice and orange fire rose up and twisted, braiding themselves together with Klaudius at their centre, and the whirling maelstrom became a twisting knot that started off bigger than a human but rotated in simultaneous impossible ways to shrink towards zero size and then it was gone.

Nothing remained. No sign of Klaudius at all.

Thanatos.

One Hades of a way to make an exit. No wonder Klaudius couldn't be bothered to dress like an ordinary guy: he wasn't one.

But he was fast becoming a good friend, all the same.

Leaving a workout incomplete wasn't Donal's way, and he'd planned on nine rounds of work, which meant two and one seventh rounds – some part of his mind tracked time and tasks automatically, ever since resurrection – remained to be done.

And I can plan while I work.

He pulled on the old kimodo-leather gloves – stained and worn and shiny, curved by years of work to fit his hands precisely – and crossed over to the heavy bag that Klaudius had placed his hand on.

The shape of Klaudius's hand remained on the canvas, palm and fingers and thumb formed of ice, with sprays of frost spreading out.

Donal moved into technical mode to restart, shifting in from distance to hit with a long jab followed by a cross and hook and slip away with a shift in angle before lunging in once more.

Brian.

The name popped into his head as he snapped the next combo into the bag. Brian's cousins – or at least Raj, if not Mary – had presumably told Brian about the planned rendezvous, and Brian had passed the info on to Aggie for some reason. Sharing information between cousins made some sort of sense, but where did Aggie fit into all this?

And why would Brian feel any kind of obligation towards her?

Three more punches snapped into unforgiving canvas.

Maybe Aggie had something on Brian. Donal had once caught Brian selling police ammunition on the side – it seemed a long time ago – and perhaps Brian hadn't kept on the straight and narrow afterwards. Perhaps Aggie had caught him out, somehow.

But the chain of gossip – call it that for now, though it might have been actual betrayal – started with the two people who should have been in that alleyway.

Raj. Mary.

Next combo, delivered harder.

Feeling good.

The two Fixtovax siblings, who knew about Talon's protection racket, or at least some part of it, and had promised to help but hadn't delivered.

Aggie.

Her, he couldn't deal with on his own. Not in a confrontation.

Lamis.

As the previous police commissioner's chauffeur – more a cover role than his real job – Mage Lamis had spent considerable time at Police HQ. He might know Aggie, at least in her previous persona of Gertie. Maybe that would help. Maybe it wouldn't.

Slamming in the punches even harder now.

A redblood would be covered in hot sweat, but Donal didn't do that any more. He felt as if he could pound the bag forever.

There's Kelvin.

Younger than Lamis and something more than a rising star at Mordanto, but a newish father – something Donal hadn't had sympathy with before, but things were different now – and badly injured the last time he and Donal and Lamis worked together, and no longer answering the phone when Donal called.

Donal had given up trying.

Or Helena Steele.

Slamming in power punches now.

If Donal hadn't been a blackblood, the emotion in that thought – the notion of seeing Helena Steele, mother of Laura – might have altered his punching rhythm, because it was Laura Steele's zombie heart that beat in Donal's chest.

Had Laura lived, things would have turned out differently. Professor Helena Steele might well have become Donal's mother-in-law.

Too bad he never met Helena – he thought of her that way sometimes, with reservations – while Laura still lived.

She might help.

Donal switched stances, and hammered in the mirror image of the combo he'd been working.

Helena had hated him at first, but the last time they talked there'd been some kind of understanding. And the thing was, as head of Mordanto, she had the resources to help him.

I'm not a cop these days.

Mordanto maintained an obligation to help Tristopolis PD on official matters, but when it came to the Guardians, ensuring the two siblings were doing okay had to be in everybody's interest: official or unofficial should make no difference.

If Donal could slip in a request for help regarding Aggie, that would help too.

So that's decided.

End of the ninth training round, and he stepped back, breathed in and out once, shrugged and shook his shoulders, and that was that. Cool-down finished: so different from the old days.

Training over.

It was time to see a mage.

SEVEN

Tumbleup Road curved around in a two-thirds-of-a-mile spiral, with near-unbroken rows of purplestone houses – grown crooked over time, subtly redolent of eldritch energies long ago absorbed by stonework – on both sides of the street. Flamesprites, bored by the quiet emptiness, barely glowed in their basket-cages atop the lampposts.

The white-haired lady walked slowly, ramrod-straight despite her age, tapping her platinum-tipped cane against the dark slate sidewalk as she progressed, alert to everything around her.

Familiarity, in this place, bred watchfulness, not contempt.

No creatures moved.

Her cane-tip tapped with metronomic regularity as she progressed.

Occasionally a white lizard would venture into a backyard, looking for scraps; but for the most part, they knew better. A squawk might sound beneath one or other of the eaves from time to time, but the small obsidian razorbats weren't truly living organisms, and for the most part performed their sentinel duty in watchful, hungry silence.

The white-haired woman smiled, noting the glistening black forms watching her from the eaves of almost every house she passed.

Some houses had domestic gargoyles, the miniature variety whose toxin and fighting ability did not suffer at all in comparison to their larger, more common brethren living atop the city's oldest and most forbidding towers.

A few ordinary people did live around here, but only the kind who knew how to keep themselves to themselves, and who possessed a certain kind of mental fortitude: a sprinkling of thaumaturgeons and the like, obsessed with their careers.

To Professor Helena Steele, this place represented childhood.

I woke up from a dream of my one great early failure, and now I'm back where I grew up.

She had played in these streets, and visited houses that looked to be pretty much the same these days: dark, curtained with deep purple drapes the same hue as the sky overhead, all of it quiet and nicely grim, because constant mental discipline was a must when two hundred mage families lived in constant proximity.

So easy for someone to slip up, to make a mistake – perhaps while they slept, in dreamtime – and tap into the quantally entangled miasma of shadow energy that grew ever stronger as the centuries passed.

Bad accidents could happen that way, and when Helena was seven years old, three of her friends had been ripped apart by darkness while two others morphed into hellish forms that no amount of thaumasurgery could alter. One of them, Tatiana, still lived – in private chambers in a rarely visited tower within the Mordanto grounds.

No public appearances for poor Tatiana: her schooldays and ordinary life had ended in a single moment, all because some stupid boy had gone to sleep without setting the ritual safeguards in place, the nine automesmeric chants that every child with mage potential learns by the age of five.

A good idea any place, and essential for anyone living around here, in Tumbleup Road.

The tiny amber amulet at Helena's throat tingled. She stopped, touched it with a fingertip, and said: "You worry too much, André."

Just checking, ma'am. The words sounded in her mind, not her ears.

"I'm going to be fine."

I can drive closer.

André would still be sitting behind the wheel of her limousine, parked at the outer end of the spiral that formed Tumbleup Road. She'd insisted that he stop there and allow her to proceed on foot.

"Stay where you are."

Ma'am.

The amulet grew cold, and Helena lowered her hand.

André, at her suggestion, had begun to look after himself better – losing weight, regaining a little of the fitness he'd possessed as a young man joining the Police Department, where he'd remained until seven years ago – and it seemed to have made him more concerned about her wellbeing also.

There were worse faults. She'd never regretted taking him on as her chauffeur.

Keeping André out of Tumbleup Road was as much for his safety as for the sake of a low-key approach.

He knows this is important for me.

For one thing, back at Mordanto, while André held open the limo door for her, she had been talking to two of her admin assistants, telling them to cancel all her appointments for today, including the seventeen o'clock meeting with councillors at City Hall.

"I don't want to see anyone," she had told them, ignoring their wide-eyed reactions. "Anything less than a priority crimson emergency, I do not even want to know about it."

Both assistants had stood there on the knucklebone gravel, nodding and answering "Yes, Professor," and otherwise keeping quiet, sensing her mood.

She had known it was going to be an interesting day even earlier, from the moment she woke up.

Then, her transition from dreaming to wakefulness had been abrupt, her eyes snapping open as she uttered aloud a name from the past: "Kandroknar."

Then, warm in her comfortable bed and staring at the shadowed ceiling, she had wondered why – after so long forgetting about that old failure – that long-dead mage's name had been on her mind. She could think of only one thing.

Kelvin, her designated protégé, had come up against a failure of his own, albeit at a later stage of his career, and it seemed to have derailed him entirely.

Maybe my greatest disaster can get Kelvin out of his mess.

That had popped into her mind as she swung out of bed, wrapped in her heavy rune-embroidered nightgown, and placed her feet on the cold stone floor. The more she had thought about it since, the more inspired her idea had seemed, even though the thought of Kandroknar – and the unusual kind of being he had allied himself with – brought a swirl of nausea to her stomach, even after all these years.

Kelvin, like Helena herself, had always been drawn to pure academic research as much as practicalities and leadership, and there had been questions all those years ago about Alej Kandroknar's abilities, which had been greater than anyone might expect, even from the most adept of the Zurinese mages.

Singletons. If anyone can get a handle on them, it has to be Kelvin.

Bad events from the past might lead to some good in the present… or she might be entirely wrong, because she had no way of truly knowing Kelvin's present state of mind, not until she sat down to talk to him.

I am far too old to find another protégé.

That was a defeatist thought, therefore unworthy of her.

Never mind.

She walked on, tapping the cane against the ancient slate flagstones, following the spiral curve until the house she wanted came into view, and at that point she stopped.

Number 47-omega looked much like all the rest: black windows in purple walls, the hint of razorbats beneath the dark roof, black shrubbery in the garden, and a glistening dark slowvine sliding serpent-like behind the wrought bone gate, along the path that led to the front door.

A modest enough home for a mage on the cusp of coming into his own, on the point of transition from promising protégé to accomplished successor: to becoming capable of leading Mordanto while adhering to standards as high as hers.

She had tried to retire once, but learned that it wasn't safe to do so – not before Kelvin became the obvious choice and no rival candidate could get a look in.

So.

Time to get on with it.

A delicate moment, but I still need to act.

Tapping the cane, she continued forward.

At first the wrought bone gate refused to budge, but she gestured hard and a hex pulse slammed the thing open, and silver sparks were still falling through the air as Helena took a step onto the front garden path.

The serpent-like slowvine uncoiled towards her, stopped, wavered, and with deliberation rolled off to the side and snaked its way to the centre of the black lawn, where it began to coil itself around the dark-grey stone pillar of the central fountain.

That fountain, currently unmoving, was filled with a dark, viscous-looking liquid: neither blood nor venom but possessing properties of both, as it ran through the arteries and veins of the house and grounds.

Helena could sense the internal architecture, could feel at a distance the arterial and veinous networks within the house walls, along with the watchful pseudo-consciousness of the house itself.

Its regard, focussed on her, felt like tiny needles on her skin.

"I see you've been making some home improvements." She spoke aloud in the empty front garden, knowing that one way or another, Kelvin would hear her words. "I suppose it's one way to spend your study leave."

Sometimes *study leave* meant just that – a paid sabbatical for self-guided research – while at other times it served as a bureaucratic euphemism for disciplinary action or recuperative necessity. Suspension or medical leave.

On occasion, it could be all of those things, or morph from one into the other.

Time to find out exactly what stage Kelvin was in.

Maybe he isn't up to the singleton research. Maybe my bright idea is one hundred percent stupid.

She walked up to the front porch and stopped.

Silver fire ran along the house number on the door, the hex-soaked metallic 47Ω glimmering with spillover radiation.

The door knocker, the colour of pewter, was fashioned into a dragon head with eyes of red glass or possibly rubies. When Helena looked at it, pewter flicked like nictitating membranes across the shining eyes: a movement so fast that someone less alert might have missed it.

Call it a warning.

"Don't try me," she told the dragon head.

Red eyes grew duller and the subtle hue of animation faded as the pewter quiesced into immobility: as close to inert as it could get, without losing its interesting properties.

A wise choice.

"Kelvin." Strengthening her tone. "That applies to you as well."

She waited for a count of nine.

No answer.

The door looked solid, the silver fire illuminating the 47Ω sign hinted at the power within, and the house's quasi-mentality was oriented by design towards implacable defence. All of this, Helena felt deep within her bones.

It could not be allowed to matter.

She raised her cane.

A silver glow, the same hue as that on the door sign, strengthened on the handle and tip of the cane. Helena began to focus.

That was when the door clicked and swung inwards, not at her command.

Another wise choice.

The hallway appeared dark and hollow, with hints of orange flamesprite light from deep within the house, but only shadows near at hand.

Not exactly welcoming, but no matter.

Helena lowered her cane and stepped inside.

EIGHT

Donal paid off the cab on Hollow Way Drive three blocks away from Mordanto, climbed out and shrugged to check the fit of his shoulder holster beneath his suit jacket, and began to walk.

Above the baroque towers on either side of the street, the sky remained its normal unchanging hue, deep purple as always, while the flamesprites in the lampposts burned pretty much the same as they would elsewhere… if you examined things objectively.

Yet the world seemed darker in Hollow Way, and that sensation would close in ever more strongly the closer Donal drew towards Mordanto. He knew this from past experience.

Doesn't matter.

He walked as far as the first corner, noting the dimly lit diner set into the ground floor of a seven-sided tower that might otherwise be residential. Curlicued niches for statues and twisted stone carvings stretched all the way up the sides, the tall dark windows mostly unlit, a full ninety-one storeys by Donal's automatic count.

Scarcely visible from down here, a handful of gargoyles crouched high above, where the roof became a spire.

Going inside the diner seemed a good idea, though his destination remained Mordanto.

I'm not hesitating.

It was a deliberate decision, though he could not have said why. A few years after resurrection, and he seemed to be acting more and more like a redblood, when it usually went the other way.

He surmised that much, not just from the zombies he'd met in the past, but from the books on biomorphics and revitalism that he'd devoured back when Mel had announced her pregnancy – something he'd assumed was impossible given his resurrected status, but turned out to be rare, not unknown.

Maybe I should hang out with my own kind.

That was a valid thought – logically – but somehow it didn't sit right, and he dismissed it as his hand touched the cold braided gunmetal handle of the diner door, pulled it open and strode inside.

No pause in the chatter. Mordanto might be nearby, but this was still Tristopolis, where most of the time everyone in sight was a stranger, and busy movement and fast tough talk were par for the course, a kind of constant urban friction that kept everyone on their toes, Donal included.

Nobody seemed to pay any particular attention as he made his way to the counter and answered the inevitable "Whatcha want, pal?" with "Coffee. Black. Large."

The big moss-skinned man nodded and turned to grab a jug of the stuff.

Donal considered adding a scarab cream doughnut to the order, as a nod to the old days, but he wasn't with the Department any more and zombies don't eat much and the sense of taste alters radically post-resurrection.

Then a thought struck and he flipped his decision around again. "And a scarab cream."

In Illurium or even Fortinium, he might have added *please*, but not around here.

"You got it." The big man, his hands like spikeball mitts, used bone tongs to place the doughnut on a five-sided plate, and put it down next to the coffee mug. "Two thirds."

Donal had already extracted two third-florins from his pocket, and clacked them down on the countertop. "Thanks."

"Take it easy. Next. Whatcha want, pal?"

A narrow-shouldered older man shuffled into place as Donal took his mug and plate from the counter. He headed for a small table next to the wall, recently vacated by a mother and child.

An unsmiling waitress, short and slight with long black hair hanging limply, snatched the detritus off the table before Donal reached it, waved her left hand over the dark surface, and hurried out to the rear of the diner.

Though the waitress's hand had been empty, a distinct smell of beetlewax polish rose from the tabletop now, and the surface looked utterly clean.

Interesting.

Donal put down his coffee and doughnut, and sat down. The chair was hard, the table small, and the proprietor – probably the moss-skinned guy behind the counter – had packed in as many tables as he could without violating regs too much.

Employing amateur witches as waitresses didn't break the rules, and maybe if you were a part-talented hopeful, you'd want to work a minimum-wage job in the vicinity of Mordanto and soak in as much indirect learning and atmosphere as you could.

Or maybe the entire experience would dishearten you. Donal hadn't been able to see the expression in her eyes, but the waitress's gait had been the same nervous rush as everyone else's. Working in a busy diner wasn't most people's idea of fun.

Donal let the sound of chatter sink in, along with the warmth of the air, then took a slow sip of coffee – hot and strong – and put the mug down, and tried to work out why exactly he'd come in here.

Did something call me?

The decision had been intuition-based: perhaps a recognition that he needed to get his mental state right before reaching Mordanto. That, or something in the environment had drawn him in.

I could do with mage help, or I wouldn't be here.

Hellah wasn't someone he could track by himself, while the other case – the real one, that of the missing Konrad Talon – seemed to involve his friend Aggie, and if there was some way to bypass his normal investigative steps with mage help, that might be a way to avoid getting Aggie into trouble.

That's why I'm around Mordanto, but why this diner?

Maybe he just wanted coffee and a doughnut, simple as that. Maybe introspection beyond a certain point turns into paranoia.

He leaned back a little, scanning everyone, seeing nothing untoward.

Almost automatically, he reached for the doughnut, bit into it, and a sweet taste explosion unfurled in his mouth: scarab cream tasting better than it had for years. Better than it had since his childhood, because treats had been rare and sensations pressed in hard and the world felt new and immediate back then, as it did for children anywhere.

He blinked three times, put the doughnut back down on the cheap pentagonal plate – a small chip marked one edge – and pulled out his handkerchief to wipe his fingers clean.

What the Hades is going on?

Zombie sensory acuity is greater than a redblood's, but also different. Doughnuts like this weren't really supposed to taste good, not the way they would have done pre-resurrection.

He looked at the rear door leading to the kitchen. The waitress hadn't reappeared.

Probably this had nothing to do with her.

And that was when a shriek sounded out back, followed by a man yelling in pain, and a loud blast of what sounded like steam escaping, and Donal was on his feet and moving while everyone else had barely begun to look up.

It was a swing door and he kicked it open with his left leg, a long heel-thrust as his right hand went inside his jacket to his holstered Magnus, and then he was through, still holding his firearm but not drawing it, not yet, because this might be a different kind of danger.

Clouds of steam, and a chaos of panicked movement.

Tendrils and tentacles amid the steam.

Big tentacles, grey and white and splotched with black, flinging pots in all directions, swiping people and saucepans and hanging knives in rage or panic or something, while clattering and screaming echoed and someone up against the tiles of the furthest wall yelled out: "Where the Hades did it come from?"

Crouched face-down with her head almost at her knees, a small black-haired woman cowered almost directly beneath the centre of the action, where the tendrils came together while moving so fast and randomly that Donal got no sense of the central body's shape.

The cowering woman looked like the waitress who'd cleared his table: call it ninety-seven percent likely it was her.

Donal started to draw the Magnus from beneath his left armpit, but his inner forearm touched a lump of hardness beneath his shirt and tie, offering a better possibility. Quickly, he reached inside his shirt, found the amulet – call crystal – and squeezed it hard.

It burned hot, just for a moment.

Not sure if it would work: there was a reason the two Guardians weren't seen more often, and it wasn't just the fear they invoked, but the fact that they couldn't simply leave their subterranean home and place of work beneath Avenue of the Basilisks, not on a whim. Not when the entities they guarded could wreak so much havoc.

Donal let go of the amulet and pulled out the Magnus, pointed it diagonally towards the floor and hoped he wouldn't have to use it.

He couldn't have said why, but he felt an overwhelming sense of fear and panic – not malevolence – coming from the thrashing tentacles and part-glimpsed central body. At least two of the kitchen staff were down and bloodied, injured if not dead, but this panicking thing wasn't targeting individuals.

But Donal had no way to calm the thing down.

Nor any idea how well his bullets would work to put it down for others' safety.

Thank Thanatos.

A swirling, braided pillar of white and orange, of snow and ice and burning flames, formed at the centre of the kitchen.

It whirled and grew brighter, larger, and a white hand reached out to touch a flapping tentacle that froze, while the other tentacles and tendrils quietened down, becoming almost motionless. A dark pentagonal eye, widening at the centre of the thing's mass, looked like a window onto a sickening void.

Donal's stomach churned.

Then the tendrils and tentacles shrank along with the central body into a twisted knot that wrapped itself up and rotated in five impossible ways at once and then it was gone.

Nothing left.

Klaudius's pale face leaned out of the swirling ice and flame, smiled at Donal, looked down at the cowering young woman on the floor, then raised his flame-irised eyes to Donal once more, and raised an eyebrow.

"I've got it from here," Donal found himself saying.

"Just as well." Klaudius glanced at the surviving kitchen staff, backing away amid the wreckage, more terrified of him than of the entity he'd banished.

Or rescued. Whatever.

Donal grinned. "Later, pal."

Klaudius said: "Later, my friend."

He was busy, or he'd have stepped out of the ice and flames. Donal appreciated the way he'd diverted his attention to this little problem.

They smiled at each other, then Klaudius slipped back inside the ice-and-flame braided pillar. It spun faster and faster and expanded and collapsed and nothing remained.

Only a ruined restaurant-café kitchen with smashed tiles and crockery and pans everywhere and wounded people sprawled on the floor or whimpering against the walls, still terrified.

Steam all over the place, clouds of it, but less than before.

Donal squatted down next to the cowering waitress.

"It's gone," he told her. "All gone."

For a moment, she seemed not to have heard. Then, in a small voice: "I'm sorry."

Lank black hair hung across her face like a greasy veil.

"Not your fault." It seemed the right thing to say. "You didn't mean to bring it here, did you?"

"N-no." Quietly.

That confirmed a lot of quick working assumptions in Donal's mind. It also raised questions, like why he'd felt that coming into the diner was a good idea in the first place.

Footsteps, heavy and fast and coming this way, sounded from out front. Donal powered himself up from squatting to standing.

Now what?

The swing door crashed open and the big, moss-skinned man was standing there with some kind of cleaver in his hand. A large cleaver with black glowing runes on its blade.

Black runes pulsing fast.

"We need to talk about this," said Donal.

The big man raised his cleaver, and growled.

"No." Donal used a two-handed grip as his Magnus came up. "Not happening."

Donal didn't want to kill a business owner whose fear and anger were understandable – maybe resenting an employee for betraying trust, as much as raging at the damage to his kitchen and the effect on his customers – but the Magnus wasn't a bluff.

A calm willingness to use lethal force always has an effect at a subconscious level – the level where body language doesn't lie – unless the other person is too drunk or ensorcelled to notice. The big moss-skinned man understood immediately.

He lowered his blade.

The black runes on the cleaver faded a little, pulsing more slowly, just like a calming heartbeat.

"Good," said Donal. "Now put the—"

"Alright, I've got it. I'm good." The big man turned as a waitress with shiny scaled skin entered behind him. "What?"

"I was going to call sixes and nines." She swallowed, perhaps expecting anger, since calling the emergency services was the obvious thing to do and she'd failed. "But Silva said there are mages on the way."

Donal had no idea who Silva was, but the big man clearly did. He reversed the cleaver and handed it hilt-first to the waitress.

"Put it back behind the counter, willya?"

"Yes, boss." The waitress didn't quite curtsy, but her body bobbed as she ducked her head, and it might be a signal that she feared the big man.

Donal didn't like bullies.

But signals can be misread and a lot was happening here.

Plus the black-haired young woman needed to be handled with care, for her own sake and everyone else's safety. Donal put away his Magnus, double-checked that it felt secure, then squatted back down by the woman.

He reached out towards her shoulder and stopped, not touching her.

"It's okay," he said. "It's going to be okay."

"No." Immersed in misery. "No, it really isn't."

Misery and hopelessness. The tone of someone who'd given up.

"You'll be surprised at how quickly you can turn your life around." Donal wished he had the persuasive powers of a seasoned witch like Ingrid Johannsdóttir or even Rilena with her blasted eye-pits.

Beneath her hanging hair, the waitress looked up.

"It called to me," she said. "It was lonely and sad and I reached out to help but what I did went wrong and it fell into the hole I made in the air and came out here and… and…"

"I understand," Donal told her.

"Maybe it called out by accident. I mean, it didn't mean to call *me*, not me in particular, or anyone else around here."

A trained witch or mage would have used some kind of vocabulary related to void geometry or thaumadynamics or something. An untrained witch who somehow could create the correct neural patterns in her brain to work with hex or whatever this was – people like her were supposed to be caught by the system early on, during schooldays. Identified and given the training they needed, at least in theory.

All procedures have holes in them. People get missed: no one to blame.

She wasn't physically hurt and other people were, but if Donal went to help the injured then her instability might cause another fracture in normal spacetime and he couldn't risk that.

He turned towards the big man with the mossy skin. "Help the injured. We're okay here."

"Ah. Yes." The big man rubbed his face. "I'm Alberto. That's Gina you've got down there. My cousin's girl."

For *girl* read *daughter*, Donal assumed.

This Alberto had appeared willing to use his rune-inscribed cleaver on Gina, but his motives might not have been entirely selfish – lives had been at risk – and maybe he'd meant only to attack the entity wreaking havoc in his kitchen.

Whatever the truth, Donal had to get Gina out of here.

Maybe she called me, somehow.

Perhaps at some unconscious level, her hopelessness had broadcast itself in the same way the void entity's emotions had called out to her.

A resonance of misery. Poor kid.

Alberto shrugged his big shoulders, rubbed the mossy skin of his face, then turned away and went back out through the swing door to the dining area.

"Get some medics here," he shouted to someone.

Not what Donal had meant when he told Alberto to tend to the injured, but never mind.

From replaying sounds he'd unconsciously heard in the background while tumult reigned in here – furniture shifting, footsteps thumping, voices sounding frightened – plus a general sense of emptiness now, Donal guessed that few – if any – diners remained out front.

"Come on, Gina," he said. "Stand up with me."

It took seven long seconds before she nodded, her long black hair slightly swaying, and reached out towards Donal. He took hold of her forearms, adjusted his squat position, and rose up, lifting her.

He kept hold until she was steady.

Then: "You can walk."

She nodded. "Yes."

"We'll go out front, and wait for help to arrive."

"But—" Looking back towards her injured colleagues.

"They're going to be fine." Possibly untrue, but that wasn't the point. "Come on."

Gina looked up at him, her eyes filling up with desperate trust.

"My uncle…" She stopped. "He didn't hurt me. He's not a nice man, but he didn't hurt me."

"Alright." Donal almost blinked. "Why do you say that?"

"Because you want to hurt him, don't you?"

"Ah." That was something he hadn't expected. "I guess I do."

But you couldn't beat niceness into people.

Punish, yes. Reform, maybe not.

Some hope.

Time to get out of here.

NINE

Surveying his marble-lined vault, its walls and ceiling swirling with pinks and creams polished to the highest of shines, Alej Kandroknar reminded himself, as he so often did, that you could get so very used to wealth that you forgot to appreciate what you had, and such forgetfulness would be a gross mistake.

We do not make mistakes.

The familiar voice echoed in his mind.

Indeed we don't, he answered silently.

Kandroknar stroked his goatee beard, took in a deep slow breath of cool air, let out his breath, and sighed.

Life was for enjoying, in the most sybaritic way possible, and ever since he'd divested himself of ordinary human involvement – after those first years in Tristopolis, getting to know the city while helping the young, ambitious Konrad Talon build a successful criminal organisation – he'd been able to concentrate on his pleasures, here in the palatial surroundings of his mostly windowless, elegantly appointed and generally beautiful home.

Secure in the knowledge that those who might bother him, particularly the mages of Mordanto, believed him long dead, exactly as he had planned.

His imminent revenge would taste all the sweeter for those long years of holding back – delayed gratification at its most sublime – while surprising the mages even more, in their moment of defeat.

For defeat, read agonising death.

"Get me a whiskey," he ordered now. "And chocolate."

One of the three wraith-slaves accompanying him slipped away, moving very fast, understanding the penalty for taking too long or fetching some inadequate whiskey blend or even an insufficiently strong dark chocolate, that last perhaps the major surviving habit from the country Kandroknar grew up in, before relocating here.

At the time it had felt like fleeing, but the subsequent three decades offered a more benign, educational perspective, given all his successes here in Tristopolis.

Luckily, imported Zurinese goods (never Surinese, not in his presence: he remained old-fashioned that way), chocolate included, were easy enough to acquire here, even for an ordinary citizen.

Alej Kandroknar, of course, lived a far superior kind of life, and that was obvious right now, as he looked over the open bone-and-platinum shelves stacked with various kinds of wealth, including actual cash primarily in ninety-florin notes, totalling some two and two-thirds million florins, wrapped and bundled in open pterahide cases, ready for transport.

I've lived here long enough.

Yes, we have.

Soon, it would be time to leave Tristopolis and start a new phase of life, with new pleasures to enjoy, funded by the wealth he could carry with him: all that could fit inside an aeroplane with a spacious cargo hold.

Such as the plane being serviced at Tempelgard right now, soon to be loaded up with portable wealth.

Bearer bonds and jewellery were more transportable than cases full of high-denomination notes, and he possessed them too – some on shelves right here – along with artworks, paintings and non-living sculptures of the less arcane kind – no hex or entrapped entities involved – which decorated the rest of his extensive near-windowless mansion.

As for the artwork, the pieces stored at the back here, such as the dark, twisted sculpture called The Seven Dying Mages, were those he had rotated out of normal view just to keep things fresh. There was no point in acquiring the best and keeping it out of sight forever.

Now, he regarded the delightfully agonised features of the dark metal figures, the mages who had in reality perished with pretty much those expressions, and decided it was time to bring this piece back into one of the lounges, where he could regard it at his leisure.

Most likely for the last time: unless he changed his mind, that particular piece wasn't going to make the journey with him.

Sir.

The wraith-slave billowed next to him, somewhat less substantial than before, having rotated enough of its mass out of the compactified dimensions to hold a crystal tumbler of whiskey and a half-skull dish filled with dark chocolate pieces.

Kandroknar, with his delicate fingers, took a single piece of near-black chocolate, placed it on his tongue and took hold of the tumbler before closing his eyes and taking a sip of the fine, smoky whiskey, feeling it wash luxuriously around the dark, bittersweet sacrament of chocolate, focussing so deeply on the pleasure—

Yes.

—that the rest of the world faded for a moment, while sybaritic sensations, heightened beyond normal mortal comprehension, flooded through his physical form and—

Good.

—he knew, with absolute solid certainty, deep down inside his conjoined self, that this was how life was meant to be lived, at least by those superior beings who understood the nature of pleasure and power, of delight and accomplishment—

The wraith can live.

Of course.

—and the true ways of the world: the connoisseurs of culture, the game masters of wealth and the lofty strata of power wielded from far behind the scenes.

Kandroknar opened his eyes, looked at the wraith-slave, and nodded.

No ordinary man would have detected the deep feeling of relief in the wraith's billowing form, but Kandroknar felt and tasted wraith emotions – he was deeply sensitive that way, and always had been – and he felt the corner of his mouth twitch in amusement.

For a second he thought of reversing his decision and killing the wraith-slave regardless, but no: that would spoil the pleasure.

I'm a gourmet, not a gourmand.

Indeed we are.

That much was obvious.

He plucked another piece of chocolate from the half-skull – it seemed almost to float in space, as the wraith-slave grew less substantial except around the half-skull bowl – and once more took ritualistic care as he placed chocolate on his willing tongue and swirled whiskey around the chocolate and closed his eyes to focus—

Yes, that is right.

—knowing that his life's purpose lay in creating moments of perfection such as this, like beautiful beads strung out along the delicate chain that was his timeline, the wonderful years and decades of his existence, and although part of him would survive when this most fleshly part of him was gone—

I will persist, indeed.

—that didn't really matter, at least not right now.

Sir.

An interrupted pleasure: every one of his wraith-slaves understood, deep in their core, what they risked by intruding on such moments, which was exactly why he rarely had to exact deserved punishment: they would weigh up the risk beforehand, and if matters weren't clearly urgent, they would wait for however long it took before Kandroknar, as their master, opened his eyes and decided to look in their direction.

He did that now, knowing that this was not the wraith who still floated in place with pieces of dark Zurinese chocolate.

"What is it?"

This other wraith was rippling with fear.

Mr Fleischmann is here.

Fleischmann's presence alone was not enough to generate this emotion, not if Fleischmann were here to report success as usual. The conclusion was simple: he had failed to carry out his mission.

So he didn't manage to kill the detective.

Perhaps we should make use of the detective.

That was a good point.

Talon's knowledge of us is years out of date.

Indeed. But this is an interesting time for him to go missing.

Their wraith-spies had been unable to provide any hint of the missing Talon's whereabouts. From their observations, no one in Talon's organisation had a clue, and most didn't even know he was missing.

We need to question Osako.

More than question, I think.

Ah, yes. That would be delicious.

There are wraith-spies and wraith-spies. Osako was an indentured wraith employed by Axelson – the number two man in Talon's organisation – and it had been a pleasure to take control of her, all the while knowing it could only be a temporary arrangement.

Keeping tabs on Talon, after all these years, had seemed marginally safer than simply forgetting about his existence.

Talon's organisation had internal safeguards that for sure weren't perfect, but at some point a security witch would perform a routine check and discover that Osako was no longer trustworthy. At that point, the suicide hex implanted in Osako's subconscious mind would activate, leaving nothing that might lead back to Kandroknar.

If not for Osako, Kandroknar might not even have learned of Talon's disappearance.

Does it matter that Talon's missing?

No answer from the other part of him.

According to Osako, Talon's daughter had recruited a useful investigator, ex-TPD. Kandroknar's first instinct had been to send Fleischmann's gunmen after the man, because Talon was better off missing than newly found and making a fuss, so shutting down an investigation seemed a good idea.

Fleischmann seemed to have failed in that regard.

With luck, the missing Talon had simply been murdered by a rival, his corpse made to disappear, and that would be that. Having him found alive and well by an ex-TPD cop, that risked questions being asked at this most delicate stage of Kandroknar's plans.

If one of Talon's underworld rivals was holding him captive, that was fine:

their focus in interrogations – if any – would be on the present, on activities which Kandroknar himself had no part in, since his involvement was all in the distant past.

Our involvement.

Of course. Of course.

A rival criminal would be unlikely to learn anything that would affect Kandroknar's plans for Mordanto, and maybe the risk of this detective learning anything dangerous was equally minimal: perhaps setting Fleischmann's gunmen on the man had been unnecessary.

Maybe we should try to find Talon ourselves.

Even if it was only to kill him: that was implied.

Send the Martina.

Yes, of course.

To warn off the detective, and find Talon herself.

Kandroknar smiled. That would be useful. Meanwhile, let Fleischmann show himself and report his failure, and experience some fear of his own.

Or better still, let him wait and worry for a while, and in the meantime summon the wraith-spy Osako here for… questioning.

Sometimes, the thing about executing minions was choosing which one needed to die, and in how much exquisite agony, over how much beautiful time.

One could of course wipe them all out in a delightful orgy of blood and aether and screaming, and there had been three or five such episodes of excess over the years, but one couldn't live that way all the time, not without surfeit deadening the sensibilities, even if one ignored the practical difficulties of restaffing after every such bloodletting adventure.

Soon, of course, it would be time for the greatest feeding ever, such glorious slaughter that he could barely wait to taste, but holding back until the right moment is always, always part of the pleasure.

Not long now…

Indeed. But not just yet.

Kandroknar handed his whiskey tumbler to the wraith-slave who'd brought this new message. The tumbler dipped in the air but didn't fall or spill a drop, which right now was good enough in terms of allowing the wraith to live.

"For now, Fleischmann can wait. Summon Osako here via the usual protocols, and notify me when she arrives."

He held up his hand, which all three wraith-slaves correctly interpreted as a command to remain still, because he hadn't finished delivering his instructions.

"Meanwhile," he continued, "I will take a little break in my bedroom. I'll have Bernedetta, Alek, and the new one."

There was no real ambiguity in referring to the *new one*: currently, only one unnamed pleasure-wraith occupied a holding cage, waiting for her introduction to her new life in this place, serving her new master in the ways that suited him, while Bernedetta and Alek had submitted to his pleasures so many times already, but remained fresh enough not to be disposed of, not yet.

Not quite.

"Now," he said, dismissing the wraiths.

As they fled, he looked over his wealth once more.

Just trinkets and tokens.

Indeed so.

It was always possible to make more of such things, but on leaving this Federation, travelling fast and incognito with portable wealth, landing into immediate luxury in his new home abroad, well, that was the superior way to do it.

That's what we are.

Superior? Always.

He smiled, chuckled to himself in what he hoped was an impish way, and with a light, happy step, he exited the vaults and turned right, into a deeply carpeted corridor that led to the appropriately named master bedroom.

Time to enjoy himself some more.

TEN

Donal and Gina went out into the front part of the restaurant with Donal slightly in the lead. Some of the chairs had toppled and tables had shifted position and glasses had spilled their contents, but the diners had made surprisingly little mess when they exited in a rush.

Alberto hulked behind the counter, a frown causing his mossy forehead to look lumpy, watching Donal and Gina but saying nothing.

Fair enough.

"They're going to want you to stick around, like," said a narrow-faced waiter.

He was standing near a window, wringing a cloth in his hands. The cloth looked dry.

Donal looked at him. "You're Silva?"

"Um, sure. I mean yeah, I am."

The one who'd apparently said that mages were on their way.

Donal was about to ask how he knew, when a small black dragon tattoo with slowly beating wings slid up Silva's neck, made its way up along his cheek, and slithered – or appeared to slither – headfirst into his eye socket.

The tip of the tail was the last part to disappear, accompanied by a faint slurping noise that Donal hoped was just his imagination.

Most ordinary people would end up in hospital with that much hex soaked into their skin, so unless there was some way to create living tattoos that Donal hadn't heard about, Silva was odd in much the same way as Gina.

That made Donal wonder about Alberto's hiring policies, but first things first.

"Come on." Donal touched Gina's arm. "Carry on walking."

But they'd only moved halfway to the outer door when it swung inwards, and a shaven-headed blue-skinned woman walked in, followed by two flint-faced men who had to be combat mages.

Behind them a red-headed gawky young man seemed to be walking on tiptoes, trying to see over their shoulders.

The mages Silva had predicted. Four of them.

The young red-headed mage at the back had a prominent Adam's apple and big eyes, widening now. He actually giggled.

"That's Lieutenant Riordan." He poked his face forward between the combat mages, and spoke in a rush. "The one who dealt with the Void Threat. Touched by white wolves, too. Works with the feds."

"Hades, kid," said Donal. "I'm not with the Department these days."

Nor did he have a great deal to do with federal spellbinders, but there had been moments, and from the look in the combat mages' eyes, having someone to vouch for him right now was pretty damned useful.

He recognised the red-headed mage. The kid had been part of a response team deployed against a much greater entity than the thing Gina let loose in Alberto's kitchen.

"Anderl." Donal dragged the name out of memory. "Anderl Havoch. I remember. You did okay that day."

The blue-skinned female mage stared at Donal, then at Gina – who shrank back and hunched up – then looked past both of them towards the rear of the restaurant. It seemed as if her eyes were focussed beyond the swing door: as if she could see directly inside the kitchen.

As if the door and wall did not exist.

Then she snapped her head towards Donal.

"A Guardian was here," she said.

"Klaudius popped in to help out."

"You know a Guardian by name?"

"They're my friends," said Donal.

One of the combat mages breathed in sharply. The blue-skinned mage stared at Donal, her eyes unreadable.

Behind the combat mages, Anderl laughed.

"Told you," he said. "He's a friend of Kelvin Johannsson's as well."

Donal wasn't so sure about that, not these days, but never mind.

"This is Gina." He gestured towards Gina while returning the blue-skinned woman's stare. "She needs your help."

"Help, is it?"

"Yes. Help."

Again, the unreadable eyes.

Then: "Alright," she said. "Help it is."

The combat mages moved to stand either side of Gina, but neither man reached out to touch her, perhaps in part because they sensed Donal looking at them and prepared to act, regardless of their power.

"Has anybody actually called for an ambulance?" said Donal.

All this mage malarky made it too easy to forget ordinary human beings who were injured and suffering. They needed a more immediate, mundane kind of help.

"Hades," muttered the waitress near the counter, the one who'd earlier talked about calling sixes and nines.

Alberto, the big moss-skinned proprietor, had shouted for someone to get medics here. Maybe everyone had assumed someone else had done it.

Right now Alberto was closest to the phone, and he surprised Donal by picking up the handset himself – no yelling at a subordinate this time – and spinning the cogs to the emergency number.

But Alberto stopped when the blue-skinned mage called out: "There's no need for that. We've already called for medical assistance."

Peripherally, Donal noticed young Anderl raise an eyebrow, and wondered which of these four mages had actually thought to signal – somehow – for ordinary medical help.

Donal winked at Anderl, who grinned back.

"That's Mage Winona Cloudback in charge of us." Anderl nodded towards the blue-skinned female mage. "I'm learning a lot from her."

Donal kept a straight face despite the ambiguity in Anderl's words. Mage Winona might have the power and intellectual sharpness, but her personality wasn't much at all.

Then again, when he rousted suspects back in his days on a neighbourhood beat, those individuals often knew him by name and maybe accorded him respect of sorts; but they probably didn't like him, and he probably didn't give them any reason to.

So, Mage Winona. It was good to put a name to someone you had to deal with.

"Enough," she said. "We're leaving now. You first."

"Ma'am," said Anderl.

Donal was half expecting some kind of portal to open up because of everything he'd experienced recently, but the truth was that few mages had the power to create such things or shift instantaneously through space at all. Of the few who could, most might manage a range of a yard or three at best: enough to pass through a wall, say, but nothing more.

Instead, Anderl opened the diner door like any normal human being, and stepped out into the darkness of the street. Donal took hold of Gina's arm and walked her out.

The two combat mages followed.

They were clustering on the sidewalk, waiting for Mage Winona to join them, when a TPD patrol car swung out across the road with its black strobe pulsing waves of darkness along the street. It halted at right angles to the traffic, which was sparse enough – by Tristopolitan standards – for the driver to get away with this manoeuvre.

Farther down the street, a second patrol car did the same thing.

Both cars set their sirens to screeching in banshee mode, and that was enough to get the traffic to pull over to the sides and bump up onto the sidewalks where possible. Every car stopped, but nobody got out of their vehicles to gawk because, well, this was Tristopolis after all.

Just another day in the city.

Mage Winona exited the diner as the first bat-winged ambulance swooped into view, curving down towards Hollow Way Road.

There was also a moving speck, black against deep purple high in the sky, looking like a second ambulance, flying this way very fast indeed.

Donal wondered exactly how Anderl had worded the emergency call, or whatever it was he'd sent.

The first black ambulance spread its wings wider as it slid down to land without bouncing, decelerated along a commendably short length of Hollow Way with engine and brakes howling, curving those wings to a concave configuration for additional braking, and then it was rolling to a halt.

At that point its wings shook and folded back and inwards with a rustle, audible only because the engine had shivered into silence. The black vehicle had halted.

A momentary pause, as if reality held its breath.

Then two grey-skinned paramedics in dark tunics exited fast, one carrying a black medical holdall, the other with only a diagnostic divining-fork made of platinum and bone. Nictitating membranes flickered across their eyes as they drew close.

They stopped in front of Donal.

One bared his pointed teeth in a smile. "Riordan."

"Good to see you," said Donal.

Behind him, Anderl muttered, "Told you," to no one in particular.

Donal pointed to the diner. "The casualties are inside, in the kitchen in back."

"Yes-s-s."

Another pointed-teeth smile, and the paramedics headed inside.

Mage Winona came out as the second ambulance commenced its descent.

"What are you grinning at, Mage Anderl? Never mind. Come on."

She strode past Donal and carried on, not looking to either side as she crossed the road, aiming to continue along Hollow Way in the direction of Mordanto.

Where Donal had intended to go all along.

Moving unobtrusively, at least compared to his usual gawkiness, Anderl slipped around the combat mages and took up position on the other side of Gina, who looked up as if startled, then tilted her head and relaxed her shoulders.

Seeing Anderl as a potential friend among these mages, it seemed.

Good.

"Let's walk." Donal tried to keep his voice gentle.

"Lovely day for it," said Anderl with a cheeky grin.

Donal shook his head, but gave a twitch of a smile.

Together, they crossed the side street to the next block of Hollow Way, following Mage Winona. The two combat mages took up the rear. In theory, their presence should have made Donal feel safer.

So much for theory.

The closer they came to Mordanto, the more gloom seemed to shroud the world.

Soon enough, they reached the perimeter.

Tall outer walls with battlements that looked even more ancient than they were. Beyond them, a profusion of baroque towers and halls and other ornate buildings ascended within the grounds. A shimmering greyness in the air extended high up and possibly formed a dome over the entire place.

Probably protection of some sort, but who knew? It formed the least of the strange features you might encounter here.

They walked slowly now, drawing closer to the gates.

The air feeling chilly and tasting… different.

No one approached this place fast, not even a mage, except in the direst emergency, for fear of triggering the defences.

Black metal formed the gates, tall and impenetrable, and even an ordinary person could feel the aura of defensive hex running up and down inside the metal, thrumming as if alive.

Alive and hungry and eager to feast.

Call it a paradox, since one of the primary stated aims of this place was to offer healing to victims of the most dire mishaps and violence involving hex, quantal manipulation, crawlspace dimensional breaches, advanced ensorcellment, and worse.

Things that Donal didn't have a name for.

Mordanto was more than that, of course. It functioned as a place of higher learning and of research that often had nothing to do with healing people, and maybe it even operated as a kind of ruling body.

Donal had picked up hints of all these things, especially when talking to Mage Lamis, his sort-of friend who'd been ostracised by the powers that be, meaning the most senior mages within these walls.

It had come as a surprise to learn that Lamis Grimstone and Helena Steele were brother and sister, which complicated an already complex situation, but that was about as much as Donal understood.

He wasn't even sure that Laura had known Lamis to be her uncle. She'd never hinted at such a thing, and nothing in her apartment had indicated that connection, or linked to the mage at all.

Another life.

Donal blew out whatever breath was in his lungs. He was with Mel now, and they had Finbar as the centre of their world, and that was that.

Mordanto's main gateway stood up ahead.

The wrought metal insignia announced the name of this place, as if anyone other than a clueless tourist could fail to know it.

MORDANTO HOSPITAL

&

THAUMATURGICAL COLLEGE

chrd. 6397

Steel shields on each gate bore runes – archaic runes that looked different from the ones you saw elsewhere – that glowed black and felt threatening to look at. Great dragon claws, that might or might not be the real thing, held those shields in place.

"Such an inviting place," said Donal as they drew near.

"I've always thought so," said Anderl.

Mage Winona stopped a yard from the closed gates and then she was standing on knucklebone gravel beyond the gates as well, or maybe that was an illusion – two of her existing in that instant – before reality steadied to reveal that she was in fact standing a yard inside the solid gates.

Just one of her now, of course.

"Quantal superposition," said Donal. "Right?"

Gina glanced up, face part-covered by her lank hair, eyes widening. Perhaps she hadn't realised there were technical explanations for these things.

"Not bad," said Anderl.

"I've been reading up."

Not the kind of books with actual hex equations or spell matrices or any of that stuff, though Libraskull Library stocked a few of those. Exactly why, Donal didn't know, since they seemed to live permanently on the shelves.

Maybe on the off chance that some child with undiscovered potential – someone like Gina, say – would borrow them and begin some self-education that might lead them into something more formal and structured.

And safe. Or at least less dangerous.

"There's a quantal tunnelling effect as well." Anderl glanced at the two combat mages, and shook his head. "I'm probably not supposed to mention that."

Then the combat mages moved very fast indeed, one laying a hand on Gina's shoulder, the other grabbing Anderl's arm, and even though Donal reacted straight away, trying to grab Gina, the mages were quicker. Donal's hand moved through empty air because no one was standing there.

No one at all.

Gina and Anderl and the combat mages were inside Mordanto's gates, along with Mage Winona, who commenced walking towards the main buildings, her back towards Donal.

"Wait." Donal raised his voice. "I've got business here."

Anderl started to call out something, but one of the combat mages shook his head, and something might have flickered in the air around him.

Whatever it was, Anderl tightened his mouth and didn't speak.

"It's why I was in the neighbourhood," added Donal.

The two combat mages inclined their heads, and Donal read that as some kind of command issued to Gina and Anderl, whose body language tensed. Then their shoulders slumped as they began to walk, following Mage Winona.

One of the combat mages glanced back at Donal.

"I have Laura Steele's heart inside my body." Donal hated to play this card.

The combat mage turned away.

All five were heading towards an arched entranceway to one of the big, old buildings.

"Tell the Professor I want to see her," Donal called out. "I mean Professor Helena Steele."

The big doors opened in the ordinary way, except that Donal could see no human intervention. Anywhere else, that would have implied indentured wraiths performing the task, but in this place, who knew?

Mage Winona was already inside, Gina and Anderl and the combat mages followed into some kind of hallway that looked blurred, as if seen through faceted glass.

The interior seemed to shimmer as the doors swung shut and that was that.

Wonderful.

Mages. What can you do?

A nightmare, the lot of them.

There were kids' books where a youngster with potential had to stand in pouring quicksilver rain or – if the tales were set elsewhere, like Norvège or Surinam (called Zurinam in older books) or even on the Lightside of the world – in blizzards of snow or else in blazing heat, for days on end. It was all about proving themselves worthy of being taken in by some ancient mystic who could teach them greatness.

But Donal wasn't a child and he wasn't here to study and he had plenty of things to do if no one felt inclined to help. Tracing a Guardian's movements and tracking down a missing crime lord: he should have known better than to expect help from the people best placed to give it but least likely to listen to an ordinary person's request.

He'd known from the start he'd need help in finding out what Hellah was up to, but tracking down Talon had seemed a straightforward case until Aggie

turned up. Being warned off by a TPD freewraith – even an old friend –
altered everything, however.

I should've gone to Lamis first.

He turned away and walked.

ELEVEN

Alej Kandroknar remained in his silk embroidered dressing-gown, open at the front while he rubbed his chest and belly, remembering the pleasure, enjoying the exhausted emptiness of another hour well spent. He had walked to this lounge from his bedroom in a warm, contented state, moving softly in a kind of sybaritic version of a tai-chi master's gait, the product of a very different kind of discipline: based on pleasure, not austerity.

Seated in a soft pterahide-upholstered chair, Kandroknar sighed, closed his gown and tied the sash, crossed his legs, and called for a cup of tea.

It was a small pleasure, seeing the fearful way the wraith-slave flew off to fetch the tea, and that was good: orchestrating moments, managing one's state and sensibilities, formed a mindful approach to deep, ongoing enjoyment and accomplishment.

Luxury as a form of discipline.

Good.

The wraith returned with a white cup containing green Zurinese tea, and held it close to the right arm of Kandroknar's chair, and waited.

After an appropriate few seconds, Kandroknar took the cup, inhaled the steam and faint floral fragrance, and took a sip: it was nicely hot.

"Fetch them both," he said. "Keep Osako in the antechamber and bring Fleischmann straight in."

There was nothing light-hearted about his command.

Soon enough, Fleischmann appeared: wide shoulders in a well-tailored suit, his hair cut too short and his blocky features too hard for blending among ordinary citizens, his thick neck indicating his background in wrestling and lifting weights in competition; but it was his ability to manage a firm of tough, ruthless operators that counted here.

None of his associates had failed in a major way before, not when engaged in any of the jobs Kandroknar had commissioned; and when minor failures did occur, Fleischmann to date had always dealt with them himself, entirely to Kandroknar's satisfaction.

Today, of course, was different.

Fleischmann stood at something close to military attention. "My apologies, Mage."

Addressing his client by an appropriate title was entirely in keeping with Fleischmann's ordered approach to business.

Kandroknar knew himself to be cut from an entirely different cloth than those idiots who occupied Mordanto and similar institutions, but "mage" was meant respectfully and was in fact what Kandroknar had started out as, back in the day, before becoming something more.

Much, much more.

"Are your men alive?" asked Kandroknar.

Fleischmann shook his head. "All three down. One hit with a triple tap, another with a single shot. This Riordan is clearly capable with a firearm. The other... No marks on him, and it'll take an autopsy to determine what kind of hex or similar was involved."

He stopped, where a more voluble or fearful man might have blurted on with irrelevant details or speculation.

Kandroknar looked at him for a long moment, then nodded, and turned to a wraith-slave.

"Bring in Osako."

As the wraith slipped out on its errand, Fleischmann said: "This is your contact in Talon's organisation?"

"My dear fellow" – Kandroknar leaned back in his chair and crossed his legs – "how delightfully astute of you. Osako is indeed the wraith in question."

Until now, Fleischmann had known about nothing other than the existence of a well-placed spy. His eyes narrowed just a little: no doubt processing this new information, that Kandroknar had suborned an indentured wraith serving someone in Talon's outfit. That was no trivial matter, given the kind of safeguards the organisation made use of, security witches included.

Soon enough, five wraiths reappeared with a sixth at their centre: Osako, floating in place but ringed with golden bands that would prevent her total rotation into the compactified dimensions, effectively pinning her to mesoscopic-dimensional space.

Kandroknar wondered how much Fleischmann might understand such concepts, then set aside the thought, because he had more immediate questions that required answers.

"Osako, my dear," he said lightly. "You look ever so fetching today."

The wraith billowed just a little in the golden bands.

I told you everything.

Her words were soaked with desperation, sweet and sour and tasting strong, and Kandroknar took a moment to enjoy the sensation before moving the interaction forward.

"Tell me again."

Again, the rippling of Osako's wraith form: surely she should know that escape was impossible here.

Axelson fetched a former police detective called Riordan, at Susan Talon's command, to look for Konrad Talon who disappeared three days ago.

For a wraith, this was a lot of words to utter in one go.

"Continue." Kandroknar knew this much already.

Riordan left in the same car he arrived in, driven by the witch Rilena, and your shield allowed me to follow.

Light pulsed inside Osako's form. The shield in question was the hex implanted by Kandroknar to hide the changes in Osako from security witches and normal protective scans.

That shield included the suicide hex that would end Osako if any witch performed a proper focussed scan, but there was no need for Osako to know that.

"Good," said Kandroknar. "And you sent back the location of a rendezvous."

Osako had passed on the information by more-or-less ordinary telephone to one of the senior wraiths here: wraiths and phone lines had an interesting relationship that most people knew nothing about.

That senior wraith had in turn relayed the details to one of Fleischmann's lieutenants.

Riordan used a phone on the corner of Crisis Avenue and Bloodway. He arranged to meet a Raj Fixtovax in an alleyway in—

"The location doesn't matter now. What else do you know about this Fixtovax person?"

A wraith could follow a person and listen in on phone calls and other conversations without being detected except by accident, and Osako had proven her usefulness in that regard, but it seemed she had now reached the limit of that usefulness.

Nothing. I've never heard of Fixtovax before.

"That's somewhat disappointing."

Dim fluorescence appeared in Osako's form: a sign of stress, a recognition of the danger she was in.

Wait... It's a restaurant. I mean, Raj Fixtovax works in a restaurant. On the phone, Riordan told someone to fetch Fixtovax from the kitchen out back.

Not the most useful piece of information to come Kandroknar's way. "Do you know how many restaurants there are in Tristopolis?"

I don't know where... Oh. I think Fixtovax is the owner. Does that help?

Kandroknar smiled, baring his teeth, enjoying the moment. Business owners had to register at City Hall, and their names were a matter of public record, available on request and for a minor fee.

"It does indeed help, Osako, my dear. You have served me well, and that is good."

Fleischmann was clearly adept at analysing tone of voice and reading Kandroknar's intent: with soft sideways steps, he moved away from Osako and the wraiths who held her.

The golden bands encircling Osako began to shrink.

No!

Fleischmann's nostrils dilated as if even he could sense the wraith's aetheric screams, so obvious – and delightful – to Kandroknar's sensibilities.

"Alright." Kandroknar stopped the golden bands shrinking and allowed them to expand a little – just a fleeting capricious thought was enough to form the neurohex resonance command – and noted the pale waves of relief passing through Osako's semi-corporeal form.

"Just one other thing, my dear," he continued. At some point he'd uncrossed his legs; he recrossed them now, and gave what might well be the gentlest of smiles. "Who else are you going to tell these things to? If you go back to Axelson, who will you tell about our little conversation here?"

A large wave of fear pulsed through Osako.

No one. I promise. No one at all.

Kandroknar nodded.

"That's the right answer," he said, and raised both hands.

It felt so good, the way the power rose inside him.

I am peckish.

Me too.

The pleasure-wraiths earlier had satisfied one kind of hunger, but there were many, especially for the connoisseur, and this particular kind had not been sated for a while.

No!

Osako's words were cut off as the golden bands expanded and dropped to the polished floor with a clang.

No restraints were necessary now.

Ah.

Yes.

He sucked her aethereal-corporeal form towards him, towards his opening mouth, vaguely aware of the horror falling upon Fleischmann's features as the big man stumbled back, having seen so very much in his violent life but not this, not the kind of feeding that Kandroknar was allowing him to witness.

She tasted so good, soaked with fear and spiced with sorrow, flavoured with desperation.

Sweet.

Very.

Osako wriggled as he took her down inside his throat, swallowing her, beginning the digestive process, continuing until she was fully down inside

him.

He sighed, and gave the softest of burps.

"You can't imagine how lovely that tastes," he told Fleischmann.

The big man swallowed, not ingesting but exhibiting fear, barely controlled.

It would take a little time to fully absorb the wraith, but digestion was well underway, and Kandroknar felt nicely replete already.

His five guard-wraiths had floated to the back of the lounge: wise of them.

A long respectful pause ensued, while Kandroknar leaned back with his eyes closed, savouring the sensations inside him, smiling to himself, all the while enjoying the nervousness he sensed from Fleischmann and the wraiths.

Finally, Kandroknar opened his eyes, and smiled: call it gentle encouragement towards lesser beings.

"What…" Fleischmann cleared his throat. "What did you learn, Mage?"

Some of Osako's words would have been broadcast in clear, the wraith equivalent of speaking aloud, while others would have been absorbed, whisper-like, by Kandroknar alone.

Kandroknar could not be bothered to work out which was which.

"Talon has gone missing," he said, knowing this would be news to Fleischmann.

There'd been no need to give a reason for wanting this Riordan fellow to die, which might in any case have been a tactical mistake.

"Konrad Talon?" said Fleischmann.

"The very same."

"Huh. The fallout from that could be… interesting."

The state of Tristopolitan organised crime wasn't actually Kandroknar's main interest, but he understood Fleischmann's perspective.

"I'm going to put someone else on finding Talon," said Kandroknar. "Not you, at least not for now. But I'd like you to meet my asset before you leave, in case you end up working together."

"Fair enough."

Kandroknar sent a mental command, a summons that had to be obeyed.

"In the meantime," he said, "I need you to question someone called Raj, probably short for Rajesh, Fixtovax. He owns a restaurant, apparently. He might have some information regarding Talon's whereabouts."

Not a gourmet establishment, or Kandroknar would have known the name already.

"And find out everything he knows about Talon?"

"Exactly," said Kandroknar, "Anything he knows about Talon himself or the organisation in general."

In the early days here in Tristopolis, Kandroknar would have known every detail of Talon's setup, but those days were gone, and thankfully so. His wraith-spies mostly operated at a distance – Osako being a short-lived exception – so any detail at all might prove relevant.

"Understood," said Fleischmann. "And after he's told me everything he knows?"

Kandroknar considered this. Clearly this Fixtovax had to die so that no one else could make use of him, but there was the manner of the fellow's passing to consider.

"Do you still have witches in your employ?"

"I do," said Fleischmann.

"Alright." Using a gesture that looked like sleight of hand, Kandroknar brought a silver wristband into view upon his palm, having fetched it from a compactified-dimensions storage pocket, something far beyond the reach of most normal mages. "This forms an ice cocoon once you snap it onto someone's wrist."

"An ice cocoon?"

"You'll see. Make sure you've asked all your questions beforehand, though."

If the victim, in this case Fixtovax, wasn't dead already, then fastening the bracelet would finish them off in a ninth of a second or less.

"May I ask why, Mage?"

Kandroknar nodded. "Call it misdirection. Death by witch, when there are no witches involved in whatever's going on."

"I see."

"Also, it's booby-trapped. If someone tries to poke at the cocoon, the corpse will fall through a persistent vortex."

"Er…"

"It'll vanish," said Kandroknar.

"I see."

Well no, he didn't, because setting up a long-term persistent portal-vortex with a portable endpoint was so far beyond normal mage capabilities that most of them couldn't begin to imagine the concepts and work involved, which meant no mundane like Fleischmann, no matter his background, could possess the faintest inkling.

Never mind. The man was useful, that was all.

Fleischmann also looked relieved that the victim's dead body would disappear if anyone tried to investigate. Scene-of-crime diviners were not to be sneered at, but Fleischmann clearly understood that if Kandroknar knew his portal to be untraceable, then it was exactly that.

A thin, porcelain-white figure appeared at the lounge entrance, looking more like a statue than a living being, except that it moved and wore a modest grey dress: call it an animated mannequin.

The Martina entity was here.

It took a while for Fleischmann to notice the new arrival, which was very pleasing because a skilled operator, hyperalert, normally processed every little detail in the environment. Martina's ability to move silently was useful, and it wasn't the limit of her abilities.

When the big man did finally realise a figure was in the doorway, Kandroknar waved a graceful hand. "Mr Fleischmann, meet Martina. And vice versa."

No features marked the blank white face in Martina's current configuration.

"I… see." Something about Fleischmann's tone indicated he knew about living-ceramic entities.

That raised him in Kandroknar's estimation: entities such as Martina were rare.

Kandroknar said, "Mr Fleischmann, you deal with this Rajesh Fixtovax. Martina, I've another job for you, which involves tracing a detective called Riordan. Tell him to stop looking for Konrad Talon, and he'll be well rewarded."

No expression showed on that blank white mask.

"I assume," added Kandroknar, "he's a sleazy ex-cop with loose morals and a need for cash, otherwise he'd still be with the Department."

Handy with a firearm, Fleischmann had said, but that was irrelevant.

Martina stood statue-still, face a blank white mask. As for the suffering behind that mask… that was something Kandroknar could always taste, sweet and fragrant and delicately flavoured.

Delightful.

Never mind.

Indeed.

Time to send these living tools out into the world. With luck, Martina's very nature would be enough to convince that meddling detective to stay away from things that went far beyond his understanding.

Fleischmann's operators had a more straightforward yet interesting objective, involving this Fixtovax person.

It might be nice to…

No.

Well, that was right. Killing this Fixtovax was a tactical move, not an aesthetic moment to savour. Let Fleischmann have the pleasure, if the brute — or his even more brutish operators — were even capable of such aesthetic pleasures.

Never mind.

He watched as everyone left: Fleischmann, the white Martina entity, the five guard-wraiths who'd brought him the tasty captive Osako, so very enjoyable.

Then he smiled, settled back in his soft pterahide chair, and closed his

eyes, ready for a snooze.
      Time to digest what he'd absorbed, so delightfully.
      Such a wonderful, wonderful life.

TWELVE

Lamis was in trouble.

Donal felt there was something wrong when he was seventeen paces from the great eleven-sided door. It looked more like a hatch in a ship's bulkhead, or the entrance to a bank vault, than what it was: the front door of a subterranean apartment.

But that in itself was normal around here.

He looked back towards the steel steps he'd come down by, exiting the descending helical bone-and-steel tunnel that led down to this level, some three and a half furlongs – call it five sixteenths of a mile – beneath the River Umber.

That made it almost a full half mile below Gallway Depths, meaning the elevated Pneumetro station, not the neighbourhood itself. Donal had sort of enjoyed the walk down.

Until now.

Hardly anyone else moved in the main tunnel, or in the branching tunnels-come-corridors to either side: only a few pedestrians and wraiths, none of them suspicious.

There was a kind of ordinary deadness to the air, but what he'd expected to feel was a growing heaviness, as if the air itself were viscous, and he needed to press through it, working harder and harder the closer he came to Lamis's apartment: part of the normal defences, or maybe just a side effect of whatever mage things happened here.

None of that today, it seemed.

As soon as Donal reached the hatch-door and took hold of the wheel-like handle, he knew that someone had turned it already to the unlocked position.

No defensive aura, and the door not even locked?

Donal settled his weight, pressing down with his heels, and hauled back on the wheel, using his back and lower body as well as his arms, working it like a barbell row-come-deadlift. The Thanatos-damned thing was heavy.

Heavy, but perfectly balanced on frictionless hinges, and once he got it into motion he eased off in case it swung around hard and crashed into the wall. Instead, he kept things slow and dragged it to a halt when it was two-thirds open, which was more than good enough.

Pale, almost transparent runes, marked the eleven-sided jamb or whatever you called the inside of the threshold. Under normal circumstances, they would have glowed; now they looked like decorative traces, nothing more.

Usually the heavy door would have opened by itself, with zero need for muscular exertion.

I can't go calling Klaudius again.

Donal pulled out the Magnus. He seemed to be drawing it too often today.

Here we go.

Stepping over the high threshold one raised knee at a time, with steady control so he could still react to any threat, he entered the wide lounge. Shelves stood empty, along with a table of bare bone and three uncushioned chairs.

Lamis's favourite chair — or at least, the armchair he'd sat in during Donal's previous visits — had gone, along with candlesticks and skeletal artefacts and books and even the coffee maker.

Donal touched an empty bookcase that stood against the rear wall, then looked back over his shoulder at a whisper of sound.

"Are you my fifteen o'clock?" A stooped figure, pale and lanky, peered through the open doorway from outside. "Mrs — I mean Mr, obviously — Mulvany?"

Donal reholstered the Magnus before turning around.

"I was visiting Mage Lamis," he said. "Has he moved out?"

"Oh." The stranger was tall. He had to bend forward while picking up his knees to step over the threshold. Like a spider if it were pale and possessed only four limbs. "My name is Kaltrikoan Balimi. I'm handling the property, as I expect you've guessed."

A West Vitrix accent. Maybe from Fortinium itself. Or an affectation.

"Yeah. I'm Riordan. So what happened to Mage Lamis?"

Balimi, all seven lanky feet of him, shifted from side to side, as if standing on something sharp. "I have the current owner as Mr Grimstone. And the first name isn't Lamis."

"He uses his middle name."

"Ah." Balimi's mouth opened and closed again. He took a moment, then: "I'm not surprised he was a mage. Is a mage. I hadn't known that beforehand, though. We exchanged correspondence and several phone calls, nothing more."

"So he's moved out."

"Well, yes. Quite."

"Do you know exactly when?"

"He made first contact a while back. Maybe the third of Quintember? I'd have to check."

"And he was gone already?"

"I can't say for sure, because it was at least a week before I came to view the property. He sent the keys and tokens by mail, you see."

"Tokens."

"To drop the hex wards. He really is a mage, isn't he?"

"Yeah." Donal looked at Balimi hard. The guy seemed to be genuine. "You got a business card or anything?"

"Oh, dear me. Of course." Balimi fumbled at a waistcoat pocket – in Fortinium they'd call it a vest, not a waistcoat, and be more likely to wear one – and he pulled out a card and offered it.

"Thanks." Donal took it. The office address was downtown, therefore not cheap, although a bit too close to Twistover Pits to be classed as top tier. "Your client's full name is Dexter Lamis Grimstone."

"Ah. Yes, that makes sense of things."

"And you got to have an address to do business with him. I mean, somewhere that's not here."

"Well, a Post Office box and bank details, which are of course private."

"I don't want to send him money," said Donal. "Just talk to him. Where's the PO box?"

"I'm afraid I don't... Is this official in some way?"

"Ah, Hades. I'm a PI, used to be a cop. Don't sweat it, Mr Balimi. And I don't have time to stake out a post office until Lamis shows up. Can I just leave a message with you?"

"Of course you may."

There was a subtle inflection there, reminding Donal of Sister Mary-Anne Styx back at the orphanage school, correcting his grammar. But Donal could snap Balimi in half like a matchstick, and he probably read more books for that matter, although not the same ones.

Balimi could feel superior all he wanted, so long as he did what Donal asked.

"Tell him," said Donal, "to call Donal Riordan when he can. Please."

"I'll remember the *please*."

"Yeah, do that." Donal looked around the room again. If Lamis had put this place up for sale, then he hadn't left anything useful behind... and this wasn't a mystery to solve, so by definition there weren't any clues, and it was time to get out of here.

"Please," he added again, this time addressed purely to Balimi. "You'll be doing me a favour, and I appreciate that."

"Well, good. There's no chance that you're in the market to buy a property, I suppose."

"No."

"Or sell one?"

"We bought an old temple off Hel Ave, me and my partner," said Donal, surprising himself. "Turned it into a boxing gym with a live-in apartment."

"Gosh. How interesting." Balimi's reaction seemed to be genuine, not sarcastic.

Maybe he was alright, after all.

"Excuse me?" An older woman's voice, piercing and slightly wavering, came from outside. "Oh, Mr Balimi. It *is* you."

"Mrs Mulvany. How wonderful to see you."

"Am I too early?"

"Not at all," said Balimi. "Exactly on time."

Donal didn't need a clock or watch to know that she was seventeen minutes late, if she was Balimi's fifteen o'clock appointment.

"I'll leave you to it," he told Balimi. "It's a very nice property. Intriguing location, and perfect security."

"It is indeed, Mr Riordan."

"Really interesting. I'll be in touch." Donal crossed to the open doorway.

The woman, Mrs Mulvany, blinked when he offered his hand, to help her step over the threshold. "Thank you, young man."

"My pleasure. It's solid, isn't it?"

"Hmm. Certainly." She stepped in and held out her hand for Balimi to shake or possibly kiss the back of.

From behind her, Donal grinned at Balimi, whose eyelid flickered in a suggestion of a wink.

Good luck, pal.

Donal headed back into the main helical tunnel and began to climb. Call it 550 yards vertically to reach the surface, which would give him time to think.

His footsteps echoed from bone and steel, and a wraith exited from the solid wall and slid right past him without slowing down, and he wondered why Lamis had chosen to live down here in the first place.

But everyone needs someplace, and Lamis didn't seem to be driven by a need for money or ostentation any more than Donal himself. Mages had their own obsessions, of course.

He climbed the easy steps. Easy, but numerous.

After two minutes climbing, he stopped, though he didn't need a rest.

It was interesting that an older lady like Mrs Mulvany had come this way. The idea of living somewhere secure might well be inviting for her, but the walk must have been dreadful, unless she was fitter than she looked or had travelled by some other means.

She wasn't a wraith.

Wraith elevator shaft, maybe.

Donal hadn't known there was one, but then he didn't know the area that well. There could be multiple shafts that connected with the horizontal side tunnels.

He shook his head. Another wraith flitted past.

I don't like this.

What if there weren't any elevator shafts? What if Balimi was in danger right now?

"Thanatos."

He turned and sprinted back down.

It took him most of a minute to reach the short corridor leading to Lamis's apartment – if you could call it that – and part of him expected to find Balimi lying dead on the floor, but he stopped before getting to the doorway.

"—the elevated station," Balimi was saying, "and the other shaft takes you directly up to the taxi rank. Easy access."

"Oh, no, Mr Balimi. I'll continue to use the parking garage. I have a young man who drives me."

An employee, or something else? There was something in her voice, but it wasn't anything to threaten Balimi; and Donal's guess about elevator shafts further along the corridors had been correct, so there was nothing to worry about.

I'm turning paranoid.

Maybe it was a wonder he was as sane and balanced as he was. If you could call it that.

Doesn't get me any closer to Talon. Or finding out what Hellah's up to.

Shaking his head, he headed back to the spiralling main stairs, and started to climb once more.

Wishing he knew what to do next.

THIRTEEN

Talon wept blood and sweated tears, and all his nerves felt twisted inside out and corkscrewed every which way, and nothing made sense any more.

"Why?" he managed to say.

Did he address the hungry things surrounding him, circling him, or the absent witch Rilena, his betrayer? He no longer knew.

Maybe it was both.

She dropped me off, did Rilena. No one else knew where I was.

He spat, tasting bile, remembering Rilena driving away as instructed, leaving him in a lonely street beneath spattering quicksilver rain, Kaldera Lane at its most inviting in a sleazy sort of way.

That, and the approaching female figure in raincoat and scarf who should have been a glamorous, enthusiastic escort sent by the agency but instead proved to be a decoy, a wraith in human clothing, just solid enough to hold garments in place.

She – it, whatever – had stood there, or rather floated in place, while other wraiths appeared from nowhere, an entire ferocious group of them, and they fell on him and he was done for.

And pain.

So much pain since then.

"Why?"

The wraiths who tortured him had nothing to say as they closed in.

And brought the pain once more.

In her lonely underground home, young Susan Talon slid her gelatinous body off the curved seat she used for study, wriggled a little inside the protective carapace that formed her back, and edged sideways to a table while trying to leave as little of a slime trail as possible.

With her three left arms she reached out to pluck six balls formed of knucklebone from the tabletop – she didn't know what kind of bone it was, from what huge creature – taking two in each left hand.

Tears grew in her eyes as she began to juggle.

Two balls looped between each pair of hands, forming three nested loops. When she was at her best, she could manage more intricate patterns than this, so that each ball visited each of her six hands in one or other of the sequences she practised.

But not today.

The knucklebone balls flew through their curved paths in the old familiar rhythm.

Soft orange glows barely held back the shadows here in her underground chamber filled with the books and instruments that brought her joy in normal times. Reflected orange light slid across the moving knucklebones as she kept them in the air, working the routine her father had devised and encouraged her to practise every day, because he cared.

Her biomorphic configuration was unusual according to the mages Dad consulted – including the horrible Alej Kandroknar before his violent death; but others, the nicer ones, agreed – and while she enjoyed the study of recombinant hex manipulation and related fields for their own sake, she couldn't avoid the practical, personal conclusion either.

She didn't know anyone else who looked like her.

Two of the knucklebone balls tapped against each other in mid-air – call it a demonstration of momentum conservation, the way their trajectories altered, although the clacking sound and air resistance drained energy from the knucklebones, of course – but she could be fast and agile when she wanted to be – that was the original reason for this practice that Dad had devised for her, this routine and others – so she corrected now and kept all six knucklebone balls looping through the air.

Dad. Where are you?

Balagron and Rilena had tried tactfully to prepare her for the possibility that Dad had died somewhere, but Susan couldn't allow herself to believe that.

Why haven't you made contact?

There had been times, though not recently, when Dad had needed to be away from Tristopolis for business; and during those absences, he had managed to phone every single day to check up on his little girl, sometimes more than one call in a given day.

Today's juggling wasn't for the agility practice, not really.

Dad.

It was a prayer and an act of love, because if she kept juggling the way Dad had taught her, he had to remain alive, didn't he?

He has to.

Or maybe it formed a kind of desperation, the juggling.

Another two balls collided with a clack and went their separate ways and this time she couldn't compensate and the entire pattern collapsed and all six balls fell to the floor and rolled to a halt on the rugs and flagstones and that was that.

All done.

"Dad," she whispered. "Daddy…"

No answer from the bookcases or the silent flamesprites in their lanterns or the arched stone overhead or the shadows all around.

Nothing.

Please…

Emptiness was all.

FOURTEEN

Donal stood on a windswept platform, considering his options. Next to him, rippling dark-blue letters spelled out GALLWAY DEPTHS on a rectangular bone sign, and you could take any of seven different directions out of here: three by Hypoway, four by Pneumetro.

Spoiled for choice, in this elevated station, but it didn't help because he didn't know what to try next.

Lamis was gone. No one at Mordanto was being helpful. Klaudius was available in emergencies, but no help in the slogging footwork of investigation.

If they had a phone at home, he could call Mel – she'd be back from the clinic with Finbar by this time – and ask her for advice. But it had cost enough to have a phone line installed at his office, not to mention the tri-weekly charge for his answering service: a phone at home, even though home was a boxing gym where people paid to train, would be extravagant.

So now what?

If he couldn't get a mage's help, maybe he should ask a witch.

"Ingrid," he muttered.

"Say what?" A gnarly-skinned man, sitting on a bench, looked up from the *Gazette* he'd been reading. "You talkin' to me, pal?"

"Saying a prayer," said Donal softly.

And let his expression go dead, the way he always did when readying for combat.

"Er, right." The guy cleared his throat. "Carry on, then." He raised his newspaper high, obscuring his face.

Some people.

Donal could call Ingrid Johannsdóttir, right enough. She was first choice for anything to do with looking after young Finbar, and she'd been there for his birth.

But in her professional life, she'd worked as a security witch, mostly at one or other of the airports, and if Donal got her involved in some dodgy investigation, she might wind up losing her Class 2 clearance.

Which would never do, if she wanted to return to her old line of work someday.

Rilena, then.

She was a witch, clearly capable, plus she worked for the missing Konrad Talon, and she'd offered her help – her and the muscular blue-skinned Balagron.

Donal looked up and down the platform. There wasn't a phone booth in sight. He could either go back down to ground level or carry on with his journey and phone later.

Before he left young Susan Talon, she'd given him a cheque for three thousand florins drawn on High Cauldron Bank, and recited a phone number for him to memorise but not write down, adding: "Someone will answer at any time."

And Rilena, before Donal had left her and Balagron, had said the answering service could always reach her. Donal had known better than to ask exactly what that meant.

Farther along the platform stood a small booth, a combination newsstand and coffee counter, presided over by a flat-faced woman with a hard expression and crimson eyes. Something about the trace of airborne scent told him the coffee would taste dire, but the book rack looked to contain maps, and that might come in handy.

Raj Fixtovax lived in an interesting area.

If I didn't know any mages or witches, where would I start?

Maybe with the person he'd been supposed to meet when he got warned off by Aggie instead, not to mention ambushed by three gunmen. That would be a good first step.

He bought an Alpha-to-Omega map booklet that covered Catastrophe Depths and Cataclysm Reaches alike, and had just returned to his place on the platform and opened the booklet when off to his right a train rumbled into sight.

Donal checked the open booklet once more, then closed it and slipped it into his jacket's inside pocket. The map was memorised, pretty much.

He had the feeling that Cataclysm Reaches wasn't the kind of place where you acted like a gormless tourist with map in hand, not unless you wanted to draw attention to yourself.

Tactical stupidity, he was allergic to.

Almost here, the train.

Ovoid translucent carriages clattered and growled, louder and louder as they approached, then brakes hissed as the Hypoway train powered to a halt, and the sliding doors rattled open in their bronze frames, and a few desultory passengers dismounted to the platform.

The carriage closest to Donal bore scratches and grime across its convex surface. The interior was redolent of old sweat and maybe worse, but that was normal, therefore okay. He climbed on board and took a dusty seat and settled back as doors whined shut and the whole thing rattled into motion.

A languid-looking woman in a grey sleeveless dress and no coat, her skin a startling ceramic white, spike-encrusted and polished-looking, sat on the opposite side of the carriage, nine seats down, reading a *Tristopolitan Gazette*.

The guy who'd been on the platform reading the same newspaper wasn't here: he'd taken the next carriage down, most likely to avoid Donal.

Raj Fixtovax's restaurant was a block away from a Spectre & Host bank, which meant Donal could go there and deposit Susan Talon's cheque on the way. But maybe he should start doing something to earn that money before banking it, and surprising Raj at his home instead of his workplace seemed a more efficient way to do just that.

He tried to surprise me in Scrapeworthy.

By not being there, but was it Raj who'd sent the three men to kill Donal? It seemed unlikely.

Raj had phoned his cousin Brian in Police HQ, and Brian had told Aggie about the meeting, at least according to Aggie herself. She had killed one gunman and hurt the other two enough for Donal to put them down, which logically put Raj on the opposite side of the gunmen.

But still…

Donal had memorised the names of the two dead shooters with IDs – Larkinson and Filafr – but hadn't tried to follow up with any of his old friends in the Department. Three men were dead and he didn't want to answer any questions about the circumstances.

But maybe he should.

Hold that in reserve for now.

It was always good to have options.

The train carriage included a stained bone panel showing all the stops on this line, which in this case meant going all the way to Abyss Cloisters. And three stops before the Cloisters was Cataclysm Reaches.

Maybe some answers were there, waiting to be found.

Loud, the train.

There was a sheer drop on either side, and the carriage – the entire train – rattled as it traversed a length of track mounted on stark pylons. Here, the West Bloodflow Line ran parallel to this one on its own pylons, and through the grimy translucent carriage wall Donal watched another train matching this train's speed.

Down below stretched the dark expanse of Clamwell Pits, which were ringed with the jagged Coalsoul Towers, like smashed irregular fangs around some ruined titan's mouth.

The white-skinned woman was sitting three seats closer than before, still reading her newspaper. By the looks of it, still on the same page.

I didn't sense movement.

Donal looked back deliberately towards the receding Pits and shrugged to disguise the unbuttoning of his jacket. Then he turned towards the woman and smiled: a low-key warning of recognising her approach.

Of not being surprised, even though she now occupied the seat right next to him.

She smiled back in what looked like actual pleasure. "Hello, Donal Riordan."

Her newspaper lay on the seat she'd occupied before, on the other side of the carriage.

"You're not here to harm me, are you?" he said.

It was an odd thing for Donal to say. Strangers are strangers, unknown by definition, yet he felt certain that if she intended violence, he'd have picked up on it.

"Of course I'm not."

"I don't know you, though."

She, whoever she was, looked innocent and a little playful and utterly deadly if pushed to it, but broadcasting her inner self through body language.

No subterfuge, no defensiveness.

The train rattled and bounced once more – another shaky section on the route – but Donal kept his attention on the stranger. She seemed enrapt, focussed on him.

He'd been tricked and even ensorcelled before, but this was something else, no trickery involved.

"The enemy of my enemy is my friend." The woman laughed, and her teeth differed from standard human but her actual laugh held melody like a song. "That's a funny phrase, but it's true."

"So what do you want?"

"I'm only allowed to tell you that hunting down Konrad Talon would be dangerous, while giving up the search will prove lucrative for you."

"Allowed by who, exactly?"

"I… don't want to discuss that."

"I had a meeting arranged with a contact," said Donal. "Three unpleasant individuals turned up instead of the person I was supposed to talk to. Did your people send them?"

There was no one else in sight, not in this carriage, but Donal didn't want to spell out his complicity in three homicides, all the same. Not to a stranger whose very nature formed a mystery.

She said nothing.

Donal said, "Since we're having such a nice chat, what's your name?"

"I'm just a friend."

"Well, Miss Friend, I think you're failing in your mission. Or can I call you Justa?"

"If you must call me something, call me Martina."

"Nice to meet you, Martina."

Again, the smile. "And I'm rather enjoying this, even though, as you say, I appear to be failing in my mission."

The train rattled to a halt.

This was Naildark Thinrow station, with scarcely anyone on the platform. Every door opened on the platform side, but all it achieved for this carriage was some ventilation, which would have mattered more for Donal in his redblood days.

Neither he nor Martina moved.

No one got on. No one on the platform had been in normal hearing range. Still, he waited for the doors to close before continuing the conversation.

"Tell me what you want, Martina."

"For you to stay safe, Mr Riordan."

"You mean I should back off from finding Konrad Talon."

"I do in fact mean that."

"Why?" said Donal. "Are you or your people responsible for Talon's disappearance?"

Martina shook her head. Her long hair played over the spikes that decorated her shiny skin. "No. It's not like that."

"Then why warn me off?"

"It's because I'm... No, I can't."

Her features blanked out.

What?

More than that...

Martina's face flowed into a new shape, blank and ovoid and pure white. The hair seemed to shrink into that ovoid and disappear from sight.

"What *are* you?" said Donal.

But the thing sitting next to him no longer possessed a mouth with which to answer.

Or human hands: what remained looked like a stylised statue with smooth curved suggestions of fingers, unblemished by knuckles or nails. Like a mannequin whose fingers weren't even separate.

The white thing, still wearing that grey dress – modish, but not enough to keep a normal human being warm – rose to its feet.

It – she? – reached out with one hand towards Donal, a movement both elegant and wistful, then allowed its/her hand to drop.

Donal liked mixing with all sorts of people and beings, but he'd never heard of anything like this.

"We're not enemies." He said this with certainty, meaning it. "Not personally. I don't know how I can be so sure, but I am."

He breathed out. The first time he met Laura, back in the day – back when the zombie heart he now considered his was beating inside Laura's body – he hadn't been himself. Ensorcellment had made bizarre actions on his part feel like the natural thing to do.

This was different.

Like a featureless statue, the Martina thing stood there, blank face towards Donal as if it could still see him, but it wasn't actually frozen in place. The carriage swayed and bumped and it – she? – remained balanced, making the same automatic adjustments as a normal person. Better, as the train hit a particularly bumpy section of track and she-it remained steady.

For all Donal knew, Martina's feet were actually adhering to the bone-and-wood surface.

"Konrad Talon was a good father. Still is," added Donal, "if he's alive."

The featureless head changed angle.

"His young daughter is beautiful and smart," continued Donal, "and different and vulnerable, and torn apart by Talon's disappearance. And nothing to do with his enterprises."

Lowering its chin, the Martina thing might have been considering this. Maybe even expressing a degree of sorrow.

"So I don't want to move against you, Martina or whatever your real name is. But I do want to reunite a girl with her father."

Or at least find out for sure what had happened.

A nod, before the Martina thing straightened up.

Then it remained static, with its blank pseudo-face turned towards Donal, until the train squealed to a halt at the next station. The door opened, then it-she-Martina was gone.

Donal pushed himself up from the seat and turned, scanning the platform outside, and saw the Martina thing standing next to a column some seventeen yards distant. A normal woman might have been shivering, dressed like that without a coat, but Martina stood entirely still.

There was a flicker as if he had blinked – though he hadn't – and she/it was standing at the head of a staircase two-thirds of the way down the platform.

Flicker once more, and she was gone.

Dear Thanatos.

Pursuit was impossible, and probably wouldn't achieve anything. She/it had been sitting right next to him already.

The train doors rattled shut.

I've had weirder days.

But none so confusing, not that he could recall.

Some investigations involved the sequential tracking of clues, while others were more about poking around until someone reacted – or overreacted – giving him something to grab hold of. Right now, he had nothing. No idea of how to proceed.

He sat there as the train rattled on.

FIFTEEN

Upthrust towers slid past the carriage. The Hypoway ran lower here, and Poignard Heights lived up to its name: tall dagger-like towers rose on either side.

Donal glimpsed a single gargoyle gliding from one tower to another – stubby wings, as non-aerodynamic-looking as the rest of its kind, but flight-capable all the same – and then the towers were past and the elevated track began to rise once more.

The motion tipped Donal at an angle in his seat.

There was something slippery about today's events. Something hard to get a grip on.

Someone else is operating behind the scenes.

Nothing unusual in that. A lot of cases back in his TPD days began with zero suspects. A few that had seemed confusing eventually boiled down to multiple criminal elements at odds with each other, trailing wreckage all over the place – both deliberate and collateral casualties – until someone shut them down.

"It's related to the past."

Those had been Martina's words, before her morphing into a featureless white shape. Or actually, no. She'd managed to say something else before that happened: *"It's… No, I can't."*

Some kind of hex block installed in her/its mind?

Maybe something forced her to change shape.

Morphing into a faceless configuration before she could say anything more.

So maybe it would help if he could find out what kind of being she/it was. Or that effort might prove to be a time sink, a distraction, jeopardising his chances of finding Talon fast.

The track straightened to horizontal, and the train's motion grew smooth, humming along, relaxing him. Warm, the air inside the carriage.

The train tilted forward and down, and Donal automatically gripped the beetle-carapace grab handles to keep him in his seat.

Here in Crinkle Cascades, the Hypoway plunged downwards past cliff-like walls decorated with baroque, intricate carvings, where wraiths and other insubstantial beings whipped in and out of sight.

They passed through the next two stations without stopping: Upper Cascades and Lower Cascades, out of use, abandoned for as long as living memory.

Curving, the track, to ease the gradient as the train entered an unlit section of tunnel, before finally drawing to a halt in a dingy station barely lit by dim orange flamesprites in sconces attached to walls of old carved bone.

The train stopped a little short, with part of its length still within the tunnel proper, waiting for some kind of signal before moving into place against the black platform.

Giant human skulls of unknown provenance, ancient and hundreds of feet tall, were scattered here and there across the Earth, although absent from the Lightside according to everything Donal had read. Tristopolis boasted several of the giant skulls, including the pair that housed the great multi-level road junctions of the Orb-Dexter and Orb-Sinister Freeways, so familiar to Donal.

This place, this entire district, grew from similar beginnings.

The whole subterranean area seemed to consist of a huge buried bone of similar provenance, but for some reason no one knew exactly what kind of bone it was – what shape overall – only that it extended for a third of a mile in every horizontal direction from here, the central Hypoway station.

Beneath the train that Donal sat in – beneath the station itself – everything was solid bone for hundreds of yards downwards, but only a hundred feet or so overhead, before bone gave way to ordinary soil.

After a moment, the train edged forward, fully into the station, squealed a little, then stopped. Carriage doors hissed slowly open, as if reluctant to do so.

Time to get out.

In the station proper, the air felt different. Some kind of edge to it, though Donal would have had difficulty explaining exactly what it felt like, if someone asked.

Some restaurant owners live directly above or below their businesses; others, like Raj Fixtovax, would hate to be trapped in the same place where they slogged for so many hours a day. Raj ran a decent-sized place off Hoardway, but he made his home here.

This was Cataclysm Reaches.

The platform beneath Donal's feet was formed of black fossilised carapace that looked like polished slate. A few translucent yellow worms slid across its surface, growing insubstantial and wriggling down into the solid platform whenever someone came too close, though only a few travellers stood or walked here.

Wraith worms.

You didn't see those every day.

Both the station and neighbourhood of Cataclysm Reaches were a mystery as far as Donal was concerned. Perhaps he needed to change that.

Not a busy place. He looked around for the way out, and spotted it.

And wondered if Raj was expecting him.

Foolish of him, if he isn't.

Which meant it would be equally foolish to approach Raj's home and expect to stroll straight in without any kind of conflict on the way. Raj might not have ordered three hitmen to take Donal out, but there was a chance he knew what was going to happen.

And maybe a bit of violence would clear the air.

Donal felt a spring in his step as he passed through the platform exit barrier – the old turnstile formed of pitted bone creaked as it turned – and into a dim waiting-room plus ticket hall combined.

Here seven sour-looking, standard-issue humans sat clumped on one of the long bench seats, huddled next to each other but lost in their individual thoughts: a family enduring misery.

A lot more wraiths than you'd see in Lower Danklyn were moving through the station, in and out of the walls and ceiling – avoiding the floor, it seemed – and all three ticket windows were manned by wraiths as well.

Interesting.

Donal exited to a pedestrian tunnel with mostly unmarked walls but grime piling up at the bottom, where they met the floor. A few individuals were standing around, talking to each other or staring at their feet.

No one paid Donal any mind as he strode past them and reached the far end, where a normal-looking street sign read Scalex Way. There were at least two other streets of the same name in Tristopolis. But overhead hung a ceiling, not sky.

The thoroughfare running from left to right was a tunnel, with bicycles moving along its length but no motorised vehicles in sight. Raised sidewalks stood on either side. Steps led from sidewalk to cycle path every thirty yards or so.

Flamewraiths trapped in overhead globes lit the place brightly, surprisingly so.

Every dwelling-place and shop and tunnel in the district had been carved out of the titanic fossilised bone, harder than granite, that comprised Cataclysm Reaches.

Feeling the map booklet inside his jacket, he left it there, orienting himself with respect to his mental image of the map pages and the route he had planned.

A soft voice sounded from his left. "You want to make love, sir?"

She was small and her face was lined but not by chronological age – probably in her mid-twenties, not the fifty-something she appeared – and she didn't meet Donal's gaze when he looked down at her.

"Not today." He kept his voice gentle.

The woman nodded and returned to her position inside a shabby-looking doorway.

Part of him wondered about the sorry story that must have led her to this place and abject state, but you couldn't save everyone. Right now he had a job to do.

Nice neighbourhood.

It was an obvious sarcastic thought, but the more he scanned the establishments carved into either side of Scalex Way – and something of the side tunnels branching off at sixty degree angles – the more complex and contradictory the place appeared.

In other districts, a streetwalker battered by life would ply her trade in dingier, darker doorways, not this close to well-lit grocer's stores and a bookshop called Nulworthy's Nook.

There were three coffee shops that Donal could see, including a Fat'n'Sugar franchise. Also a sporting goods store called Iron & Bone, and his and Mel's boxing gym could do with a couple more pterashrike-sinew jump ropes and decent bag gloves, and for that matter his tracksuit had seen better days, but giving into temptation would be pure indulgence.

He quelled the desire by a kind of internal mental twist and shove, forcing the thought into a different slot within his mental architecture, deactivating it for now.

Not something he'd have done pre-resurrection.

So I am still a blackblood.

Which made him think of checking his watch, so he did just that, because his time sense might be accurate but energy usage was something else.

The black pie-slice on the bone-grey dial looked slender, which meant he would need to recharge his heart within the next three hours, preferably not at the last minute.

It's only Raj, and he's probably at work.

If no one was at home, Donal could use his lock-picks and plug himself into a wall socket – recharging at Raj's expense – confident that he could react in time if someone turned up while his chest was pulled open.

Not something he'd want to make a habit of, all the same.

Remembering the way from his Alpha-to-Omega map, he took the seventh side tunnel, descended a spiralling staircase and traversed a lower-level corridor. There he passed a row of lock-ups with hex-guarded carapace doors and two security golems on watch, their featureless yellow eye-slits tracking Donal's progress.

Finally he reached a flamesprite-lit residential tunnel, the place he was looking for.

Far cleaner than expected. Maybe this part of Cataclysm Reaches was okay.

Number 329 boasted a sturdy door, and if there'd been more people about then Donal would have had no chance in working the locks unobserved. Right now, the place looked quiet.

He strolled past Raj's place while the last few people entered their residences – subterranean houses or multi-level apartments: Donal wasn't sure what to call them – apart from two who exited the tunnel without looking back.

Donal went back to Raj's front door and knocked like a civilised normal person.

Nobody answered the knock, so Donal slid out the monogrammed kimodo-hide tool-wallet that Mel had given him for St Magnus's Day, extracted his new rune-engraved lock-picks – powerful enough to deactivate most domestic hex defences, according to Spikeworthy Bob who'd sold him the tools – and got to work.

It took thirteen minutes to get through all three locks and soak up the remaining defensive energies from the door with a hex-blotter mini-skull. When it grew icy to the touch, he dropped the mini-skull back inside his pocket.

He slid his tool-wallet back inside his unbuttoned jacket, and used his left hand to slowly push the door open.

Sparse, the hallway.

Donal took in a long, controlled breath, relying on his zombie sensory acuity to pick up any scent traces: the aftershave of a waiting thug, a woman's fragrance, the earthier smell of the recently deceased.

Or even just a hint of gun oil.

It's empty.

Intuition and experience told him it was almost certain – call it ninety-seven percent – that he was alone; but three percent uncertainty wasn't zero, so he took his time closing the door in something close to silence.

Step by careful step, he advanced along the hallway, jacket unbuttoned but hands in front palms-forward. He was, after all, the intruder here.

Nothing and no one waiting.

It was always strange, searching someone's home when they weren't in it.

The windowless lounge looked tidy, with a small bookcase, an old-fashioned but comfortable settee, and a fake Surinese shield and halberd on the wall, which should have looked ridiculous but actually felt cosy, reinforced by the old porcelain crockery collection, decorated with tiny black roses and skulls, on display in a glass-fronted cabinet.

An old fashioned telephone carved from mammoth ivory – the kind where the mouthpiece blended with the upright stalk you held it by, and the dialling cogs were set in the same stalk, while the earpiece formed a separate part, linked by a cord – stood on a small table.

Beyond stood a standard lamp with parchment shade decorated with pictograms as fake as the shield. A batwing armchair was positioned beneath the lamp, just right for reading.

None of it to Donal's taste, but comfortable all the same.

I don't know what I expected, but it wasn't this.

He was in the right place. On top of the crockery cabinet stood a single purple-and-white photograph showing Raj in his younger days, along with the gawky smiling girl who would later become his wife and more latterly his ex-wife and bitterest memory, from the way he spoke these days.

The photo – the fact of its still being on display – hinted at deeper, contradictory feelings.

He might not have set me up.

Raj had made a phone call that resulted in Aggie's appearance, but the hitmen were something else. Working assumption: no need for violence when Raj appeared.

Three things to do: check that every room was empty, take a look around for any hint of Raj getting involved in something he shouldn't – bank statements and letters or any kind of contraband stashed away – then choose a plug socket for recharging his heart.

It's cold. How come?

He drew the Magnus as quietly as possible, because the icy sensation on his skin hadn't been there a few moments earlier.

Nor did it feel like Klaudius making an appearance somehow: this cold had a deader, static feel to it.

A second earlier, he'd felt nothing, yet the cold held steady as if it had been here forever.

The nearest opening led into a kitchen, as windowless as the lounge but subtly warmer, therefore not the source of whatever he was sensing.

Back out in the hallway, the doors to a utility room and walk-in cupboard felt ordinary: nothing behind them. Normally Donal would have opened both to check, but he couldn't do it silently, and right now stealth felt like an excellent idea.

Diagonally opposite the lounge door, a tiny square carpeted landing led to carpeted stairs leading both up and down: Donal's working assumption was that there were three floors in total and no other ways in and out, only the front door.

But he might be wrong and he'd better stay alert because Mel would be Death-damned furious if anything happened to him.

Focus.

He edged his way to the small landing and reached out slowly, slowly with his left hand, feeling the air.

Like redbloods, because the placement of arteries and veins and capillaries remains unchanged, zombies transfer heat most easily through three areas: the lower half of the face, the soles of the feet, the palm of each hand.

Resurrected folk possess lower body temperatures but greater sensory acuity, which evens things out in terms of sensing cold.

Donal sometimes wondered how different his life would have been if he'd read textbooks so intently back in the day – his mind had never been so full of facts and theories regarding physiology and so much more – especially if, like now, he simply hadn't needed sleep.

Cold from downstairs.

He checked again, growing more certain. The cold was rising from below, although technically that meant thermal energy was flowing downwards; but the point was that something odd was happening one floor down and he was going to have to look.

Slowly, slowly, he descended the steps.

A minute later, and Donal knew he'd been one hundred percent wrong.

Raj Fixtovax was not in fact at work – neither cooking nor supervising nor doing the accounts in the restaurant he'd worked so hard to build up from nothing – nor would he ever be there again.

Death puts a crimp in everyone's career plans.

"I'm sorry," Donal said aloud.

Sorry, because coincidences exist, but unexpected events during an investigation usually mean something else.

I rang you for a meeting and now you're dead.

This was going to be bad, because of what was hanging in mid-air.

Some roughly ovoid, near-transparent volume of… something… hovered in the centre of a room that Raj had probably called his den. The floating shape looked like ice but probably wasn't, and might not even be of ordinary matter.

This close, the slick aura of hex felt unmistakable.

Whatever it was, it enclosed the splayed figure of Raj Fixtovax – of the dead thing that had until recently been Raj.

His corpse hung at the centre of the ovoid.

There was such a thing as stasis, but this wasn't it. The merest glimpse of Raj's grey face and opaque eyes was enough to tell you he'd given up his life, and not easily. Twisted limbs and angled neck and prominent sinews all spoke of agony during those final moments.

Donal put his Magnus away.

It wasn't going to help anybody now.

Someone's going to pay for this.

An ordinary civilian might find his values odd – Donal knew that – but having hitmen coming after him was in some sense part of the game, because it was his investigation that provoked the response. But when some essentially innocent bystander suffered, that took things to a whole new level.

Time to phone this in.

I thought I was done with HQ.

He could call the nearest precinct, but he'd rather deal with detectives he knew, and with luck call in a favour: get Viktor or one of the other guys to swing past Mel's Gym and let Mel know that Donal was going to be late home, but not to worry.

And damn the expense: they needed a home phone. He'd get right on it when this case was done. First, he needed to report a homicide.

"Sorry," he told the floating corpse once more.

Then he climbed back up to the lounge, picked up the faux-antique telephone that Raj would never use again, and spun the cogs with his thumb.

"Tristopolis PD," he heard. "We protect or avenge."

"Detective Harman, please," said Donal. "It's about a homicide case. My name is—"

"Hades, I know who you are, Loot."

"Eduardo. It *is* you."

"Sure. I been taking what you might call elocution lessons, remember?"

"Thanatos."

"Yeah, tell me about it. Okay, you gotta case to talk about, so I'm putting you through. Later."

"Yeah. See you."

Clicks and buzzes, overlaid with hums from anti-ensorcellment sprites working the line. Finally, a louder click and background silence.

"Detective Harman."

"Viktor, it's Donal."

"Hey, pal…"

"I'm standing in a dead man's home, and the man in question is Raj Fixtovax."

"Is that—"

"Brian's cousin, yeah. 327 Septakon Ductway, Cataclysm Reaches."

"Oh, Hades."

"You don't know the third of it."

They were friends. Donal could tell Viktor things that would never make their way onto a scribed report; but that didn't mean he had to share everything.

"I was supposed to meet him," Donal began, "but never mind where. The whole thing was a setup, an ambush, and I was lucky to get clear. I was in two minds as to whether Raj dropped me in it deliberately, so I came round his house and the front door was, er, open…"

"That sort of open. Okay."

"So I came inside and that's where I found him, and he's in some kind of hex field or something, stuff that looks like floating ice, and it's sucking the heat out of the place."

"Don't move until I get there."

"You got it." Donal hung up the phone quietly.

Still have to recharge.

It was a Hades of a thing to do in a dead man's home, but Detective Sergeant Viktor Harman had told him to wait here, so what else could he do?

No free sockets, so he unplugged the standard lamp, pulled the slim black cord from his pocket, and plugged it in.

Sat down in the batwing armchair with the other end of the charging cord draped across his thigh, undid his tie, and slowly unbuttoned his shirt.

One Hades of a thing to do.

SIXTEEN

Donal was still recharging when Viktor and two uniformed officers showed up. He remained in place, listening, while they let themselves into the hallway and entered the lounge.

As always, a stubble of beard emphasised Viktor's hard features, and his glasses with the round pale-blue lenses removed any last trace of softness. His ever-present leather coat hung off square shoulders while leaving access to the twin Grauser machine pistols holstered beneath his armpits.

He was also Dr Harman these days, an actual ThD, and possibly the smartest person Donal knew.

"Don't get up," Viktor told him, then turned to the uniforms. "Secure the premises, by which I mean don't mess up my crime scene before the SOC diviners get here. No trampling, no spitting, no picking your noses and flicking snot."

"Sure thing," said the younger officer, and tapped her colleague on the shoulder. "We'll guard the front door. No other way in or out of these places."

The older officer gave an easy-going nod that Donal read as one hundred percent deceptive: the relationship between the two wasn't what it seemed, but either way they looked competent and sharp enough.

After they'd exited the lounge, Viktor made a show of looking around – at the bookcase, the husband-and-wife photograph, the old-fashioned telephone, the quaint crockery in the glass-fronted cabinet – although he'd almost certainly analysed the place already, down to the tiniest fraction of an inch.

Sitting in an armchair with his black heart plugged in and his pectoral muscle and skin flap pulled back, Donal ought to have felt vulnerable; but this was Viktor and they'd been through stuff together and neither of them could be bothered to sweat the small stuff.

Plus Donal could unplug and shift into action in a ninth of a second.

Relaxation through vigilance.

Peace through badassery.

"You think Raj chose the furniture," he asked. "Or was it his ex, back in the day?"

Viktor's mouth twitched. "He was your snitch, not mine, but I always figured him as being a lot like Brian. And Brian's a bit of a slob, except when he's organising inventory."

By which Viktor meant weaponry and ammunition, plus auxiliary kit like targets to shoot: something Viktor himself did very well indeed, except that the Grausers tended to obliterate those targets, turning them into confetti.

An unspoken question hung in the air. Donal decided to address it directly. "My client is innocent and a civilian, but her family isn't. I'd rather not drag names into this, if I don't have to."

"Alright, got it. I'll take a look at the corpse, but is there anything beyond what you said, down there?"

Donal shook his head. "He wasn't a criminal, was Raj. Not as far as I know."

Viktor's face grew even harder. Sometimes that just meant he was thinking.

"Restaurant kitchens need expensive fittings when they get started, and food supplies all the time." Viktor stared at Donal from behind those pale-blue lenses. "If he wasn't buying dodgy supplies, which would be a criminal act, then I'll bet he was paying protection money."

"In my book," said Donal, "that would make him a victim."

"If he wasn't a victim before, he is now."

"Yeah." Donal breathed out exactly as if he were a redblood, and never mind his exposed zombie heart and the glistening black cord that led to a wall socket. "Killed because I wanted to talk to him about that protection."

"Unless it's random coincidence," said Viktor. "We both know that happens."

Donal shook his head again. "Go down and take a look. Then we can discuss the chances of a random burglar being caught in the act by Raj."

"Alright," said Viktor.

He was a big man but even with zombie sensory acuity, it was hard to detect even a whisper of sound as he slid out to the stairs and disappeared from sight.

Donal settled back.

One hundred and twenty-seven seconds later, by the automatic time sense Donal took for granted these days, a faint thud sounded from below.

By the hundred and twenty-ninth second, Donal was halfway down the stairs, Magnus in hand and shirt gaping open, slapping his chest muscle into place left-handed, with the charging cable back in the sitting-room.

Over seventy percent recharged, more than enough for a full day's worth of action, moving as fast as he could without creating a racket.

Into the dead Raj's den, looking for trouble and finding it in the form of Viktor's prostrate body but no enemy to shoot: nothing and no one at all.

Really nothing.

What the Hades is all this?

The den felt cold, as cold as before, but the glowing ovoid hex field – or hex-impregnated ice, or whatever the stuff was – had disappeared completely.

As had its contents. No sign of Raj Fixtovax's body.

Only Viktor, lying there.

"You better keep breathing, pal." Donal went down on one knee, pressed fingertips against Viktor's carotid artery, checking the pulse while scanning the room with his weapon still raised.

Still without a target.

Metronome-steady, the pulse, at least by redblood standards: Viktor had simply drifted into sleep.

I probably looked like this when Rilena dropped me into sleep trance.

Not good, but it could have been worse.

"Death in Hades, this is a mess."

He jammed the Magnus back into his shoulder holster, shifted into a squat position, grabbed hold of Viktor by the lapels of his leather coat, and powered himself up to standing, much as he had with Gina in the diner kitchen earlier.

Viktor felt heavier: hard-boned even while unconscious.

Donal dipped and pulled Viktor over one shoulder – firefighter's carry position – and started up the stairs, with Viktor still unconscious. This was going to make a funny story one day, but not right now.

He carried Viktor all the way up to the sitting-room and hallway, where he lowered Viktor to the old-fashioned carpet and looked up at the two uniformed officers staring wide-eyed.

"No smart remarks." Donal rose up to standing. "Something put Viktor to sleep and snatched the murder victim, and we need more than scene-of-crime diviners here. You need to call for—"

On the floor, Viktor moaned and moved from side to side.

"He's waking up," said the female officer. "Besides, the diviners have medical training, and they'll be here soon."

"You might want to do your shirt up," said the older cop. "Might start some odd rumours about you and Detective Harman here, otherwise."

"Hades." The younger cop shook her head. "I really can't take you anywhere."

Shirt undone, Viktor at his feet, and with two uniforms ladling out sarcasm here at a homicide scene, Donal felt an odd thought crystallise.

I miss this.

The dark banter that let you cope with unpleasantness. The sense of camaraderie, of shared knowledge the rest of the world preferred to ignore.

Behind the round blue lenses of his glasses, Viktor's eyelids flickered.

"I don't think he's going to be happy," added the female cop. "He's got quite the reputation."

The older cop sighed, and something changed in his demeanour. "He's not the only one round here." He nodded towards Donal. "Right, Loot?"

"Do I know you?"

"Worked a couple of scenes in the background, Lieutenant, back in the day. But we never really talked, like."

You didn't always get to know the uniforms securing a crime scene: fair enough. "I'm not with the Department, not any more."

"Don't look like you're a civilian either."

"No, I don't suppose I am." Donal shook his head as Viktor, still lying on the floor, grimaced and squinted upwards.

Conscious once more.

"Thanatos," rasped Viktor. "Things are never boring when you're around, are they?"

The older cop looked at the younger one. "Told you."

"Crazy. Absolutely crazy," she said, and grinned. "I love it."

Donal looked at her. "You'll do okay."

She nodded, accepting the compliment.

Viktor rolled onto one knee, then up to his feet. The twin Grausers showed, dangling beneath each armpit as his leather coat swung open, and then he was fully standing and his face looked harder than ever.

"I'm not happy," he said.

The younger cop's eyes were twinkling, but she clearly knew not to add a smart remark of her own, not now.

"Me neither," said Donal. "Time we found out what's going on?"

"Oh, yeah."

"Good."

Maybe things would start making sense.

SEVENTEEN

The chief diviner was a Bone Listener Donal had never met before, and she stared at him for a long time after entering the premises.

No indigo ribbons marked the front door as a crime scene, not yet, but the two uniforms were standing outside in the corridor once more. The scene-of-crime team would have had no difficulty in seeing which apartment to enter.

The chief SOC diviner nodded three times without a word, then brushed past Donal on her way to the stairs that led downwards to the basement level: down to where Raj Fixtovax's body had hung in some kind of hex field.

Both assistant diviners were young – they looked as if they ought be in school – but only one had the bulbous-eyed gawky look of a Bone Listener. The other was dark-skinned and looked standard human apart from the suggestion of pointed ears.

A look that Mel had briefly possessed following Finbar's birth, though it had faded and they hadn't really talked about it since. Not properly.

Not really addressing the details of her ancestry, and therefore that of their son.

Focus.

This was a crime scene, and Viktor's voice floated up faintly from downstairs. "I took maybe one step into the room, and that's all I remember."

A murmured question from the Bone Listener at low volume, low enough so that even Donal couldn't decipher the words.

"No, I didn't see it." Viktor clearly felt no need to keep his voice down. "Or if I did, I don't remember. But if Donal Riordan says there was a body floating inside the thing, there was a body, okay?"

Donal's mouth twitched.

Up here, the dark-skinned diviner held a small platinum trident in one hand – she'd extracted it from a pocket of her tunic – and now she waved it back and forth near Donal's chest. Then she stopped, with the divining trident hovering close to Donal's heart.

She looked straight into his eyes, and frowned.

"What's wrong?" said Donal.

A silent pause, then: "Nothing."

The diviner turned to look at her colleague, who gave a slow nod that might almost have been a ceremonial bow.

"Your resonance is unusual," said the other diviner, the young Bone Listener. "Perhaps if you'd care to wait outside, Mr Riordan?"

Part of Donal wished she'd addressed him as lieutenant even though he wasn't one, not any more. "What does that mean? About the resonance."

"Just that we need a clear space in which to work."

"To find the traces of what happened," said the other. "Traces left by individuals and phenomena other than yourself, sir."

Donal let out an unnecessary breath.

Then he grinned. "I don't think anyone's ever called me a phenomenon before."

"Er." The diviner blinked and shifted her weight from side to side, clearly losing her composure. "I didn't mean—"

"Relax." It was the younger female cop, leaning in from the corridor outside. "He's teasing you. You *are* teasing, right, Lieutenant?"

"I wouldn't dream of it." He winked at the dark-skinned diviner.

After a moment, she managed a half-smile in return. Her Bone Listener colleague showed no reaction.

Wonderful.

But Donal wasn't here to make friends, and the scene-of-crime diviners weren't paid to chat with civilians to no good purpose, so he added: "I'll get out of your way. Call me back in if you need me."

He smoothed down the front of his tie, buttoned his jacket – no one had questioned his right to carry a concealed Magnus – and walked along the hallway.

The female cop drew aside to let him through the doorway, out into the pedestrian corridor.

"Smells different out here," said Donal. "Not fresh exactly, but not stale either."

"I know what you mean," said the older cop. "Had an aunt used to live here. Not a bad place, as neighbourhoods go. Despite all the weirdness."

Donal looked left and right, up and down the long bone corridor of Septakon Ductway that stretched for maybe a third of a mile in total.

A few residents had exited their apartments to stand in the corridor and stare at the cops, which meant little in itself: rich or poor, law-abiding or shady, citizens felt some kind of curiosity in the aftermath of crime or tragedy.

As an investigator, you could make use of that curiosity, if you approached people carefully. Donal didn't think a door-to-door enquiry would yield much today, but you never knew.

Near the back of a small crowd gathered some ninety yards away, a tall figure shifted and turned away.

What the Hades is he doing here?

The figure wore a long coat plus a wide-brimmed dark hat that Donal had never seen before, but the wraparound shades looked the same as always. Maybe in his redblood days Donal wouldn't have recognised Mage Lamis from this distance, but those days were gone.

Lamis – it had to be him – walked farther away from the group until he reached a side-corridor on the left hand side. There, he hesitated for the count of three – a child would have said three Mixadriptotrixes, or Mixadriptotrices if they went to an old-fashioned school – then moved out of sight.

It looked like an invitation.

After the Martina thing morphing shape earlier, maybe it would be a good thing to stay alert. Just because that figure looked like Lamis, that didn't mean it was him.

So: invitation or trap.

"I don't feel right," Donal told the two uniformed cops. "I need to walk a little, clear my head."

He said it as if he didn't mean it, because he might not be coming back, and wanted them to know that.

"You need to—" the younger cop began.

"Sure, Loot." The older cop rubbed the side of his nose. "You take some time. Not like you're a stranger, right?"

The younger cop blinked twice but said nothing.

"See you in a bit," said Donal.

He shrugged his shoulders and unbuttoned his jacket, a gesture that wasn't lost on either of the cops.

"Just going for a walk," he added.

"Uh-huh," said the younger cop.

But neither cop followed or tried to call him back.

He upped his pace as he walked.

Donal caught up with Lamis five blocks away, if that was the correct way to think about subterranean layouts. Call it five intersections, maybe.

Either way, the tunnels were wider but grimier here, though you'd be hard put to say exactly where one neighbourhood transitioned into another.

Lamis was standing beneath a ceiling-mounted basket of flamesprites, with his hands inside the pockets of his long coat. In rural areas, people would call it a duster.

He turned to look at Donal through those wraparound shades whose only purpose, as far as Donal could tell, was to conceal blasted eye pits. He remembered those scarred sockets as less angry looking than Rilena's, but just as empty.

The wide-brimmed hat would be good for keeping off quicksilver rain, if they weren't in a tunnel deep below ground.

"You were looking for me." The sepulchral voice resonated as deeply as ever. "Or you were you just dropping in for tea?"

Donal considered asking Lamis how he'd tracked him down, then realised there was no point. You dealt with mages, stuff happened.

"No, I was after your help," he said instead. "You know, I don't actually expect you to help me out for free."

Three cyclists pedalled past, their bicycles carved from bone in old-fashioned but serviceable designs. None glanced in Donal or Lamis's direction.

Lamis asked, "How much are you being paid for your current case?"

"Um, well, for the one I really need your help on, nothing at all. What percentage cut would you like?"

"I'm homeless from choice right now, not poverty. Not desperate for money."

"So I presume that Balimi talked to you. The guy selling your apartment."

"Indeed. He told me you helped persuade the buyer, a Mrs Mulvaney."

"Not that much help," said Donal. "But the deal's going through, is it?"

"It is, in fact."

Enough of financial small talk. "If an entity," said Donal, "can transit through crawlspace dimensions, like a mage portal but different, is there any way to track their movements?"

Wraparound shades and facial muscles that didn't move: no readable expression on Lamis's face. "There might be. What kind of entity are we talking about?"

There was no avoiding the next part. "How about a Guardian?"

Lamis opened his mouth, then closed it, looking grim. Finally an expression Donal could read.

"You have a strange sense of humour, Donal Riordan."

"I'm really not joking."

"No, I don't suppose you are."

Donal jammed his hands inside his trouser pockets. "Klaudius and Hellah have become friends of mine, over the past few months."

Lamis lowered his chin but said nothing.

"I'm closer to Hellah than Klaudius in general," added Donal. "But Hellah's been transporting herself to somewhere unknown, and I'd like to know where."

No need to mention that Klaudius was the one worrying about Hellah. Both Lamis and Kelvin went up against the ensorcelled Klaudius that time, so neither was likely to remember him fondly.

"There are easier ways to commit suicide," said Lamis in a tone like rumbling thunder, "than facing an angry Guardian."

"Like I said, we're friends."

"But not so close that Hellah tells you her every move, by the sound of it."

"Well, no."

Again Lamis just looked at Donal, or seemed to: you never could tell, because of the shades.

Finally, "I'm going to have to think about it," said Lamis. "At best, it wouldn't be straightforward."

"Alright. How long do you need to—"

"Unknown. There's no way to tell which detection method might work unless I carry out some experiments. So give me a day or a year, whatever it takes."

Donal controlled himself.

Instead of protesting, he said: "Would getting a wraith on board help in any way? I mean, if it's all about crawlspace dimensions, the way Guardians transport themselves from one place to another."

"Hmm. It might help, at that, when I've carried out some preliminary work. Do you have any wraiths you call friends?"

At one time, Gertie would have sprung to mind.

"The one I know best," said Donal, "has been acting very strangely recently. She warned me off this case." He gestured back in the direction of Raj Fixtovax's home, now out of sight. "I take it you saw the cops."

"A crime scene," said Lamis. "Or so it appeared. What happened? And do you think Hellah had anything to do with it?"

"Uh, no, that case hasn't got anything to do with her. I'm kind of working two things simultaneously."

He gave a brief description of the Talon case: concerned daughter, missing crime boss, and Aggie warning him off while at the same time saving him from the ambush at the rendezvous location.

And Raj Fixtovax's body, floating in a translucent ovoid cocoon or something that looked like ice, but disappearing – corpse and enclosing stuff alike – when Viktor Harman went to look at it.

"Like ice," said Lamis. "You say the floating volume looked like ice."

"Uh, yeah. That's right."

"And you said this is a separate case, this Talon investigation, that has nothing to do with a Guardian behaving differently than usual."

Donal wasn't sure he had a handle on what constituted normal behaviour for a Guardian, but he answered, "Sure. You've got it."

A group of foundry workers in oil-stained coveralls were heading this way, trailed by a golem with a glowing yellow eye-slit. Lamis and Donal moved close to the tunnel wall, allowing them to pass.

None of the workers paid much attention to Lamis or Donal, apart from the golem, which turned its head to stare at them without changing its walking speed, until it was several paces past them, at which point the stone-like head rotated to face forward once more.

When the group was out of hearing range, Lamis stepped away from the wall. "You said the cocoon or enclosing bubble looked like ice. Who else do you know with a penchant for manifesting ice and frost?"

"I don't—You can't mean Klaudius."

"Don't be too sure that the siblings can't manifest each other's usual phenomena."

Hellah's skin was the colour of fresh glistening blood, and whenever she caused visible energies to appear, it was usually in the form of flames. Only her eyes, with seven-sided irises of orange fire, looked identical to those of pale-skinned Klaudius.

Both Guardians carried out the same job, of course: pacifying or controlling the great eldritch entities below One, Avenue of the Basilisks.

"I don't see the connection," said Donal.

"That doesn't meant there isn't one."

"No." Donal turned to stare in the direction of Raj Fixtovax's home. "No, it doesn't."

Behind him, Lamis said nothing.

In fact, the subliminal sense of human presence seemed not to be there, and when Donal looked back, no one stood there. No one at all.

Lamis was gone.

There'd been none of the energy emanations associated with a portal, so maybe Lamis simply possessed a way of shielding himself from view and hearing as he walked like an otherwise normal human being.

I could shoot a few rounds along the tunnel. See if anything happens.

Not the kind of idea to act on.

Mages. Still a nightmare.

But at least he'd learned one thing, or a hint of something, and maybe set a useful process in motion. Provided Lamis could come up with a way of tracking a Guardian's movements through the crawlspace dimensions.

In the meantime, the exact circumstances of Konrad Talon's disappearance remained unclear. Susan hadn't been able to shed a great deal of light in that regard. Perhaps Donal needed to go back to the beginning; or perhaps there was some other way to move things forward.

Time to figure it out.

EIGHTEEN

Konrad Talon existed in a nightmare beyond exhaustion, his world a fractured mass of agony, a mess of tortured sensations: scarcely able to see, his vision permanently blurred – or so it seemed – and he could no longer tell whether he felt hot or cold or anything other than pain: every kind of pain that could exist, did so inside him now.

Writhing on the cold, blue-grey flagstones for what seemed eternity.

Finally, the wraiths pulled their slithering tendrils out of him and moved away and sank out of sight into solid stone.

Were gone.

Oh…

A silent moan inside his head.

They're going to let me rest.

At last, some kind of surcease.

All around, the purple flames were drawing back, receding from him, opening up space on the stone floor with its impossible pentagonal flagstones. Maybe the departed wraiths wanted him to move about, to exercise; and maybe that was to keep him alive and suffering for longer, nothing more than that.

Neither charity nor mercy existed in their nature, as far as he could tell.

Doesn't matter.

He was too exhausted to move. Wrung out and battered and violated, and this was no way to live, but still he didn't want to die: not here, not now.

Not yet.

Give me one chance.

Any slip on the wraiths' part, and he would seize it. They might kill him if he looked like escaping, but that couldn't be allowed to matter.

Cold, the bluish grey floor on which he lay.

It was miserable, but at least it formed a feeling other than pure pain.

Susan. I've failed you, like I failed your mother.

She should have been safe, and maybe that traitress Rilena would show some kind of mercy towards a fourteen-year-old girl, but wishful thinking was for weaklings. Konrad Talon might be injured and damaged beyond repair, but he was never that, not weak.

Everything hurt, so very much.

There was a hiss, and a tight column of orange flames grew into being in front of him, twisting like some tornado formed of fire, while the original purple flames drew further away still, almost to the seven walls of the chamber, and seemed to dim: whether in contrast to the new flames' brightness or in absolute terms, it was impossible to tell.

Whiteness spinning around, mixed with the orange blaze, like a twister of ice and fire, and it rose and grew and Talon could only stare at it, unable to think coherently as it brightened and faded and twisted from existence, leaving only a tall figure standing there.

Her skin glistened the exact hue of freshly spilled blood.

Thanatos, no.

Eyes of flame: seven-sided irises burning orange.

Death's blood, help me.

Her voice, when she spoke, went through him like a knife, like a multitude of knives. A torrent of fear swept through him, like every terrifying moment of his life brought into one moment and magnified beyond all recognition.

He'd never understood how deep fear could run inside you, could shear you into slices and claw you into shreds, not until this moment.

I can't…

Exactly what he couldn't do, he didn't know. Confusion. Couldn't think, couldn't breathe…

Could no longer form coherent thoughts.

Can't…

Hideous and awful, the emotional cascade ripping him apart more thoroughly than the most invasive of torturing tendrils, and it came to him that the agony inflicted by those terrible wraiths would be preferable to what he felt in this moment.

When she spoke, every word felt like death.

"Talk to me," she said, the entity who seemed like horror personified.

Talon's mouth worked, but nothing came out.

Can't…

The Guardian raised one eyebrow, causing the blood-red skin of her forehead to glisten even more, while the orange fire of her eyes grew brighter still, becoming blazing heptagons of golden flame, ferocious and implacable.

"You will tell me."

"I…" He managed that much, and a croak.

Nothing more.

The entity known as Hellah – unless this was a different Guardian, one from some other part of the world but similar in appearance – spoke louder, each syllable a crashing torrent of pain and torture and overwhelming fear, rocking the structure of reality at its roots.

"Tell me about the singleton behind it all."

"I…"

"Tell me what you know of the composite, most foul."

Talon cried and tried to turn his head away, but couldn't.

That was when the pain started in his chest.

My heart.

Maybe that was good. Salvation of a sort.

"No. I will not let you die. Not yet."

His heart felt hardened, like a rock.

What's happening to me?

Heptagons of orange flame, those overwhelming irises, and as he glanced at the eyes of Hellah the Guardian, every vestige of will and determination shrivelled up like fragments of burning vellum, and flew away like ash upon the wind.

"Tell me what you know of The Draxoleth."

All he could do was cringe and sob.

No.

"Tell me everything."

Talon possessed no will of his own. Not any longer.

Then, without volition, he opened his mouth and began to speak: less like a human being than a record player replaying the music laid down as tracks inscribed in thin bone disks; no more than that.

Relating everything he knew, while tears flowed almost unnoticed, and he wasn't really thinking any more at all. His confession, if that was what it was, seemed to go on and on and on, a continuing release of things he had held onto for far too long, and even with the pain and fear, a thread of comfort ran through his sobbing words, letting go at last.

And then he was done: empty of words and memory.

Exhausted.

"Good."

The word sounded finally, minutes or aeons after his exposition began.

"Now sleep."

And the world went away.

NINETEEN

There were more mage-like methods, but for the sake of blending in with humanity and similar kinds, Alej Kandroknar often employed the telephone, and instructed his various associates to do the same.

Still, it brought a sense of surprise to find himself sitting at his amber-slab desk – the one with tiny proto-human remains trapped inside, shrunken over ten millennia ago and beautifully preserved – and answering his skin-covered telephone to Fleischmann, who normally preferred to visit here in person.

Perhaps the way Kandroknar had eaten a live wraith before Fleischmann's eyes had put the poor fellow off, just a little.

Kandroknar said, "Tell me there's good news to report, why don't you." Not a question, however light-heartedly he pitched his voice.

Fleischmann sounded deeper-toned through the handset than in actuality. "If you're referring to the customer" – voice code for the target, Rajesh Fixtovax – "then he's gone, and he didn't tell me anything that's going to be of use, I don't think. Still, here goes."

That made Kandroknar look up at the ceiling, scarcely seeing the wide-mouthed silent yells of the frozen petrimorphs embedded in the crystal ceiling as a deliberate aesthetic counterpart to the amber-slab desk.

Those petrimorphs were hired street soldiers who'd failed to live up to expectations, and therefore failed to live, instead being frozen at the moment of their deaths for decorative purposes.

But Kandroknar's eyes were defocussed as he listened carefully to Fleischmann's recited details of the so-called protection racket as it applied to the dead man's restaurant, including any gossip that other restaurant owners might have passed on.

Neither the people and procedures that Rajesh Fixtovax had dealt with, nor the snippets picked up second-hand, bore any kind of decent clue to Talon's whereabouts or the manner of his disappearance.

The detective, Riordan, had been chasing a dead end, or something very close.

"His co-owner," Fleischmann went on, "is his sister Mary, and we could pop round and have a word with her if you like."

By *a word* he meant shouts and screams and finally death: understood.

"No," said Kandroknar. "She'll probably have company by now."

Meaning police officers questioning her and perhaps offering protection.

"Sounds right. I don't think there's anything interesting there." There was some kind of edge to Fleischmann's voice on the line. "The investigator, though. The detective. He was there, and he didn't look like the kind to give up."

"Ah. This Riordan fellow."

"Right. Two of my men stayed in the neighbourhood afterwards, to see what happened. Riordan turned up, went inside the... location, and wandered off later to talk to someone I'd swear was a mage."

"Alright," said Kandroknar.

"He had the look, you know?"

"What kind of look is that?"

"Capable," said Fleischmann.

"Alright..."

"I'd say a killer."

"Hmm. Interesting." Kandroknar had assumed this Donal Riordan would turn out to be a sleazy loser. Clearly that was wrong. "No need for you to follow that up."

"Your Martina failed in its mission."

Kandroknar wondered why Fleischmann felt the need to point out the obvious.

Perhaps it was all about the price of failure, given the wraith's fate earlier – and the warm feeling that remained inside Kandroknar's torso, faded though it was by now.

"I'm not going to punish her," he told Fleischmann. "If this Riordan is a more useful man than I'd assumed, then that's good to know."

Switching tactics when the situation changes: that was the kind of thinking Fleischmann would understand.

"I'll recall Martina," added Kandroknar. "and find a more fruitful way to deal with Riordan."

"Got it."

"Any more interesting news to tell me?"

"No, that's it," said Fleischmann. "That's everything."

Kandroknar listened carefully.

Sprite defences be damned, if he needed to strike remotely down a telephone line, he could, although he would need to destroy the entire line afterwards, and obfuscate the location so no engineers could trace the pathway back here.

Not that anyone would venture down into this part of the city.

His mansion might gleam, but what lay beyond the windowless walls…

"Then thank you very much." He decided that Fleischmann had passed the test: he was phoning from afar out of prudence, but remained professionally trustworthy.

That was good enough.

Kandroknar hung up the phone, stroked the skin-covered handset for a moment without really thinking about it, then made a decision.

A new player I don't really know about.

His stomach gurgled, and he laughed to himself.

Variety is everything.

Maybe it was time to meet this Donal Riordan.

TWENTY

Donal felt puzzled yet again.

Questioning himself, for one thing, as he sat in a booth in a small seedy bar with a black Surinese coffee in front of him.

Outside, a pedestrian tunnel ran past, briefly visible whenever someone entered or left through the narrow doorway, otherwise obscured by windows stained so dark they might as well have been boarded up.

This area was still a part of Cataclysm Reaches, albeit three levels down from the dead Raj's home, and a good bit closer to where the tunnels ended. Beyond lay only fossilised bone blending into ordinary stone and nothing but solid matter – if you could flow through it like a wraith – until you came out into the deadly air of Cataclysm Chasm, a place that didn't bear thinking about.

He took a sip of hot dark coffee. It tasted surprisingly good.

Why am I worried about Hellah?

If any of his acquaintances besides Klaudius said their sister was popping out to unknown places with a false cover story, he'd treat that as some kind of gossip, not a cue for an investigation.

Yet he hadn't even questioned Klaudius's rationale when Klaudius asked for help.

Because they're not just ordinary folk.

He settled back, the cracked pterahide upholstery creaking beneath him. The whole bar smelled of beetlewax and old booze, the tables were shiny with polish but old and scarred, and the stains on the floor could be anything.

There were seventeen other patrons and none were paying attention to him, meaning he was effectively alone: the place might feel downmarket, but it gave him the opportunity to think.

Alright.

Hellah wouldn't feel a need to lie about her activities, not to her brother, under ordinary circumstances. When a Guardian was up to something, that wasn't like a normal human being engaged in some kind of private project or affair.

So maybe it did mean trouble of some kind.

I should talk to Mel.

She'd be home by this time, and he really wanted to hug her and play with Finbar, and that would take precedence over any investigation. So yes, Mel would in many ways be the best person to mull over the case with, but going home would be a form of marking time, and what he needed right now was forward progress.

He wondered what Lamis was doing to help – if anything – and how Lamis might make contact if he found something.

Lamis had known earlier that Donal wanted to see him, and anyone else would have responded by leaving a message with Donal's answering service, no more than that. Instead, Lamis had popped up here in Cataclysm Reaches.

I wonder how he found me.

About to take another sip of coffee, Donal paused with the cup halfway to his mouth.

No. Can't be.

He lowered the coffee once more.

He's got some mage's way of locating me, that's all.

No way was Lamis responsible for Raj Fixtovax's death. That wasn't why he'd been in the neighbourhood.

It couldn't have been.

Sweet Thanatos.

He let out a long unnecessary breath.

Not liking the way his thoughts were going.

"You're sitting in my seat, pal." A gravelly voice.

Donal had scarcely noticed the big man's arrival.

Not just him, but the two lowlifes hanging back behind him and smirking.

"I'm really sorry," said Donal, looking up at him.

"Well now, maybe that's not good enough. Maybe—"

The Magnus was in Donal's hand and aimed between the big man's eyes, and everyone stood stock still.

Around the periphery of the bar, conversations dipped and petered out.

"I'm sorry that I'm in a bad mood," said Donal.

No one said a word.

"If we start a fistfight," continued Donal, "I'm worried that I'll beat you to death, you for sure and maybe your pals if they don't run away in time."

Still no reply.

"So I might as well escalate," Donal went on, "to lethal force up front. You follow my thinking, *pal?*"

At last, a reply of sorts: "Er…"

"You're going for a walk," said Donal. "You don't have drinks yet, so go work up a thirst. When you come back, I'll be gone."

"Look." The big man started to say something else, then stopped and nodded.

"Go on," said Donal. "The first round will be on me. I'll pay the barkeep when I settle up."

A smirk started to spread across the big man's face. "So you are scared of me. You just happen to have a pistola. Lets you act like a hard man."

Donal felt a big smile spreading across his face, as if all of his birthdays had come at once: middle-class birthdays with presents, not the kind he'd experienced back in the orphanage.

Moving slowly, he put the Magnus away.

And stood up.

As Donal rose, the blood drained from the big man's face and he stuttered as he added: "N-never mind ab-bout the drinks. You s-stay there."

Then he backed off without taking his gaze off Donal, several paces until he bumped into one of his pals, at which point the three began a stumbling exit, looking back over their shoulders, clumsily getting in each other's way at the door, and finally getting out: the big man first, then the other two.

The last gave a rat-like stare in Donal's direction before he, too, was gone.

Maybe that's okay.

Burning off steam might have been welcome, but it wasn't making progress in either investigation.

Time to see the Axe.

The Talon case began with Axelson's appearance at Donal's office. According to Rilena, Axelson and his people had searched the area around Kaldera Avenue, the last place Talon had been seen, at least by Rilena.

Maybe the Axe had learned more than he realised.

Or maybe he was responsible for Talon's disappearance in the first place.

He could have brought Donal on board simply for the sake of appearances, going along with Susan's idea of using a private investigator. Perhaps Axelson didn't expect Donal to get anywhere.

So far, that was about right.

I'm not going to find out anything just sitting here.

Murmured conversations rose around the bar, and a woman said: "About time, too."

A local, talking about the three guys Donal had just faced down.

Several smiles were directed towards him as he finished his coffee and went up to the bar and paid. The barkeep nodded. Maybe if Donal had beaten the three troublemakers to a pulp, the coffee would have been on the house.

He left, cranking up his alertness in case the big man had screwed up his courage or fetched weapons or reinforcements, but the tunnel looked almost empty in both directions, with no one dodgy in sight.

Mildly disappointed, Donal headed right, back towards the centre of the district.

The attack took place exactly where he didn't expect it, and it wasn't human beings who came for him, but wraiths.

Dozens of wraiths, a huge number, coming for him all at once.

One moment Donal was simply walking, and in the next instant everything changed.

They poured out of the central shaft that joined all the levels of Cataclysm Reaches like a spindle.

On any given level, such as this one, each shaft was a circular building in appearance, wide enough to contain three separate helical staircases and three elevator shafts, able to accommodate multiple indentured wraiths on duty, twenty-five hours a day.

The whole thing ran vertically from floor to ceiling/roof/whatever within a larger underground space.

The number of visible wraiths right now was growing huge, impossible to count.

What the Hades?

A mob of wraiths.

Time slowed down to what felt like glacial pace: subjective, not hex-induced.

All around the immediate vicinity, ordinary solid-matter citizens — standard human and otherwise — were staggering and coming to a halt at the sight of translucent wraiths rushing en masse towards a single point.

Not even remotely normal behaviour.

In most parts of the city, you rarely saw more than one wraith at any given time, and often not at all. Riding an escalator, most people forgot that all the motive power came from a hidden indentured wraith.

And yet here were dozens of them appearing in one place.

A floating, translucent mob intent on committing violence on a single person — *they're looking straight at me* — during the busiest part of the day — *every one of them* — on a major thoroughfare in the heart of a populous district.

A deliberate attack before a considerable number of witnesses.

No subterfuge at all.

This shouldn't be possible.

Donal processed the shock on the faces of the passers-by without feeling any panic himself.

Somehow.

For him it comprised a moment of clarity.

He'd once seen a newspaper photo of a tidal wave rearing over a beach formed of scattered bones, and it came back to him now — a momentary flash — as the rearing wall of translucent wraiths rushed forward and fell towards

him.

Grew huge, so very quickly, as subjective time sped up.

More wraiths joined the rising mass.

Impossible.

So vast, like a cosmic phenomenon: no point in feeling angry or even afraid.

It was just too large to generate emotion, something you had to accept, for it was going to happen regardless.

The vast wave halted, just for an instant; and then it dropped towards him.

Wraiths, falling en masse.

So many of them.

Mel, I wish—

A tsunami of wraiths engulfed him.

TWENTY-ONE

Every now and then, from her crouched squat position – a nice isometric exercise for the thighs, a welcome side effect – Mel looked over at the cradle, its carapace a kind of silvery mother-of-pearl, with a rune-embroidered blanket covering Finbar's sleeping form.

She couldn't help checking visually, even though she felt one hundred percent certain that if Finbar wriggled or grew disturbed in any way, she would sense it regardless of where she happened to be looking at the time.

Back to work.

With her left hand, she raised the battered spikeball mitt, and said to the young boy in front of her: "Just jab."

Young Oliver gave a serious frown, one that belonged on someone older than his nine years, and popped out a jab. It snapped against the mitt.

"Nice," said Mel.

Oliver had been working hard combinations, but you needed to lower and raise the intensity and complexity in waves.

With a grown-up, Mel would have asked for deeper focus on the punch, greater penetration, but young bones are still growing, knuckles included. Plus Oliver was already capable of dropping bullies his own age.

Schoolyards have never been that fair, of course, not to mention the streets and alleyways between school and home. But Oliver looked well-balanced while remaining light on his feet, which boded well for facing older or multiple opponents.

This wasn't just a matter of sport.

"Now moving." Mel shifted the mitt to one side.

Pop.

"Again." Moving the mitt to the other side.

Pop.

"Double jab."

Pop, pop.

"Double jab."

Pop, pop, and she raised the second mitt with her right hand.

"Jab cross."

Pop. Smack. Jab into her lefthand mitt, longer cross to the right, good swivel action.

"Jab cross."

Pop, smack.

"Double jab cross."

Pop-pop, smack.

"Jab cross hook uppercut."

Smack. *Smack*. Smack, thump.

"And done. Good job."

Oliver, backed off two paces, breathing hard, his face glistening with sweat, and nodded twice. Smart enough to know he was getting there.

"*Good* job," repeated Mel.

She looked over at Gladys, perched on one of the wooden folding chairs against the wall – Oliver called her Auntie Gladys, though she was really just a neighbour – and nodded.

Gladys's facial lines deepened as she gave a smile back.

No longer as equivocal as when she first took Oliver here for lessons: she'd already seen the benefits of his training, and said as much to Mel more than once.

Over in the far corner, a somewhat podgy grey-haired man was encouraging a nine-strong group of kids through rounds of jumping rope and push-ups. His name was Fred Delacroix, and he was a retired physical education teacher who'd started coming three months ago in order to get back into shape, and ended up training for free in return for helping Mel coach the kids' sessions.

He was fitter than he looked, and by now the kids knew it, even though he never showed off.

"Don't go too easy on them, Fred," called out Mel.

"Wouldn't dream of it."

Two of the kids doing press-ups, a dark-skinned boy and a moss-skinned girl, laughed aloud without changing cadence, while most of the others smiled. A good sign: you needed to maintain an element of fun and play at that age. Maybe at any age.

The side door opened to reveal a tall, high-shouldered figure in a long coat and wide-brimmed hat, with wraparound shades and grim-looking features.

"Hey, Oliver." Mel kept her eyes on the newcomer. "Go jump rope with Fred's crew, okay?"

Peripherally, she could tell that Oliver's answering nod was wary, picking up her mood. He went towards Fred without a word.

Still sitting on her chair, Gladys made the sign of the axe with her fingers as the stranger strode inside. He didn't appear to look around, but he didn't look like the kind of man someone could sneak up on, either.

Gladys's lips moved in what might have been a prayer to Saint Magnus. It looked like one of the more bloodthirsty litanies: *Perdition to mine enemies/Glory in their howling*, and so on like that.

Mel straightened up, loosening her shoulders, preternaturally aware of the distance and angle between her and Finbar's cradle.

Nothing and no one could be allowed to threaten her child.

"You don't know me." The newcomer's voice echoed and rumbled as if rising from the catacombs.

"Too right I don't."

"I regret not visiting." He raised a hand. "Congratulations on parenthood. Donal changed for the better while he was in Illurium, and it happened because he met you there."

She knew him now.

"Lamis," she said. "Mage Lamis."

"Indeed."

The half-renegade, half-respected senior mage had been deeply involved with the case Donal was working when Mel met him, but only behind the scenes. Lamis had helped Donal before and since as well, and they were sort of friends, but only sort of.

Or maybe I just don't trust mages.

There was more to self defence than a tight guard and fast hands. Attitude and awareness plus aggression trump most other factors.

Also timing, targeting and distancing; but sometimes you just have to listen to the other person hard and be careful what you say.

Tone of voice can be telling too, in the pre-physical stage of combat.

"I can't find Donal," continued Lamis. "I talked to him earlier, in Cataclysm Reaches, but now his location is obscured in ways that shouldn't be possible."

Mel shook her shoulders. "Explain."

"When he met with the White Wolves Council that time," said Lamis, "back during the encounter with the Void Threat, they… Well, you could say, they left their mark on him. A trace. But it's more a neurohex pattern capable of producing a resonance effect."

"Oh, sure. One of those." She knew something of the encounter that Lamis was talking about, without understanding much of it at all.

"I'm aware that explains next to nothing." The sepulchral voice deepened. "My point is, once I eventually realised Donal had been – well, let's call it infected, though that's not quite right – I had a way to sense his location whenever I wanted. Except that it takes some effort, so no, before you ask…

I had no reason to keep track of him on any kind of ongoing basis."

This was a wordier explanation than Mel had expected, if she expected anything. From Donal's description, she'd always imagined Lamis to be taciturn, not talkative.

She blew out a long breath.

In his cradle, Finbar shifted, but it was a natural movement during sleep, nothing more.

"So you've lost him," she said, meaning Donal. "The wolves' scent has worn off, or you've lost your grip. Or something."

Fred was taking the kids through a mobility drill, mostly as a cool-down, but he was keeping an eye on Lamis too: Mel could see it from the edge of her vision.

"It's not a scent," said Lamis. "And it won't wear off naturally, although it might be eradicated by a massive dose of hex or else fine manipulation. I can't be sure of that, mind you. The quantal field calculations are non-trivial, to say the least."

He had quite the vocabulary, but clarity didn't seem to be his strong point.

Mel said: "Are you telling me Donal's in trouble?"

"Yes."

Hades. Plain speaking could hurt like a punch.

No problem.

Getting hit is a sign that you need to fight harder.

"And you don't know how to help him?" she asked.

"Nothing simple I could act on immediately, or I would have done so. I've started some… processes… in the background, but I don't want to rely on them. Partly because they're inherently slow, or at least unpredictable in duration." A slight pause, then: "Due to the *Hexentscheidungsproblem*, as they call it in the Bayerisches Magisterium."

Mel understood him just enough to control her growing frustration. "So, what, are you here just out of courtesy? Or is there something we can do?"

"You have friends I don't," said Lamis.

"Right." Mel blinked. "Ingrid Johannsdóttir, if a witch can help. But you know her brother Kelvin anyhow, don't you?"

"I was thinking of the Guardians."

The words rolled like thunder, or maybe it was just the thumping of Mel's heart. Sweat began to spring out on her face and neck.

"Not them," she said.

Like taking an uppercut to the stomach exactly on an inhalation: that paralysis of the diaphragm, the ferocious upwelling of actual panic.

They're friends.

Forcing herself to think that.

They're our friends.

Not just Donal's, and Hellah had in fact saved them all on the day of

Finbar's birth, when some strange entity started to burst through from somewhere beyond ordinary reality, right here in the gym.

For reasons Mel didn't want to think about.

Someday, maybe, she would have to face her past for Finbar's sake, because of the legacy he *might* have inherited.

But Hellah frightened her, that was the point.

Oh, for Death's sake.

Mel had managed to make tight-voiced conversation with Hellah for several minutes at a time, which was considerably more than most people managed; but that was as much through loving Donal – who possessed zero fear in either Guardian's presence, uniquely so – as any kind of courage Mel herself could muster.

Another conversation, nothing more.

Surely she ought to manage that.

She breathed out through her nose, then: "What do you suggest?"

"A trip to Avenue of the Basilisks, I think."

"Why would they let either of us in?"

Lamis might be a senior mage, but he no longer worked for Tristopolis PD. There was no way he could simply stroll through the Headquarters doors, never mind descending to the deep off-limits levels.

He said, "I'm sure you're friends with some of Donal's former colleagues."

"Yes, but—" She stopped, thinking about this.

Meanwhile Lamis was turning his head, clearly examining the inside of the gym and perhaps the people in it.

"Interesting," he said after a moment. "Some rather unique entities once worshipped here."

"*Were* worshipped here, you mean." Worshipped *by* the congregation: surely a mage would get that right.

"Hmm, that too."

Well, alright. The deeds described the building as a deconsecrated temple: no real details of its former incarnation. She'd never thought of investigating further.

Never mind all that. "There's a couple of detectives I could ring."

"Very good," said Lamis.

Mel looked over at Gladys, then at Fred with the young boxers around him, and shook her head. "I'm going to need a babysitter first."

She might trust the people here to look after Finbar for a few seconds, but no longer than that. Going out without Finbar worried her, and she'd only done it twice so far, and failed to enjoy herself on both occasions, despite Ingrid keeping watch, along with her young apprentice Ludka.

"I've already taken the liberty." Lamis gestured towards Finbar's silvery cradle, without actually turning his head. "I know you and Donal are parents now. My felicitations again, belatedly."

"What do you mean, you've taken—"

The doors at the far end of the gym clattered open.

Ingrid.

Some kind of pale red aura surrounded Ingrid, like blood in swirling water, and even from here Mel could see she looked mad.

Ingrid's fingers twisted into mudra gestures full of menace. "Who the Hades is responsible for this?"

Lamis bowed forward from the waist, just as the aura around Ingrid grew paler, more translucent, and faded incrementally until clear air remained, free of all traces.

"My apologies." Lamis's voice rumbled. "I'm sure you recognised the locus of attraction."

"Of course I did, or I'd have sent death-fire back along your summoning geodesic, you bloody fool."

Meaning Lamis had summoned her here, to the gym: Mel understood that much.

"Indeed." Lamis stood straight and tall now. "And I am truly sorry, but Donal is in trouble and Mel here needs your help."

Ingrid growled in a way Mel had never heard before, not from her.

"Tell me." There was a hard flatness to Ingrid's eyes, also unexpected.

"You're aware," said Lamis, "of the neurohex potential he possesses. I mean the field pattern in Donal's mind. The one that didn't used to be there."

"I…" Ingrid flicked a glance in Mel's direction, then: "Let's say I know what you're talking about. Continue, Mage."

Again Mel was preternaturally aware of Finbar's cradle and his sleeping form, knowing that she would throw herself between him and danger, should the crackling tension between Ingrid and Lamis erupt into something more.

"Actually" – Lamis's voice switched to a musing tone – "there was a prototype seed for that pattern there already, now I think of it. Perhaps because he had earlier contact with the White—"

"For Death's sake," said Ingrid.

"My apologies, Ingrid Johannsdóttir. Let me start again. I am Lamis Grimstone, and I regret the necessity of summoning you in this fashion. But I established a resonance with the pattern in Donal Riordan's mind, and a short while ago my receiving pattern grew quite still."

Ingrid's mouth opened, and she looked at Mel again.

"No," continued Lamis. "If Donal died suddenly, I'd expect a kind of shivering harmonic, a final pulse. Nothing of the sort occurred. One moment the link was active, then it was gone."

"Thanatos," muttered Mel. She pointed towards the ten kids grouped around Fred, but addressed Lamis and Ingrid: "And watch your tongues, both of you."

Rage was building inside her, and she could drop Lamis before he might cast a defensive spell or whatever mages did, because even the youngsters punched faster than conscious thought, and she was twice as fast as them.

Donal had knocked out a Guardian. She could manage Lamis.

"You need to watch your step, Mage," said Ingrid. "You're in more danger than you realise."

Lamis's mouth twitched. "Then Mel Carson and myself should be able to leave Finbar here, knowing he's well guarded."

"No. Seriously?" Ingrid's voice lowered into a growl once more. "You want me here to babysit? Me? *That's* why you brought me here?"

Mel spoke fast. "He's talking about getting Hellah or Klaudius to help."

Ingrid's mouth opened, then closed.

Lamis said: "That will require a trip in person to Police HQ at One, Avenue of the Basilisks. Unless you know of another way to request their assistance?"

Ingrid shook her head.

After a moment, she said: "I can only point out the danger involved." She inclined her head towards Fred and the children. "Without going into squeamish details."

"Do you have an alternative suggestion?" Lamis's voice rumbled, as deep as ever. "One that doesn't involve the Guardians?"

Ingrid let out a shaky breath. "I wish I did."

And that was that.

There are times to ignore expert advice, and times to go along with it. The trick lies in knowing which is which.

Right now, Mel felt certain.

Something had happened to Donal, and a senior mage like Lamis couldn't help, but maybe one of the Guardians could.

"We're going to Police HQ," she said.

Staring at baby Finbar in his cradle, tucked up beneath a blanket inscribed with defensive runes, needing a certified security witch for protection, and maybe the world shouldn't be this way, but it was.

She was determined to be a good mother, and part of that meant making sure Donal was here in addition to her: she knew this with a certainty so deep that her actual love for Donal felt like a bonus on top.

"Give me a moment," she added, "to fetch my purse."

The dark satchel-like handbag Donal had given her on Oathgiving Eve: that would do nicely, because of the bespoke hand-stitched holster inside, cut to fit her Draken .39 exactly.

A girl needs the right accessories when it's time to face the world.

TWENTY-TWO

A great granite block rose up from the floor of the Police HQ foyer, reaching several feet above head height. The entrance hall itself arched high overhead like some kind of cathedral, but it was the burly police officer, his upper body appearing to grow out of the top of the tall granite block, who captured Mel's attention.

"No one said nothing, I mean, no one said anything to me about this." Sergeant's stripes adorned his sleeves. "It's not regular procedure, neither."

"Honestly, Sergeant." Mel had to keep her head craned back to look at him. "I talked to Harald, I mean Detective Hammersen, on the phone."

"I thought you said you was – you were – going to meet Detective Sergeant Viktor Harman."

"Yes, that's right." Mel kept her voice level, and wished Lamis had come in with her.

She shrugged, shifting the shoulder strap of her handbag, getting it comfortable.

"Well, I'm confused," said the sergeant. "Let me call up."

A slow breath out. "Harald said he was about to leave, heading for a crime scene or something." She'd rung him from the corner call box near the gym, before catching a taxi on Hel Ave, her and Lamis. "But Viktor was on his way back and would meet me here, apparently. Right here at your desk, Sergeant."

"So you're on first name terms with—"

That was when a low growl sounded, and Mel held herself very still, swallowing.

From the direction of the great doors behind her came the sound of paws padding – plus the click-clack of claws, the non-retractable kind – on the polished marble floor.

Breathing softly, the deathwolf stopped next to her and raised its head, but not to bite.

"S-s-sergeant." The deathwolf's tone was sibilant.

"Yo, Lupo Nine."

"This-s-s is-s mate to… Do-nal Ri-or-dan."

The sergeant, leaning over from the block, said, "Get away."

"This-s-s is-s my pos-st."

"No, yeah, I mean right, I know that." The sergeant shook his head. "I just meant I'm surprised, is all."

"S-s-aaa."

Not an actual word, as far as Mel could tell. Just an exclamation regarding human slowness.

"Thank you," she managed to say.

"Yes-s-s," said the deathwolf.

Mel wondered how it knew about her and Donal, then considered its capacity to perceive the world through scent, wished she hadn't bothered, and pushed the thought away as hard as she could.

"I have a mage friend waiting outside." She was going to have to bring this up sometime: no point in waiting. "If you know Donal, then I'm guessing you know Mage Lamis as well."

The deathwolf padded back towards its position by the great doors.

"Him," said the sergeant. "Yeah, I know Lamis, alright."

"He's here to help."

"There's help and there's help, lady."

"My name's Mel. You know Donal and I have a baby boy now? His name's Finbar."

"Well." A genuine-looking smile appeared on the sergeant's face. "I did hear something about that. Call me Eduardo, provided there ain't no senior officers around, like."

"Pleased to meet you, Eduardo."

"Yeah, likewise. You say Viktor Harman is on his way?"

"Supposed to be."

"And the mage is right outside?"

"Unless he's moved," said Mel, "he should be a few yards down the street, by a lamppost. This side of the Avenue."

"Maybe Sergeant Harman will fetch him inside. No way he'll miss noticing a mage hanging around the building."

Sergeant Harman, not Viktor. Not on first name terms, then, but respectful.

"I guess not."

"He's pretty sharp," said Eduardo. "You know he's Doctor Harman too, these days?"

"Yeah. Donal said Viktor reads hard textbooks for fun, you know?"

This was gossip, but she had nothing better to do, unless it was to worry herself sick wondering what the Hades had happened to Donal. She knew nothing about resonances and hex patterns or whatever Lamis had said, but Ingrid clearly knew a lot, and was taking Lamis seriously.

A metallic groan sounded from behind her, which made Eduardo straighten up above his block. The doors had opened silently just a minute ago, so maybe something was wrong.

Or maybe they just didn't like admitting certain people.

When Mel turned, she saw no danger, simply two familiar figures striding through the high open doorway: Viktor in the lead, Lamis diagonally behind him.

Viktor looked hard and grim, even more than normal.

"Mel," he said. "Are you okay?"

"Donal's in trouble."

"Yeah." With a glance back at Lamis: "So I heard." He came close and stopped. "We were at the same crime scene in Cataclysm Reaches, me and Donal. Then he went off for a walk or something, never came back."

Mel felt chill, and not just because of the draught from the dark, chill boulevard outside.

"Was he supposed to come right back?"

"Not as such, actually. Why exactly are you worried about him?"

Unspoken: in the normal run of things, having Donal out of contact for a matter of hours was just another day at work.

Mel looked at Lamis, but directed her words at Viktor. "Can we talk about this at your desk? It's kind of complicated. The kind that needs a senior mage to explain."

"Hades." Behind his round blue glasses, Viktor's eyes narrowed. "I can get a squad car and you can tell me about it while we're driving."

Lamis shook his head but said nothing.

"No," said Mel. "The kind of help we need, we need to talk about it right here."

Viktor looked from her to Lamis and back, muscles tightening around his mouth. "Tell me it's not related to an unusual guest at your party, the one you threw after the Void Threat thing."

Mel knew exactly who he was talking about. She herself had been terrified of making conversation with Hellah but managed it, only to learn that Hellah sensed her pregnancy, long before anyone else knew, even Donal.

"We need help," she told Viktor. "Really powerful help."

Finally Lamis spoke: "She's telling the truth."

His words were deep and resonant with certainty.

After a moment, Viktor looked up at Eduardo. "They're with me."

"Sure thing."

About to address Eduardo by name, Mel realised that perhaps he wouldn't appreciate that with Viktor here, so instead she deliberately warmed her voice and said: "Thank you. Very much."

"Any time," said Eduardo. "And good luck. All of you."

He nodded towards Lamis, and Lamis returned the gesture.

Maybe Mel had helped Lamis rehabilitate himself, just a little, in the eyes of Tristopolis PD, or at least some small part of it. Or maybe that would depend on their success in finding Donal, which was all that really mattered here.

I hope to Hades this works.

Not knowing what to expect, she followed as Viktor led the way towards a bank of elevator shafts. Three of the openings were filled with waiting, billowing wraiths.

Lamis strode alongside her.

"Thank you for this," she said.

"For Donal's sake," he told her.

Words to frighten her as much as reassure.

We wouldn't be here if it wasn't serious.

Lamis could be up to something, but instinct told her otherwise: Donal was in trouble and all of this was to help him. Just that, with no ulterior motive.

As they approached the elevator shafts, the waiting wraiths grew still.

Because of Lamis?

It seemed that way, but their stillness was impossible to read. Nervousness, fear, resentment or something else entirely: no way to tell the difference.

She held her breath and stepped inside an occupied shaft.

Trusting the wraith enveloping her to do its job, to hold her safe and not let her plummet to her death in a shaft that went down more than two hundred levels, to Thanatos-knew-what kind of depth.

She swallowed, and closed her eyes.

And waited for seven long seconds before she felt the wraith start to move, beginning a controlled descent.

They stepped out onto a landing, all three exiting separate shafts pretty much at the same time.

"You haven't seen our team's offices before, have you?" asked Viktor.

Gothic silver numerals on the wall, looking recently polished, indicated this was the minus twenty-seventh floor.

"I haven't actually been in this building before," said Mel.

"No, I guess not. You ever visit Tristopolis before hooking up with Donal?"

Mel shook her head. Everyone knew she'd met Donal in Silvex City, which people thought of as the capital of Illurium even though it wasn't. Much like Tristopolis and the Federation.

Viktor was making small talk but not delaying: instead he was leading the way through an open plan area, all the way to a desk set with its back against a hard carapace partition that reached to mid-chest height. Above it, pebbled glass rose all the way to the ceiling.

No other detectives around, which seemed strange until Viktor added: "Everyone's at a policing conference, at least the ones who couldn't get out of it by working urgent cases."

Donal had worked alongside Viktor as part of a task force that sounded like a small team, unless Mel had misunderstood, but there were desks for maybe twenty people here, plus two enclosed offices that seemed empty right now.

At any other time, she might have wanted to learn more about this place which had meant so much to Donal, or at least figured in his life to such a significant extent.

But not now.

She sat in the visitor's chair that Viktor indicated. Lamis preferred to stand.

"We need Hellah's help," she said. "Her or Klaudius. Hades, if those things you keep in the depths are quiet today, let's ask both of them to help. I mean both Guardians."

Not like her to babble. She inhaled sharply through her nose, and blew out a long exhalation. She added: "Sorry, Viktor."

"Tell me," said Viktor, taking his seat behind the large black desk. "What's going on, exactly?"

Mel looked up at Lamis.

"I was previously able, with effort," said Lamis, "to track Donal's location through a resonance effect, and I was doing so today because he'd been trying to get in touch with me."

"Alright." Viktor steepled his fingers. "Where was he?"

"You know because you met him at Rajah Fixtovax's home. I was in the vicinity."

Viktor's eyes narrowed behind the pale-blue lenses of his glasses. "Were you indeed."

Not sounding like a question.

"When Donal left the crime scene," said Lamis, "he saw me and we talked, and we went our separate ways. Some time after that, the resonance link that joined us suddenly dropped."

"You're talking quantal field patterns?" said Viktor. "Was there a shutdown pulse?"

He looked like a hard case and was apparently deadly with the twin Grausers Mel could see beneath his coat right now, sitting in shoulder holsters: a trained thug on the side of law and order.

But it sounded as if he actually was as smart as people said.

"No pulse," said Lamis. "He's alive."

Mel blinked, trying to make sense of the words, then remembered that a pulse in this case meant the link being severed by death. A last blip of energy or something.

Lamis had also said something about a crime scene, and Donal being there.

"I don't know anything about this." Mel looked from Lamis to Viktor. "Are you and Donal working on something together?"

Viktor said, "He found a homicide victim and called it in. Mage Lamis, did Donal tell you anything about it?"

"Indeed, and the manner of death is… highly unusual. But we still need their help. The help of one of them."

Meaning the Guardians, presumably.

The lines in Viktor's face deepened. A hard face, pondering a hard decision: that was what it looked like, but it made no sense.

"We have to help Donal," said Mel. "I know the Guardians are scary, and you don't have to meet them with us. Lamis and I can talk to—"

"That's not his problem." Lamis's voice rumbled even lower than usual. "His problem is knowing which Guardian to trust."

Viktor stood up slowly behind his desk, and faced Lamis directly. "Trust is a hard-earned commodity, Mage. And hard to regain once lost."

"I'm not the problem here, Sergeant."

This was enough. Mel flung herself up to standing, kicking back her chair.

"What the Hades is going on, guys?" She looked from Viktor to Lamis, loosening her shoulders, wanting to thump the pair of them. "What *is* your problem?"

You couldn't tell what Lamis was thinking, not with those wraparound shades and all, but he flattened his tone as he said: "Most detectives would not understand the issues, and in fact I hadn't expected anyone to grok the mechanisms involved. But you do, don't you, Sergeant Harman?"

Viktor's lips formed a grim line.

Then: "*Grok* isn't a real word," he said.

"I think you'll find it is."

"*Guys*," said Mel. "What the bleeding Hades is going on?"

Lamis said: "Sergeant Harman thinks the Guardians are suspects in the homicide that Donal discovered."

Mel opened her mouth, shut it, and swallowed. "Say what?"

Viktor looked at her, then did something she thought he never did: he slowly took off his glasses and laid them on his desk. His irises, when he stared at her, were a polished silvery grey.

Probably not the way they'd looked when he was born, but Mel had no idea what kind of modification this might be.

"The mage is right," said Viktor.

"Oh."

Whatever difficulty she'd been expecting, this wasn't it.

"But my opinion still stands," said Lamis. "In the macroscopic dimensions, the resonance is gone forever. To find Donal – to *maybe* find Donal – we need someone able to detect entanglement of crawlspace properties, and I can't do that."

Viktor still looked grim. "Any specialists at Mordanto who could? Or what about the feds?"

"Maybe," said Lamis, after a moment. "Of the two, the federal spellbinders are the biggest unknown. But how much time will that take, getting hold of them and organising some kind of operation?"

"Thanatos," said Viktor. "Look, how certain are you that the resonance remains in the crawlspace dimensions?"

Lamis shrugged his high shoulders. "Thirty percent probability at a guess. Maybe a lot less. But I'm a hundred percent certain that I can't think of any other way to find him."

"Other than old-fashioned police work."

"Yes, other than that."

Not making any negative comments about police capabilities, which was probably smart.

Why can't they just get on with it?

Mel forced her fists to open, telling the flexor muscles in her hands to relax.

"Is Hellah involved in Donal's disappearance?" she said. "Or maybe Klaudius? Is that what you're saying, Viktor?"

"The Guardians are unknown in many ways," said Viktor, "but ethically, no one has any doubts about them. None at all. They're straight arrows, committed to protecting Tristopolis and by extension the world."

Meaning presumably that if the entities got loose and went wild, more than one city might be lost.

"So they're loyal," said Mel.

"Maximally so."

"Unless," said Lamis, "they consider Donal to be an enemy of the city."

Mel turned to look at him, while even Viktor seemed surprised.

"Whose side are you on?" said Mel.

"Yours. And Donal's. I was thinking the matter through logically, that's all."

"Right. Have you guys ever heard of analysis paralysis?"

"Some things can't be solved by jumping into—"

"No, she's right." Viktor shrugged his shoulders, maybe to settle the cross-draw holstered Grausers beneath his armpits. "Sometimes you just have to make a move."

His leather coat swung as he rounded the desk, then he strode back the way they'd come, heading for the landing and the elevator shafts.

"Death on a broomstick," said Mel, the expression from her childhood just popping out. "Come on, Mage."

She was five paces past him before she sensed him getting into motion and trying to catch up. They followed Viktor past empty desks and through the open-space office door and the short hallway beyond, and came out on the landing, opposite the elevator shafts: a row of dark openings, none currently occupied.

A wraith shot upwards, visible for a split second, its passenger a dim outline, no more than that.

"Which way are we going?" said Mel.

"There's a limited number of places," said Viktor, stabbing his forefinger at the call pad on the wall, three times over, "where I can send a pneumatic-tube message down to the lowest levels. Commissioner Sandarov's office, the emergency response command centre if it's unlocked right now, maybe a couple of other locations."

"Okay..."

"All of them will take time to get to, which you've just pointed out is a bad thing."

Beside them, Lamis's form was starting to glow with a kind of faint white aura.

What's that about?

She didn't want to ask. If Mage Lamis felt worried enough to cast some kind of protective shield around himself – and for sure, that's what it looked like – then maybe she was better off not knowing any details.

It looked like the same three wraiths bobbing in the same three shafts they'd arrived in a few minutes back, but how could anyone tell for sure?

Donal would know.

He always did have a way with strangers of all kinds. It was one of the first things she'd noticed about him, back in Silvex City, in what seemed another life.

"All the way down." Viktor projected his voice: not so much loud as carrying. "As far as you can get us. Emergency access, please."

It sounded like a command, apart from the word *please*. There was a lot going on here that Mel didn't understand, but she didn't have time to figure everything out.

Viktor stepped straight ahead, into the shaft in front of him: the centre of the trio. Lamis headed right at pretty much the same moment Mel went left.

Like warm mist on soft mossy ground: that's what it felt like, cocooned inside the wraith's levitating form. Mel slowed her breathing, knowing that actually holding her breath would be unnecessary, and wondered whether Viktor or Lamis could explain how that worked: the wraith holding her up in empty air while her lungs were still able to—

Thanatos!

The bottom dropped out of her stomach, or felt that way, as she plummeted downwards with the wraith wrapped all around her. Weightlessness took hold of her – she could no longer feel the wraith pressing upwards against the soles of her feet – yet she was still surrounded by wraith-stuff, whatever its body was made of.

Freefalling, her and the wraith together.

I don't like this.

Falling faster now.

I really don't like this.

And faster still.

Faster than any nightmare of falling she'd ever had.

TWENTY-THREE

Helena was feeling her age but determined not to show it. Kelvin was leaning back in the opposite armchair – twin to the chair she sat bolt upright upon – facing her at an oblique angle, while the crackling flames in the fireplace complemented the faint orange glow of flamesprites dancing in their ornate sconces, set high upon the walls.

"You're looking better," she said.

"Which isn't saying much, Professor." The flames produced shifting orange highlights on his face and short, untidy hair. "We both know that."

Helena didn't know which made her more uneasy: the short but messy hair instead of a cleanly shaven scalp, or the weary tone of his voice, so different from the bouncing, enthusiastic energy she'd grown used to.

"Where's Olivia?" She kept her voice gentle, though she knew her patrician accent sounded like cut glass to others, no matter the emotion she intended to convey. "Is she out with young Claude?"

"You could say that. Out of the house, for sure."

Helena controlled her breathing. "Don't tell me. Gone to stay with her mother."

"Nothing so cliched." Kelvin managed a twisted, momentary smile. "Her sister's putting her up."

"And how often do you—"

"In Fortinium," said Kelvin. "So I can't just pop round for tea or playtime with Claude. Not that I've been a playful father lately. Or any kind of decent husband."

"I'm sorry."

"Claude. What kind of name is that, anyway? Certainly not my choice."

"Kelvin, please."

"I suppose if you'd had a son, coming from an upper crust family like yours, Claude would have been up at the top of the list for possible… I'm sorry. Oh, Thanatos, Professor."

Helena refused to blink. "I called my daughter Laura and she's gone. We both know that."

"And I feel really bad. Rambling on like that. Thoughtless. I just forgot."

"Yes," said Helena. "You should feel bad."

Placing subtle emphasis on the last two words – semi-hypnotic suggestions to do just that: feel bad. The side of Kelvin's mouth twitched, just a little, in recognition of what she was doing.

"I deserve that," he said.

"Yes, you do."

The dark room around them looked tidy enough – the lizard skulls arranged on a bookcase in front of old classics, bound in mammoth hide, that Kelvin had actually read; the snake-dragon painting depicting an entity from Zhongguo mythology; the Higher Arkanian-system runic scrolls hanging either side of the knotted-shield sculpture carved from Lightside obsidian.

All that cleanliness meant only that Kelvin's cleaning wraiths hadn't abandoned him when his wife and child departed.

Kelvin's rune-embroidered wraparound robe looked decent enough too, but the rumpled clothes underneath – revealed where the robe came loose at the front – plus the slumped posture and weak expression, indicated something different.

Inside, where it really mattered, Kelvin – her star student, her protégé – had become a total mess.

I need to shake him out of this.

So much could be accomplished covertly, using applied psychology with only a touch of neurohex manipulation, that an ordinary-seeming conversation – a verbal exchange whose written transcript, if such a thing existed, would look totally innocuous – might produce profound and lasting change in a person who had been suffering from trauma or neurosis, even conditions that a thaumasurgeon might class as parahex possession or psychosis, although there were definite limits.

Several cases came to Helena's mind, but she dismissed them all, because the people she'd helped in this way – profoundly and without their knowledge – had been mundanes, not senior mages trained in those very same techniques.

No shaking him up. I need to lead him gently.

Catching his interest: that was the trick, if she could manage it.

I woke up saying Kandroknar's name aloud.

But the threat back then had come from more than a mage, that was the point.

On taking her seat, she'd leaned her cane against the arm of the chair. She regarded it now: the platinum knob, carved with a fine design only a handful of mages in the world might recognise.

Sometimes she thought she might have been at home directing a spy agency, perhaps one of the federal intelligence services, given how the most interesting parts of her career — most of them, at any rate — amounted to operations within an eternal secret war.

Or what felt like a war, in any case.

"I made a mistake," she said. "Actually, during a particular early phase of my career, I made many mistakes, but I only made each kind of mistake a single time. My mentors allowed me a lot of leeway, so I was always trying things I'd never done before."

Kelvin was looking at her. Not hanging on her every word, but not dismissing her either.

Perhaps he sensed the difficulty and trauma behind her controlled tone of voice.

"There's a wraith genus called *spectrae taxolotlae*," continued Helena, "though you may not have come across them except in reading old books. What's unique about them — the older books aren't clear on this subject, not truly — is that each individual is a singleton, meaning it's the sole representative of a separate species."

Kelvin raised an eyebrow. "I didn't know that."

She had not expected him to know anything of singleton wraiths.

Another way of describing them would be that each birth involved a major mutation, but Helena didn't need to belabour the point. Let Kelvin mull over that aspect for a few seconds.

"As I said" — she glanced again at his bookshelves — "the older books aren't clear on the subject, and the newer reports are classified. Not all are beyond your clearance level, but if you didn't know they existed, you wouldn't know to look for them in the shadow archives."

Kelvin said nothing.

No way to read what he was thinking.

"Most people consider wraiths a single species," added Helena, "unless they've been to somewhere like Cataclysm Reaches or the purple light district in Nether Kalix, whereas I'm not sure that even classifying them as a kingdom, the way we normally do, is truly sufficient."

Still nothing from Kelvin, except that he continued to pay attention.

It was possible he knew just a little of this.

His first degree would have included a third-level module on wraithkind and heptadimensional geometry, but the emphasis would have been on the physical side: tau-matrix transformations, particularly the rotation of mass into and out of the mesoscopic dimensions.

Not the plethora of wraiths and wraith-like beings: that kind of taxonomy and evolutionary analysis remained a more specialised area of study.

"The spawning of new singletons is entirely understood," she went on, "and we know there's a variable number of parental wraiths involved, sometimes just one. But even a parthenogenic spawning needs to be considered an act of speciation as much as reproduction, due to the amount of mutation that occurs every single time."

Back to that aspect of their birth process.

Each individual differed greatly from the parent or parents that spawned it.

"If that's so," said Kelvin, "then shouldn't they figure more prominently in the syllabus?"

So he too had been thinking of formal study and the mandatory requirements for student mages at Mordanto and similar (if lesser) institutions like Collosso or Shadeford.

"Some areas of study," said Helena, "are obscured for reasons of security rather than shallowness of scholarly enquiry."

That brought something like a smile from Kelvin, at last.

"Nicely worded," he said.

"Yes, well." Helena turned her head to stare into the crackling flames in the fireplace, seeing memories of what seemed another life. "There was a wraith-like entity we called the Draxoleth. Always *the* Draxoleth, using the definite article with the name capitalised, which is the correct way to denote a singleton."

"Is this going to be on the exam?" he asked.

"In a way." Now it was her turn to smile. "If you choose to help me, then maybe so."

Was this a briefing? Or simply a way to confess old sins?

All those deaths, on my hands.

Unburdening herself wasn't the intent here. She needed to be clear on that.

"Was it bad?" said Kelvin.

The question threw her, though not for long.

"You could say that," she told him. "A lot of people died, including senior mages, and maybe if I'd been quicker off the mark, most would have survived. Maybe even all of them."

This was going to take some time, because without context, little of what happened then made any kind of sense at all.

"Let's start with the geopolitics," she said, "so you understand how things were at the time. Probably the main thing happening was the embargo against Surinam – usually called the Zurinam back then, including the definite article again, and nothing whatsoever to do with wraiths and singletons. Except that parahuman rights abuses in one of the Zurinese provinces triggered the Federation's protests in the first place."

"That seems a bit hypocritical," said Kelvin.

Good. The comment meant he was engaged.

"Tristopolis for sure has had its dark moments," said Helena, "and not just the Unity Party's time in office, but during the period I'm talking about, the Federation really was taking a decent moral stand."

"Alright."

This was off the main point, but Kelvin would need the background to understand everything else.

"The thing is," Helena went on, "a lot of opportunities opened up in the criminal world, driven by the growth of smuggling routes to bypass the embargo. Goods of all kinds travelled both ways, exports and imports that were equally illegal, and unfortunately the smugglers graduated to shipping people and other sentient entities as well."

She paused, listening to the crackling flames and checking that Kelvin was still paying attention.

"One of the people who came here via the smuggling routes," she went on, "was a mage who'd committed several aleph-level transgressions and was being hunted by the Surinese Collegium Veneficium and their Sorcery Enforcement Agency's seeker squadrons."

In Surinam, SEA operatives worked in a more paramilitary fashion than the federal spellbinders here, but their abilities were almost on a par when operating solo, and their effectiveness when deployed in teams was legendary.

Kelvin's gaze remained steadily focussed on Helena, so she continued: "The mage's name was Alej Kandroknar, and he was quite a piece of work."

That was when Kelvin sucked in a breath and said: "He was there when my father died. And my uncle."

Not the disaster Helena had played a part in: those men had died in separate earlier incidents; but the details had been classified, although in a deceptive way. As a boy growing up, Kelvin would have learned only that they died in the line of duty, brave mages both.

Kandroknar had been a menace pretty much from the start.

"So you have heard the name," she said. "Or read it. What else do you know?"

"Nothing else." Kelvin shook his head. "I dug around when I was a novitiate and found an old report. It was an investigative case gone wrong, and the name Alej Kandroknar featured in it as a collateral casualty, another fatality in the same hexplosion, but I thought from reading between the lines that he might have been the real cause of it all."

"I see," said Helena.

"But there were no details to speak of, and could it all have been an accident."

"Sure. Just an obscure case that happened to end badly." Helena leaned back in the armchair, focussed on Kelvin's expression. "That's how you really hide the truth. Not by simply classifying it or burying it completely, but obscuring the report and making it appear shallow and routine. You yourself never dug to the point of triggering security blocks and redaction hex."

Now she really had his attention.

Classified information was one thing; cloaking it with disinformation was another, usually to protect some person or entity, sometimes to cover up misdeeds or lack of competence.

A dangerous glitter was growing in Kelvin's eyes.

This, I must handle carefully.

Get it wrong, and he'd dismiss her from his house, and never mind the consequences for his entire career. Get it right, and she'd regain the most important asset she could possibly provide for Mordanto: a capable senior mage worthy of leading the institution when she finally stepped down.

Carefully, with deliberate calculation in every word, she began to talk once more.

"It was on the outskirts of Black Iron Forest, the rendezvous," said Helena. "I was considerably younger than you are now, and I was on perimeter guard duty, hidden among the trees but watching Hardhammer Heath, where they were supposed to meet.

"I'm talking about seven of Mordanto's top enforcement mages with remote backups linked to them, while I was there because of my studies regarding singletons and the Draxoleth in particular."

She paused, rebuilding the scene in her memory, before continuing: "All I could see was black grass beneath a nearly black sky, with only a few fluorescent moths flitting here and there, and at first I thought our team was early."

Another pause, getting things straight in her mind.

"They'd set the whole thing up," she went on, "with all sorts of other people involved, police included, and one of the mages – Susan Silverton, who'd been a liaison with federal spellbinders for several years – laid down a threadfield beneath the soil, one that even I couldn't detect, despite knowing it was there."

Kelvin, listening intently, tilted his head. "To stop a wraith coming up through the soil from underneath, is that what you mean?"

So he did understand.

"That's right," said Helena. "We knew the Draxoleth was particularly skilled with its matter-binding manipulations, so having it appear from nowhere would have been disastrous. And we knew it had been helping Kandroknar."

She saw the way Kelvin's eyes narrowed as he heard the name.

"Anyway," she went on, "he, I mean Kandroknar, was even earlier for the rendezvous than we were. It took me a long while to realise he was already out there on the heath, waiting for our people to turn up."

"Out in the open, a long way from nowhere," said Kelvin.

"Like an obvious trap, sure," said Helena. "But he was used to taking precautions, and according to the briefings, all sorts of realistic and real details had been put in place beforehand to make it seem a genuine meeting."

She inhaled, then let out a breath.

"Plus, you see," she added, "none of that was supposed to make a difference. Seven top mages in place, with remote backups linked to them and ready to transmit whatever they needed, and with all necessary attack-hex cached and ready to be loosed, all of it supposed to overwhelm any kind of detection or shield or weapon that Kandroknar might deploy."

Kelvin said nothing.

"Of course he was Zurinese," continued Helena, "therefore with a different background and capabilities, but our people knew that and had liaised with Zurinese SEA officers beforehand, all that kind of thing. We were supposed to be prepared."

Helena closed her eyes, held them shut for a moment, and opened them again.

She went on: "Right until the entire Hardhammer Heath exploded, I thought we were. Prepared, I mean. Prepared for anything."

The memory remained sharp in her mental focus, but the room and Kelvin grew blurred, and she wouldn't cry in front of anybody else but perhaps today, in this place, she could let her guard drop just a little.

"They all died," she whispered. "A huge explosion, five corpses in pieces, the other two plus Kandroknar simply gone, blown into mist and flying soil, and maybe Kandroknar hadn't intended to kill himself along with everybody else, but there was no surviving that."

She stopped, and realised she was breathing hard.

"Most of the remote backups died as well," she added after a moment. "Some kind of blowback."

"You were junior," said Kelvin. "This was hardly your fault."

Helena closed her eyes, remembering the beetlewax smell of the tribunal room, the endless too-patient questions, the too-sympathetic look in the inquisitors' eyes, and the final analysis and verdict that, on the professional front, exonerated her entirely, even though she knew better in her heart.

"Without the Draxoleth's involvement," she said, "there was no way Kandroknar could have defeated our seven best mages, not even by sacrificing himself."

That was the thought that had haunted her, back when it happened and every day since. No single mage could have accomplished what Kandroknar did that day, even though he died in the process, and good riddance.

Kandroknar had required a very particular and powerful kind of help.

"Which means," she went on, "that the singleton wraith, the Draxoleth, must have passed through my detection aura. There was no other way for it to reach that Death-damned Kandroknar, but I detected nothing. Not a single thing."

She wiped her tears away.

Stupid old woman.

And looked at her protégé.

"I'm going to have to retire at some point," she said. "I hope you'll be there to take over the reins. But if not, what I do need from you is a reliable singleton detector. There, I've said it."

To an outsider, this wouldn't even sound like a confession; but to a fellow mage, someone on the same journey although starting decades later, the implications were plain to read.

It was her one great technical failure, the one disaster she had failed even to comprehend, and she sorely needed some form of closure before she gave up her work for good.

A way of detecting singletons. If Kelvin could manage to develop such a thing...

She blinked, suddenly surprised.

Thanatos.

Twin tracks of silent tears were glistening on Kelvin's cheeks.

Indicating a new motivation, something to make him turn his life around?

Or have I made things worse?

She waited, not knowing what to say.

TWENTY-FOUR

Pressure everywhere: against Donal's face, his chest and back and entire body, and he thought he was suspended in a chest-down horizontal position, prone yet moving, but acceleration kept surging in different directions so he couldn't even be sure of that.

Without the cushioning effect of the wraiths pressed against him, he'd have been battered and snapped apart: the sudden shifts in movement were that abrupt.

I'm in the middle of a mass of wraiths.

Eyes squeezed shut, because he didn't want wraith-stuff pressing against his eyeballs: you could lose your eyesight that way, if the wraiths weren't careful.

And it was a good job he didn't need to breathe, because this wasn't like being carried by an elevator wraith: a redblood cocooned in wraith flesh as solid and tight as this would suffocate. He felt almost sure of it.

Another sickening shift in direction.

They could have killed me.

Not a good thought, but a mass of wraiths falling on you felt more like an act of nature – the disastrous kind – than a physical confrontation.

Losing a fight always feels bad, but in a flood or landslide, simple survival counts as victory: it's all you can hope for.

Something to tell Finbar's kids when I'm a grandpa.

An odd thought, daring to think that far ahead, but maybe he could survive this after all.

There was no telling where the wraiths were taking him or what he would face when he got there, and maybe they were just looking for someplace to dump his body; but the whole action had been public in the extreme: a mass of wraiths snatching someone off the street.

Even in a district as odd as Cataclysm Reaches, that had to attract attention.

People will be looking for me.

Yet short of a fully fledged task force of federal spellbinders – or military sorcerous operators like Omega Force – getting a captive free from a combined mass of a hundred, maybe three hundred wraiths, didn't seem like something the authorities could achieve.

Not even if they knew where to deploy.

So I'll need to be ready.

The dictum that protection officers drum into civilians is simple: in a kidnap situation, fight back before getting into a vehicle or other enclosed space, since afterwards will be too late.

Donal had missed the first opportunity, and you rarely got a second, but that couldn't be allowed to matter.

Make your own luck, laddie.

That was Sergeant O'Connell, back in the day; and someday Donal should track him down and thank him, because his teachings had saved Donal more than once – and with luck might do the same again.

The amulet.

Right now he couldn't move, but at some point this mass of wraiths would pull apart and release him – surely that's what they intended – and it would only take two ninths of a second to reach inside his shirt and grab the crystal.

Klaudius had said it was a call crystal and not an amulet, and if he could come through and rescue Donal then he could call the Death-damned thing anything he liked.

Even if Donal himself fell to his death or perished in some other way, there'd be an angry Guardian to avenge him.

Not good enough. I want to live.

Another sideways lurch and upward bump and what felt like a surge of acceleration along some helical path, which might indicate the mass of wraiths was flying like some titanic single organism along a tunnel somewhere, constrained by the world of solid matter only because of the tiny human being in their midst.

They could translate their body mass into the crawlspace dimensions but they couldn't take Donal with them, or at least not in one piece.

Then their flight levelled out and Donal felt sure they were flying through clear air.

Something's not right.

He was a resurrected man, a blackblood with discipline, and something in his internal perceptions had continued to register motion in the same way he subconsciously tracked time.

We can't be that high up.

A pressing against the top of his head and shoulders indicated a hard deceleration, and he had the idea that soon enough they would be coming in to land somewhere, and that would be time for action.

But even as he had that thought, another came crowding in, and this one made his skin crawl and his body feel cold even as he felt the slow, almost gentle descent begin.

Because he knew how to resolve the seeming paradox: how he could be flying through clear air – within this mass of wraiths – and yet remain far below the normal ground level where most of the ordinary people of Tristopolis led out their ordinary human and parahuman lives.

I'm down inside the Chasm.

Words he never thought he would utter, not even silently inside his head.

Oh, sweet bleeding Thanatos.

This was going to be interesting, at best.

Cataclysm Chasm.

Where nothing normal lived, not even by the standards of Tristopolis.

Gentle now, the slowing motion, and then the feeling against his skin changed in character, and he knew the wraiths were preparing to disengage, to float away from each other into their separate selves once more.

For several seconds – seven and a third, or thereabouts – he hung in place, still with eyes squeezed shut, but feeling his lips tighten in what he'd been told looked like a predator's grin.

He might not have any chance at all, but if there was one, it was almost here upon him.

And then the loosening—

Yes.

—and the sickening sensation as he dropped through the air—

Now.

—with eyes snapping open, wide as a cat who's falling or in a fight, and his hands whipped inside his clothing in the kind of double cross-draw that Viktor used to whip out his twin Grausers and start firing.

But Donal's right hand pulled at his shirt en route to grasping his Magnus in its shoulder rig, while his left hand went inside the part-opened shirt and grabbed hard, clenching the amulet – crystal, whatever – as hard as he could even as he dropped feet-first to grey-blue flagstones and took the impact crouching.

He whipped the Magnus up right-handed and pulled the trigger fast.

Rapid fire.

Five shots banged, flat and hard in the cold air, and the tall smooth-skinned, round-featured man in front of him stayed seated on what looked like an executive's swivel chair formed of polished bone and lizard hide, situated on an open-air dais of some kind, with the chasm walls far off to either side and stretching into the distance.

You couldn't see the sky at all without looking up and that was the last thing Donal intended to do with his target right in front of him.

A target that remained unharmed.

I thought so.

The man was dressed in a high-collared tunic that might have looked exotic in most parts of the city but right now seemed all of a piece: his twinkling eyes and straight-yet-relaxed posture even while sitting, plus a smile of gentle, almost quizzical amusement.

Here was the reason for Donal's being here: the man – more than that, the mage – who had bent so many wraiths to his will.

I know I didn't miss.

Donal hadn't been the best shot in the Department, despite spending so much time on the firing-range beneath Avenue of the Basilisks, but he'd been a long way above average in those days, and he hadn't slipped since.

He knew that for sure.

Five shots fired, and he needn't have bothered, because they didn't faze this mage in the slightest.

Let's see what he can do against Klaudius.

Grasping the crystal very hard indeed.

"Please, Mr Riordan." The stranger spoke with a mild tone, his accent patrician, his bunched cheeks almost cherubic. "There's no need for that, not at all."

Twinkling humour in those eyes: corrupt yet cheerful all at once.

"Yeah, there is." Donal put the Magnus away, released his hold on the call crystal that hung around his neck, and rebuttoned his shirt. "Call it making a point."

Either the crystal had sent its signal or activated its resonance or whatever the Hades it was supposed to do, or it hadn't.

There was nothing more he could do about it.

"Indeed." The answering smile was gentle. "And so eloquently delivered. Five to the heart, I believe."

"More like none," said Donal.

He had no idea how this mage's defences worked – the stranger had to be a mage of some sort – but Donal was certain of one thing: somewhere between exiting the barrel of his Magnus and reaching their intended target, all five bullets had disappeared.

Evaporated, rotated into crawlspace dimensions, or otherwise taken out of local existence.

This was more than a simple hex shield, for sure.

"But you did, in fact, intend to kill me. Or have I somehow got that wrong, Mr Riordan?"

"I had a hunch you were protected," Donal told him. "But if you killed Rajesh Fixtovax, I don't much care if you die right here and now."

They were in open air, but surrounded on all sides by cliffs.

Part of his awareness – using a kind of split focus that came more easily now than in his redblood existence – took in the strange, dark surroundings of Cataclysm Chasm, whose walls formed a complex mix of natural, canyon-like crevasses and later artifice.

Craggy buttresses featured everywhere, pocked with jagged openings too sharp-edged to be ordinary cave mouths.

Normally, eldritch shapes flitted around the Chasm, while howls and groans twisted like ribbons through abnormally cold, still air; but today the place felt hushed, almost silent, as if entities in the not-cave openings and the solid rock were holding their collective breath – if any of them did actually breathe.

Donal had a bad feeling this mage had a lot to do with the quiet stillness.

Anyone who could frighten the denizens of this place had to possess power far beyond the ordinary.

I've faced your kind before, mage.

A small twitch at the corner of the mage's mouth seemed to answer Donal's unvoiced thought.

"The enemy of my enemy," said the mage, "is my… temporary ally."

"Who you might stab in the back now or later on." Donal kept his gaze steady. "Why would you even try to enlist my help? Assuming that is what you're getting at."

"Let's say it's a possibility, and maybe even a desirable one for someone in your shoes."

"So who's the common enemy?" said Donal.

Not bothering to hide his scepticism.

Protection officers say a second thing to civilians under training: besides taking the first opportunity to break clear, to fight your way out of a trap, you must also disbelieve the words of the person who promises not to hurt you provided you do what they say.

Untrained people do give in with a kind of fearful gratitude despite the total illogic at work, since anyone who breaks civilised protocols by attempting kidnap – or by breaking their way into your home or otherwise violating your private space – is the last person to trust.

In Donal's experience, trusting criminals usually ended badly.

Playing for time was a possibility, but Donal had a bad feeling that Klaudius wasn't going to turn up. This mage had somehow blocked the call crystal's signal or severed its quantal connection or whatever.

"When I say enemy," said the mage, "I mean the people who could have saved the woman whose heart beats inside your chest right now. People who could have stopped Blanz and all his comrades, had they worked *with* your police department instead of hoarding their power and hiding their secrets."

There was no skipping a beat or accelerating Donal's pulse, because black zombie hearts don't work that way; but he felt sickened inside at the mention of poor wonderful Laura.

Her head had been blown part in a cloud of grey mist by a single shot fired by that bastard Senator Blanz, who was really Mage Blanz but *not* Mordanto-trained: a product of some dark illegal counterpart.

"And the irony is," continued this unknown mage right here, "that your dead lover's mother was one of the worst, a leading figure in that conspiracy of power and corruption. Had she and her kind acted against what you called the Black Circle, Blanz and his allies would never have made the gains they did, or achieved any kind of success at all."

Donal wanted to shoot again, even though it wouldn't work.

"You're saying" – he wanted to be certain of the details, even if the whole thing was a lie – "that Mordanto is the enemy."

"Mordanto and the greater enterprise of mages' political and secular power, yes. That's exactly what I'm telling you."

"Greater enterprise?"

"Wider enterprise, let's say. Social institutions of various kinds. They, I mean the mages of Mordanto and their ilk, influence more than you realise in the corridors of power." A hint of a twisted smile, then: "I'm not saying that Helena Steele deliberately sacrificed her own daughter. Only that her neglect allowed the whole tragedy to be possible in the first place."

They say the skill of telling a convincing lie involves wrapping it around some solid nugget of truth, and Donal could pretend to follow this step-by-step verbal journey as if believing it – by focussing on the part that sounded as if it might be right – but in the end he wasn't that gullible.

No point in pretending that he was.

Shapes were moving in the distance now, but nothing that could help: just a handful of large wraiths or wraith-like beings flitting through the dark air of the Chasm, intent on their own purposes.

"I'm not buying your act," Donal found himself saying. "You haven't even told me your name, which I thought was Rule One for you narcissistic mage types. I mean the ones who've fallen off the hard moral path because you haven't got what it takes to wield power and remain a good man."

A slow shake of the head. "My name doesn't matter, Donal Riordan."

"True enough." Donal almost laughed, feeling a weight lift off his shoulders. "I don't care who you are."

"What matters is that our interests are aligned in the matter of Konrad Talon."

The mage paused.

Alright…

Maybe this changed everything.

And maybe it meant nothing at all, unless it offered Donal a chance of getting away from here.

TWENTY-FIVE

As the mage sat there in his executive's chair against the strangely fitting backdrop of Cataclysm Chasm, fallen-cherub features bearing a whimsical smile that matched the twinkling of his eyes, he seemed to be pausing deliberately, as if used to lesser mortals needing time to understand the sparkling brilliance of what he offered.

It allowed Donal to make a strategic calculation, reversing some previous assumptions.

Part of him had taken it for granted that this mage was behind Talon's disappearance.

Maybe that was wrong.

"I feel guilty," the mage finally went on, "or at least discomfited by my former client's predicament. Had I remained the power behind Konrad Talon's throne, no one could have made a move against him." A strange, satisfied smile grew on the mage's face. "Not successfully at any rate."

As if remembering the blood he had spilled and enjoyed so much.

"So." Donal looked at the mage, all senses zeroing in. "You're concerned for your former client's safety and well-being."

"Of course." The mage smiled with a twinkle in his eyes.

"Yeah, I don't buy it." Donal settled into himself, fully on balance, totally in the moment.

"My dear fellow…"

"Someone's made a move on Talon, and you're worried they're really after you."

For a moment, the mage held totally still.

Then, "It seems you're even better than they say, Mr Riordan. So. My name—"

That was when Donal made his move.

Now.

It was a lunging drop-step punch, moving very fast towards his target with no precursor twitch of the shoulders and the human eye and brain don't process an onward approach as accurately as an angled incoming attack while in any case the dictum is that action beats reaction every single time.

Except that this time it didn't, not at all.

Donal had dropped bigger adversaries from further away than they thought possible, launching his attack from what looked like being out of range while closing distance very fast indeed, and those enemies were streetwise thugs used to swift and random attacks.

Got you—

But Donal was bouncing back and his fist had struck something but not the mage's face and whatever it was had pushed against Donal's chest as well and the whole repulsive hex field threw him backwards, away from the mage.

Donal's heel struck something on the ground and he spun around a vertical axis, almost a full turn just to stay on his feet because falling flat would grant his enemy even more of an advantage than he already had.

"—is Alej Kandroknar," the mage continued, "and it's rather lovely to make your acquaintance, Donal Riordan. I haven't enjoyed myself so much in… well, several days at least."

Donal tilted his head from side to side and shrugged his shoulders once, just to loosen them.

He shifted to the left a little, noting where the stone lay on the ground, the one he'd come near to tripping over when the mage's defensive shield flung him back this way.

"I can't trust you," said Donal. "Let's not pretend here."

"Well of course you can't, dear boy." Again the twinkle of non-innocent eyes. "What kind of dark mage would I be if I went around keeping my word to mundanes? Even interesting mundanes like you."

"Sweet bleeding Thanatos." Donal almost smiled at this corrupt flash of honesty.

"Indeed. But you can make use of any information I give you, and profit from any, let's say, influence I might wield to clear your investigative way." With a delicate shrug: "Helpful little snippets like that."

Chattiness and twinkling eyes: this Kandroknar guy wasn't like any dark mage Donal had confronted in the past.

Makes him more dangerous.

Because a kind of knowing confidence accompanied that pseudo-charming manner, and in Donal's experience, such confidence came from bedrock-certain power and repeated past success, many times over.

"Tell me about Konrad Talon," he said.

Still not trusting the mage: that would be stupid.

"A goodhearted soul from a rough neighbourhood," said Kandroknar. "Or at least that's how he sees himself, but the ordinary folk he gives back to

– the ones he supports financially and in other ways – are grateful out of greed and fear. It's not because they actually like dear Konrad, not at all."

So nothing new here. This was business as usual: crime bosses wielding influence by placing whole districts in their debt, by the granting of favours and protection that always – eventually always – came with a price.

The return favour might involve any kind of act that benefited the boss in question, and while often that act was pretty much legal, everyone knew that it might not turn out that way, not at all.

But they would return the favour regardless, out of fear.

"So who are his enemies?" Donal could guess some answers, but not all. "Spike Kurosawa? The Mangianero clan? Oddball Orcana and her sharks?"

Not literal sharks, but oddly formed parahumans with razor teeth and thick grey skin and eyes incapable of holding pity, always dressed to the nines in wide-shouldered suits and silk ties, along with eyeball tie-pins that tended to blink when you least expected it.

They'd clashed with Talon's people over dockland control, to the extent of mutual bloody slayings that made all the papers, from the *Tristopolitan Gazette* to rags like the *Chronicle*, bringing exactly the kind of public – and Tristopolis PD – attention that made business awkward for the underworld.

"All of those conflicts were notionally settled." Again the twinkle-eyed smile you might mistake for innocence and warmth. "Truces in place, and so on. Right now, however, I sense some naughtiness among all those groups you've mentioned, Mr Riordan."

"Huh."

"But I also surmise this… restlessness… is a reaction to a lessening of activity in Konrad Talon's manifold business enterprises. I wouldn't say there's a rumour of his disappearance, more a growing question mark over whether Konrad still has his hands on the reins of power."

That could mean several things, including a challenge from within Talon's own organisation.

"Axelson," said Donal. "The one they call the Axe. You think he might betray his boss?"

Just because Axe had brought Donal in on this in the first place, that didn't make the man innocent in this matter. Not wanting to be seen to move against Talon wasn't the same as not moving against him at all.

"Interesting question," said Kandroknar. "Let's think about this."

Was it tactically and strategically feasible for Axe to take over? It depended on how the loyalties of the street soldiers and lesser bosses worked, and even when Donal had been a detective lieutenant with an active network of informants, his knowledge of Talon's outfit – about the inner workings, the hierarchy of personnel – had been vague and shadowy at best.

"The naïve idea of leadership," continued Kandroknar, crossing his legs as if getting ready to expound at length, "is that it consists of giving orders which subordinates leap to obey."

"Uh-huh." A seminar wasn't what Donal needed right now.

"Axelson is a great enforcer," said Kandroknar. "Maybe the best I've ever seen. But he isn't a true general, and I believe he's smart enough to know that."

"Okay." Maybe this was going to prove useful after all.

"You asked about Kurosawa and the others, and again, I believe they're getting ready to move now, but only to take advantage of this new opportunity. None of them is actually behind Konrad's disappearance."

"Then who is?" said Donal. "You're not going to blame Mordanto, are you?"

"Thanatos forbid" – Kandroknar uncrossed his legs, then crossed them the other way – "that the great and the good would cause a known criminal overlord to be snatched and interrogated somewhere out of sight, without due process and lawyers and all the rest."

"Or that you would just come out with what you're really thinking, Mage."

Kandroknar sniffed, with perhaps a hint of reaction in those pseudo-gentle eyes. "Careful, my nearly human friend. Careful."

"Warning noted. And?"

"I have people," said Kandroknar, "who can help you track down Konrad. People and… others."

"Why?" Donal felt some kind of change in the still air, accompanied by a faint sound diagonally behind him, but not close. "Is that who you're talking about?"

He jerked his head backwards at an angle, in the direction of the sound.

"Your auditory acuity is impressive, even for a resurrected man. As are your speed and, I suspect, physical work capacity."

"I'm too busy to compete in athletics," said Donal, "or listen to this crap while I've got work to do."

"Oh, well. We should take time to enjoy the good things in life, pleasant conversation included, but barbarism so often mars one's attempts at civilised discourse. I gather young Susan Talon has blossomed intellectually. Perhaps I should bring her here to——"

"Leave the girl alone, Kandroknar."

"Ah. I will do that, Mr Riordan, while I have your full cooperation. I do have it, don't I?"

Donal let out a breath, more from habit than as a calming measure. "Right now we're on the same side. That's good enough."

"I can accept that. Susan Talon will remain untouched." Kandroknar shifted his attention, looking past Donal's shoulder. "Martina, you will work with the detective, and furnish every assistance in the matter of finding Konrad Talon, but only in that matter, nothing more."

Even before turning, Donal knew approximately who – or what – he was going to see.

Dressed differently than before, now wearing a long grey coat over a dark-grey skirt suit and pale pink blouse, here came a white-faced elegant woman whose features were different from before, but had to be the shape-changing entity he'd encountered on the Hypoway train.

"Hello, Mr Riordan." It was the same cultured voice as before, currently affectless, although capable – Donal remembered – of containing emotion.

Or maybe it just simulated feelings.

"You tried to warn me off," said Donal. "Looks like we're working together now."

The Martina thing looked at Kandroknar as if for an answer, then back at Donal without a word.

"You'll find," said Kandroknar, "that it has interesting capabilities in terms of shifting through space as well as morphing."

Donal remembered the way that this Martina had appeared to shift instantaneously within the train and later on the station platform.

"So it's a good burglar," he said.

No change of expression occurred on Martina's face. While still, it looked like a porcelain statue with coloured-glass eyes, even though Martina could speak with normal mouth movement, or something much like it.

If referring to Martina as "it" caused any emotional reaction, none of that showed on the surface. Donal wondered if she-or-it was something like a golem in nature, despite the radically different appearance: small and elegant as compared to huge and lumpy with either two yellow eyes or a single yellow eye-slit.

Other denizens of the Chasm were moving in the distance, but Donal couldn't spend time focussing on them.

"Martina's abilities are in fact well suited to burglary," said Kandroknar, "though that wasn't the original purpose of this design."

Something happened then on Martina's features, some microscopic flicker of reaction that in his redblood days would have escaped Donal's notice entirely.

You didn't like the word "design", did you?

That might be useful information, provided Donal didn't screw up the rest of this encounter, because he needed to be clear: Kandroknar possessed enough power to wipe him from existence here and now, if it became expedient.

Donal focussed on Kandroknar. "What about *my* abilities? Why bring me here at all?"

"My dear fellow, you're an exemplary investigator, are you not? Why wouldn't I want to make use of you?"

"Yeah, right. And what else? Is it just that you don't have many actual people under your control these days? Now that you're living in this place" –

Donal waved a hand at the Chasm in general – "without a real organisation to be part of."

Whether Kandroknar actually called this place home was unknown, and his reaction to Donal's verbal prod might have revealed the truth either way, but no such luck: the eyes twinkled and a full-lipped twitching smile followed.

None of that was helpful.

"You really are quite entertaining." And then, for maybe two-thirds of a second, the genial mask evaporated, giving a glimpse of cruelty in Kandroknar's expression, before the courteous veneer slipped back into place. "Our time together will be amusing, I think."

"What can Martina do that I can't, or" – with a glance at those still porcelain features – "vice versa? She looks quite capable to me."

Not of normal human interaction, but Donal's remark had a purpose, part of which was to see if he could elicit a reaction from Martina: a hint of gratitude or annoyance or anything in her expression.

Nothing occurred.

"In your own respective ways," said Kandroknar, as if musing to himself, "you and Martina are both more human than one might expect. How that affects the game, we'll just have to see."

"Game," said Donal.

"With mortal stakes, of course, my dear fellow, else what would be the point?"

Depraved tastes require ever greater stimulation, Donal supposed, but he'd had enough of this conversation. Talon's disappearance might be some mild diversion in Kandroknar's world, or it might be something more, but either way Donal had a job to do.

A job whose scope was growing ever more blurred, but that couldn't be allowed to matter.

"Enough dancing around." Donal's voice tightened, albeit mostly as a conscious adjustment: he remained a resurrected man, after all. "Time to point me in the right direction and let me go."

Assuming Kandroknar had meant what he said.

"My wraith-spies will report to you." Kandroknar gestured, and five translucent wraiths rose straight up from the ground and hovered in place, billowing slightly. "And to me, of course, but they will do your bidding and tell you what they see. Right?"

Yes. Commands will be followed.

Wraith voices didn't work in the normal human way, and they never sounded exactly human either; but this wraith's words hung wreathed with heaviness, as if all its joy had long ago been sucked away, replaced with hollow hopelessness.

You have a lot to answer for, Kandroknar.

Perhaps Kandroknar understood the thought, for his eyes filled with humour as he said: "You'll take advantage of them, whatever you think of the way I've broken their spirits and bound them to my will. Or are my words too florid for an orphan raised in Danklyn?"

Hex defences could be made to work against wraiths – witness the energy trap that had nearly killed the freewraith detective called Xalia, and perhaps actually had, given that her identity had merged with that of her rescuer Gertie, thereby forming Aggie – but in general, a wraith could slip through solid walls and all the rest, and rotate so much of their mass into the crawlspace dimensions as to become almost invisible.

That would make them ideal spies if people considered them reliable for that kind of work… except they didn't, not normally.

There was an icy feeling against Donal's sternum.

It's the call crystal.

He'd thought it inactive, cut off by whatever defences Kandroknar employed here, or simply by the unnatural strangeness of Cataclysm Chasm itself; but something was happening now.

Kandroknar looked the same as he had a few seconds ago: no sign that he'd detected anything odd occurring.

The cold was replaced by warmth, growing against the skin of Donal's chest.

With luck, he was betraying no reaction either.

"None of this helps," he told Kandroknar. "Martina, these five wraiths, plus whatever else you can give me – none of it makes any difference if I don't where to start."

"You start with their kind." Kandroknar gestured towards the floating translucent wraiths.

"What do you mean?"

"To enable Konrad Talon's rise to power, a certain amount of bloodletting was inevitable."

"Okay…" Underworld mob wars, out of the public gaze as much as possible: call it a known process, the natural selection of one group of gangsters competing with another.

"The use of kill-wraiths made all the difference in Konrad's case, and those wraiths were controlled—"

"By you," said Donal. "I got that much."

The crystal was growing cold once more, but he didn't allow himself to shift position or alter his posture.

"The ones I… recruited, let's say, came straight from the crawlspace realm. The ones who never normally came into our macroscopic dimensions at all. The best raw material for my purposes, you might say."

If he'd been a redblood still, Donal would have blinked.

"You kidnapped and enslaved them," he said.

"And bent them to my will, reshaped their cognitive processes, and made them entirely mine. Indeed, that is exactly what I did."

The cherubic humour in those eyes seemed monstrous now.

"No wonder you both have enemies," said Donal. "You and Talon."

"Poor Konrad was seduced by power, as so many people are."

"He thought he was using you." Donal nodded. "When it was really the other way around."

"My dear fellow, you *do* understand. How delightful."

"And I should start," said Donal, "by checking out the survivors from the gangs you and your twisted wraiths decimated, back in the day."

"Well, you might try that… However, a more lucrative avenue of exploration might be relatives of the others involved in all that lovely suffering."

It occurred to Donal that Kandroknar spent most of his days alone, or at least giving orders to entities he held total control over, hence this almost whimsical conversation that was lasting so much longer than expected.

Talking to Donal about his accomplishments, sharing them with someone who disapproved but at least understood something of the effort involved in his long struggle.

And perhaps giving Donal the chance to end all the mystery here and now, if Klaudius could make contact with the call crystal, because a Guardian's appearance would surely trump all else, even here in the Chasm.

Warm again, the crystal between his skin and his shirt.

"Relatives," he said, repeating the word Kandroknar had used, and then he got it.

Kandroknar smiled more broadly, bunching up his cheeks.

"Wraiths," Donal went on. "You're talking about other wraiths."

Aggie had tried to warn him off the Talon case, so that was clear enough.

She'd also saved him from three gunmen, presumably sent by Kandroknar – or some subordinate acting on their own initiative – before Kandroknar decided to recruit Donal instead of dropping the hammer on him.

More than that: Donal's surviving the hit would be one of the things that brought him to Kandroknar's full attention.

"Blood vengeance," said Kandroknar with an almost delighted tone in his voice, "is one Hades of a motivating force, I find."

The crystal was alternating between hot and cold more rapidly now, and Donal had the odd idea that it was searching for a particular frequency in some sense, looking for some arcane harmonic to lock onto.

Someone's looking for me.

Klaudius, with luck.

Maybe it was some kind of automatic emergency process taking place inside the crystal because it had been out of normal contact for so long. Maybe that was it: not someone trying to contact the crystal, but the crystal attempting to establish outside contact.

Either way, it might be best to keep Kandroknar talking.

"You mean blood as in family," said Donal. "Among wraithkind."

For all his recent reading and long-accustomed interest in other people's stories – for a broad definition of "people" – his knowledge of wraith procreation and upbringing was almost zero.

Maybe less: the little he thought he knew was probably plain wrong.

"A place to start," Kandroknar told him. "And these five will identify the individuals for you."

There was something cold in his voice, and Donal wondered if these wraiths would in some sense be sniffing out – or something – their own relatives as the next stage in this investigation.

Faster again, the alternating heat and cold against his chest, and soon enough it would be resonating with Donal's heartbeat, not that that would matter: no way did his heartrate count for anything in the world of quantal field equations and hex matrices and all the rest.

He looked at the wraiths, then at Martina, and made a sudden decision.

"Alright," he said. "You're my team for now. For the duration."

Slipping his fingers inside his shirt as if to scratch his chest, he pressed the crystal between his thumb and forefinger three times, holding it for a count of nine Mixadoptrixes on the last squeeze, hoping that this call crystal's shutdown procedure worked the same way that the ones used by witches did.

Klaudius hadn't exactly provided operating instructions when he handed the thing over.

The transition was instantaneous: the call crystal suddenly felt the same temperature as his skin. He slipped his hand out from his shirt and smoothed down his tie.

"Wise decision," said Kandroknar. "I really would not have allowed it to establish contact. Not without knowing who was on the other end."

Donal stared at him for three slow heartbeats. "You knew all along I had a call crystal."

"My dear fellow, are you still underestimating me that much?"

Such corrupt cheerfulness in those seemingly warm eyes.

"For the last time," said Donal. "I promise you that."

Meaning every word.

"Delightful," said Kandroknar. "And now our meeting is over."

"How do I—"

The world disappeared.

TWENTY-SIX

Mel had grown up in a tough neighbourhood and learned to use her fists, first when Uncle Dorax taught her how to stand up to bullies, then in the Gravel Pit Gym under Mary Balisto's tutelage, fighting in the ring as an amateur.

Winning trophies meant less than the true prize of courage and self-knowledge and the relentless discipline that kept her world intact and purposeful before Donal and most wonderfully Finbar came along.

Her work as a transportation crew chief had occupied the fringes of organised crime, she knew that, and her peers and subordinates as she rose through the ranks had been tough people, all of them, and every now and then some action had plunged her and her team into real danger – they had, let's face it, crossed the line into actual larceny more than once – and sometimes people died.

All the things she'd been through in her life, but she'd never known she could feel this scared.

"We're in the Pits of Hades," she said.

Droplets of glowing orange magma dripped *upwards* towards the high ceiling that was coated with a roiling black mist in which flickers of yellowish light moved in time with discordant screeches right at the upper limit of Mel's hearing.

It sounded like suffering, but what was making the noise, and for what reason, was impossible to know.

This was a cavernous place, half-natural, half-artifice and wholly *other*, the blue-grey stone covered in column after column of black runic symbols that looked jagged and nasty, unlike any Mel had seen before.

A cold icy draught moved turbulently through this dark cathedral-like space, chill against her face and causing Mage Lamis's long coat to stir and flap, even as a silvery white shield seemed to brighten around him, forming an upright ovoid of light.

Mel felt her mouth tighten, hating to feel defenceless but damned if she were going to ask for help, for Lamis to share his shielding defensive hex in some way: creating a duplicate for her, or spreading his shield wider to cover them both.

Then Viktor – with the usual round blue glasses on, despite the darkness predominating even with the fiery magma-drops off to either side falling up to meet the black mist overhead – rubbed his stubble-bearded chin and spoke in a rasping voice.

"Don't be envious of the mage," he said. "The hex makes him a target as much as anything."

What with Lamis's wraparound shades and the still-brightening hex, Lamis's expression was hard to read, but his deep gravelly tones sounded tighter than usual: "Doctor Harman is right, and you should run back this way if anything drastic starts to occur. Get moving straight away. The entities might not notice you at all."

The word *entities* made Mel's spine crawl, because of the way he said it.

"I don't see anything." Her voice sounded high and odd to herself. "Or feel any… beings nearby."

She looked back towards the empty elevator shafts – the three they'd used, and another ten in sight, ranging across the foot of the rearing stone wall – as if one or more of the wraiths might have reappeared, but no chance: the poor things had fled silently upwards as soon as they deposited their human loads here.

Feeling sorry for wraiths wasn't part of her normal life, but what the Hades was normal now?

"We aren't in the Caverns yet," said Viktor. "This is what you might call the antechamber."

"Indeed." Lamis inclined his head, a gesture still visible despite the white glow around him. "That is the usual term for this place."

Something caught in Mel's throat then, before she forced herself to ask: "How much time have you spent here, Mage?"

"Little enough, and far too much." A kind of sepulchral sorrow drenched Lamis's words.

Mel felt her guts tighten, and decided she didn't want to know any more.

Viktor said: "Mage Lamis was once officially the police commissioner's chauffeur, back when it was Commissioner Vilnar in charge."

That commissioner had died in Donal's arms, pretty much, although Mel couldn't remember the details of the story she had heard because more immediate sensations were swirling through her now, all tasting of fear.

For herself, for Donal – the reason she was here, she and these two men risking their lives as well – and for Finbar who might grow up an orphan if anything went wrong in this awful place.

"Chauffeur," she said, more an automatic reaction than a deliberate prompt.

"It gave me physical access to this place," said Lamis. "I mean HQ in general. My duties were… various, let's say."

In the ring, you learned to read people, at least if you'd been trained by Mary Balisto whose primary dictum was to fight wide-eyed like a cat, and that brought a sudden insight now: Mage Lamis was talking because he didn't want to get moving, even though he was here for a reason and knew there were actions he needed to take.

He's afraid.

Sweet bleeding Thanatos and all of that.

A senior mage with a renegade reputation knew enough to be scared of this place, these Caverns; but he'd agreed to come anyway so that was what she had to work with now.

"Which way do we go?" she said.

Viktor sucked in a breath, and his thin lips tightened. Inside his hex shield, Lamis's mouth might have twisted to one side as if trying for a grin.

"I guess," said Lamis, "I had better lead the way."

All around this huge cavernous space that was apparently just a taste of the greater Caverns ahead, the air seemed to darken – no, not seemed, was actually darkening as if the inky black mist near the ceiling was sending out a thin vapour to fill the air below – even as the inverted-teardrop, upward-falling lava shapes grew a brighter, fiery orange that sparked highlights in the lenses of Viktor's glasses, and the thin screeches from high overhead shifted to a steady high-pitched whine that hurt the ears and made Mel shudder.

She really didn't like this at all.

The stone wall should have creaked when it pulled itself open, but it didn't.

Imagine that a titanic creature lying on its side decided to yawn like a predator, to slowly open its dark fanged maw to form a vertical opening: for a second, that was what seemed to be happening, as part of the cliff-like wall drew apart and caused a warm, sickly draught to wash over Mel.

It made her blink five or seven times before shaking her head and snorting in a breath to reset herself.

Like regaining equilibrium in the ring after being on the wrong end of a flurry.

A faint crackling sound grew from Lamis's direction, and Mel had to squint against the brightness of his hex shield to make out the angular patterns revolving within the light.

With luck, Lamis had conjured these deliberately, the complex configurations acting as the key that caused the solid stone wall to open this way.

Or more likely they were something like reflections or harmonics of the real neurohex patterns conjured inside his brain, the kind of stuff Donal had been reading about while she'd been too busy to care.

Better not ask.

Viktor looked grim enough, and he had a much better idea of what was going on, so Mel could in theory ask him questions; but right now doing anything that might break Lamis's concentration seemed like a very bad idea indeed.

She could hear a kind of bubbling hiss from Lamis's hex shield, but very faint and growing fainter.

The opening in front of them became a tunnel – or the gullet of a vast creature formed of stone and eager to swallow three morsels of flesh – and the thought of walking inside scared the Hades out of Mel, but she was going to do it anyway.

She took a step forward, but Viktor touched her arm, so she stopped.

The brightness surrounding Lamis faded to a glimmer: still present, still with shimmering highlights, but transparent enough to reveal his expression, unreadable though it remained, his wraparound shades adding to that effect as always.

A faint scent of rust and sulphur caused Mel to wrinkle her nose, before the warm draught shifted and only the smell of dampness remained.

I'm here because I have to be.

Mary Balisto used to say that it takes a girl to do three things at once, which normally referred to pumping out punches while keeping a tight guard at the same time as using footwork to dominate the fight.

Here and now, neither Lamis nor Viktor looked about to speak, and Mel would be damned if she were going to break the silence out of nervousness.

This was their area of expertise, or the closest to expertise anyone apart from an actual Guardian might possess, and she needed to trust them in this.

On the surface, Lamis didn't look afraid, but intuition told Mel that the faint shifting patterns of light in the air surrounding him, manifestations of arcane hex field manipulation, represented a form of triple-checking his defences: not backing out, but not exactly eager to proceed.

Or maybe he knew what he was doing.

We can't ask for help if we don't survive the journey.

And turning back was no kind of option at all.

It took a while before Lamis made the decision to move – if Donal were here, he could have said exactly how many seconds – but when Lamis did get into motion, his forward stride looked purposeful, his long coat swishing from side to side as he went straight for the tunnel.

All hesitation gone, walking like a man with a goal.

Mel took in a deep diaphragmatic breath, and followed.

Behind her, she heard a kind of fast rustle that she recognised: Viktor had cross-drawn the twin Grauser machine pistols from inside his coat; and maybe they wouldn't do any good here at all, but in extreme circumstances the smallest factor can make a difference.

Blood rush was dampening her hearing as she entered the tunnel behind Lamis, but she remained aware of Viktor following behind, and she felt grateful that someone as dangerous as him was acting as the rearguard.

Except the danger almost certainly lay ahead.

Can't stop now.

Strange patterns of light moved across Lamis's back as he strode forward: patterns in his long coat or more likely in the hex shield itself.

Shapes that looked both angular and hooked, abstract in form yet somehow provoking a mix of feelings that boiled down to a single word.

Threatening.

TWENTY-SEVEN

"I need a clock," said Donal.

It was a weird thing for anyone to say the moment they woke up, especially in public surroundings: a blue-walled coffee shop, the smell of Surinese roast beans heavy and comforting on the air.

There was a murmur of polite conversation from what you might call a middle-class clientele, all of this at first glance, but Donal had grown used to his automatic time sense operating flawlessly, that was the thing.

He couldn't tell how much time had elapsed since blanking out in Kandroknar's presence.

I don't like this.

The sudden need for recalibration felt unsettling.

Never mind. Settle down.

He was leaning back against the wall of a booth, the fittings formed of black carapace taken or grown from some kind of giant beetle, and at least he wasn't alone.

Martina, sitting next to him with a dark scarf over her head and wearing orange-tinted glasses, still with the dark grey coat over a skirt suit, could pretty much pass for standard human, certainly in a place like this where the lighting was subdued, in this case from dancing flamesprites in sconces high up on the walls.

The booths stood in a kind of half shadow.

Without a word, Martina pointed to an antique grandfather clock standing against the wall near to the counter.

Donal checked the carved-bone hands, down to the visibly moving second hand – normally he could make out a minute hand's movement also, provided he took the time to watch with patience – and he felt a kind of mental twist, an internal readjustment of components like imaginary cogs, as his time sense settled back into place.

Nine minutes past fourteen o'clock, exactly.

Seventeen and two-thirds minutes elapsed.

His transition from Cataclysm Chasm to here – wherever this was – had been nothing like instantaneous.

No one appeared to be within easy listening distance, so he said: "How did I, we, get here? Did Kandroknar conjure up a portal? Or did you do this?"

This didn't feel like Cataclysm Reaches or a similar neighbourhood: there was an ordinary dark street outside, not a brightly lit tunnel, and he suspected they'd travelled several miles at least.

Surely part of that transition had been instantaneous, or close enough, to move so far in so short a time.

Martina's voice sounded like a sigh. "I cannot carry people when I shift, not without damaging them beyond repair."

"Okay." That might be tactically useful to know at some point.

"I cannot tell you how my master put us here."

And a statement like that held even more implications – the word "master" sounded plain nasty – but the time for unravelling all that was later.

Donal shrugged his shoulders inside his jacket, feeling the comforting snugness of his shoulder holster harness and the weight of the Magnus beneath his left armpit.

Not that firearms were always the answer, not when you kept bumping up against mages and wraiths and Thanatos knew what else.

He placed his hands flat on the small nine-sided table in front of him.

Scanning his surroundings, checking the place out – half-posh, you might say, with seven-foot-high paintings on the walls, on elongated paramussel shells hanging like shields, depicting ancient purple-skinned warriors with spears and the like – and you would have called the place peaceful and utterly respectable, if it weren't for the fact that an unconscious man could be brought here and placed in a booth to wake up all by himself, while no one appeared to notice a thing.

A bulky man stood behind the counter, in white rolled-up shirtsleeves with a black waistcoat – that made Donal think of the waistcoat-clad estate agent guy at Lamis's place: Balimi with the West Vitrix accent who'd probably say vest rather than waistcoat – while this man here was busily wiping cups and not looking over this way at all.

Even as he kept an eye on the rest of the place.

It's not always obvious which details turn out to be tactically relevant, so Donal took in everything, scanning these new surroundings, all the way down to the smooth feel of the wormskin upholstery beneath him.

"Is there anything special about this coffee shop?" said Donal. "Besides being a discreet place for me to come back to my senses, kind of thing."

"It is not part of the investigation," said Martina.

"Alright. Fair enough."

Mel would have finished up the children's class by now. Unless she'd gone out with Finbar in the stroller, she ought to be home at the gym, and while taking time out for personal calls had never been part of Donal's professional life in the TPD, things were different now.

He looked around for a wall phone, and spotted one at the rear, close to a half-hidden door that might have been the one he'd come in by, if Martina or someone had been carrying him.

Maybe it was the five wraiths who'd done the actual lifting, although he couldn't see any sign of them right now.

"Give me a minute," he told Martina.

"Ringing a snitch?" she said.

"Oh, boy. Have you been reading *Purple Mask*?" It was the most popular of the pulp magazines, featuring Dax Hamlett and others like him: hard-bitten tales of improbable heroes.

"Yes." No emotion in her voice. "I needed to do research in order to work with a detective."

Wonderful.

"Well… Not a snitch. Not this time. Stay there, and I'll be right back."

He slid out of the booth and headed for the phone, checking for coins in his pocket and taking out three bits – three thirteenths of a florin should cover a short call – even as something occurred to him, something that might prove important.

An entity capable of reading fiction was surely conscious.

While some folk treated golems as voice-commanded construction machinery incapable of true cognition or actual emotion, no one could judge Martina that way, whatever she-or-it might be.

Feeling unsettled, Donal lifted the pewter earpiece, spun the cogs to one of the few personal numbers he remembered, and shoved in three coins when a gruff "Hello?" sounded at the other end.

He leaned closer to the fixed mouthpiece. "Hey, Fred. It's Donal."

"Sodding Hades, pal. You heard what happened?"

"What?" Donal blinked as hard and suddenly as if he were a redblood still. "What's going on?"

His idea had been to ask Fred Delacroix if he could pop back around to the gym – Fred would have been helping Mel with the kids' class – and relay a message about Donal being all right but maybe not home until tomorrow.

"Mages and witches and I don't know what else."

"Is Mel okay?" Donal felt his voice tighten. "Finbar?"

"Oh, dear Thanatos, sure they are. I didn't mean to frighten you."

"Well, you kind of did. Slow down, Fred. Just tell me."

"Er, this tall dude with, like, shades and a long coat came in, and after a while Ingrid came in because the tall guy, the mage, had called her. Somehow. She was spitting mad, pal, I tell ya."

Fred might have been a teacher before his retirement, but sometimes his diction lapsed to that of his childhood. The streets of Brinklyme where Fred grew up were as tough as any around Danklyn, even though Donal wouldn't admit it in casual conversation.

Except this conversation now felt serious.

Fred said, "The mage said something about tracking you, how it had failed but not in a way that meant you were dead. You know anything about that?"

Donal thought of the call crystal against his chest, then shook his head, even though Fred wasn't here to see it.

"Mages," was all Donal could think of saying. "You never know where you are with them."

Even the ones who are supposed to be your friends.

"Mel headed out to your old place of employment, Donal. Avenue of the Basilisks, and she took the mage with her."

"She did what?"

"Looking for help in tracking you down, pal, is all I know."

This didn't make sense. Not yet, at least.

Donal turned to check the coffee shop environment.

No significant changes: the clientele talking softly or reading newspapers, the flamesprites casting soft orange light as before, the big guy behind the counter preparing an espresso, Martina sitting like a mannequin in the booth, her eyes impossible to read behind the orange-tinted glasses.

She looked unanimated, lifeless: no hint of her ability to move in the ordinary way, never mind the sudden shifting through space Donal knew she could accomplish.

No immediate threats, so Donal brought his attention back to the phone conversation.

"What about Ingrid?" he asked. "Why did Lamis need to call her?"

"That's the mage?" said Fred. "He called her in to babysit Finbar. She wasn't best pleased at first."

Ingrid was a fierce witch with Class 2 clearance who'd previously worked airline security, but she'd also grown protective when it came to Finbar, and when Finbar grew old enough to speak he'd be calling her Auntie Ingrid: that thought put Donal at ease, just a little.

"She's at the gym with Finbar, then," he said.

"Sure is." A faint hiss sounded on the line, then Fred came through clearly once more. "Ask me, I reckon your boy is safe as houses."

"Yeah." Donal felt his mouth twitch, not quite in a grin. "You wouldn't want to cross Ingrid, especially when she's grumpy."

"I'll say. She's got older kids of her own, right?"

"Er, sure. Two of 'em, in school."

"But she's, what? Divorced? Widowed?"

Now Donal did smile. "Maybe you should ask her yourself, pal."

"Yeah…"

"Later."

"Later."

Donal replaced the earpiece on the hook.

All the weird surprises he'd encountered today, and now this from Fred: something ordinary, a reminder of the real, everyday world and how important it actually was.

Finbar must be okay, guarded by Ingrid Johannsdóttir, and Mel was with Lamis, heading for or actually inside One, Avenue of the Basilisks, and you couldn't get much safer than that, so everything was fine for now.

Then he stopped.

No. Can't be. Stupid thought.

For a second he'd had a brief mental image of Mel chatting to Hellah in whatever Hades-like environment occupied the Caverns on the minus two hundred and seventy-third floor of Police HQ.

Not that he'd ever been down there, or knew anyone who had, except perhaps the late Commissioner Vilnar, and that was only a maybe.

But the thought was ridiculous, because for all Mel's bravery, he couldn't actually see her going to talk to either of the Guardians voluntarily, not for anything.

Whatever kind of resources she and Lamis had decided they needed, they surely had more to do with ordinary policing than the world of eldritch entities and the two Guardians tasked with keeping them under some kind of control.

It was more likely she'd gone to see Viktor or Harald, the guys who'd been on the same task force that formed Donal's last assignment in the TPD.

Or maybe an older colleague like Levison, although she didn't know Lev or the others quite as well.

He spun the cogs to the direct line for Viktor, and after a second the ring tone came, accompanied by the usual sigh of line-sprites guarding against hex intrusion, but no one was picking up, and after seventeen rings, Donal put the earpiece back on the hook to end the call.

Martina still hadn't moved, back in the booth, and Donal wondered what would happen if he just headed straight for the exit, maybe at a run.

If Martina served Kandroknar as exactly that, a servant – or worse, a disciple, or worse than that, a slave – then she would be here to keep an eye on him as much as to help.

I'm supposed to be tracking down wraiths.

It seemed that in Kandroknar's rise to power, at least when he came to Tristopolis and decided to make his mark in the criminal underworld – having left his native Surinam and come here for Thanatos-knew-what reason – he'd pulled in, well, let's call them slaves: slaves from the crawlspace dimensions.

Assuming Donal had understood Kandroknar correctly, and that

Kandroknar had been telling the truth in that regard.

"Aggie," Donal muttered to himself. "That's why she tried to warn me off looking for Talon."

Abused wraiths, across the years.

Other wraiths, Aggie for sure and maybe a whole group of them, wanting justice or vengeance: that had to be it.

That's a motive for snatching Talon.

Especially if they didn't know about Kandroknar operating in the background... or even if they did, given that Kandroknar's involvement with Talon had ended long ago, assuming everything Kandroknar had said was true.

Donal stared at Martina over in the booth, vaguely aware of the continuing conversation of the other clientele, and the overall warmth of the coffee shop, the clink of cups and the like, but his real focus was internal and tactical.

Whatever else was happening, Aggie – or at least her previous sort-of-incarnation as Gertie – remained his friend.

No way was he going to let Martina or any tool of Kandroknar's near Aggie.

Avenue of the Basilisks.

Funny that Mel was supposedly going there, to the very place that Donal needed to visit next... except that maybe he didn't actually need to travel there.

I don't really know wraiths, not the way I know other beings.

He almost bit his lip, but he wasn't a redblood and everything he did was potentially under conscious control, or at least that was the theory: it more and more didn't feel that way.

"Alright," he said, still talking to himself. "Alright."

He turned back to the phone, lifted the earpiece, and spun the cogs once more.

Raj Fixtovax was dead, but his cousin Brian surely wasn't.

"Firing range." The familiar voice answered on the second ring.

Donal shovelled in another three bits – each coin clunked in turn – then two more just in case. "Brian, it's Donal Riordan. Bad news, I'm afraid. I wanted to check you've heard about Raj."

"Ah, Hades, Loot."

"You have heard."

"Yeah, sure. I know it's somethin' weird, too, but that's like all I know."

"I was the one who found him, Brian."

"Yeah..."

You weren't supposed to share details in a homicide investigation, but Donal wasn't actually a detective lieutenant any longer, while Brian Fixtovax was a TPD employee, even if he wasn't a law enforcement officer as such.

"Don't tell anyone I told you," said Donal, "but Raj was floating in some kind of cocoon thing, best I can describe it."

"A what? You mean like a spider or something got him?"

"Not a real cocoon. More like a hex thing, and I do actually mean floating," said Donal. "As in, hanging in mid-air kind of thing."

"Thanatos' bones." Brian sounded more exasperated than sad. "What was he mixed up in?"

"I really don't know. I wanted to talk to him about restaurants and protection, but I can't say more than that."

"Yeah, sure, Loot. I understand, like."

"You know I'm private these days."

"I… Yeah, I guess."

"Listen, Brian, you know I'd arranged to meet Raj in Scrapeworthy."

"Huh? I heard he was… found… at home."

"Um, yeah," said Donal. "Because he didn't show where he was supposed to, I went to Cataclysm Reaches instead."

"Oh."

No point in pursuing that line of questioning: clearly, whoever else Raj might have informed about the arrangement, Brian wasn't part of it. Or maybe Donal would need to question him in person, just to be sure.

"Listen, pal," said Donal. "I've maybe got a handle on something that needs a wraith to make sense of, but I don't know any wraith detectives these days."

"They don't spend much time in the shooting range," said Brian. "Like, never."

"Makes sense. You know Aggie, works the elevator shafts?"

He knew damned well that it was Brian who'd told Aggie about the meeting, but there was no need to bring that out into the open. Not when he needed Brian's help.

"When she feels like it," said Brian. "Sure, I know Aggie. Used to be Gertie, right?"

"And she was also Xalia," said Donal, as if he was in no kind of hurry whatsoever, "who was a detective second grade. Some kind of merged-identity thing."

"Say, yeah, that's right."

This was taking time, but some things, you need to lead the way carefully or it doesn't work at all.

"Maybe if I could talk to her," said Donal, "she'd remember her Xalia stuff, be able to help with some actual investigation. Which I'm sharing with Viktor, by the way. Viktor Harman."

"Sure," said Brian. "Makes sense."

If Donal came right out and accused Brian of complicity in whatever was going on, Brian would most likely hang up. This way, he might actually do what Donal wanted him to do.

"So this might sound a bit mad," said Donal, "but I've kind of heard of wraiths being able to talk on the phone. Never from someone who was actually there when they did, mind you."

"Huh."

"I don't suppose…"

"Oh, no."

"What?" said Donal. "What is it?"

"You're not going to ask me to bring no wraith to the phone, are you, Loot?"

"I want to know what happened to Raj. You do too, don't you?"

The sound level had risen in the coffee shop, just a little, but not enough to mask Brian's sigh in the earpiece. "You want any wraith at all, or does it have to be Aggie?"

Donal squinted, trying to parse the undertones in Brian's voice. "Some kind of problem there? With Aggie in particular?"

"No…"

"Brian."

"Well, kind of… But I'll get her. Alright? I'll get her now."

"I'm on a payphone, but I can hang on."

"Oh, okay. I'll just—"

There was a clunk but no sounds of a sudden scuffle or anything else untoward. Donal cancelled out a rising urge to sigh in exasperation, checked Martina was still sitting in the booth – she was, exactly as before – and dug in his pocket for coins, and pulled out a full florin just in case.

Donal exhaled and stood there waiting.

Perhaps an impartial observer would see him as unmoving and lifeless as Martina over there. Fidgeting here wouldn't cause Brian to move any faster in Police HQ, though.

Hey, lover.

Wraiths didn't exactly speak with normal sound, but what came through the rounded earpiece wasn't just clearly wraith-speech: it was recognisably Aggie herself.

"Rajesh Fixtovax is dead," said Donal. "In case Brian didn't tell you and you didn't know already. Killed."

Unfortunate. Bad news.

"How come you were in that alleyway in Scrapeworthy, and Raj wasn't? How did that happen, exactly?"

Surf-like hissing filled the earpiece. No actual words at all.

"I need to know," added Donal. "Unless you're the killer here, which I've been hoping you aren't, whatever you can tell me will—Hades!"

He flung the suddenly icy earpiece away from him, then hammered the edge of his hand down onto the hook, almost hard enough to pull the entire payphone away from the wall but not fast enough to break the connection in time.

Not fast enough to cut short whatever was happening here.

Too late.

She billowed outwards from the earpiece and the braided connecting cable all at once, expanding and translucent, growing fast and large to double human size, floating a yard above the polished floor, wriggling a little as she manifested bigger and stronger than usual.

Aggie rotated more and more of her mass out of the crawlspace dimensions, hanging there without anything like a face, and yet it was somehow obvious that all her attention was on Donal.

You wanted to talk, I believe.

"Bleeding Hades, Aggie."

She must have followed the phone connection, through telephone exchanges and all the rest.

Donal hadn't realised wraiths could do that.

Maybe most of them couldn't.

There might have been a blur, or perhaps it was some artefact of human vision – resurrected human vision – because Martina was suddenly standing next to Aggie in a crouched position, and there might not have been any actual motion between her original seated position in the booth and her appearance here.

Just a transition between two states with nothing in between.

You.

"Yes." Martina's voice was feminine yet inhuman, all at the same time.

A new kind of fear swirled inside Donal's guts. His clever idea of phoning a wraith had turned into something else entirely, and it felt like a disaster, an imminent catastrophe.

You know you deserve to die.

"Yes," said Martina. "I know I do."

Donal raised a hand.

"Stop," he said. "Both of you, just stop."

Aggie rose higher, expanding and brightening, while startled customers pushed back their seats and the ones closest to the exit were already beginning to stumble out, like some horrible replay of Donal's earlier encounter with the waitress Gina, the untutored witch in that place on Hollow Way near Mordanto, and the entity Gina inadvertently summoned in the kitchen.

But this time Donal was the one who'd made the mistake and anything that happened here was going to be his fault, and his alone.

Too late, old friend.

"Yes," said Martina. "Too late."

White fire exploded in the air, and Donal knew they were right and he was wrong, so stupidly, stupidly wrong.

Coruscating energy, blinding brightness everywhere, and nothing he

could do.
    Too late, too late.
    Mel. Finbar…
    Far too late.

TWENTY-EIGHT

Talon hung in place from a harness that he couldn't see, suspended over the impossible blue-grey pentagonal flagstones, while all around, the barrier of purple flames had died down to little more than candle brightness, a ring of inch-high fire flickering along the floor.

The walls of the seven-sided chamber stood blurred in dark shadows now.

Beyond pain, beyond agony, he hung there: worn out, wrung out, with nothing left.

No resilience, no force, no anger to strengthen him.

All of it, gone.

I'm sorry.

Was that a thought, or had he managed to say the words?

"I'm... sorry."

There was no visible doorway, but how could that matter now? No way was he leaving here alive. Not after all the things they'd done to him, when the violating tendrils of all those ravening wraiths had turned out to be only a precursor to the deepest horror of all.

He'd confessed everything to that creature from Hades, the woman-thing with the glistening scarlet skin – the colour of freshly spilled blood – and those eyes: seven-sided irises of orange flame morphing into blazing golden fire.

Perhaps he'd spent his life burying old fears inside him but nothing compared to the awful terror suffusing every cell and fibre of his being in the presence of that... thing.

She'd torn everything out of him, using only words, as far as he could tell, for his memory was in shards that seemed to be tumbling in his mind like falling broken glass from a high-up window and if that didn't make sense then he couldn't help it because his world was over now.

And worst of all was this realisation: he deserved it.

So much pain I've caused.

Doing what you had to do in order to achieve your goals: none of that had felt evil at the time, none of it, and if anyone had dared to ask him if he thought he was a good man at heart, he would have answered yes... before beating up and maiming the one who asked the question, or more likely killing them.

Because anyone who dared to speak up like that would have formed a threat and needed to be taken off the board.

I tried to do right by Susan.

His daughter, one of a kind in so many ways, and he had always cared for her as best he could, including insulating her from as much of the reality of his working world as possible, and maybe that had been the chink or crack in his armour that the wraiths and the Hades-spawn woman with glistening blood skin used to rip apart his psychological carapace and throw the pieces away, before getting to work on the soft remaining innards of his defenceless self.

If he'd truly been a good man, he wouldn't have needed to hide his world from his daughter, which meant the wraiths and that blood-red woman with orange-fire eyes had the right of it, and he, Konrad Talon, had been wrong all along.

"I'm..."

No getting around it.

No time for illusions anymore.

"...sorry."

For the hurt he'd caused collaterally in the real world, to ordinary folk he mostly never saw, and directly to his enemies and even his own people in the world of criminal enterprise, and the creatures he and Alej Kandroknar dragged from that place, the what, crawlspace dimensions that the red woman asked about—

Tell me what you know of the Draxoleth.

—and her words burned in his mind still, and always would, for whatever small amount of time remained before his death.

His well-deserved death, following all that pain and torture that had after all – he understood so clearly now – simply been what he deserved.

Something shifted.

What...?

It hurt, but in a distant way: the harness that held him up had shifted somehow.

No sound.

Perhaps he'd imagined that external change: perhaps it was his own internal organs giving way, his physical self shearing apart after all it had suffered, and no wonder. Amazing that the meat-stuff of his own body had held up so long without disintegrating.

Another shift, and this time it hurt more.

Finally, the end.

A third movement, and suddenly he no longer felt the unseen harness – it just wasn't there, not any more – and without any kind of strength remaining he simply dropped to the blue-grey flagstones, and they seemed to come up to meet him with a smack that should have been jolting but instead was simply one more tally mark in the ongoing count of things happening to him.

Cold and hard, the stone pressing against his face.

With one eye squinted open, he saw purple flames diminish to the tiniest of flickers, and then they were gone, as if snuffed out.

Time for me to die.

It was all that he deserved, and waiting was all that he could do, and nothing mattered now: none of it at all.

No more struggle left.

Time. At last.

And yet…

As he lay there on the floor nothing happened, except that the flagstones beneath him were perhaps growing even colder, that was all.

Still, he did not try to move.

I'm done.

Yet the longer he lay there, the more nothing happened.

Done?

Minutes or hours or aeons passed: the duration of time no longer made sense. Had long ago stopped meaning anything at all.

Am I…?

At some point a decision occurred, and he began to move his limbs, feeling far too weak to stand but maybe, just maybe, he might be capable of crawling.

Drew in a sobbing breath, and tried to muster strength.

Finally, he drew himself an inch along the flagstones, and then another inch.

Can't…

But it was some kind of progress, except that he deserved to die here so why should he move at all?

Susan.

Something melted inside him at that thought.

Protect Susan.

Dragged himself forward, one more painful inch.

And again.

TWENTY-NINE

Mel had no idea what she was seeing.

It's all impossible.

Immense things swirled, a chaotic purple vastness that might have been tendrils or might have been something else entirely, twisting through impossible transformations, as if the Caverns contained no earthly geometry but instead held fast to the laws of nature belonging to some other realm, a place of cold and heat and sickening, distorted perspectives no ordinary person could possibly comprehend.

She rocked unsteadily on a wide stone ledge above a precipice that plunged even deeper into the Earth itself, and it was Viktor's strong hand on her upper arm that allowed her to keep her balance.

Then she nodded hard, and Viktor let go.

Impossible shades of reflected light bounced back from the round lenses of his glasses.

"I can't..." she started to say.

"We're okay." Viktor's words seemed to curve around in the air, to manifest as some kind of twisted glow, before being whisked away by a sudden caprice of wind or something else, something beyond the edge of human perception.

A few feet away, Lamis was standing with one arm upraised, leaning forward as if against a hurricane wind that only he could feel, surrounded by his white-light shield that seemed to be taking a battering from unseen forces.

In front of him rose the purple-dominated living mass that looked bigger than most houses and more fearsome than a tsunami or volcano, some huge phenomenon filled with unstoppable power drawn from the stuff of primordial chaos.

Lamis's voice sounded deeper than human, and it would have been overwhelming in any place other than this.

"I... need... to..." He seemed to gather more power within himself. "See... them."

A whirlpool, a maelstrom of wind and living matter and energies beyond naming, confronted him.

"Now," added Lamis. "I mean *now*."

There was more going on here, some kind of communication or battle along axes or dimensions beyond touch and vision, a back-and-forth play of swirling energies without any counterpart in the everyday world.

How Mel understood this she could not have said, but she knew with rock-hard certainty that it was happening.

How long the confrontation/negotiation/duel or maybe even some kind of war persisted, Mel had no idea, because it took all her strength to stand here and wait while all her nerves were screaming for her to hunker down on the ground with her hands over her head or simply run in terror from this place.

If it hadn't been for the thought of Finbar and Donal, mental images of the people she loved that she tried to hold onto, she would have done just that: fled and wept and afterwards felt no shame, for no one should be expected to go through this experience.

No one.

Then the big purple mass twisted in on itself, was sucked into solid cliff-like rock, and was gone. Out of sight. No longer there.

Just… gone.

Mel fell forward, went down on both knees, and retched.

"Ugh." Even Viktor was rocking and swaying, his hands out to either side as if for support that wasn't there.

Lamis stood in place, head tilted forward as if in thought.

"Sorry." Mel rubbed her face with one hand while the other remained on the ground – it felt hard beneath her kneecaps – then she went up on one knee, the genuflection position, before rising straight up as if performing a split squat with dumbbells, and then she was herself once more. "Everyone okay?"

"Just an ordinary afternoon in Avenue of the Basilisks," said Viktor, which would have been convincing except for the greenish pallor of his skin and the white fleck of spittle at the corner of his mouth, along with an unexpected weakness in his tone.

He rubbed the spittle away with the back of his hand, and nodded, presumably as a way of indicating he was in fact okay.

"Mage Lamis?" said Mel.

Lamis turned to look at her, or seemed to: with the wraparound shades you could never be entirely sure.

"All is well," he said.

"So you've done it," said Mel. "Hellah or Klaudius or both are being summoned now, right?"

Lamis said nothing.

"I don't think," said Viktor, "it's quite that straightforward."

Mel looked at him. "You've got to be kidding."

But Viktor nodded in Lamis's direction, and neither of them was smiling.

After a moment, Lamis said: "That was a lesser entity. A minor being, more or less child-like, and nowhere near reliable enough to fetch a Guardian here to meet us."

"Hades," muttered Viktor.

Mel looked from one to the other.

"Tell me," she said.

"We have to go on." When Lamis gestured to where the end of the ledge met the cliff-like rock, white light played around his arm and hand, adding a surreal, almost dreamy touch to his motion and words. "Through there, and get through several more encounters, most likely."

Mel let out a breath. "With non-lesser beings, I suppose. Even bigger things than that huge bugger we just encountered."

"Indeed," said Lamis.

"And I apologise, Mel," said Viktor. "Everyone's kind of heard what this place is like, but the reality is more than that, plus you didn't even grow up here. I mean in Tristopolis. You don't know the stories."

Mel frowned at him. "Why would you need to apologise?"

"Because I should have warned you, is why. Warned you about these Caverns."

"You're saying it gets worse than that." She waved a hand in the direction of the rock face where the huge purple entity had disappeared. "When we meet these bigger entities."

"Oh, yes," said Viktor. "A lot worse."

Lamis finally bore a readable expression: a grim smile beneath his wraparound shades.

"It's too late to turn back now," he said in his normal sepulchral tone. "If we flee having caught the attention of even one entity, we'll never make the exit alive."

Mel looked at him for a long moment, saying nothing.

Then she said: "Good."

"Excuse me?" Viktor stared at her from behind his round blue lenses.

"Easy choice," she said. "Go forward or die. Makes things simple, right?"

After a moment, Viktor smiled.

"No wonder Donal fell for you," he said. "You're as bad as he is."

"I'll take that as a compliment."

Lamis shook his head but said nothing, and presumably he knew more about the trials they faced than Mel or even Viktor, but Mel didn't care.

Then he nodded.

"You're ready," said Mel: more command than question.

Lamis nodded, and the white light began to brighten all around him once more.

Time to continue on.

Soon they were wading along a rotating tunnel of… stuff.

It whirled like water but sometimes looked like orange rock or grey wood and other times like helical streamers of brightly coloured silk while the air smelled electric, and when Mel glanced down she couldn't tell if it flowed under or just around her feet, but every instinct told her to avoid sticking her hand into the flow because at that point it would manifest as deadly, not just a conduit.

Its arcane nature would overwhelm and dissolve ordinary human flesh, sucking her inside to form part of that whirling flow.

The tops of her ears itched, a strange and maddening sensation, but she didn't reach up to touch them because oddities didn't matter here: all that did matter was pressing onwards, her and Lamis and Viktor as a team, and while Lamis walked in front of her, hex shield glowing, and Viktor trailed right behind, she knew that in some sense she herself commanded here.

If her will faltered then their unity would break and all three of them would most likely die.

So.

No going back.

The rushing flow, the circling tunnel-like wall, seemed stronger now, with glimpses of random objects – here part of a desk lamp, there a child's carved-bone spinning-top, a fragment of a red wool scarf: flotsam and jetsam in some tidal flow that had nothing to do with water – grew stronger now, hissing louder and louder, yet it didn't tug at her feet as such, so she would keep her balance.

Forward.

No choice now, not when failure meant death for all of them.

Only forward.

It occurred to her that the tunnel-stuff was like some portal of a mad, insane variety, meaning if she jumped into the flow then parts of her would be ripped off and extruded into other locations in the world, the normal world, and she imagined gobbets of flesh and fragments of bone falling out of thin air onto someone's kitchen table or the middle of a crowded sidewalk.

Just for a second she felt a bizarre desire to jump into the maelstrom regardless, drawn by a kind of extreme vertigo.

But in that second Lamis came to a halt, and squinting past him, Mel saw only a kind of falling curtain of silver light, some form of barrier they had to pass through, and she hoped it was something Lamis knew how to deal with.

She dared to glance back, to check Viktor was okay – he seemed to be, though his face appeared grimmer and harder than ever – and she managed to keep her balance despite the whirling sights all around.

A low moan sounded, and a vibration started in the ground below her feet.

Keep balance.

All those Death-damned years of training and fighting in the ring: no way was she going to let a little ground tremor throw her off balance and tip her into the rushing reality-maelstrom.

It was *not* going to happen.

Then a scream rose in front of her, not from Lamis but from the silver curtain itself as he drew it apart, creating an opening with his hands, and it was impossible to see what lay beyond except that it appeared both shadowed and steady, which was good enough for now.

Lamis leaped forward and she tried to spring right after him but the silver barrier was starting to close up. She whirled and grasped the sleeve of Viktor's leather coat as he nearly tripped up, and she almost lost him but tugged him forward and they fell through the opening in the silver barrier, out to the other side.

Behind them the silver stuff hissed and flowed.

For a second Mel felt a strong sensation of frustration coming from the barrier, a sense of hunger unfulfilled, and maybe it had wanted to keep her and Viktor and Lamis inside itself.

"You're okay?" she said.

"Thanks to you," said Viktor.

She nodded.

And turned, wondering what the Hades they were coming up against now.

"No," she said.

They'd come out in some other Cavern, it seemed.

A polished marble floor lay in front of her, and beyond it rose golden doors encrusted with spikes that were stained with what might have been old blood and other fluids, inhuman ichor of various hues, while the air felt cold and smelled unaccountably like rotting rhubarb.

It looked and felt utterly weird but the main thing was what she *couldn't* see.

Lamis was gone.

THIRTY

Miniature gargoyles and obsidian razorbats shifted uneasily on the rooftops, one house after another as Helena tip-tapped her way with the platinum-tipped cane along the dark, curved sidewalk of Tumbleup Road.

She followed the old spiral route while holding in – holding tightly inside herself – the same kind of tempestuous, baffled rage she had felt as a schoolgirl just starting to come into her powers, back when she had felt helpless to control her thoughts and feelings, except no, that wasn't quite right…

She had never entirely lacked self control: if she had, the stern grandparents who raised her here would have shipped her off to somewhere safer for all concerned.

I have control now.

Helena could feel, deep in her trained awareness, the roiling eldritch energies concentrated in the purplestone houses here: the houses and the very land they stood on.

So many mage families had lived in this place, so many generations; and while it was impossible for actual coherent memories to remain soaked in the ground itself, it certainly felt that way: decades and centuries of experience permeated the entire street.

There was no need to look over her shoulder to know what number 47Ω looked like right now: glowing with a pale, silver-grey light, from the wrought-bone gate to the kraken-ivory window frames and the carapace guttering where the razorbats nestled, normally keeping watch but unsettled by the changes occurring inside the house.

Gathering energies cause spillover: in a place like this, some things cannot remain invisible, however unknowable they might be to mundanes, to those who were not blessed (and cursed) with magehood.

I hope I've done the right thing.

Trauma can break anyone, even the most stout-hearted of mages, and Thanatos knew that Kelvin had been through his own kind of Hades of late.

The Draxoleth and Kandroknar were my failure, not his.

Impossible to know why the old memories had suddenly popped into her dreams, but as a topic for academic research, the added emotional baggage from her past might help motivate Kelvin to deal with his own issues even as he picked up the burden of discipline once more.

His power, if turned inwards and used chaotically, could prove his fatal weakness; and if that happened, Helena knew – felt with a deep certainty in every bone and creaking sinew and overwrought nerve in her too-old body – that she would never, ever forgive herself.

What if it goes wrong?

All leading-edge research in areas like this came with dangers. What if Kelvin perished because of her, because of the things she had told him here today? All the while, she had been telling herself it was all for his own good as well as the city's, as well as Mordanto's: to the benefit of magekind and maybe even humanity.

No. Don't exaggerate.

Existential crises are part of living, now and in the past and always: that happens to be a given.

Flamesprites appeared to snuff themselves out in their baskets overhead, one after another as Helena passed each lamppost in turn; but again she knew, without turning around, that after she had passed, each flamesprite would begin to glimmer again: softly, a fraction of normal intensity even for this shadowy place, waiting for her to be gone entirely before they would dare to brighten once more.

She stopped.

To her right, a slinking black shadow also froze, and she knew it for an obsidian cat: a feline formed of living volcanic glass through an act of species creation she had studied in depth – it formed the subject of her ThD thesis, back in what felt like the immensely distant past – and which no one had duplicated in a thousand years, but which used an unusual hex maze with a half-life of nearly a million years, located in Eastern Umbrastan.

That energy pattern blazed in eleven visible dimensions in a secured cavern deep below ground that few individuals dared to venture close to, never mind attempting to enter: only a few highly trained teams of dedicated weapon mages kept watch on the place, ready to alert the world if something happened to its stable configuration.

It was strictly illegal to use that distant energy pattern to bring forth more individual felines, and it was also dangerous in the extreme to the few individuals capable of sensing, latching onto and attempting to communicate remotely with the hex maze itself.

To use it successfully was something else again, and while there was more than one living mage capable of bringing this creature into existence, she could pretty much count them all on the fingers of one hand, and never mind the arthritis in her knuckles.

Until now, she would have excluded her protégé from that list, despite all his progress and successes.

But this obsidian feline was Kelvin's creation, that was obvious, and it formed an act of defiance as much as a tour de force of power and ability.

The maze and the pseudo-cat species might be a thousand years old, but this individual cat born of the maze's energies was far, far newer – perhaps just minutes old.

On the other hand, its creation – its instantiation from the species pattern within the distant energy maze, using so-called factory spells and constructor conjurations – must have been some time in the planning.

Considerable time in fact, with a manic focus that might have bordered on the self-destructive, meaning Kelvin had not much cared whether he lived or died.

"Watching me, are you?" she said.

The black-glass cat did not answer.

"I know what you are," she added.

Her patrician tone remained unflinching, and the sternness of her grandparents had proven in the end to be an advantage, just one more source of strength against the dark chaos that has always threatened the world, while she had – on growing up – joined a long line of mages pledging service to help humanity, no matter the personal cost.

Are you alright, ma'am?

For a second she tensed, thinking these were the feline's words sounding in her mind; then she relaxed by the smallest fraction, recognising the tone and energy harmonics in the signal that she herself had tuned via her throat amulet.

This was André, her chauffeur, checking up on her.

She touched the small amber amulet, still watching the static crouched feline of black living glass, and spoke aloud, although it was not actual sound that André would perceive through his counterpart amulet.

"I'm on my way back to you," she said. "Please start the car up, but don't move yet until I give you the word."

I'm getting ready.

That was not exactly a code phrase, but it held something of his police training in its wording, and it meant that André understood that circumstances were in some way fraught, which meant engaging the car's defensive hex among other precautions.

He would be loosening his holstered handgun, a dreadful long-barrelled thing that fired depleted-bone shells containing cursegel cores, suitable for some of the most out-of-control threats that someone in her position might face.

It would also create a public relations disaster should he accidentally shoot a mere miscreant witch or rogue parahuman with mage-like abilities, because a hit with one of those particular bullets was like unleashing a section of Hades here on Earth.

The legal consequences for Helena herself would be awful, but she would consider herself deserving of any punishment should the worst happen.

She was the one who had decided that protecting the head of Mordanto – meaning herself as the premier mage in the Federation in terms of political power at least, not her as an individual person – was worth the risk of using normally-proscribed weaponry and placing it in the hands of a non-mage human being, albeit a former TPD detective with considerable training in sorcerous investigations.

"Alright," she said. "Alright."

Her posture remained as ramrod-straight as ever as she resumed her walking, while to her right it seemed a black shadow flowed like liquid: the obsidian cat in motion once more, now matching her pace exactly, keeping a constant distance from her.

"You're a dangerous creation," she went on, "and maybe that's what I deserve, so don't worry – I will work with you, and do my best."

It seemed to turn its head to look at her, to stare with black-in-black eyes that might not exist at all or more likely saw all the way within, beneath all surface appearance, to the inner truth of whatever it regarded.

Matter-binding: the Draxoleth had been a master, and the cat's existence showed that Kelvin understood enough of the techniques involved to potentially create a reliable detector for singleton-wraith presence.

Helena knew she might be judged, here or in the near future, by this creature brought forth from a chaos of hex and otherworldly energies by Kelvin who, like all of his generation, simply had not experienced the world that she herself had operated in when she was his age.

So many details lost to time, so much context she could never explain in words without sounding like a tiresome old woman.

And so many hard things done in the name of Mordanto.

Maybe it is time I retired.

And maybe, just maybe, Kelvin would rise to his natural position as a result of what they were engaged in now; and maybe she wouldn't survive the coming battles: either political manoeuvring would topple her from power or she would actually perish through hands-on hex manipulation, either in combat or simply in trying to get weapon-grade hex mazes ready for use by others.

Rounding another section of arc in the widening spiral of Tumbleup Road, she saw the long dark limousine waiting for her, its hooded headlamps glowering, engine running and ready to leap forward if she signalled appropriately.

Instead she shook her head and continued to walk.

André – always called Big André by his TPD colleagues, although he'd shed the convex belly that had been part of the reason for that name – stepped out of the car and around to the passenger side, where the rear door opened by itself while he held onto it as if guiding the motion, purely as a form of courtesy.

His tie and suit were black as always, his shirt a pale bone grey.

"We're going to have a passenger with us," she told him. "It's perfectly okay."

"Ma'am?"

Helena gestured, and André jerked a little as he suddenly perceived the black feline shape at the edge of the sidewalk: it had slunk beneath dark hedges all the way, so stealthily that even a trained ex-detective had not seen its approach.

"Please," she said, and now she was addressing the living-obsidian feline. "It's easier if you simply ride with us."

When it remained still, the feline might have been a kind of solid shadow, an absence from the world more than a present, living entity.

"And I'll be glad of the company," Helena added, giving a gentle smile and surprising herself by doing so.

Perhaps that was the deciding factor: in any case, the living-obsidian feline flowed across the sidewalk and into the rear seat of the limousine and curled itself up into an inky volume of what looked like nothingness.

André was staring at her. "Ma'am? Are you sure about this?"

"It'll be fine," she told him.

"You expected something like this to turn up?"

"Yes and no. You know people sometimes tell you to expect the unexpected?"

"Yeah… Like that, is it?"

She had not explained in detail – or even overview, really – what she had intended by visiting Kelvin in his house; but André was smart, kept his eyes open, and had been with her for over seven years that sometimes felt like twenty-seven, even forty-seven years together.

"Truthfully, I'm not sure what I've started," she said.

"But it had to be done?"

"It had to be done."

André grinned at her, and it felt as if the world had settled back into its rightful orbit.

"So you did the right thing, ma'am, yet again."

After a moment, Helena lowered herself through the open limo door to a seating position – the older she got, the harder and more painful such simple bending of the joints became – and swivelled her feet inside, and settled the platinum-tipped cane beside her.

The living-obsidian feline remained curled up, and might even have been asleep, assuming its kind slept at all: there was so much that Helena didn't know here.

"Thank you," was all she said as André closed the door for her, but she meant a great deal by those two simple words.

Then André was behind the steering-wheel, and he flicked the bone handle of the indicator switch even though there were no other vehicles around, not even a pedestrian to see the turn signal; and then he turned the limo slowly and steadily, navigating his way out of the spiralling Tumbleup Road.

Soon they reached the curved and criss-crossing roads of Shadowknot Parkway, with André keeping his speed low until they came to a nameless wide road that after a mile morphed into an on-ramp leading to the Orb-Sinister Highway where they merged into the half-busy traffic flow, at which point André accelerated smoothly into the fast lane, his driving as masterful as ever.

Beside Helena, the living-obsidian cat had not moved, yet even in its possibly-asleep state, it most likely understood all that was happening around it.

Kelvin. Choosing you to mentor was the finest decision of my career.

André sped up, still in total control of the limousine.

I just hope—

It is hard to squelch a thought before it is fully formed, because ideas like to spring into the awareness already complete; yet she managed to stop this one from elucidating the things she hoped would *not* happen to Kelvin as he embarked on the mission she had set him.

So many, many bad things were likely.

I—

It was hard not to foresee all the many, nasty, painful ways that he might die.

So very, very hard.

THIRTY-ONE

Donal had no idea what was happening, only that it hurt.

I died.

Well, no, because here he was thinking, forming thoughts despite the pain permeating his entire body, from his scalp all the way down to the tips of his fingers and toes alike, his torso feeling tight, his eyelids squeezed shut and reluctant to open, not wanting to find out if the blazing white light had damaged his sight, because it surely had.

Such a cascade of energy, and he had no idea whether it was Aggie or Martina who'd called it forth.

Maybe it was both or neither: some unintended collateral consequence of mutual aggression using crawlspace energies or something similarly unknowable to a simple human being like one Donal Riordan, who'd clearly stumbled into – or actually caused – a situation far beyond his areas of expertise or even half-baked competence.

Is it possible to set the air alight?

That's what it had felt like when the white explosion happened.

I'm lying on the floor.

Cold, hard stone lay beneath him.

Something told him that he wasn't in the coffee shop any longer, although he couldn't be certain until he actually managed to get a grip and open his eyes and get to his feet and for Thanatos' sake take a look around, and start to take some Death-damned action.

He felt battered and in pain, but that couldn't be allowed to matter.

Step one. Do it.

Lying on his side, ignoring the cold hardness beneath him, Donal squeezed his face into a grimace, then relaxed and forced his eyes to open wide, and for a second his fears came true: a deep sense of semi-blindness fell on him.

No. It's alright.

The chamber was dark, that was all. That, and his eyes had required a moment in which to regain focus.

I'm fine.

Step two was getting upright, which started with pushing himself up into a half-reclining position, then he tucked one foot across as if to sit cross-legged on the blue-grey flagstones, but went up onto the other knee and, with careful focus and using no hands, he slowly stood up, all while unbuttoning his jacket so he could reach the Magnus fast if needed.

Nothing here.

No single source of light provided the dim illumination.

Instead, the stonework all around him – floor and ceiling and walls – gave off a faint, spectral, silvery glow, just bright enough to lend a hint of colour to the flagstones beneath him – bluish grey or greyish blue, something like that – and he didn't know what exactly drew his gaze to those flagstones… except suddenly he did.

They formed five-sided shapes, regular pentagons that fit together precisely in what looked like a natural configuration and yet also deeply unnatural and twisted, all at the same time. No gaps showed between the pentagons, which ought to be impossible.

It was a geometric effect he'd seen before, but only in very particular types of location or circumstance, including St Jarl's the Healer, the hospital where he'd once spent time in the acute ensorcellment ward.

Mages.

Or maybe witches, because you never could quite tell, but for sure he was in some place frequented by people who thought of ordinary folk as mundanes; and while they didn't necessarily consider mundanes to be inferior beings, that didn't matter much to anyone caught up in dangerous conjurations.

I'm not liking this.

Well, tough. It was time to find out what Aggie or Martina had done to him.

Already his pain had faded almost without his noticing, which meant most likely the transition to this place had activated the pain receptors in his body without actually – he was pretty sure now – causing any real damage. He shrugged his shoulders and shook his entire body, feeling loose and well and capable of normal movement once more.

Looks like a dungeon.

Not the kind of place anyone would want to wake up in.

And dungeons have doors, with luck.

If you were a mage capable of using portals, you could deposit someone inside a space that had no openings apart from minor apertures for ventilation, unless you were okay with your prisoner suffocating to death, in which case you could go for a totally isolated chamber as your dungeon of choice.

There were seven sides to this chamber, and in one of them, an opening revealed itself as an area of darkness from which a chill draught emanated.

A soft, distant scrape of sound came from beyond.

Here we go.

The Magnus was in Donal's right hand almost without thought.

Call it a subterranean maze: a place of low-ceilinged corridors or tunnels that curved in some parts and ran straight in others, all of it illuminated by the faint silvery glow of the stonework itself, and not a flamesprite in sight.

The air was chill, and odd draughts flowed in unpredictable directions, perhaps as some deliberate design feature – if you thought following the flow or going against it would lead you to an exit, you'd find out soon enough that you were going around in circles.

That was what Donal calculated in the first two minutes of edging his way along a mostly-curved tunnel while checking each of the three intersections he passed; and while he could tell that a kind of soft turbulence was involved in the flow of air, what he couldn't get was a sense of how big this place might be, how long these tunnels or corridors might run for.

It confused his sense of hearing, that odd airflow, and there was something possibly alive here in the maze – somewhere – except it was hard or maybe impossible to tell the direction for sure: the sounds occurred intermittently, for one thing.

He moved slowly and carefully forward.

Only in the third minute of his exploration did he pick up another definite, unambiguous scrape of sound, this time distinct enough that he could follow the direction with a good sense of certainty.

Some of the openings he passed on the way led to empty shadowed chambers that appeared, as near as he could tell without ducking inside to check, to be identical to the one in which he had awoken. Why anyone would construct a place like this, he had no idea, but maybe you could store things here.

Things or people.

Around the next corner.

A low moan accompanied by a soft scrape sounded as Donal rounded the curve in the tunnel-come-corridor, and he guessed what he would find just a second before he saw it: a crawling man, moving pitifully slowly, dragging himself inch by painful inch along the smooth stone floor.

"Thanatos," muttered Donal, knowing that at some point, if he remained trapped down here without some way to recharge his heart, he too might end up in some near-death state, reduced to feeble movement and, in the end, no deliberate movement at all.

He crouched down into a rock-bottom squat on the crawling man's lefthand side and touched the man's left shoulder.

"Ugh!" The man twitched and whimpered, and began to curl up on the stonework.

"It's alright," said Donal. "I'm on your side."

"Huh…"

Coherent conversation wasn't going to happen here, clearly.

If it weren't for the lack of visible spilled blood, Donal would have guessed torture.

Then again, given the distorted geometry of the pentagonal flagstones back in the chamber he woke up in, this was mage or maybe witch stuff, and some of those folk could get pretty creative when it came to punishing people or getting them to talk.

So what was it here? Punishment or interrogation?

Maybe an element of both. Or torture for the pleasure of inflicting agony on others, but Donal hoped to Hades that wasn't it, not if Aggie were involved in this.

"My name's Riordan." Donal made the words forceful, just in case the guy was too wrapped up in pain to pay attention to outside sounds. "I'm going to get us out of here."

Making a promise he might not be able to keep, but it seemed the right thing to say. Thanatos only knew what had been done to this poor guy.

Then Donal added, knowing it weakened his stated promise but needing information: "You know where the exit is?"

Another whimper, then a tiny shake of the head from the man. He had pulled himself almost into a face-down foetal position, as if scared even to look up at Donal.

Not good.

I'm going to have to carry him.

Internal injuries can be worsened by a firefighter's carry, but when an actual fire is involved, the alternative is leaving the injured person to be consumed by flames.

Here the question was less clear, but if this place truly formed a subterranean maze, then leaving the man behind in order to find the exit more quickly, well, that risked being unable to find him again, or at least not finding him in time.

Medical treatment had to be priority: that was clear.

"Alright, buddy." Donal took hold of the man's shoulder and tugged to roll him partly face-up: head to Donal's lefthand side, his feet to Donal's right. "I'm going to grab hold of both your arms, okay?"

Zombie sensory acuity is a fine and wonderful thing.

Bleeding Hades.

The suffering man's features were lined and sweat-soaked despite the chill air, his eyes held knowledge of things that should have remained unknown and unguessed at, and his trembling wasn't going to stop anytime soon; and Donal was seeing all of this in gloomy surroundings: seeing by the inexplicable spectral fluorescence of the stonework all around.

Yet even with all these disadvantages, and despite having seen only a single blue-and-white photo portrait for a short period of time, Donal knew exactly who this was.

"Talon," he said. "Konrad Talon."

"Ugh." Talon jerked again as if struck in the stomach or cramping up, wanting to curl up more tightly, unable to face any kind of human interaction whatsoever.

At least, that was how Donal read Talon's reaction, but it was all guesswork, and a shocked and traumatised man is never going to behave exactly predictably.

What the Hades have they done to you?

Who or what "they" might be was another question that would need to be answered, but the first priority was exactly what Donal had already asked about, without success.

They needed to find a way out of this Death-damned awful place.

There are ways to carry an unresponsive victim to safety that involve taking excessive care not to exacerbate any existing injuries, taking things slowly and carefully, preferably involving more than one rescuer.

When there's only one of you doing the lifting, it helps if the victim is at least partly conscious and willing to do what you tell them to do.

Right now the whimpering victim was a crime lord with a vicious past, and this was closer to a battlefield situation than an accident scene: in an actual open battle, moments and areas of calm often exist in the midst of ongoing carnage, and that calm is destined to evaporate sooner or later.

Lessons learned in situations of high adrenaline stay embedded in the mind and body forever, and there were some skills that Donal had learned while on overseas deployment alongside the Shadowborne Rangers, back in the day.

He knew how to do this fast.

Talon, curling up once more, was again almost face-down in front of Donal: head to Donal's left, feet to the right. From his squatting position, Donal rolled Talon onto his back, straightening him out; then Donal changed to kneeling on both knees as if about to drop his chest on Talon's.

As he leaned down, Donal moved his left hand across to hook under Talon's knees, and kept rolling clockwise so that it was the back of his shoulders that made contact with Talon's chest, while Donal himself was facing the ceiling, being careful to keep the movement going.

Momentum and technique were everything.

It was a sideways shoulder roll that brought Donal back to kneeling once more, except that now he was on one knee, not two, and he had effectively wrapped Talon around his shoulders, behind his neck, as the roll progressed: he was now kneeling with Talon draped chest-down across his shoulders.

Keeping the legs hooked with his left hand, gripping Talon's sleeves with his right hand, Donal took in a breath, held it, then powered himself up to standing.

Easy.

He shifted once and adjusted the weight, centring the load, and then he was ready.

A single soft groan sounded from Talon, but he didn't struggle, which was okay: a limp weight is easy enough to carry once you've got it on your shoulders. It's the lifting part, getting the weight up there, that's tricky.

Alright.

Time to orient himself.

A way out of here would be nice.

He took a step forward, then another and another, getting used to the weight across his shoulders, the feel of Talon draped there, before upping the pace to a fast terrain-crossing march, like jogging – in terms of speed – but with a stronger gait, suitable for load-carrying across an extended period of time.

Talon hiccupped, just once: some odd reaction in his body, nothing more.

It was the kind of detail that might amuse Mel later, if Donal survived to tell her the story of what happened here, but right now he wasn't smiling.

He'd never been one for solving maze puzzles in newspapers, the kind where you draw a pencil line through the diagram, and right now he was in a three-dimensional reality, an actual maze with tunnel-corridors formed of spectrally glowing stonework and no obvious clues to follow, not even the air flow.

Doesn't matter.

Any kind of movement would count as progress here.

Come on.

One foot after another: all he had to do was march, with Talon on his shoulders.

Just keep going.

Over and over until he found a way out or fell down and perished: the very lack of choice made this easy from a certain point of view.

Just keep going forward.

Discipline was all.

THIRTY-TWO

"How do we get through?" asked Mel.

She touched the rearing golden door – it was wrought into patterns, convolute and horn-encrusted – while making herself ignore the purple-and-green ichor streaks on the horn nearest her face, not knowing what to expect from the door itself, other than immense solidity.

The metal felt as cold and hard as it looked. It might also have been conducting some kind of faint vibration, or possibly that was just her own hand trembling.

"Good question." Viktor had stepped back farther from the door, and was looking up towards its top, some twenty-one or twenty-three feet overhead, where it was framed by solid rock.

"Or around," said Mel. "If you can spot a way to squeeze past somehow."

Perhaps there were small natural tunnels not filled with great heavy barriers or deadly sheets of hex or some predatory kind of being that would eat them alive or worse, or arcane hazards of kinds she could not imagine at all until one of them got hold of her and then that would be it, her life story finished, over and out, the end.

Not happening.

"Avoiding this door is the only thing I can think of," said Viktor. "But I just can't see a way."

"Off to the sides." Mel waved towards the shadows stretching beyond and behind him.

"Maybe, but how good is your sense of direction if we start following some tunnel curving up and down and sideways, twisting every which way?"

"I have no idea."

After a moment, Viktor nodded. "We won't find anything if we don't look, so heading off to one side or the other would be a good Plan B."

"Right. Let's keep plugging away here at the door until we've definitely had enough."

Unspoken: they were better off sticking together than going off in different directions. The Caverns were dangerous enough as they were. Dangerous enough to have snatched Mage Lamis, for all his power and experience, right in front of them.

She hadn't expected any of this to be easy, but losing Lamis so soon, that was a nasty surprise.

"Blood stains," muttered Viktor.

"None of them look wet," said Mel. "Some might well be dirt or rust."

"And no bones or exoskeletal carapace remains."

Mel blinked. It was easy to forget that a stubble-bearded tough guy could also be smart enough to have earned a ThD.

"Something took away the bodies," she said. "We already know the Caverns aren't exactly deserted. It's kind of why we're here."

If they got through the huge, horn-encrusted door, then they would presumably meet whatever it was that had been able to snatch a senior mage from right in front of them, but it was no good thinking that way because there was no other choice, not now.

"Doorway, doorway, doorway," muttered Viktor. "All we need to do is open a Death-damned door."

Mel blinked hard, then again, and after a moment, a third time.

"That's right," she said.

"Say what?" The round blue lenses made Viktor's eyes look hard, or maybe that was how they looked regardless.

"Or almost right," she said. "Maybe you don't have to die to open the door. Just bleed a little."

"You've got to be kidding."

"I like a good joke as much as the next girl" – Mel took a step to her left, looking for a curved horn that might be relatively clean – "but this time, no, I'm not really" – and braced herself, tightening her abdomen – "*joking!*"

The exclamation helped her slam her left hand forward, palm first against the point of the horn, and she yelled against the pain of it, yelled with ferocity, because she had no other choice: she had to do this, for Donal and for Finbar's sake as well as her own and that of their friends.

Did it.

It penetrated deeply enough, the point of the horn embedded in her hand, and for a second or three it hardly hurt at all, because pain is in the brain and right now hers was flooded with adrenaline and the absolute need to make this work.

Have I damaged a nerve?

There was no way to tell.

Broken bones?

She hoped not.

No big arteries in the hand.

So long as the blood vessels were small enough, she could contain any bleeding, but that was in the near future, not right now. In this moment, shedding blood was the entire point of this.

Of course it was hurting now. Her left hand burned with pain.

"Thanatos." Viktor, seen as a tear-blurred figure, came close but did not reach out. "You want help to pull the hand away?"

"No." She waited a beat longer, then another. "Get ready." Speaking was hard, with her hand impaled like this. "If it opens, move inside."

She forced herself to keep on breathing hard.

"Look for openings," said Viktor. "Get through, both of us, and worry about your injury afterwards."

Good. He got the point.

Alright.

Now all she had to do was pull the left hand away from the golden horn that pierced it.

I'm ready.

Knees dipped a little, tightening the abdomen, preparing to lunge backwards, powered from the legs and core, determined to do this right.

Now.

She yanked back.

There might have been a liquid slurp but her yell covered any other sounds and slick redness remained on the tip of the golden metal horn and that was all she needed.

Good enough.

She grasped her left hand in her right while taking another few steps back, making herself look up at the rearing golden door, patterned and horn-encrusted as it was, knowing she needed to put her attention there, not in her pain-filled hand that burned and frightened her with the idea of possible long-term damage but the point was she'd done it now.

Whatever the damage, it was something to be dealt with later.

Right now she only had one job to do and that was get through to the other side of this bloody door – literally bloody now with her own lifeblood on the hungry golden metal – and that was a strange thought, the notion of lifeless metal possessing hunger or thirst or any kind of feelings at all, but that was the kind of place this was.

She knew that.

She'd known it the second they stepped out of the elevator shafts back in what seemed like the distant past, her and Viktor and Lamis, knowing from that moment in her heart that she was placing all of them in mortal danger.

Because of her both Lamis and Viktor might so easily die, and so could she, of course she could, but risking her own life was okay when she knew the reason, and hers was the best reason of all.

So she could take this burning pain, this agony filling up her left hand like boiling hot blood filling a bucket, which was a weird way to think but she was feeling sick inside and everything was whirling and why the bleeding Hades wasn't the Thanatos-damned door even starting to open?

"I'm sorry." Distant words, probably Viktor's, though it could have been some other part of her fractured mind, talking to herself, because defeat and pain were swirling together inside her.

I thought it was going to work.

Stupid, stupid, stupid.

Caverns and entities and Guardians and all of it beyond me.

Call it hubris, the way Donal once explained the word to her. Stupid pride, thinking she could come to this place and get something done, when the truth was she'd been in over her head from the very beginning, and now Finbar was going to grow up without a mother as well as without a father, and it was entirely her fault, no one else's.

Her fault alone.

So stupid…

Blood-rush in her ears, oceanic sound of pain and stress and bewilderment, filling up her senses so it was impossible to hear anything else, anything like…

Something.

I thought I heard…

So very hard to blink her way out of tear-blurred confusion and dampen out the stress sounds of her own making and listen for something out in the world, but she had to do just that, she really had to.

I thought…

There.

A creak?

No. Nothing.

I'm imagining…

A definite creak.

Oh, dear Thanatos.

And the door began to move.

THIRTY-THREE

Donal was hurting.

Mostly it was the weight across his shoulders – the barely conscious Talon, with enough residual muscle tension in his body to indicate he remained alive, but mostly forming a mass of slack flesh draped like a heavy sack behind Donal's neck.

The subsequent stress and strain centred on Donal's lower back, which was where you needed to be careful when speed-marching long distances under a reasonably heavy load.

Still, he marched on.

He'd carried heavier men than Talon, both in training and actual emergency situations, but the problem here, in the spectrally lit maze of stone tunnel-corridors that seemed to wind on forever, was not knowing the end point: the exit could be minutes away or many, many hours.

There might in the end be no way out at all, not for anyone incapable of summoning up a mage-style portal; and while he knew that kind of thinking was pointless, it still lapped away at his mental defences, threatening to erode his will.

Talon seemed to be growing heavier, but that could only be an illusion, nothing more.

One step at a time.

Grinding difficulty teaches patience, and Donal had learned so many lessons over the years. Here and now he needed only to apply them, to keep on going: simply that.

Nervousness and fatigue were his enemies.

Pain was an illusion.

I'm a zombie.

A resurrected person can shift their mental architecture around, given enough internal discipline, and he'd done it before, although less and less often these days.

It makes a difference.

As he marched on, his footsteps sometimes echoing back and sometimes lost to the random turbulent air-draughts, a web of shifting mechanical forces was at play throughout his body, the lumbar region – around the lower spine – included.

That would have been true for any living human or bipedal animal, but the point right now was that he could interpret the sensations as ongoing pain or simply as an internal measurement of force vectors exerted and experienced, nothing more.

Call it a form of recalibration.

Done. It's okay.

Nothing changed as he continued to speed-march his way along the curving maze, and yet subjectively everything felt different: Talon's weight remained but the notion of it hurting was gone, entirely evaporated.

Gone for good.

He upped the pace, although only by a little, for he'd already been operating at near-optimum speed.

Yard after yard, he continued to cover distance, and this was the absolute best he could manage: traversing tunnel-corridors with no strategy or tactic beyond making sure he didn't start covering the same ground more than once.

That was where zombie acuity and awareness stepped in once more, because he knew for sure that if, for some reason, he needed to retrace his steps all the way back to the chamber he'd woken up in, he would in fact be able to do just that: replay and reverse his movements in this place.

There was no reason to pick one route over another at any branch point or intersection within the maze – the idea of always turning left or some such nonsense was exactly the kind of thing a maze designer would keep in mind, assuming that really was the intent of this layout: making it hard to find way a out – and so he made what felt like random choices, so far with the comfortable knowledge that he could remember each one.

At some point he would presumably reach overload and maybe then have to reconsider, devise some new way of picking routes from that point onwards.

I can keep going.

Just marching, keeping things physical: it really was like being back in the Army.

Another intersection, this time a branching into three onward corridor tunnels – two twisting off to the left, one to the right, a wedge of stone preventing forward movement directly ahead – and he was about to choose the leftmost tunnel when a screech of some sort sounded from way off to the right, and in that instant everything changed.

Time to run, but Talon was coming with him.

You've done it before.

Sometimes on hilly terrain with muddy rising slopes, and at least the stone floor ran level throughout the maze, with so far no trip hazards either: as a challenge, this almost counted as easy.

Which meant Donal could run faster, that was all, even with Talon's weight pressing down across his shoulders, trying to slow him down but he could *not* allow that, not at all, because the screech sounded louder and closer and if there was a chance of taking decisive action here then he could not allow it to slip away, not now.

Running harder.

Yes.

And a little harder, like a battlefield sprint to remove a casualty from danger, upping the pace again as urgency flooded through him along with the hope that this might be it: a chance to escape from this place if he acted fast enough.

Footsteps echoing back from the walls as he pounded around a rightward-curving arc in the route.

Come on.

A short straight length of tunnel-corridor and then a kind of elliptically shaped intersection with one exit wider than the other four and that was where things opened out into a different kind of chamber than the ones he had passed before or the place where he woke up.

This was bigger than the others, a chamber that stretched at least three times longer and wider, and possessed either seventeen or nineteen sides. Normally his sensory acuity and precision would have offered up a definite answer in the first fraction-of-a-second glance, but his visual foreground was taken up by a maelstrom of blazing light and shifting confusion, and that made things harder.

So very bright, and confusing.

It shone. It whirled.

Donal had no idea what he was seeing, but he couldn't look away: it was a swirling vortex of light with glimpses of random objects, visible then snatched away – there a man's hat, there a hand with shirt cuff and cufflink showing for a split second in the rush, a blue umbrella, a violet leaf, a white lizard's thrashing tail, a patch of black soil, a scarlet ribbon, two purple fish, a paving stone, a portion of grey cloud, an angry-looking cat, a torn book, a mop of hair that might have been a wig, a broken headlamp, a human skull with three eye sockets, another book, a stained sword-blade bent in the middle – amid a rushing, circling flow of liquid light, glowing white and blue and fire-orange.

The air smelled of ozone and roses.

What the Hades?

Donal half-squatted under control, and let Talon slip from his shoulders. Without taking his attention off the whirling reality-vortex, Donal kept a grip on Talon, finally letting go when he sensed that Talon could support himself in a half-sitting position.

The screech sounded once more, and it appeared to emanate from the flowing stuff of the vortex, as if the whole thing were a kind of mouth giving vent to furious pain.

It felt deeply unpleasant, a vibration that went all the way through Donal's body, causing him to clench his teeth, while beside him Talon simply groaned.

This could be a way out.

It didn't look like a mage portal, not really, yet there was some kind of similarity in the way it distorted the stuff of actual reality, so there was a possibility you could step inside and be transported somewhere.

But not, he suddenly decided, if you wanted to arrive in one place intact. *We'd get torn to shreds.*

He felt sure of it, or almost sure, but still he waited, unable to look away or move from this place.

Movement inside.

A different kind of movement: a shape at the centre of the whirling that appeared to be growing closer, a bundle of dark material and paler flesh that looked to be a human corpse, tumbling around and around as if caught in a hollow spinning drum.

Then one hand moved independently of the overall rotation, which meant they were alive, whoever they were: helpless in the vortex that was flinging them this way.

In this direction, straight towards Donal.

Bleeding Hades.

He flew out of the vortex mouth, the man — it *was* a man, tall and gaunt in a long, flapping coat — and Donal caught him, rotating and absorbing some of the momentum, taking a step and then another step before everything steadied and he could lower the man to the floor,

At that point, Donal sucked in a breath as if he remained a redblood, because there was no mistaking those features, even without the usual wraparound shades.

"What the Hades?" Donal wasn't expecting an answer.

This was Lamis, but Donal had never seen him looking like this.

A hint of a moan came from Lamis's throat, but you couldn't tell if he was awake or unconscious because of the lack of eyes: only scarred, blasted eye-pits featured in that long, familiar face.

"Lamis? Can you hear me?"

But Lamis said nothing.

This eyeless mage, his friend, was clearly out of it.

Beyond him slumped Talon: a trembling, useless, broken crime lord, the original target of Donal's search. Straight ahead hung this whirling reality-vortex that looked like some kind of one-way transportation mechanism, with this chamber here forming the destination.

Something told Donal that Lamis's shades had come loose inside the vortex, flicked away and ending up in some other part of the world, or as separated pieces in scattered locations.

I'm looking for a way out.

The vortex looked like a bad bet, but on the other hand, this whole place formed a literal maze and there might not even be an exit, not in the normal dimensions of reality.

Do I chance it?

He started to lean forwards, readying himself for the possibility of a forward dash – nothing more than that, just considering the possibility, especially since he would have to drag both Lamis and Talon with him – and he could have sworn that the motion made the vortex notice him, as if the whirling thing possessed awareness and maybe even will of some kind.

The vortex-tube reared up like a worm or snake, then pulled back, and suddenly it was shrinking and pulling away from Donal and there might have been a kind of hiss in the air as it withdrew into itself, sucked itself down into a narrow point of light, and hung there, shining steadily, as if waiting for Donal to make a move.

Still the smell of rose petals intertwined with the oceanic tang of ozone: such an odd mixing of scents.

Taunting me.

That was an odd thought to have about something that looked mostly like an unearthly weather phenomenon, but you couldn't discount intuition when it came to dealing with the unknown.

"Damn you," he said, and in that moment whipped out his Magnus and squeezed the trigger.

A flat percussive crash sounded in the chamber.

For a moment the light-point wiggled in what looked like shocked surprise, then it twisted around on itself, shrank even further, and continued shrinking all the way to non-existence.

Gone.

"Don't come back," added Donal.

Well, that had told it.

Lamis. Talon.

Now he had two men to look after, still with no idea of how to get out of this place, not really. Tramping around until he stumbled on an exit: that was all he'd come up with so far, and the appearance of Mage Lamis didn't alter that, at least not until the mage woke up and produced some kind of amazing solution just like that.

Still slumped on the stone floor, Lamis began to snore.
"Oh, for Thanatos' sake."
This was all too much.

THIRTY-FOUR

Tempelgard Airport: it had been a long time since Kandroknar had seen the windswept runways, stood in the lee of the hangars, and watched the propellors slow down on one of the shiny silver cargo planes, while the beetle-carapaced unloading cranes rolled into their ready positions.

He owned – via multiple layers of corporate proxies – a small fleet of cargo aircraft, while the interesting thing about this particular aeroplane was its additional fuel tanks and long-range capability.

Blinking against the faint quicksilver rain – everyone who worked at Tempelgard was fully vaccinated against the rain's effects – the stocky transport chief, Braunkin, assured Kandroknar that the plane could be made ready to fly anywhere in a matter of hours.

"As far as Silvex City?" asked Kandroknar, enjoying the feel of metallic droplets against his face.

"Silvex—? Well, sure," said Braunkin. "If the permits are in order."

"They're in order."

Braunkin's surprise was natural, given how seldom Kandroknar's companies did business with Silvex City or anywhere else in Illurium, but the permits had been in place for years, kept up to date by teams of tame lawyers and their bureaucrat assistants.

"Keep it ready, then," said Kandroknar. "For a flight to Silvex City, full cargo load, at what you might call a moment's notice."

But not actually a panic evacuation: he was *the* Alej Kandroknar, and far too settled and powerful to require an actual retreat.

He had truly been thinking of making a new start for some time. The fact that Mordanto's mages might learn that he had survived that years-old confrontation on Hardhammer Heath, even though their best seven mages hadn't, that wasn't the reason for his relocation.

That very confrontation was depicted in the sculpture of seven mages that he kept at home, and perhaps he would take with him after all, along with the easy-carry crates of cash and valuables.

"Very good, sir," said Braunkin. "And the pilots and crew? Keep one crew on standby at all times?"

"Exactly so," said Kandroknar, glad he'd chosen his transport chief so well. "Exactly so."

As Braunkin started to turn away, Kandroknar surprised himself by adding: "I might accompany the cargo too."

He hadn't intended to announce that in advance, but it would ensure decent supplies of gourmet food and drink on board, for Braunkin understood something of Kandroknar's normal requirements for personal travel.

And then, because he couldn't resist, he added: "After a rather spectacular leaving celebration just to start off the trip, I should think. Something spectacular."

Braunkin nodded, stocky and stolid. "I understand, sir. Very good."

Except, of course, the poor clod understood nothing at all.

Something spectacular.

Enough to make a mark on Mordanto.

And on the city.

Exactly so.

If he was going to fly away from Tristopolis, he might as well wreak some revenge and artistic destruction on the way.

Martina.

Yes. A good choice of weapon.

Definitely leaving his mark.

And a trail of rather wonderful destruction.

THIRTY-FIVE

"Talk to me," said Donal.

He'd been dragging both men along yet another tunnel-corridor by their collars – the collar of Lamis's long prairie coat, the kind some folk call a duster, and the collar of Talon's suit jacket, which seemed to be made of sturdy fabric that surely hadn't come cheap – but Talon's body had grown stiffer with tension in the last few minutes, and he'd begun muttering actual words.

Until then, he'd been a slack weight that could barely moan or mumble. Maybe now he could actually communicate.

I could do with a break, anyway.

Donal was nowhere near the limit of his physical endurance, but even disciplined blackbloods can benefit from a recuperative short break.

Plus, with a modicum of luck, he might actually learn something useful.

"What? No," said Talon, then gave a moan.

Donal stopped dragging the men, then he rolled Lamis onto one side – into something like the recovery position – in the centre of the tunnel, and hauled Talon towards the wall and propped him there, legs outstretched along the floor.

"Alright." Donal settled into a rock-bottom squat facing Talon. "Susan is worried about you."

"Huh?" Blinking, then squinting, Talon attempted to focus. "Su-Susan?"

"Your daughter."

"Yes-s-s." Talon's chin tipped down to his chest.

Donal waited.

There was no way of guessing how quickly a tortured man could regain a semblance of normal cognition, could manage to drag himself back to a place where he recognised his own thoughts, where he might regain some sense of his previous identity.

Personalities can be shattered, like rocks in a quarry. There was no telling what Talon had been through, but whatever it was, it hadn't been pleasant and it hadn't been easy.

"D-danger." Talon gave a whimper and shook his head, eyes closed. "Susan."

"She's alright." Donal tried to make his tone soothing. "She's fine, Talon. I talked to her. She sent me to find you."

"No." A moan from Talon. "No. Where?"

For a second, Donal thought he'd said *nowhere*, but maybe Talon meant to ask where Donal had met Susan. That might make sense.

"In her rooms," said Donal. "That's where we met. She's safe there."

"Ri-le...na."

Donal couldn't help glancing in Lamis's direction. Here was a mage with blasted eye pits, while Rilena was a witch who also sported burned ruins where her eyes should have been.

"Rilena's helping in the search," said Donal. "Her and Balagron."

Not that he'd made much use of their offered help, or given them any information that might have helped them mount a search of their own. All these resources he might have used: Rilena, Balagron, Martina – whatever she/it was – and even those five spy-wraiths that Alej Kandroknar had assigned to obey Donal's commands.

He'd had the makings of a team, yet here he was, on his own once more, saddled with one unconscious mage and an addled torture victim, and the idea of getting useful information out of Talon suddenly seemed laughable.

"Witch," said Talon. "Traitor!"

His eyes opened wide, and for the first time he focussed on Donal.

"No," said Donal.

"Betrayed..." Talon slumped.

"Are you sure? How do you know?"

"I..." For a second, Talon almost looked sure of himself, then he shook his head and leaned back against the wall, still with his legs stretched out on the stone floor, and closed his eyes.

This really wasn't going well.

Was it Aggie who sent me here?

It had to be, because it wasn't Martina acting under Kandroknar's orders: he was almost sure of that.

"Kandroknar," said Donal. "Tell me about Alej Kandroknar."

The more he thought about that fallen-cherub-like mage, the more uneasiness spread through him.

"No!" Talon shook his head from side to side, three times over, eyes squeezed shut and with a hint of tears. "Not again. I told you..."

"What? What exactly?"

It came out as a sob. "I told you *everything*."

"Thanatos," muttered Donal.

Someone or something had captured Talon, tortured him yet kept him alive, and even left him unguarded in the aftermath of interrogation, although it was still unclear whether anyone could actually get out of this Death-damned maze: perhaps being brought to this place amounted to a death sentence in itself.

Still squatting, Donal stared at Talon's suffering features, evaluating the man and the tactical situation.

Maybe you weren't the end goal.

There was an awful lot that Talon could spill to TPD officers in a normal interrogation cell, but maybe the "everything" he'd told his torturers here had little to do with his years as a crime lord except in one particular regard: his past association with Alej Kandroknar, the twisted mage-or-similar whose wraiths had taken Donal to the Chasm and who'd promised all that help which hadn't, in the end, come to much at all.

"Alright," said Donal. "Alright."

Call Talon a kind of collateral damage in someone else's private operation against Kandroknar. Donal's job was to find Talon – now accomplished, sort of – and get him back to his daughter Susan, nothing more than that.

Aggie. Is all this your doing?

That didn't seem right, but speculating in the absence of facts wasn't going to get anyone out of here.

He looked over at Lamis, whose muscle tone and slack features indicated a kind of sleeping state, meaning he was no use whatsoever right now.

Wonderful.

Donal needed to take action, to make something happen, but that was an awful lot easier when there was some kind of path to follow. Random movement was still movement, therefore better than inaction, but sub-optimal all the same.

What would Sergeant Zelavitch do?

That was a question that went right back to his earlier days in military action, sometimes resurfaced during his time on the beat as a uniformed cop after leaving the Army, and only occasionally popped back into his mind in more recent times.

In the past, asking that question had effectively saved his life, several times over: asking the question and hearing, in his mind, the succinct rules that hardbitten sergeant would drum into soldiers' brains.

If there's something to shoot, shoot it.

Long stone tunnel-corridor, arcing to the right in one direction, leading to a three-way split in the other, no useful features in sight, certainly no other living being besides Lamis and Talon and Donal himself.

If the enemy forces are weaker than yours, advance aggressively.

He could probably rule out that one as well.

And if the enemy outnumbers you, search for their flank and then attack it.

Yeah. That one, if he could find a way to apply it in his current situation.

"Forget about escape," he muttered.

What he needed was someone or something to fight.

When all else fails, you can drop your guard.

That had been Coach O'Brien in the boxing gym, not Sergeant Zelavitch, but the old coach's rule came with an important proviso.

So long as you know what you're doing.

Right now, there was an enemy out there but Donal didn't know how to attack them, so he could do the next best thing: get them to attack him, so at least there'd be something to latch onto.

"Dangerous, always dangerous," Coach O'Brien used to warn his young boxers. "But always sweet when you get it just right."

So. How to apply that now?

"I could shout and yell," muttered Donal, but Talon here was proof that that wouldn't work: there must have been howling and screaming when the torturers got to work.

What would make an adverse party show their hand? What would draw them here because they needed to destroy one Donal Riordan?

So far, they – Aggie or whoever – had dumped him here and then departed, without even bothering to lock him into one particular chamber of this maze. You only attacked someone when they were both an immediate threat and also revealing an opening, an unprotected target you could aim at; or at least, that was some kind of ideal.

I didn't smell ozone earlier.

And there certainly hadn't been roses when he woke up in that chamber lying on impossible-pentagon flagstones.

Maybe I didn't come through a vortex like Lamis.

Or he had, and the scent hadn't lingered, but he needed to work with something.

"Lamis, you stupid bugger. Why won't you wake up?"

No answer, and those long features remained slack, the burned-out eye pits as unreadable as ever.

"Okay." Talking to himself, and maybe in part to Talon, who looked at least semi-conscious, if so far no use at all in finding a way out of here. "Maybe there are two ways to transport someone into this place."

Wraiths couldn't transport a person via the crawlspace dimensions, so that was out.

Wait a minute.

He only knew that – or thought he knew that – because he'd asked Aggie about it, and she'd replied that transporting humans that way was impossible if you wanted them to arrive alive at the other end.

Maybe she lied.

On the other hand, humankind and wraiths had co-existed for millennia, which meant if such transportation were in fact possible, it would surely have become known by now.

Amulet.

He was an idiot. The call crystal, the one Klaudius had given him, hadn't worked in Cataclysm Chasm because Alej Kandroknar had been blocking it somehow; but this was a different place, and if anyone could get in here without problems it was a Guardian.

"Oh, for Thanatos' sake."

His hand went to his chest, but he knew without even slipping his hand inside his shirt that the call crystal was gone. Whoever or whatever took him to this place had known what they were doing: they'd taken the Death-damned thing off him.

I still should've thought of it earlier.

Donal had thought he was operating at close to peak efficiency, but if he'd missed this, then what else had he blundered past and totally ignored?

Something's messing with my concentration.

You want to keep someone quiet, you might consider giving them a sedative… or employ neurohex induction with a Mickey Finn conjuration, if you were a witch or mage kind of person.

He took in a breath, then looked at Lamis and Talon, considering the obvious.

We're all alive.

All three of them had been totally helpless, unable to defend themselves, and while Talon had clearly suffered, it would have been easy to get rid of all of them entirely.

I wonder…

What if it was more than mercy?

Could be.

What if the being or person unknown, the one who'd brought them here, actually wanted or even needed all three of them to stay alive?

This could go badly wrong.

More than that: it could turn into the most tragic disaster of his life.

"Alright, both of you."

Donal moved across to Lamis, half-squatted and took hold of the duster's collar, and dragged Lamis to the wall.

"Mages," added Donal. "A scourge on the Earth."

When Lamis was propped next to Talon, Donal checked neither man was likely to shift position for a while – not via conscious movement – then stepped across to the opposite wall.

"Nah," he said. "Too easy at this distance."

He shrugged his shoulders a little, then walked a slow seventeen paces along the spectrally lit stone corridor, then stopped and turned back.

"Alright. This'll do."

Slowly, as if he were in the kind of competition where fast drawing doesn't count, he removed his Magnus from its shoulder holster, stood sideways-on towards his target, and gradually raised his weapon.

Its weight felt just right, the grip as comfortable as any handgun could offer, the long barrel forming a reassurance of accuracy as well as stopping power.

"You both need to face justice," he said, projecting his voice. "And I might not make it out of here, which means it's up to me to make sure you get what you deserve."

Letting real venom drip into his voice: easy enough to do if you knew what Talon's victims had endured at the hands of his street soldiers in the past.

Aim just right.

A zombie can stop breathing and hold a totally steady posture.

"And here it comes."

Donal started firing.

Has to be done.

Squeezing the trigger over and over.

Shots crashing and echoing.

Again and again.

Okay.

Until every round was spent.

THIRTY-SIX

Mordanto's gates could behave in strange ways, but not – except in the direst of emergencies – when a more-or-less ordinary limousine needed to make its way through.

Sitting ramrod-straight in the rear, comforted by the familiar feel and polished smell of the pterahide upholstery, Helena looked past the rear of André's head and through the windscreen, seeing those tall gates now and simultaneously through the eyes of her nineteen-year-old self, when she transferred here from Darkbridge – so very long ago – newly arrived and suffused with awe at the ancient surroundings and their deep aura of power and intellect combined.

I love this place.

For all its dark secrets, for all the compromises that came with leadership and dealing with the outside world of ordinary human affairs – not to mention the more arcane worlds that only magekind could handle, and none better than the tenured members of this institution – she could no longer imagine belonging elsewhere: Mordanto had become her life.

The gates swung open, taking their time, understanding their protective duty.

Nothing in Mordanto was quite what it looked like to mundane eyes: no non-mage could ever appreciate this place, not really.

Orin. You knew all of it.

Thoughts of her approximately late husband surfaced in maudlin moments, but these rarely occurred during the working day. Her visit with Kelvin had disturbed her equilibrium.

She forced sentiment aside, just as André worked the dragonbone gear shift and rolled the limousine forward, through the tall, imposing gateway – Helena felt the tingle of the gates' searching regard sweep all the way down through her nervous system – across the crunching gravel, heading for the grand south wing as usual.

"Wait," she said. "Not today."

André slowed the car. "Ma'am?"

"Drive widdershins to the second east entrance."

Entrance meaning doorway, since they were already in Mordanto grounds.

"Ma'am."

Keeping to the slow pace, always best when breaking usual protocol, André headed right, circling anti-clockwise around the dark, rearing towers and crenelations, the jagged buttresses and baroque colonnades: so sombre, so old, so redolent of learning.

And power, of course.

The doorway whose image had popped into her mind appeared ahead on the left, guarded by two pillars of flame and a hovering black bat carved from Surinese ebony and animated, back in the day, by good old Professor Sturton: Helena's favourite tutor of all.

Most such conjurations would bleed energy in a matter of days at most, but this bat had persisted for over four decades, hovering as strongly as ever, fully alert; and maybe it was the need to see it again, to remind herself that some things endure, that brought her here.

No. That's not it.

There are technical terms for images and impulses surfacing from the subconscious layers of the mind, including specific labels for varying levels of neurohex involvement, but in this case the details did not matter: Mordanto itself had communicated with Helena, subliminally but surely, having decided that something here held interest for her.

Specifically for her: she felt it intuitively, deep in her old bones.

Not an emergency.

That would have held a specific urgent taste or flavour, a kind of inner tang along with the mental image and the impulse to be here.

Something intriguing.

No single mage, with the possible exception of Kelvin before his recent travails, would truly have a handle on those aspects of the world that interested Helena most deeply; but Mordanto itself, that was another matter.

André rolled the limousine to a halt, with a scrunch of bone gravel.

"I'll enter by myself," said Helena.

"Ma'am."

Of course he got out so he could open the door for her: it would upset him if Helena told him to stay behind the wheel. Taking her platinum-topped cane in hand, she swivelled out as André pulled the door open, then she slid both feet to the ground, and raised herself to standing without putting much weight on the cane at all.

Good enough.

Scrunch, *scrunch*, scrunch, *scrunch* went the knucklebone gravel beneath her shoes and cane-tip as she made her way to the pillars of flame and the hovering ebony bat.

"Hello." She smiled up at the featureless bat. "Good to see you."

It gave no visible sign of recognition or anything else, but she sensed a faint warm resonance all the same, and it reminded her of old Professor Sturton's indulgent smile to his favourite students.

The twin pillars of fire rolled aside, making more room, as the tall door clicked and then swung inwards, revealing a stone hallway with a mosaic floor that often raised at least a twitch of a smile from Helena.

Today its pattern featured impossible triangles twisting back on themselves, while small dark shapes flitting through the triangles morphed from simplified fish shapes – formed of shifting tesserae – to idealised bird silhouettes and back again, over and over as Helena watched.

"Nice show," she told the floor. "Very nice show."

With a pleased, fluid ease, the shapes continued to flit and flow.

"Excuse me, as always," added Helena.

Most novitiates just tramped along the corridor without thought, and sadly continued that ignorant practice if and when they graduated to become fully fledged mages.

Now, she moved slowly along the mosaic, tapping gently with her cane.

Which way?

Room 17 in the corridor leading to Tarquin Hall, close to one of the junior common rooms: the thought came to her most naturally.

"Thank you," she said, this time to the larger pseudo-consciousness of the building all around her.

She walked on slowly, gathering her thoughts.

Tapping the door with her cane, rather than simply opening it, seemed the right thing to do. From inside, Helena sensed an aura of exasperation, female and ill-controlled, which meant there was no surprise when the door whipped open and a scowling young mage with long black hair started to snarl something along the lines of: "What the Hades do you want?"

But the young mage's words caught in her throat, and her eyes widened in instant recognition, something Helena had forced herself to grow used to: being known by far more people than she herself could name.

That kind of unidirectional relationship could siphon away a person's necessary humility if they failed to guard against exactly that.

"Weren't you going to invite me in?" Helena kept her voice soft, almost toneless.

Still, the young mage jumped as if the words contained acid. "Um, sorry, Professor. Of course I—"

Awkwardly she shuffled backwards, away from Helena, further inside the dark-panelled room.

Helena, trying not to smile too much, followed.

Are you the interesting thing Mordanto believes I should look at?

It felt deeply unlikely.

Partly it was the lack of threat or other potential from the young mage, but mostly it was the sight of another young woman whose hair was also long and dark – it had been a long time since Helena's own hair shone anything other than white – but lank and badly combed.

This newcomer sat hunched in a dark-green armchair near a fireplace filled with white and purple flames. From high shelves running around the room, sprites shone inside hollow rat skulls instead of the sconces you might find in the mundane world outside, and their orange-amber glow softened the atmosphere of the room, making it feel cosy.

Not to the strange young woman sitting here, however.

"My name," said Helena, "is Professor Steele. And who are you, exactly?"

"I'm…" She stopped.

"Her name is Gina Antonelli," said the young mage. "Mage Winona brought her in. She's a primitive, I mean, a wild untutored, er… A high potential who was failed by the search and selection system."

Helena nodded. "And you are?"

"Novitiate Irina Yuschenka, Professor."

"I take it you're Gina's welcome advisor." Such a stupid term, different from the old days, but this wasn't the place to deride or try changing the nomenclature.

"Er, yes, ma'am."

The new discovery, Gina, remained hunched over, failing to look up at Helena, while shaking a little. It looked like the aftermath of a more hysterical episode.

A significant potential.

Gina's aura smelled like oranges, and blazed in Helena's synaesthetic hexsense brighter than the flames in the fireplace.

It was time for the voice of command. "Look at me, girl."

Gina's chin jerked up, her eyes widened, and she slammed back in the armchair as if someone had pushed her shoulders in that direction.

"Whatever happened," said Helena, using a downward-pressing motion of her free hand to emphasise her deepening words, "was other people's fault. Here and now, you are in a safe place, and you can let go of the old unhelpful feelings because it's the right thing to do right now."

Here sounds like *hear*, and she'd used tonal emphasis on that word along with *now*, followed by other verbal techniques that a mundane psycho-counsellor might recognise.

They might also comprehend the subliminal effect of her posture and hand movement, but no mundane would sense the rest: Helena's setting up a low but powerful neurohex resonance between her own amygdala – the emergency-response centre of the brain – and Gina's.

There had been a whiff of trauma, not to mention a fading stink of otherworldly distress from whatever creature Gina here had managed to summon into the mesoscopic dimensions, so it was not exactly mind-reading to assume this event had led to Mage Winona finding Gina and removing her from whatever mundane place she had been in, and bringing her here.

After which, Mage Winona had left the new discovery, this wretched Gina, in the care of someone far lower in rank, which did not surprise Helena in the slightest: humility and compassion were far from the strongest features of Winona Cloudback's personality.

Still, she might have found someone more experienced than Novitiate Irina here to do the job.

Ah, well. We need people like Winona, too.

You did not staff a place like Mordanto with people experiencing warm, fuzzy feelings all the time. Sometimes, the low-empathy nasty types were exactly the kind you needed to deploy for everybody's sake, citizens in the mundane outer world included.

Helena turned to Novitiate Irina, looking deeply, because she wanted the answer to a question that should not be asked aloud.

Ah, yes. You did question Gina and get details of the disturbance.

Alright. Helena returned her attention to the wide-eyed Gina who was now sitting up much straighter, while her breathing had grown more regular: a sign of increasing calm.

You do not calm down a trauma victim and then immediately force them to relive every painful detail, not if you want them to recover as quickly as possible. So, good. If Helena needed to find out more, she could take Novitiate Irina out into the corridor and ask her what she'd learned: an ordinary conversation.

No need for any esoteric techniques.

"I hope," Helena told Gina, "you feel much better already."

Again, she used gentle commands hidden inside ordinary-seeming words. *You're still a mystery, though.*

As an institution, Mordanto had provided refuge for wild, untutored talents many, many times across the centuries. While Helena did like to take an interest in unexpected newcomers, and while Gina's latent level of power felt unusually high, none of this felt strong enough for Mordanto itself to have suggested she come here.

What am I missing?

Helena felt the corner of her mouth twitch.

Ah, Mordanto. It's part of the game, isn't it?

She always enjoyed solving a good mystery, and Mordanto knew that about her.

I am so very, very lucky to be here.

Perhaps, in time, young Gina would come to feel the same way.

"Sleep now," said Helena.

Gina's chin dropped and her eyes were already closed and her shoulders raised a little before lowering as a long breath came out and she went very deep indeed, nice and fast: a good sign in multiple ways, both in terms of mage potential and therapeutically, because the best kind of healing often occurs in trance.

Helena looked at Novitiate Irina, then tilted her head towards the door.

Novitiate Irina understood, reaching the door before Helena, holding it open as Helena passed through, then following. As they faced each other in the chilly baroque corridor, the door to Room 17 swung slowly and silently shut.

"Tell me what you know," said Helena. "Where did Mage Winona find the girl, and what happened to bring the girl to our attention?"

"Er, it's a coffee shop and, um, diner kind of thing. I've been there myself—" Novitiate Irina started brightly, then swallowed and stopped, blinking.

"Go on."

"I wasn't there today, but I have sensed, well, they hire staff with potential but not the kind to actually study here. At least, not mostly…"

Helena let out a gentle, calming breath.

"Relax," she said. "There was some kind of encounter. Tell me about that first, whatever Gina or Mage Winona told you, and we'll proceed from there."

"Alright, well, it started in the diner kitchen—"

What followed was a technically interesting but not astounding description, involving a subconscious cry of loneliness that spanned the mesoscopic and compactified dimensions – Novitiate Irina just managed to stop herself saying crawlspace like some mundane – and Helena decided to keep occasional track of Gina's forthcoming progress, assuming the girl did enlist here: it wasn't entirely mandatory.

Helena didn't recognise the location that Novitiate Irina described, and that thought came with a sad pang of realisation: it had been a long time since Helena walked the streets of the nearby districts like an ordinary person.

Establishments come and go, and perhaps some of her own favourite haunts – from when she was Novitiate Irina's age – no longer existed in the forms she remembered.

This is no astounding surprise, however.

She looked up at the arched ceiling overhead, as if that was where the vision-sense of Mordanto itself was located, so it might read her feeling of exasperation.

"That's all I know." Novitiate Irina blinked several times as she came to the end of her account, and there was dampness in her eyes.

For Thanatos' sake.

Making young novitiates cry didn't give Helena any sense of pleasure, but this was Mordanto where the spineless have never lasted long.

After a moment, Novitiate Irina got her feelings under some measure of control. "Sorry."

"What state was Gina in when she first arrived?"

"Calming down, I think."

"Not terrified." Helena kept the words neutral: not quite a question.

Perhaps Winona had quietened Gina down in order to make her more tractable, but subduing a person that way wasn't the same as inducing true calmness.

"I think Anderl had an influence. That's, er, Mage Anderl, ma'am."

"Do I know him?"

"Mage Anderl Hav—"

"Ah, young Havoch. Yes, of course."

Helena looked up at the ceiling again. It was static, not motile like the mosaic near the entrance door, yet its geometry seemed to curve all the same, somewhere between a suggested smile and a hinted wink.

She returned her attention to Novitiate Irina.

"Before you go back in to check on Gina, I want you to contact Mage Anderl, and tell him to meet me in my study straight away."

"Er..."

"I mean immediately."

Novitiate Irina straightened up, her spine growing as vertical as Helena's own. "Understood, Professor."

"Good." Helena started to turn away, then: "Just one thing..."

"Ma'am?"

"Nice work in getting the details out of the girl. Keep it up."

Novitiate Irina blinked hard once more, but this time not out of fear. "Thank you."

Making sure not to smile – because that would have been too much – Helena started walking, tapping the floor lightly with her cane as she went, as if to signal: *Alright, I will play your game.*

At least this was no emergency: neither Mordanto nor any mage within its walls would dream of playing games when time was of the essence.

Her gait felt lighter and easier than it had for a while, as she continued along the Third Minor East Colonnade, past the Outer Heptangle and the third-year dining-hall she hadn't been inside for years.

By the time she reached her study, flames were alight in the fireplace and the place felt nicely warm. A kettle steamed, freshly boiled: filled with water by whichever novitiate tidied the room earlier, but activated by the room's splinter of pseudo-consciousness or that of the greater Mordanto itself, all nicely timed so she could make a pot of helebore tea for herself.

A fresh jug of squallnut milk stood next to her china cup and saucer atop the krakenshell credenza. All good.

With a sense of ritual, careful of her posture and movements – as much to keep her musculature balanced, for the sake of her joints, as for mood control – she placed her cane aside and went through the precise motions of warming the teapot first, tipping out the water into a bowl placed nearby for that purpose, spooning in the leaves – a weresilver spoon in the shape of a smiling skeleton, smoothened with age – pouring in the water, setting down the kettle, placing the lid on the teapot and leaving it all to steep for a while.

Cosy. Comforting.

She chose an old book to read – as always she had several volumes on the go – this one written by a predecessor as head of Mordanto, knowing its words and wisdom would echo across the decades and feel utterly alive today, and placed it on the rigid righthand arm of the straight-backed ironwood chair near the fireplace.

Then she returned to the credenza to pour her tea and fetch it back.

Helena settled, breathed in the tea's sweet aroma, took a sip, and set the cup down on the lefthand arm of her chair, and picked up the book she intended to read. Her bookmark was a sliver of deep-red bone, its colouration a mystery she had yet to solve: she still did not know whether it was dyed in some way post mortem or came from a creature whose skeletal structures looked red while it lived.

She opened the book and began to read.

Three knocks on the door took her out of the book and back into the world of her study, the warm fireplace and the remains of some tea in the cup beside her. She would need to throw that out and pour some more – it would be fresh enough in the pot – but that could wait until she had finished talking with her visitor.

"Let him in," she murmured.

As the door to her study swung inwards, she replaced the red bone bookmark in her book and closed it on her lap, and focussed her attention on the gawky, red-headed young man who stepped inside.

"You called, um, wanted to see me, Professor." His words stumbled a little and his widened eyes shone brightly: signs of a slightly awkward, excited curiosity more than actual nervousness or fear. "About the new arrival, Gina Antonelli, I think."

"Anderl," said Helena. "Tell me about your day. You accompanied Mage Winona as her assistant, I believe."

"Me and two combat mages, who I think turned grumpy coz they didn't get to fight, but, um, I probably shouldn't say that, should I?"

Helena regarded him for a moment. "Probably not."

"She's got a lot of potential, has Gina. She—"

"Somebody got a call or sensed what was happening, and your team turned up at a diner or similar, and I'm guessing you all went inside."

"Uh, yeah. That's what we did."

"What happened next? Slow down and give me details."

Mage Anderl stood there, slightly rocking, and closed his eyes but managed to keep balanced.

"Um, well, everyone had cleared out, I mean the customers. I'd call it more a restaurant, maybe, than a diner?" Making it sound like a question.

"Continue."

"So Mage Winona went in first," said Anderl, "and sniffed things out – she seemed to pick up vibrations before that, from a long way back, at least a couple of blocks before we reached the place, which was awesome, really – and one of the first things she said was that a Guardian had been there."

Anderl paused, then continued: "That was why the combat mages didn't get to see any action, because the Guardian had already sent the summoned creature back where it came from, kind of thing."

Helena allowed her eyebrow to raise a little: no more than that. "Slow down a tad, but carry on."

"Okay, right. Um… Well, the untrained person who did the summoning was there, that's Gina, along with Lieutenant Riordan, except he isn't really a lieutenant any more because he's like a private eye, kind of thing, which I've got to say is really cool…"

This time Helena raised her hand, which was enough to stop the flow of words.

Donal Riordan.

In the aftermath of a Guardian's appearance.

"I think he wanted to see you, Professor. But Mage Winona… Well, we kind of came inside and left him out on the street."

Casual visitors were discouraged at the best of times, and today Helena had given strict instructions that her appointments be cancelled and she should not be disturbed. Still, it bothered her that Donal Riordan had tried to see her and it was only by luck – with Mordanto's encouragement – that she was learning about it now.

Not that she would necessarily have invited him inside: that was not the point.

"Alright." She pointed towards the credenza. "Look there. Open the lefthand door, Mage Anderl, and fetch yourself a cup and saucer."

"Wow. Um, I mean, sure."

Controlling the twitch that wanted to become a smile, Helena picked up her own cup and held it out. "And you can refill mine while you're there."

"Oh, sure. Thank you."

Anderl took the cup and saucer off her, and carried it over to the credenza, while she summoned a visitor's chair from the armoire, activating the cached transition-hex with a choppy control gesture.

The armoire's silver-chased door swung open, and a chair slid across the flagstones and rug to settle down opposite hers.

The upholstery was ancient, green and still plush: a more comfortable chair than the one she herself sat on, at least if you were young like Anderl Havoch here.

Gawky though he looked, he managed to fetch her a fresh cup of tea without slopping anything into the saucer. She took the cup off him, and sipped from it as he went back to get his own cup.

It tasted just right. She looked up at the concave stone ceiling.

You helped him, didn't you?

If Anderl was sympatico with Mordanto itself, he was most definitely worth keeping an eye on.

He sat down on the visitor's chair and balanced his cup and saucer on his lap, looked up at Helena, then all around her study, and said: "Gosh."

Now Helena did smile, for real.

"Let's chat," she said.

And so they did.

THIRTY-SEVEN

Donal had fired every round from his Magnus. Attached to his belt at the small of his back, he had a kimodo-leather holder with spare rounds, enough for one complete reload, but there wasn't going to be enough time for anything like that: he felt suddenly sure of it.

And then the feeling reversed to complete uncertainty as nothing whatsoever occurred.

I don't understand.

He waited.

Lamis and Talon remained where they were, slumped at the foot of the wall further along, although both were twitching now. Neither one had been cut by flying shards of stone, which was lucky.

Although Donal had aimed with care, ricochets are tricky things.

Silence seemed to pulse in waves, an impossible trick of the senses in the aftermath of crashing sound, and surely the gunfire would have echoed for miles, if the maze stretched that far.

No one appeared.

No person, no entity of any kind.

Damn.

Perhaps the unknown enemy had some way of sensing whether captives here remained alive, using some esoteric sense that worked from afar to detect life-signs and see through Donal's attempted ruse, his pretended execution of Lamis and Talon both.

Of the two, Talon most likely did deserve to die, except that he'd already been through torture and Donal's job was to get him back to his daughter Susan, so never mind.

Damn it all to Hades.

Donal cracked open the Magnus and began retrieving rounds one by one from the small of his back, and thumbing them into place. Once he had fully reloaded, he holstered the gun beneath his left armpit, straightened his tie and rebuttoned his jacket.

Maybe it was always a longshot.

In any case, if an enemy had appeared it might so easily have been wraiths, and he had no way of fighting them, not until Lamis fully woke up.

A rustle sounded from behind Donal, and he spun around and moved fast, heading for the source: an opening some yards ahead on the righthand wall. When Donal passed it earlier, it had led to what he now considered a standard chamber here: the kind of place he'd woken up in.

The kind where Talon had been through Hades at the hands – or non-human equivalents – of implacable torturers.

Donal stopped at the threshold and held himself still.

Creaking, more rustling, and he peeked around the doorway to see the impossible taking place, except that those floors had always existed beyond ordinary rules, consisting of regular pentagonal flagstones that somehow fitted together exactly without leaving any gaps, which you just couldn't do in any normal way.

Now those flagstones were rotating one way and revolving another, like some seething mass of leaves, partially stirred by a helical current, partly moving individually, changing in ways that somehow slipped beyond the edge of visual processing, beyond making geometric sense.

As Donal continued to watch from the righthand edge of the doorway, the flagstones began to drop a little around the edges of the room and more deeply towards the centre, forming a concave depression that continued to deepen, and releasing a pungent smell of sulphur that caused Donal to stop breathing, thanking the Thanatos he didn't believe in that he no longer had to breathe, at least not all the time.

More like clacking now, the sound, as the flagstones continued to twist and rearrange themselves, before settling down to a near-stable configuration.

A few more shifts and taps, and everything went still.

"I don't bleeding like this." An ordinary voice rose up from that opening in the floor.

Donal considered entering the room and edging around the circumference, but it looked as if some stairway or ramp or some such had opened up, and someone was climbing up from a lower level, and maybe the best place for ambush was out here in the corridor, the moment they exited the doorway.

He rolled back out of sight of whoever was climbing up.

The opening – to his right – dictated the geometry of the coming confrontation.

Wait a minute.

With his back against the stone wall, Donal stared at the spectrally luminescent stonework across from him and all around, defocussing his gaze as he mentally replayed those words he had just heard.

I don't believe it.

Maybe there was a funny story behind all this, but Donal felt zero amusement right now, and the damage done to Talon and maybe even Lamis meant this wasn't any kind of game but serious.

Two sets of footsteps rising, and one might belong to a stranger, but the other almost certainly did not.

Son of a witch.

Donal waited, totally still.

Waiting…

Two people for sure, not talking now but breathing hard from the exertion of climbing up from whatever lower level they'd been on, and as the first one stepped into the corridor Donal moved fast, sinking his weight and twisting fast and hard, hooking his left fist into the first man's left kidney, then grabbing the man's collar at the back and slamming him into his companion.

The first man had blue skin while the other looked mossy, both in cheap serviceable suits that Talon's goons would be embarrassed to wear.

Donal kicked the back of the first man's knee, whipped out his Magnus, and aimed it in the second man's moss-covered face.

"Stand perfectly still," he said.

"I—"

"And shut the Hades up."

The man's mouth opened – rather than individual teeth, he possessed a solid curve of white up top and another on the lower jaw – then closed, his jaw muscles locking rigid.

Donal looked at the blue-skinned man who was down on one knee.

So I wasn't mistaken.

"You, on the other hand" – Donal felt his voice tighten up – "better start talking."

"I don't know what—"

"Brian Fixtovax, either you tell me everything, or I end you right here."

Words can have powerful effects sometimes. Everyone knows that.

But Donal hadn't expected to break a man's spirit with a single sentence.

"I, I…" started Brian.

He stayed kneeling on the floor, surely in pain from the impact of kneecap on stone, making no attempt to rise.

And then he began to cry.

It took Brian three attempts to say sorry, gulping so hard that simply joining words together into a sentence clearly formed a challenge, but Donal felt only a rigid anger inside and approximately zero sympathy, given everything that had happened.

"I don't care," he told Brian. "I really just don't care."

Meaning the apology, not the situation: that, he cared about a lot.

"You kidnapped three people," Donal went on, "and one of them was Mage Lamis, and another one was me, so tell me why I shouldn't blow your head off right this minute."

Brian was shaking, still not looking up. "I… No, I didn't do that."

"Three seconds to live," said Donal.

The moss-skinned man remained very, very still. Perhaps he understood just how acute a resurrected man's peripheral vision could be, and how fast his reactions, if he were highly trained and kept up the discipline.

"No!" Brian's voice rose higher, and sweat glistened on his pale blue skin. "I didn't kidnap anyone. I mean…"

"Time to go to Hades." Donal pressed the end of the barrel against Brian's temple.

"Lieutenant, I just, just… re-enabled the storage labyrinth. Started everything back up. Didn't ask questions."

"What?"

"I mean I didn't *know*."

Donal jabbed with the Magnus, just a little. "What didn't you know?"

"What they were going to do down here. Who they were… Who they were going to take down here, you see?"

Now Brian did look up, fear and pleading in his eyes. "If I'd known you or your wife were in danger, I wouldn't have—"

"My *wife?*"

Donal's left hand snapped into a pinch grip around Brian's throat, while the Magnus went back to aiming at the moss-skinned man, because you never ignored a secondary threat no matter how much you wanted to kill the primary enemy in front of you.

"She came with, with Mage Lamis and Sergeant Harman." Brian's voice went hoarse, even though Donal hadn't started to really squeeze, not yet.

"*What?* Are you talking about Mel?" They technically weren't married, but no matter.

"Y-yes. That's the name Eduardo said."

Rage was whirling upwards like a maelstrom inside Donal's torso. "You're saying Eduardo's in on this?"

Perennially on desk-sergeant duty, ever since the incident that caused his lower body to blend into that solid block of granite, Eduardo had always seemed the most down-to-earth and honest of officers.

"N-no, he didn't know, Loot. It was more like, what, like gossip, you know?"

None of this was making sense.

Suddenly hot rage was replaced by icy coldness, seeping through Donal's entire being now.

No. It's not possible.

He stepped back, releasing Brian's throat, then stepped around Brian towards the moss-skinned man, who said: "I don't know nothing, man."

"Right," said Donal.

With a quick gesture, he raised his Magnus high, pointing it towards the ceiling, and the moss-skinned man reacted like an amateur, jerking his head up to follow the movement with his gaze.

Donal's left hook came in tight and hard, his two big knuckles straight into the side of the man's jaw, Donal's elbow bent at a rigid ninety degrees – a hook punch done right is effectively a straight thrust from the side, the tangent of a sweeping radius – hitting the sweet spot that whips the head around so that torque inside the brain case delivers that knockout shock.

The moss-skinned man fell back and thumped against the stone floor.

He wouldn't be waking up anytime soon.

And that meant Donal could focus entirely on Brian Fixtovax, still down on one knee like genuflecting in a temple of some kind, and still looking afraid for his life, which – given that he'd mentioned Mel – formed an accurate reading of his situation.

Donal brought the butt-heel of the Magnus to rest on his left palm, taking up a two-handed combat stance, and knew that he was capable of emptying the entire weapon of its load once more, and this time not a single round would miss.

"Right," he said. "Just where the Hades are we right now?"

Brian gasped and blinked.

"Y-you mean you don't know?"

Donal really, really wanted to open fire.

"Tell me," he said.

Strictly speaking, Brian had already answered, at least by implication; but Donal needed to hear the words, and to make a decision regarding Brian.

"We're—" started Brian.

From along the corridor, a soft moan sounded.

About Death-damned time.

That thought was more internal banter than actual annoyance: Donal felt the side of his mouth twitch, not quite a smile.

Now we're making progress.

In a place like this, you couldn't ask for a better ally than an angry mage ready to vent some fury; and with reasonable luck, here came that ally.

Lamis was waking up.

THIRTY-EIGHT

Mel passed through a Cavern filled with horror, and Viktor made the passage with her, and afterwards that was pretty much all she could have said: swirling, gigantic horrors all around, sights that made no sense, colours that should not exist, eerie screams and sibilant whispers throughout.

A deep vibration of her intestines corresponded to a pervasive subliminal moan that never, ever stopped.

Vast tendrils moved, bigger than houses; great eyes stared, larger than cars – one of them pus-yellow with a nine-sided centre of nothingness, not even black: pure void-stuff – all of it impossible to make sense of.

In front of her, high up and to the sides and all around and everywhere she looked – besides the twisting stone path beneath her feet – reality sickened into madness.

She walked, somehow.

Sometimes she froze and sometimes she burned and everything felt awful, and if she could have ripped the skin off her body and plucked out her eyes just to shut off these sensations then she would have done just that.

So utterly, utterly awful.

The crystal-encrusted roof of this place hung a hundred, two hundred feet overhead, and in at least two places seemed to twist upwards towards dark infinity even though the entire complex was supposed to exist on the minus two hundred and seventy-third level beneath the rearing tower that was Number One, Avenue of the Basilisks.

Down here, none of that seemed possible.

This was a place all its own, like nothing else on Earth.

I can't do this.

Meaning it felt impossibly hard simply to keep walking without sinking to her knees and letting her whole world fall apart, because the eldritch maelstrom all around was far too much for anyone to look upon and hear, to sense through the skin and even to smell.

There were scents here, heavy and piercing and *different*, quite beyond naming.

Overwhelm.

All of it: sheer overwhelm.

At one point she truly gave up and started to lower herself to the ground, giving in to weakness, before Viktor's hard grip fastened on her upper arm and offered more than support: it sent a message that she read by pure intuition.

We need to move on before one of them notices us.

Because the great eldritch entities moving here and interacting among themselves might be too much for ordinary human senses to perceive, but the dangers went far beyond that.

For sure, any of the great beings here could obliterate her and Viktor in an instant – could end their existence faster than blinking – but that wasn't in fact the worst danger here: Mel knew that now.

Looking upon the surroundings: that was it.

She might die or become twisted in ways beyond her current imagining in a process that could last for subjective years or centuries or longer, perhaps even an infinite duration of subjective time; and maybe it went beyond subjectivity to actual objective eternity.

You couldn't think these entities were bound by any of the laws of nature identified by tiny puny human beings. So small and soft and ephemeral: every person manifested as less than a insect by comparison.

Awful, awful, awful.

I hate this place.

A sickening feeling dropped through her at one point on the twisting path, and it wasn't the impossible sights but the realisation that Viktor was no longer with her.

Viktor?

He was gone.

Where the Hades is he?

She looked back, and there he was: standing frozen on the stone path, looking up at some huge collection of purple and green tentacles – plus other, impossible extrusions – twisting and wriggling high overhead.

Viktor's eyes were hidden by shining unearthly hues reflected from his round-lensed glasses. His mouth – usually a tight grim line across his features – hung half open as if he couldn't believe what he was seeing, and who the Hades could, in this place?

I can't move.

She was scared to go back, to retrace even a few steps, in case she faltered the way Viktor had; but he'd led her out of her own moment of overwhelm or weakness or whatever it was – something beyond fear, because that was already present, filling every cell of her body – so her feelings of fear or even terror didn't matter at all.

Time to go back for Viktor regardless, because she had to.

And it had to be in silence, because words would be dangerous in this place: every instinct told her exactly that.

Come on.

Mel took hold of Viktor's coat sleeve and tugged: once, twice, three times, but he just stood there, riveted in place, frozen by the impossible sights his brain was trying and failing to process.

For Thanatos' sake come on.

It was all too much for ordinary humans which was why they needed to get out of here, but she couldn't leave him behind: you simply could *not* abandon a fellow human amid this vast inhuman cacophony of sights and sounds and sensations beyond imagining.

The worst happened then.

A vast tendril reached down and touched Viktor's head and then carried on pressing down, all the way to the stone floor – Mel let go of his sleeve just in time – and simply crushed him from existence except no, whatever happened, it wasn't exactly *crushing*, but he was gone all the same.

When the tendril rose, there was nothing left of Viktor.

It wiped him out completely.

Not even a stain marked the spot where Viktor had been standing.

No. Not…

Her thoughts spun, unable to cohere.

Not possible.

But he was gone, Viktor was gone, and it was all her fault because she had brought him here, him and Mage Lamis who might or might not have died already, and she'd done it because there was nothing else she could do, but this was failure so maybe she'd been a fool to try at all.

White lightning flashed.

She looked up, trying to focus on the vast rising tendril, and realised there was a dark, struggling, man-shaped shadow *inside* the tendril-stuff, for it had absorbed Viktor somehow, like a jellyfish taking some tiny morsel inside itself, and now it was taking him away.

No, no, no!

All her fault.

But lightning flashed once more, this time shining silver and burning orange, brighter and harder than before.

Then a deep, awful voice made the entire Cavern's air come alive.

"ONE MORE WARNING, NO MORE."

It shook every part of her, threated to vibrate her eyeballs to jelly, and she thought the very sound of it might end her life.

"RELEASE THE HUMAN. NOW."

Ozone stink surrounded her.

Such powerful energies existed here: she'd been an idiot filled with ignorance, daring to trespass in such a place.

But incredibly, the tendril lowered, slowly and with – somehow she knew – a measure of gentle control, and it lightly touched the ground instead of obliterating the solid stone, instead of smashing it into rubble and dust the way it could so easily, this vast impossible being.

Yes. Impossible.

When the tendril rose once more, it left a tiny-in-comparison shape behind: Viktor, crouching there in place, head hanging low.

Like some chastened puppy.

Blinking through tears, Mel grabbed his coat once more, and pulled upwards, either hauling him to his feet or simply prompting him to stand up by himself: everything felt unsteady so it was hard to process even simple things exactly.

"You're alright," she said.

Talking no longer felt like a dangerous mistake, not after the greater voice that had manifested here.

Viktor's grim face looked down at her.

"What the Hades happened?" he said.

"You got blobbed," Mel told him, fighting back an urge to giggle, because that way lay hysteria and uselessness, which really wouldn't do.

"Say what?"

"Blobbed." She gave a thumbs-down gesture, feeling almost giddy. "You got sucked inside a tentacle, kind of thing. Right inside the stuff."

Viktor shook his head.

"I thought you were a goner," added Mel.

"So why aren't I?"

A sharper ozone stink still hung upon the Cavern air, and the great eldritch entities perhaps moved more slowly, but the change was a subtle one so Mel might be mistaken: it could be just her own feeling of relief that some kind of help was finally at hand.

"Looks like Hellah saved us," she said. "Saved you, for sure."

Cold hissing arose behind her, like quicksilver rainfall in chilly weather, and when she turned it was to see a great billowing column of icy steam, along with flickers of orange – like miniature lightning flashes – amid that steam, along with a person-shaped shadow inside.

As the steam rolled back and dissipated into wisps and fading streamers, the Guardian stood there, revealed: pale of skin, long-haired, with a sardonic asymmetric smile upon his features.

He wore a high-collared black tunic and matching trousers, quite plain: unusually so for him, from the little that Mel knew.

"I can see how you'd mistake me for my sister." The heptagonal irises of his eyes blazed orange like miniature flames. "We look so much alike, after all."

The thunderous voice that commanded the entities here had been deep-toned, but Mel had thought it part of the manifestation, or maybe she hadn't been thinking straight at all.

"Klaudius," she managed to say. "I'm sorry, I... I'm sorry. Thank you."

"What she said." Viktor stepped up beside Mel. "Thank you, Guardian."

It was hard to look at Klaudius, and Mel felt her eyes blur as she dropped her gaze, swallowing but unable to fight the swirling terror inside her, and something about the rigidity of Viktor's stance said he felt the same way, even if he hid it better.

Just as well.

That was an odd thought, yet clearly correct.

If Klaudius wasn't terrifying, he wouldn't even survive down here.

She'd never really thought about the Guardians that way before.

"My charges like to play and feed at times." Klaudius's voice sounded light with humour that might or might not be cruel: it was hard to tell. "Mel might not have appreciated the dangers in advance, but you did, Detective Sergeant, didn't you?"

"Yes, sir." Humility and respect were uppermost in Viktor's voice. "We were desperate for help."

It didn't sound like the hard-faced, frightening Viktor Harman who'd visited Mel and Donal's home from time to time; but still, Viktor was doing better than Mel: she no longer felt able to speak in Klaudius's presence.

He terrifies me.

Deep in her stomach, the fear kept increasing rather than settling down.

As bad as Hellah.

The sister – Mel remembered her appearance exactly – possessed glistening skin that shone the exact colour of freshly spilled blood, while Klaudius's skin tone here was that of a very pale standard human, which meant it had never been Hellah's colouration that terrified, because Klaudius invoked the same amount of horrified fear.

It was the sheer overwhelming nature of a Guardian that beat down at human senses, inducing fear all the way down, at what felt like the cellular level.

Truly, truly terrifying.

More than ever, she simply could not grasp the way that Donal acted around the two of them, as if Klaudius and the currently absent Hellah were ordinary human beings, people who'd become good friends.

"Donal's in trouble," she managed to say, although her voice sounded like a squeak in her ears.

"I—" started Viktor, then froze.

Klaudius had raised a pale hand wreathed in icy steam. "Wait."

He inhaled, visibly and diaphragmatically – Mel was used to reading people's breathing, especially in the ring – and after a moment, the orange fire brightened in Klaudius's eyes.

"You're right," he added. "I gave him a call crystal to use, but its capability, let's say, is diminished, in a way that most likely means he's no longer wearing it."

Mel realised that *capability* referred to something technical that she wouldn't understand, so she shouldn't take it as an insult.

Viktor said: "Was it abandoned, the crystal? Or is it cached inside an insulator?"

"I sense it's the latter," said Klaudius. "Well reasoned, sir. And before you ask, Donal's not inside that insulator with it. The harmonics would feel quite different."

Mel barely perceived Viktor's nod. He seemed to be finding it easier to speak in Klaudius's presence than she did; but Klaudius did appear to be on their side, so maybe she herself could make more effort here.

"What does it imply?" She was trying to think tactically. "Who would have a… whatever-it-is, insulator box?"

"That's a good question," said Klaudius. "As is, who would know to use it? And how did they remove the crystal from around Donal's neck?"

Mel felt her heart thump.

"My apologies," continued Klaudius. "I imply nothing about Donal's current state of health."

It might be easier to remove a power-token – or whatever they called such things in general – from around a dead man's throat than from a living, combat-trained detective; but she had to push that thought away, to believe that Donal remained okay, in the absence of definitive tragic evidence.

"Sir?" Again the diffidence in Viktor's voice, so different from his usual persona. "If you sense the crystal, even dimly, does that mean you can pinpoint its location?"

Klaudius emitted a chuckle. "Donal chose his friends and family well. Nicely reasoned, Detective."

Viktor inhaled hard, a reaction that Mel couldn't quite read, but she'd been out of her depth for some time now and details didn't matter.

Klaudius is going to help.

At least it looked that way: he hadn't actually made a verbal commitment, not yet.

Thunder sounded.

Klaudius looked off to his right – Mel and Viktor's left – at a distant rolling motion within one of the huge shapes hanging there in the vastness of this Cavern, a tendril-edged mass that whirled at its centre, and it might have glowed an eldritch green or it might be something else entirely beyond human vision, manifesting as some kind of colour-harmonic or overtone-analogue of its true, imperceptible nature.

"No," said Klaudius. "She wouldn't."

The words made no sense.

Those long pale features tightened, and the fire-irises of his eyes tightened into slender heptagons of fire, like glimpsing a furnace through slits.

"What's happening?" Mel had already asked the question before she realised her ability to speak up had returned.

"My sister has done something very stupid." Rumbling undertones now deepened Klaudius's voice: hints of the thunderous vocalisations from before. "That, or something very smart and brave. I don't know which, not yet."

"What—"

"But she's stirred up the denizens and left them for me to deal with, single-handed."

Mel's stomach felt as if it had jumped inside her, and she wanted to be sick.

We're in trouble.

As if they hadn't been in trouble from the start, but Klaudius's reaction was unnerving her all over again.

Klaudius looked grim.

"It's going to get interesting," he said. "I'm going to have to cage you in."

"Do what?" Mel wasn't sure she'd heard correctly.

"For your own protection, both of you."

At that point Mel opened her mouth, but whether it was to speak or cry out in fear she could no longer tell as white fire blazed up in a solid sheet before her and to either side and overhead – solid-looking planes of brilliant whiteness, of light that shone hard enough to almost blind – and the air went still while the light-stuff crackled and she was on her own in this cage of light.

Surrounded by blazing white.

A similar construct presumably encased Viktor by himself.

It's a shield, sort of.

That was the last coherent thought for a while as the ground shook hard enough to topple her and she went down hard, almost knees-first but straightening out and taking the impact with her hands, before pulling herself into the tucked-in, face-down configuration that her wrestler brothers used to call the loaf-of-bread position.

It had been a long time since she thought of them, so very long, but everything was shaking now as if artillery shells were exploding all around with hard stone vibrating underneath her as she squeezed her eyes shut and thought of Finbar and remembered Donal and all the good times they had together and prayed, prayed hard, meaning it for the first time since childhood.

Let me live a few years longer, a few more decades, please…

Surely it was a small thing to ask for in the immensity of the cosmos but reality was crashing around her while this whiteness blazed harder than ever and she hoped this wasn't going to be the end: not yet, not now.

Outside her protective cage, unspeakable energies raged.

THIRTY-NINE

After Helena dismissed Mage Anderl – so young-looking, so much a gawky schoolboy in appearance, but with a definite quirky potential all his own – she remained in her study, letting her helebore tea grow cold, thinking about the things young Anderl had told her.

On a shelf, a platinum-bone skeleton clock ticked off the seconds with metronomic swings of a miniature scythe, as if time itself were a thread that could be severed into tiny sections, hinting at a mystery that the finest theoretical thaumatists had been trying to solve for a long, well, a considerable length of time.

I could have done that.

Not so much the solving of a particular mystery as devoting her professional life entirely to research while staying away from engagement with the outer world and the rigours of working with actual people of all kinds.

It would have meant less worrying about budgets and income and operating expenses, more pondering the deepest nature of the universe – the deep intellectual wonders that made her, when she was young Anderl's age, work so very hard to become the best mage she could be.

She leaned back, to the small extent that the ironwood chair allowed, and let out a long controlled breath through her mouth, and relaxed just a little.

Getting married and becoming a mother twice over – the second time under such traumatic circumstances – had perhaps made her more practical, but the change in perspective began earlier than that... and maybe she was growing too old for this position, because nostalgia and reverie can be useful and positive experiences but living in the past would be a step too far if she wanted to remain head of Mordanto.

So it was time to get her head right, as Kelvin might have put it, had he been here supporting her.

Kelvin.

Flames crackled in the fireplace, and the sweet scent of burning stormwood grew stronger for a second or three, before fading once more.

You'd better be okay.

It would have been better for him to work here instead of from home, at least when it came to facilities and backup, but he had been isolated for a while and used to his own company, and there were security aspects to singleton research that did in fact lend themselves well to working offsite.

So long as nothing drastic went wrong.

The long-term safety of Tristopolis and the greater Federation were primary concerns of Mordanto in its outward-facing aspect, but some matters needed to be conducted in deep privacy, without fuss and without huge numbers of mages becoming involved, even though a part of Helena felt ready to deploy all of Mordanto's resources en masse at the slightest hint of its becoming necessary.

"So," she said aloud. "It's time."

On the shelf, the skeletal clock seemed to tick louder, to swipe harder with its miniature scythe, as if agreeing with Helena's assessment.

She nodded to the clock in acknowledgment, appreciating the encouragement.

Reaching out her hand, she summoned her platinum-tipped cane, and it snapped into her grip, having transitioned from its resting-place by the door in a process that took some three milliseconds to complete: effectively instantaneous from a normal human perspective, but not in fact infinitely fast.

It was a distinction that mattered, here and now, given the energies she needed to summon and work with, directing configurations via the resonance of her own neurohex patterns, using all her expertise and certainty to steady her thoughts as she stood up and took three paces forward, then stopped.

Silver fire began to spread across the floor in a straight line before her feet, running left to right, stopping when it was one and two-thirds yards in length, holding its position.

Underneath the silver flames lay a rug from Scyntilla Straits that a Ralkinese seer, the head of his order, gave Helena during her official visit there – nearly seventeen years ago now: so hard to believe – and the subdued ochres and maroons of the rug's predominant pattern were intricate enough to engage her spatial-logic appreciation whenever she stared at it in contemplation, and she hoped that she wasn't going to ruin the thing now.

Never mind.

Harmless and scarcely audible, the silver flames danced in place; but this was just the beginning of the conjuration, and portals are always tricky things, even in the most ordinary of circumstances.

This portal was going to be different, allowing passage to some air molecules and phonons of mechanical vibrational energy – otherwise known as sound – along with photons of light but no bulky matter: constraints that would normally make things easier, but not today, because of the nature of the endpoint.

Helena kept the line of silver fire as it was, burning softly and steadily, technically in the construction phase that preceded portal initialisation, allowing it to settle in while her thoughts took their time to strengthen, the entire procedure feeling natural, like the act of breathing or blinking one's eyes.

The air of the study felt warmer, almost certainly a subjective phenomenon as the stormwood fire continued to crackle steadily in the fireplace, no different than before.

In the particular technical idiom of this conjuration framework, bringing the manifestation into its operational state consisted of a three-phase process: construction, initialisation then startup, each technically distinct.

She had used this approach in enough different contexts that it came naturally, and maybe Kelvin's generation would replace it with something better – probably some equally old approach coming back into fashion – but so far this worked well, even in rigorous environments where the cost of failure would be catastrophic.

Time to initialise.

In this context, her invocation of the next step resulted in narrow columns of silver fire growing upwards from each end of the floor-level line of flames.

The columns grew to a height of two and one-third yards before halting their upward growth and strengthening in place, becoming thicker and stronger until it was time for the cross-piece to occur at the top.

When that too had grown into place and steadied, a vertical outlined rectangle of twisting silver fire stood in front of Helena, rippling with energy, ready for the next stage of invocation.

Before calling the startup, Helena reviewed its constituent steps, which would end in the concurrent conjuration of three linked processes, enabling bidirectional communication while a dedicated hex-thread listened for control commands such as resize, shift, intensify/diminish, and – most importantly – shutdown, a command that could be invoked with one swift chopping motion, for safety.

So. It's time.

She gestured and stepped into an L-stance, using movement and mudras to help control the neurohex patterns within her brain, then pressed both hands palms-downward to invoke the startup, and waited.

From here, the whole thing went very fast, which she more or less expected but could not have guaranteed, not given the spacetime separation between the endpoints and the major environmental differences between both ends of the portal connection.

That last manifestation, the connection construct itself, was created within the startup and remained in scope for her control commands to access.

If anything cataclysmic occurred at the far end — cataclysmic to ordinary humans at least — then she would run the shutdown which would destroy the connection before doing anything else, in order to prevent a blowback that might override the limited-matter-transfer constraints of the portal.

It was not her own safety that she thought of: a gushing inflow of lava or swirling ocean water might grow large enough to fill this study and burst out through its door to the corridor beyond and do all sorts of damage before someone threw up containment shields strong enough to stop the lethal deluge.

Had there been a mundane here to observe, some ordinary citizen taken from the street, they would probably think this whole thing was easy for a mage, a matter of just waving hands and causing something interesting and wonderful to happen; and as always, they would be mistaken: utterly, utterly wrong.

Blind to the wonderful, intricate and dangerous realities of conjuration science.

That was the joy and beauty of it, that made facing arcane dangers thoroughly worthwhile.

Focus now.

The startup completed.

Here we go.

Like a living portrait inside a frame, the centre of the silver-fire rectangle filled with something to look at, sight and sound from the other end of the portal connection, and the background was filled with columns of twisting yellow smoke and a cliff-like or cavern-wall backdrop down which rivulets of white-hot lava flowed, and shadowy winged shapes flitted among the sulphurous clouds but that wasn't really what dominated here.

Even for Helena, looking upon such beings remained hard, and it took all of her internal discipline and practised mental routines — installed automesmerically — to operate approximately as normal while drenched in feelings of overwhelming fear.

Blood-red skin, glistening as if liquid-fresh, was only part of it.

Heptagonal irises of orange fire in eyes that saw too much, and an overwhelming aura of power that manifested even through a constrained portal connection such as this: she stood tall and strong and — there was no other way of putting it — utterly magnificent.

Too much so.

"Greetings, Guardian," Helena managed to say.

"And the same to you, Professor."

Within the portal, the Guardian, Hellah, gave a smile that she might have intended as an expression of ordinary warmth.

Ice rippled inside Helena, despite the hot-looking backdrop in the portal. *Oh, dear Thanatos.*

Half a world separated them in reality, but even that fleeting thought failed to help.

Helena felt so very much afraid.

Some moments passed without either of them speaking, and Helena endured this without feeling any kind of embarrassment, despite the pause being entirely for her benefit, to allow her to grow used to the sight of Guardian Hellah, so powerful and so thoroughly terrifying – simply by nature – that even a superior mage, head of Mordanto, needed leeway and time for adjustment and a lot of understanding on Hellah's part.

Still, Guardians must be used to human weakness.

"Are you ready?" asked Hellah eventually. "You look ready, Professor."

"I… Yes," said Helena. "I can talk now."

"Well, good."

"I, er, I know you have the city's best interests at heart, Guardian."

"Maybe. I'd like to think so."

Helena bit her lip, wanting to cry, to actually weep tears, and for a split second she thought of the young neophyte she herself had frightened earlier – the novitiate assigned to look after an untrained newcomer – and she regretted it now.

"Or maybe," added Hellah, "I'm simply being human. In my own way."

"Yes." Helena swallowed, feeling old and desiccated and very, very tired.

"Ah well," said Hellah.

In the portrait-like connection, framed by silver fire, the Guardian laughed in a way that should have sounded pleasing – perhaps – but instead just terrified, despite all Helena's wishes to the contrary, including her desire to interact with the Guardian as if she were in fact just a human being, however different.

It's hard.

But then again, it had always been hard, and the head of Mordanto dared not shirk difficult tasks, ever.

The arrangements for this conversation had been made by courier-delivered letter, and without spelling out specific reasons for Hellah's long journey, but a subtle hint and the nature of her destination were more than enough for Helena to work things out.

There were few reasons – very few – for a Guardian to return to the island of Crepuscula, and Hellah was neither old nor ill, which narrowed the possibilities still further: the letter's hint had scarcely been necessary.

Reading that letter had been one thing: here and now, however, the simple act of conversing felt like a skin-shredding, gut-hammering ordeal she wished could be over.

A Guardian who does not terrify could not do her job.

That was a thought to hold onto, for some reason.

Helena calmed down, just a little.

"Tell me what I can do to help," she said at last.

At the far end of the portal connection, Hellah placed one hand on her own abdomen, and smiled, perhaps with a touch of sadness, understanding that Helena could still feel only fear even when conversing remotely, like now.

Some of the sulphur stench had entered the study. It had been inevitable, but that didn't make the smell any less disturbing.

"I'll need a secure environment there in Tristopolis," said Hellah. "With some distance from Avenue of the Basilisks, but not too far."

Helena swallowed and blinked. "Within, um, within the actual Mordanto grounds... Would that be sufficient?"

"That," said Hellah in the portal, her face glistening crimson, "is too much to ask, but if you're offering then it's perfect. Absolutely perfect, Professor."

"There's the matter of..." Helena gathered herself. "Staffing is something to sort out, but I'll get it done."

People able to operate while in a state of inevitable terror: not every mage could cope, not even here, but that was a soluble problem.

"I heard..." This was something Helena did not want to say, but it had interested her earlier when talking to Anderl, and she had determined back then that she ought to raise the subject at some point. "I heard you and Detective Donal Riordan are, well, friends."

Again, the tinkling laugh that should have invoked warm feelings instead of terror.

"Good friends." Hellah smiled, while lava burned brightly behind her. "My brother gets on with him too."

"No negative, um..." Helena stopped, not knowing how to complete the question without causing offence.

"Yes," said Hellah. "Donal's unusual that way. Sees us for who we are, sort of thing. Completely natural."

That was more than unusual: it was unique, as far as Helena knew.

How could that be?

Mixed feelings had always swirled inside her when she considered the resurrected man who walked around with the dead Laura's heart inside his chest.

Paramedics initiating resurrection needed to do so as soon after death as possible, and if there were a resurrected-now-deceased corpse nearby, dead of a devastating gunshot to the head, of course the paramedics would utilise that still-beating zombie heart, since its first owner no longer had a use for it.

Rationally, it was the right thing for them to do; but that was little help.

Oh, my daughter.

It felt as if she had abandoned Laura somehow, even if that made no actual sense.

"Are you okay, Professor?"

Helena blinked, and realised there were in fact tears in her eyes. "I beg your pardon, Guardian. My daughter Laura…"

"Donal told me all about it. Of course your feelings about him must be mixed."

With a shake of her head, Helena tried to reset her emotional state, while processing the fact that Donal Riordan and this Guardian must truly have become friends if they were discussing private details like this.

But the incident earlier in the diner kitchen on Hollow Way Drive, the event young Anderl had talked about, had apparently involved Klaudius – rather than Hellah here – coming to the rescue, which made it weird that Donal Riordan had apparently wanted to come here and see her, the head of Mordanto – a request that Winona and her combat mages had ignored: correctly so, according to normal protocol as well as Helena's specific instructions about not being disturbed today.

Hellah was speaking again.

"Motherhood changes everything, I guess." In the portal, she put her hand to her abdomen once more. "Duty complicates things for our kind, but we have all the same feelings as anyone else, as near as I can tell."

Helena nodded, knowing that she in some sense possessed superior knowledge here, having been through the experience twice over, but still feeling out of her depth because Hellah was a Guardian and that changed everything.

"My brother's going to be occupied for a while," added Hellah. "Because of the duration, I needed to make sure he had a lot to deal with. All the previous trips were short, but this time he might have been able to interfere. Try to make me reconsider."

Helena shook her head, although not in denial. She simply had no idea what to say, nor any clear picture of the sibling dynamics here, although the most likely factor was Klaudius's concern for his sister's safety.

"So it might be wise," continued Guardian Hellah, "for you to send some people to Avenue of Basilisks. Have them posted nearby, in case some lesser entity slips out while Klaudius is busy with the bigger guys."

Using *guy* to denote a vastly powerful entity whose full nature escaped even mages' understanding said everything one needed to know about Guardians in general and Hellah in particular.

"I… I wish you well," Helena managed to say. "I'm sure you'll be fine, Guardian."

"Thank you, Professor."

The portal filled with silver fire, a sheet of lambent silver flames, as Hellah shut down things from her end, while Helena stood there for a full five seconds before making the downward gesture that invoked the controlled shutdown procedure, thoroughly releasing every hex component, letting all the energies dissipate, closing down the portal.

Silver flames dropped downwards, briefly remaining as a line across the floor, then narrowed to infinitesimal then zero width, and out of existence.

All done.

Safely complete.

I know it's risky for you, Guardian.

A hint of sulphur smell remained upon the air, but fading.

I'd like to do more to help.

There was a lot that Helena did not know, in part because Guardians wished to keep things that way: it had been over a century since they last invited a head of Mordanto to visit Crepuscula, where Guardian Hellah was right now, involving a long, arduous voyage across the Umbral Ocean and the Penumbral Sea, all the way to the Terminator Line.

But historical records from around the world, meaning mage documents in the more developed Darkside countries, indicated a clear numerical truth.

Childbirth – always on Crepuscula Island – was a long way from straightforward for their kind, the Guardians.

The mortality rate during the birthing process – for mother and child alike – remained far higher than among standard humans, simply because ordinary medical advances did not help in this case.

Good luck.

She blinked, and returned her attention to her surroundings: the placid study, the stormwood fire merrily dancing in the fireplace, the skeletal clock ticking off portions of eternity with its miniature scythe, the book with its redbone bookmark holding her place, her ironwood chair, the bookcases where three sleepy furbats nestled high up – they had not even stirred when the portal manifested – and all the rest, carvings and memorabilia that held so many personal memories, unshared with anyone.

A knock sounded on the door.

Really?

She gestured, and the door swung inwards.

"Mage Anderl," she said. "Why have you come back?"

The young redheaded mage swallowed. "Er, I don't know, ma'am."

"What do you mean, you don't know?"

"Um… Something told me I should come back, kind of thing. Like I really ought to."

Helena took in a breath and released it, considering this.

Interesting.

She glanced up at the ceiling, then returned her attention to young Anderl.

"Come inside," she said, knowing what she had to do.

Anderl did so, and the door swung shut behind him. "Ma'am?"

"I have a job for you." Helena felt certain about her decision. "And you're going to need a team to help you. You might want to use that novitiate who handled the waif you brought in. What was her name?"

"Gina... Oh, the novitiate," said Anderl. "Um, Irina, I think."

"It's an important job, so you'll need to build a team you can trust."

Anderl swallowed, his Adam's apple prominent. "What do I have to do, Professor?"

Helena waited a moment before telling him.

"You have to build a creche," she said.

"A... creche? Like a place for babies, sort of thing?"

With a smile she could not help, Helena nodded.

"That sort of thing," she said. "Except this particular creche is going to be fully armoured, stealth-shielded and as close to impervious as anyone can make it, with facilities for round-the-clock sentinel mages and all the rest."

"Wow."

"Exactly."

"And you want *me* to do this? Lead the project?"

"Do you want the chance to show what you can do, Mage Anderl?"

"Oh, yes, ma'am. Um... How many kids are we talking about?"

"It will need to be quite a large facility," said Helena. "But we're only talking about a single baby."

A crackle sounded in the fireplace, a pop as something burst in a stormwood stick.

Helena looked at the wide-eyed Anderl.

"Then again," she added, "I suppose she might have twins, so we ought to be prepared."

"I don't..."

She gestured for the visitor's chair to slide into place.

"Sit down," she told Anderl. "We have a lot of details to discuss."

The beginning of a new project.

Anderl looks so excited.

Once, she herself had been a young mage entrusted with a project that seemed far beyond her rank at that time, and maybe those were the best years of her life; or maybe *this* was her time: right here, right now.

"You won't have heard much," she said, "about what goes on beneath Number One, Avenue of the Basilisks."

Anderl paused halfway through sitting down on the visitor's chair. He looked more wide-eyed than ever.

"You mean the... entities that live down there?" He finished taking his seat.

"And the Guardians."

It might be argued that Guardians were eldritch entities in their own right, but people normally regarded them as a separate category, if they thought about the matter at all.

"Oh, no," said Anderl. "You can't mean…"

"You know Guardians aren't immortal, don't you? Just very long-lived?"

"Um, sure. I guess so, Professor."

"But there have always, I mean for millennia, been Guardians in this land. Always at least one, sometimes as many as five, although that was—"

"Seven centuries ago," said Anderl. "But sure, basically there's always Guardians."

"And where do you think new Guardians come from?"

Anderl blinked three times, and looked at her for another few seconds.

"Oh," he said.

"After the birth comes childcare." Sometimes one has to spell out the obvious, as a lead-in to the interesting part.

"I… guess."

"Well, childcare," Helena told him, "is a non-trivial proposition in such cases."

She let Anderl ponder this for a few moments. He would know something of an adult Guardian's powers and capabilities, though even the usual tall tales fell a long way short of the tremendous actuality.

Such powers they wielded!

Helena felt so very glad that no mage, not even herself or Kelvin – nor even federal spellbinders, with their narrower but deeper focus on the combative aspects of conjuration science – experienced the responsibilities of wielding those energies beyond imagining, of remaining ever watchful, fully vigilant, and always – absolutely always – living up to their name: guarding the world.

Some of that, she could see Anderl already understood.

The rest would come in time.

New beginnings.

This could be a good thing, if everything went well.

"Wow," said Anderl finally.

"Indeed," said Helena.

And for the first time in far too long, she actually laughed out loud.

FORTY

The Magnus felt reassuring in Donal's two-handed grip, but Brian was clearly too frightened to do anything other than talk, answering any question Donal or the awakening Lamis might put to him, so Donal slowly reholstered the gun beneath his left armpit, smoothed down his tie and rebuttoned his suit jacket.

When he spoke, his voice echoed in the spectrally-lit stone corridor, carrying further into the subterranean maze. "So tell us. Where the Hades are we?"

Brian had indicated the answer was obvious, and Donal half-expected him to reveal this maze's location as being beneath Police HQ, some subterranean level that everyone had forgotten about.

"It's the seven-oh-ninth." Brian's light blue features looked paler than ever. "The precinct that we used to call the Armoury, even though it wasn't supposed to be one."

"Huh," said Donal. "The 709th. Right."

The *defunct* 709th, more precisely.

Being under Police HQ would have been too easy, not to mention unlikely, although Brian had always kept his devious fingers in all sorts of unsuspected pies, so you never really knew with him.

As for this place, with all those mage-crafted pentagonal tiles in chamber floors and the general nature of the subterranean maze… Maybe you *would* store dangerous confiscated items along with Tristopolis PD's more esoteric and powerful weapons in a setup like this.

Especially if you combined those responsibilities with questionable practices regarding prisoners – not necessarily standard human prisoners – and unusual interrogation methods.

And maybe sensible minds would decide to shut down such a facility and shift weaponry and confiscated goods to better-organised environments.

The 709th precinct had apparently operated in a unique way, with a reputation for trickiness and oddness. Even though it got closed down years before Donal left the Army and joined the TPD as a beat cop, he'd heard a bunch of stories and believed maybe a third of them, but that had been enough.

"Not exactly a normal precinct," said Lamis in his usual deep, sepulchral tones. "Maybe there's a quick way to get back to Headquarters from here, given the nature of this place, but I haven't sensed one yet."

His scarred, burned-out eye sockets should have been hard to look at, but Donal didn't care about trivia right now, not if Mel was down in the fabled Caverns beneath HQ where all those powerful entities lived.

"Can you open a portal?" said Donal. "To somewhere on the Avenue, if you can't reach into the Caverns directly?"

Lamis rubbed his face, which looked more lined than usual.

"Right now," he said, "I could just about manage to make a foot-wide opening to a location a few yards away. Maybe. Even then it wouldn't be safe to travel through."

Not what Donal wanted to hear, but you have to deal with reality as it happens, not the world as you wish it might be.

Around a curve in the chilly corridor, Konrad Talon remained sitting on the flagstones of the corridor floor, with his back against a wall – the stone blocks faintly outlined with the palest of glows – looking a little more recovered than before. He might be capable of walking, although maybe not quickly.

It was cold down here, or at least it would feel that way to a redblood, but whether that would help or hinder Talon's progress was impossible to tell.

Donal nodded, mostly to himself. "So what's the quickest way out of here?"

"I would think Mr Fixtovax here," said Lamis, "knows better than anyone."

Brian swallowed, his pale blue skin glistening with fear-sweat. "Sure. I mean, right, I can show you."

He glanced at his moss-skinned friend, who still lay unconscious on the floor, dropped by Donal's effortless left hook less than three minutes earlier.

"Never mind him," said Donal. "He'll come around eventually."

Not necessarily true, but Mel was in danger and that overrode all the usual considerations.

"Right. Um." Brian rubbed his sweaty face. "We, er, have to go down before we go up, kind of thing."

He gestured in the direction of the chamber he and his moss-skinned friend had come from, using the entrance that had opened in the chamber's floor: the head of a spiralling ramp, from the little Donal had glimpsed around the doorway's edge.

"Alright." Donal shrugged his shoulders and tipped his head to one side then the other to loosen up, as if getting ready for one more round in the ring. "Lead the way, and do it carefully but fast."

"S-sure, Loot. Sure thing."

There was a decision to make regarding Talon, and the one that Donal made now was provisional: he would try to get Talon out of here, but if their progress went too slowly then Talon could go to Hades, because Mel was more important than some crime lord moron who'd allowed himself to be captured and tortured, and never mind the daughter praying for her father's safe return.

Time to get moving.

Progress down the winding stone ramp was slow, because the slope was formed of uneven blocks, distorted over time or because of some powerful event, with occasional cracks and even, here and there, a missing block, like a pothole in a badly kept roadway.

The spectral light from the curved walls seemed blotched and patchy here, and the further they descended, the more dark areas occurred. Still, neither Brian nor his companion had required torches to climb up to the chamber inside the maze, so they shouldn't need anything to help them navigate the way back down.

Donal followed right behind Brian, glancing back often to see Lamis and Talon help each other past obstacles, picking their way over broken stone blocks and avoiding the gaping, distorted four-sided holes. Neither of them looked steady on his feet, but mollycoddling was not an option, not today.

Sweat glistened on the back of Brian's neck.

Good.

A little bit of fear was quite in order here.

They continued to descend.

Donal had expected a stairway at some point — knowing that indentured wraiths in elevator shafts were unlikely here: the shafts would have been abandoned, the wraiths deployed elsewhere, when the powers-that-be shut the old precinct down — enabling them to climb up to street level, having understood all along that the maze existed at some considerable depth below ground.

Instead, he and Brian, with Lamis and Talon trailing behind, followed a series of sloping shafts, now round in cross-section except for a narrow flat strip running along the bottom, just wide enough to walk on in a single file. The curved walls grew increasingly dank.

Soon enough, they came out into a long dark place, a gloom-filled tunnel running transversely left to right that Donal recognised straight away — not this specific location, but most certainly the kind of place he felt at home in

– causing him to regard Brian with some measure of surprise, before returning his attention to the surroundings.

Old rectangular shapes within the gloom stretched in both directions along the catacomb, along with open shelves where more flimsy protection had long since rotted away, leaving only desiccated bones, too far gone for use in the reactor piles.

No one would want them now.

Once, those remains would have been guarded, the sentinels' salaries paid by wealthy relatives of the newly deceased, but over time the need for such services would have faded as the dead became forgotten, gone from living memories just like the vast majority of deceased citizens, the ones who were processed by the Energy Authority in the usual way.

Whispers sounded from all around, whispers morphing into faint, beguiling songs, as stray natural necroflux resonated with the diffraction patterns laid down during life in the bones within the old sarcophagi, collapsed and intact alike.

Donal knew that only he could hear the whispers or feel the attraction of the songs.

It was something he had never discussed with anyone, not even Mel, but he felt certain that no one else experienced the call of the bones.

Why just me?

And why did he seem to be the only person unafraid of Guardians?

Doesn't matter.

There were other things to worry about right now.

He said, "Seriously, Brian? You come down here?"

"Um… Sure. When I, um, have to."

Donal shook his head. "I've never seen you."

Miles and miles of catacombs ran beneath the city, of course. Donal had no idea how far the network of tunnels stretched.

"You've…" Brian's voice trailed off, presumably as he worked out the implications of Donal's words.

For a long time, the catacombs had formed Donal's usual running routes, since his TPD detective's shield had allowed him access from any of the street-level entrances, and you simply didn't have to cope with pedestrians down here: he'd almost always been entirely alone on his long endurance runs.

After experiencing deep ensorcellment – while assigned to guard a famous performer, Diva Maria daLivnova, the target of dark mages – his subsequent sensitivity to the bones' songs had rendered the catacomb environment less pleasant, although that preceded his being shot in the heart and subsequently resurrected, which altered the experience yet again.

He'd never really regained the catacomb-running habit.

Partly, though, that came about because zombies don't need sleep, and during the sleep hours of normal folk – Mel and baby Finbar included – the sidewalks stood almost entirely deserted, even in the heart of Tristopolis, so long as he steered clear of Hoardway.

Also, he no longer carried TPD ID, which meant in theory the street level doors, usually set in miniature towers – or large pedestals – little more than the diameter of a phone booth and anything from seven to seventeen feet high, should no longer grant him access… although in practice, most of them still opened if he placed his palm against the ancient stones or ironwork and asked for permission.

Old guard-wraiths seemed to consider him a kindred spirit, in some way he had never tried to analyse too closely.

Now, back in the catacomb environment, he felt oddly at home, even though he could not have said exactly where this particular catacomb led, not from looking at this section alone.

The whispers and haunting harmonics grew more prominent, soft as silk trailed along his peripheral nerves.

Do you feel our song?

He wanted to call back yes, but not with Brian here and Lamis and Talon puffing along behind, catching up.

Do you hear our invitation?

Of course he did, but that didn't matter, because he had more important things to deal with.

"Left or right?" he said, dismissing all songs and whispers. "Which way do we go?"

"Um…" Brian was frowning for some reason.

"What is it?"

"Well, if we're going on foot beneath ground, that way" – Brian pointed left – "is the quickest way to Avenue of the Basilisks. It's how we, I, got here."

Perhaps he didn't want to discuss the moss-skinned man's identity.

"And if we go right?" Donal didn't care about Brian's dodgy accomplice, not right this moment.

Brian bit his lip, then: "We, um, we *should* be able to get up to street level, which would, well… It might be faster."

Donal possessed a zombie's sensory acuity, but even the most dull-witted redblood would have picked up the hesitation here. "So what's the problem, going that way?"

"I…"

Brian's eyes rolled up in a way that Donal had never seen before, and then Brian collapsed straight down, like a puppet with its strings severed all at once, which in a human being normally indicates sudden death as all muscle tension stops.

When nothing is left, limbs are like sticks and the spine is a loose stack of marbles and it all falls down, the way Brian had just now.

"Holy crap," said Donal.

But Brian was still breathing, that was the thing, so even though it had looked like sudden death, his falling down was something else entirely.

Donal looked around, because Lamis and Talon had caught up.

"Some kind of hex shield," rumbled Lamis. "Induced what you might call a fainting spell, if you'll pardon my little pun."

"I don't feel anything," said Donal.

Not quite true, but he didn't think Lamis was talking about the bones.

"There's a defence in place, there must be, somewhere along the tunnel. Some defensive setup that Brian here encountered at some point in the past, and it induced an event-observing spell, one that persisted inside his brain. It's an aversion to trespassing beyond that outer defence."

"Yeah, sure," muttered Donal. "First thing that sprang to my mind."

Lamis managed a grim smile, made grimmer by his ruined eye sockets. "There was an implanted spell in Brian Fixtovax's head that lay there in place, waiting to be triggered by a well-formulated thought or intention or action, in this case a decision to venture in that direction."

He pointed right, along the catacomb's gloomy length.

"Thanatos damn it," said Donal. "You're saying that way's impassable."

Behind Lamis, Talon moaned and rubbed his face, but said nothing. It looked as if standing upright was taking all of his energy and focus.

"It would be impassable and impossible down there" – one side of Lamis's mouth twitched – "if you didn't have a tremendously powerful mage to help you."

"Huh," said Donal. "Are you sure you're recovered enough to deal with something like that?"

"Let's find out, shall we?"

That was more like the old Lamis, at last.

"Okay." Donal took a step further into the catacomb. "Let's do just that."

"And leave Brian lying here?"

Donal stopped and looked down at the collapsed blue-skinned man. Brian's chest rose and fell slowly, and he didn't look to be in a critical medical condition, but you could never even be sure in the case of someone dropped by, say, a sweet left hook, never mind some weird kind of hex induction Donal had never heard of before.

"I'm tempted," he said. "I'm really tempted to leave this idiot here."

"You can probably walk just as fast while carrying him as I can alone."

Donal looked at that long face with those ruins where eyes should have been. "That means the quickest way would be for me to carry you piggyback-style."

"That," said Lamis, "is not going to happen."

"Well, then," said Donal.

"Yes?"

"Oh, for Thanatos' sake."

Donal crouched down, rolled the unconscious Brian onto his back and straightened out his legs, and prepared for the same manoeuvre he'd used earlier with Talon: the Shadowborne Rangers' technique for lifting an unresponsive person onto your shoulders, ready for a firefighter's carry.

"What are you—" started Lamis, then stopped as Donal scooped the legs and shoulder-rolled sideways along Brian's torso and rose to kneeling with Brian across his shoulders.

After a brief steadying pause, Donal powered himself up to standing, still with Brian draped across him, now holding Brian's sleeve-cuffs and ankles with the same hand.

"I'm ready," he said.

"Interesting," said Lamis. "Have you got any other tricks like that?"

"Mostly I just shoot people or sock them in the jaw."

Lamis shook his head, with only a hint of a smile on that long face.

"That's what I'd always figured," he said.

Donal turned, being careful not to swing around too fast, because of the extra weight across his shoulders. "Talon, are you okay to walk on?"

"I can manage."

There was a kind of annoyed weakness in Talon's voice, as near as Donal could tell. It was probably a good sign: earlier he'd been too far out of it to get frustrated or generate any kind of emotion that might drive him onwards.

"Alright," said Donal. "Let's go."

He shifted Brian's weight, centred everything correctly, and then began at his speed-march pace along the gloom-filled catacomb, not quite breaking into a run, impressed that Lamis was able – after a moment to catch up – to match his pace using long brisk strides.

Do you heed our call?

Not really.

Do you feel the need to join us?

Sometimes, but not today.

Can you—

No more: Donal pushed aside the mind-whispers and beguiling harmonics, because he had a mission to accomplish and it was all about Mel's safety so nothing else mattered, and all the banter he'd exchanged with Lamis became irrelevant except as a way of getting them to work together well, and that was okay too.

I'm coming, Mel.

Moving faster now, footsteps upping their rhythm, with attenuated echoes bouncing back from the catacomb walls on either side, the ceiling overhead.

I'm coming.

Faster again.
Speeding up because he had to.

FORTY-ONE

Donal smelled the booze before he saw it.

Up ahead, this catacomb ended in a T-junction, and it looked as if a similar catacomb ran in each direction, left and right, lit by the usual faint phosphorescence, and under normal circumstances he wouldn't have slowed, but Brian's weight across his shoulders – along with the ongoing strain on his lower back – formed a warning that things weren't as benign as usual down here.

He'd left Lamis behind, but the sound of Lamis's footsteps drew closer as Donal slowed right down, which was probably a good thing: if you're going up against sorcerous defences of an unknown kind, having a senior mage at your side tends to help.

Fainter sounds indicated that Talon was farther back but still making progress in this direction, so fair enough.

Donal stopped and breathed in, concentrating.

Smoke. Woodsmoke and alcohol fumes.

Whiskey or gin or both – or maybe neither, maybe some other kind of spirit – but any way you looked at it, operating a still or actual distillery down here in the catacombs was a long way from legal, and while Donal didn't care about any of that right now, this might be the reason for the hex-defence thing laid down in Brian's brain and activated by the thought of entering this part of the catacomb system.

Under other circumstances, this might even be something to laugh about.

Donal lowered himself into a squat and tilted sideways, letting Brian slip off his shoulders and onto the stone-paved floor, with one of Brian's sleeves going into a small black puddle, but never mind.

There was something on the air beyond the distillery smell, a faint electric edge that tickled the spine, and while that wasn't necessarily a sign of hex nearby, it was probably a clue.

Lamis came alongside, walked around Brian's slumped form, and stopped.

"I'm going to deactivate the hex-shield," said Lamis.

"Fair enough." Donal didn't want to collapse in a faint like Brian here. "How long will that—"

"All done. Come along." Lamis's long coat swung as he strode forward.

"Wait," said Donal.

Lamis stopped and turned. On the floor, Brian began to moan, his hand scrabbling in the puddle.

"He'll wake up now," said Lamis. "With the hex shield gone, the induced spell is timing out. There was some kind of resource-polling hex-thread running deep in Brian's brain, and with the shield down the polling failed."

"Er…"

"So," said Lamis, "that thread's ending under error conditions is de-registering the listener hex as part of its shutdown."

Donal shook his head. "Of course it is."

Surely Lamis realised he was essentially talking to himself, and maybe that was part of getting back to his normal mindset or something, which brought up an interesting point that might be tactically important.

"Look," added Donal. "Before we rush on… How exactly did you end up here? That vortex portal thing was in the Caverns under HQ, right? I mean the other end of the portal."

No doubt he was getting the technical terms all wrong, but so long as Lamis understood what he was getting at, the rest didn't matter.

"Indeed," said Lamis. "Call it a defence that I tripped over, or a booby trap. Like Brian here but on an altogether different level."

"And how did I get here? Through the same kind of thing?"

Two vortex-portals or portal-vortices or whatever the Hades you were supposed to call them, with their entrances in very different places but exiting to approximately the same location: different chambers within the maze located below the 709th Precinct building, officially closed down and theoretically decommissioned in full.

There was no obvious connection, yet the shared destination couldn't possibly be a coincidence.

"I don't…" Lamis halted. "My dear chap, I hadn't even thought of checking you for resonance."

It had been a long time since Donal heard anyone say "dear chap" – and never at all from someone he assumed was Federation born and bred – but he didn't feel like making any smart remarks right now.

"I had an amulet," he told Lamis. "A call crystal kind of thing, that Klaudius gave me. I'm talking about the Guardian."

"And I would have assumed as much, from the name alone." Lamis's features went stony, no doubt remembering his last encounter with Klaudius, which had not gone well at all.

Not for Lamis.

"When I woke up here," said Donal, "I mean back in the maze, the crystal was gone. Someone or something must've snatched it off me as I fell into the portal or when I was inside it, if that's possible."

Time was running out and he itched to keep moving, but this information might be important, and Lamis hadn't been properly awake and thinking clearly before now.

Call this a mission briefing partway through an extended operation: sometimes you had to stop and do just that, or risk catastrophic failure.

Mel. Finbar…

Donal forced himself to take a calming breath.

"I was in a coffee shop in Cataclysm Reaches," he went on. "Except no, I had been in the Chasm, then I woke up in the coffee shop which I thought was probably some miles away, but I never actually got around to asking."

He thought about what to say, then continued: "I'm not even sure if it was a portal that got me from the Chasm to the shop, or just this white-coloured, shape-changing being called Martina. She can shift through space somehow, although maybe not long distances."

If Lamis still possessed eyes and eyelids, he might have blinked: that was the impression he gave as his forehead wrinkled and his twisted eyebrows and scar tissue rose up, widening the ruined eye sockets, or appearing to.

"I know I'm babbling," added Donal, "but I don't understand any of this, which means I've no idea what's important, or whether we should even be standing here instead of moving on as fast as possible, okay?"

A bunch of ordinary criminals, if that was who operated the out-of-sight distillery, didn't seem like any kind of threat at all, not compared to everything else that was going on.

On the other hand, underestimating any kind of enemy can lead to disaster.

"I understand," said Lamis. "We need to re-orient ourselves."

Brian was up on his hands and knees now, and Talon was splashing through a shallow puddle just a few yards behind Donal, finally catching up.

No new sounds came from the catacombs running left and right up ahead, only a faint hum of machinery. Perhaps there were no actual people manning the thing, not at the moment.

"Right," said Donal. "Um, Aggie was in the coffee shop when it all kicked off. I mean Aggie the wraith from Police HQ, and she came through phone wires to get to me."

"Are you sure?"

"I was there, so yes. And it's something to do with a mage called Kandroknar."

Lamis sucked in a breath. "Not Alej Kandroknar."

"Yeah, that's the one."

"The day he died," said Lamis, "a lot of mages breathed a collective sigh of relief."

Before Donal could say anything, Talon began to laugh, except not in the normal way, because part of it was sobbing and part of it was almost like hiccups, and all of it sounded awful, as if it were tearing him apart inside.

"Died," Talon managed to say. "So much for your Mordanto crowd. Died, right."

"What do you mean?" Lamis's question sounded like the voice of doom.

Even though Donal already knew the answer, his skin chilled when Talon laughed again in that odd tortured way, before telling Lamis what he had probably just guessed.

"That," said Talon, wheezing faintly, "is what Alej wanted you all to think. And I… I wanted him out of my life, and he'd had enough of establishing himself here, so it was a kind of freedom, you see, for both of us."

In the phosphorescence of the catacomb, Talon's rivulets of tears glimmered like quicksilver, and he made no effort to wipe them away. Perhaps, after all the torture and everything else he'd been through, he was no longer capable of noticing or caring.

"Who tortured you?" The words just came out of Donal, as unplanned and spontaneous as if he were still a redblood, not a zombie with blood as thick and black as fountain-pen ink.

Talon squeezed his eyes shut – clearly remembering, maybe trying not to – and opened them once more.

"Wraiths," he managed to say. "Wraiths at first, and you wouldn't believe the things they, they… But then *she* came, and that's when, when I…"

Donal looked at Lamis, but couldn't read Lamis's expression.

Aggie?

It was hard to picture the freewraith he'd known for so long, who'd carried him up and down elevator shafts so often at Police HQ – albeit mostly before her transformation from her earlier identity as Gertie – doing something so harsh and violent as torturing a human being, even if the human being was a long-time crime lord with blood on his hands and an awful lot to answer for.

Aggie, a torturer?

No, that couldn't be right. It just couldn't.

Lamis's voice rumbled, deep and sepulchral: "Who do you mean by *she*?"

Significance lay heavily in those words, as if he already knew the answer, yet its confirmation would carry great import.

"Oh, Thanatos," moaned Talon. "I can't… Those eyes, the way they burn. And her, her skin…"

"What about it?" said Lamis.

Donal felt something twist in his gut, and his skin chilled again for no good reason.

"Like blood. Shining red all the time like, like…"

Talon stopped and began to gasp, the way babies do when they've cried themselves out to the point where they can't breathe, although Finbar wasn't like that at all and the thing about irrelevant thoughts is so often they're defensive mechanisms as much as stray ideas, because this couldn't be right, not at all.

"No," said Donal. "It doesn't have to be her."

Lamis seemed to exhale through his nose, before taking in a breath and inclining his head towards Talon. "How many individuals can induce terror via the nature of their being, with no torture required?"

Donal shook his head.

No.

It was bad enough that Aggie might be involved.

"Hellah's my friend," he said.

None of this was making sense.

"She and Klaudius must be at Police Headquarters," said Lamis, his voice cavern-deep and steady. "When I tripped the vortex trap in the Caverns, they'll have sensed it."

"What are you telling me?" said Donal.

"You're worried about Mel and Sergeant Harman, but if the Guardians are your friends, they'll be motivated to protect the people you care about."

"I've still got to—" Donal's voice trailed off.

A different kind of danger was approaching: the kind that offered physical violence instead of hex gobbledygook and entities beyond ordinary understanding.

Here we go.

This was the kind of situation he could deal with.

Ordinary enemies.

Seven, no, nine men who were mostly standard human filed out from around the lefthand corner, and spread out across the catacomb in a concave arc centred on Donal and Lamis, smiling and shifting and saying nothing whatsoever.

Teenage would-be thugs and drunken amateurs would be coming out with verbal challenges and insults at this point, but these were professionals of a sort, and making conversation wasn't in their repertoire, not during confrontation.

Start with the three on the right.

Donal knew with absolute certainty that he could drop those three during his first two paces diagonally forward and after that he would be spinning among them, using them for cover as things escalated wildly beyond the limits of easy prediction; and that didn't matter one tiny bit because this was it: life on the edge where he became utterly, one hundred percent alive.

Nine pairs of eyes scanned the environment before settling on him, Donal Riordan from Danklyn with all those years of relentless training made deeper by his post-resurrection discipline and capabilities, and even if he didn't survive this encounter, a minimum of five of these men would die before he did.

Most likely, he would deliver shock and awe at a speed and ferocity level these nine guys had never witnessed before, meaning all of them would perish in the next few seconds.

No one spoke.

Or moved.

Donal had no idea what Lamis might be up to, and no sound came from Talon or Brian behind him, but that didn't matter.

Utter calmness filled him.

Do you want to die today?

This was a conversation deeper than words, a primeval dialogue of posture and maybe airborne pheromones, of body language operating at a level where lies become impossible, and a gloomy catacomb was a good place for this kind of encounter, in part because right here, Donal felt entirely at home.

Maybe not all nine would perish.

Which of you wants to die so your buddies can live?

But the calmer Donal felt, the more likely it became that even that question became irrelevant, as the chances he could kill all nine of them – operating on a timescale measured in ninths of a second – kept rising in his certain estimation.

Shoulders loose, jacket unbuttoned.

Magnus beneath his left armpit.

Totally ready.

Well?

Something shifted.

It identified the leader for sure, the big man who took a step back, and it was like breaking a paralysis spell as the others got into motion, also backing off albeit out of step with each other; but still, they moved almost as a synchronised group as they filed back out the way they had come.

Most had disappeared around the corner already.

Okay.

Donal continued to wait, because everything could change if someone tripped or made some other mistake, but that didn't look likely to happen.

I'm still ready.

Only their diminishing footsteps sounded as the nine men made their tactical retreat into the cross-corridor, heading in the direction presumably of their distillery, and their footsteps continued to attenuate until not even Donal could hear them.

His calmness remained as he turned to look at Lamis.

"Screaming Hades," said Lamis. "I can't believe I saw that."

You could call it an incongruous remark coming from a mage with blasted eye sockets, and it would be nice if Lamis managed to replace his usual wraparound shades at some point, but Donal appreciated the sentiment.

"They knew what was what," he said.

The encounter was over, and details didn't matter any more, so it was time to move on.

"We need to get out of here." Lamis turned back towards Talon and Brian. "You two will be okay."

Both men were shaking and looked unable to speak, in a way that felt quite different to the silence of the nine strangers just now, not to mention Donal's own wordless state during the standoff.

He looked at the T-junction ahead, and thought about the sounds he had heard, the footsteps and the echoes, and came to a realisation.

"The exit upwards," he said. "We get to it before we reach the distillery."

"I don't… Oh," said Lamis.

"Right. Those guys didn't want to die, partly because we just need to get out of here, not destroy their business."

There was more to it than that, because most of them — this was likely, though not certain — wouldn't consider the distillery setup worth dying for, but the main point was they weren't prepared to pay the price of lethal confrontation.

They would still fight back if attacked, of course.

I'm not a cop any more.

Shutting down an illicit distillery was TPD's job, at least on learning of the place's existence, and Donal might pass on the information when and if it became convenient, but for now there were more important things to worry about.

"Time for us to move," he said.

Soon enough they were at the foot of the exit shaft, which turned out to possess a helical stone staircase with misshapen steps and no safety rail or rope, but Donal didn't care about that part.

Sprinting up any kind of stairs is a nice athletic challenge, and this stairway looked to wind upwards for a good hundred and fifty feet at least, which meant Lamis and Brian and Talon were likely to make slow going of the ascent, so there was nothing really to think about.

Donal began his solo upwards run without another word, focussing hard in the gloomy light — the faint phosphorescence of the curved stone walls just about illuminated the inert, worn steps — knowing that any kind of slip would ruin everything, but pushing fast all the same because he had to get out of here.

His ostensible job was almost finished – he'd found Talon, which was the main part – but his real objective was always the safety of Mel and Finbar, and even though Alej Kandroknar's name seemed to swirl through the confusing background of everything that was going on, that twinkle-eyed mage had been charming in a corrupt kind of way and hadn't killed Donal when he clearly could have, and all of these thoughts whirled as an analogue of this winding Death-damned spiral staircase, curving over and over—

Watch it.

—as he slipped but corrected himself—

Too close.

—while increasing the effort, thighs pumping harder than his lungs because his redblood days were done, pushing hard, seeing only the next three steps at any given moment because focus was all, focus and effort, so that—

Yes.

—soon enough the hollow cylinder of the street-level exit was drawing close and then he made it, gasping hard as he stepped onto the small floor area of uneven stone, and placed both hands against the cold iron door, pressed hard, and waited for it to move.

Nothing.

Come on.

Still nothing happened.

"I need to get out of here," he said.

But there was no response, and no sense of any wraith regarding him from inside the solid stone or the heavy black iron door right in front of him, maybe centuries old and as solid as you could get.

Oh, for Thanatos' sake.

A locked metal door: after all the obstacles he'd been facing, this seemed laughably straightforward and mundane, but that didn't help because he still couldn't force his way through.

His hand went inside his jacket to his Magnus, although he couldn't see anything good coming from firing at ancient iron and stone like this.

So what do I—

A faint call rose from below, deep-toned and hard to hear, in part from echoes, but he made out: "…away, quickly now," and reacted just in time, pulling himself back to the head of the spiral stairs as the air seemed to ripple in front of him, and then purple fire was burning around the lock in the black iron door.

"Lamis," he said. "Nice work."

The purple fire faded out and he reached the door and pushed hard, and it was heavy but finely balanced and somehow still greased so it began to move, though slowly.

It took a full nine seconds to widen the opening enough for Donal to

squeeze through.
    And then he was out.

FORTY-TWO

A black cat tapped and pawed on the window from outside, and for a second Helena felt totally afraid – shocked at the sudden appearance, unable to tell whether the sudden rush of fear was for herself or the feline outside, because her study was located at the top of a rearing baroque tower, therefore high above ground level, albeit with buttresses and statue-niches and all sorts of dark decorative stonework outside, but still a sheer drop for the most part.

A long way to fall.

She was standing with a cup of deathrose-scented helebore tea halfway to her lips, saucer in the other hand, and she stopped now, replaced the fine porcelain cup on its saucer, and placed both down on her desktop, in between a proto-human skull and a fossilised claw of mysterious origin.

The cat meowed in silence outside.

"Well," said Helena. "I almost forgot about you."

She gestured, and the platinum-and-bone window-catches glowed briefly as their runes activated, then clicked and turned and the leaded windowpane swung inwards – the reverse of its usual direction when opening – and the black cat flowed inside like a liquid shadow.

Not a true feline, of course, although this living-obsidian form contained a consciousness of sorts, bound within by Kelvin as a demonstration of technical prowess.

A weaker form of this type of conjuration was often used on indentured wraiths to make it more likely they would work to the terms of their contract, but true binding to matter in this fashion came from a high level of skill in a difficult, abstruse area of study that most mages wouldn't even consider trying to learn superficially, much less master.

The cat sat up on the floor and stared in her direction, or seemed to: with its eyes as black as the rest of it, you could not be entirely sure.

"I left you asleep in the car," added Helena. "I trust you were comfortable there."

Small twin ripples of black-on-black movement indicated a slow blinking action, perhaps a deliberate signal.

You're going to want to answer that.

Now it was Helena's turn to blink, confused by her own thought, then caught by the realisation that the words in her head came from the living-obsidian cat, not her own subconscious mind.

Either the door was about to be knocked upon or the telephone was about to ring: that was what the message had to mean; and if it originated with Kelvin, well, even he was not capable of entering Mordanto without someone informing her.

She turned towards the skin-covered phone.

Very good.

Shaking her head at the living-obsidian cat, she placed her hand on the handset, waited for the vibration to start, and plucked the handset upwards before the bell proper had begun to ring.

"Nice to hear from you, Kelvin," she said into the mouthpiece.

Something between *hmmph* and a chuckle sounded in her ear, followed by Kelvin's tired-sounding voice. "You know this singleton-wraith-detection work could take years to even approach the prototype-testing phase."

"I believe I understand the scope of the problem."

"Because you've been at this stuff for way longer than me, and all that. I appreciate that, Professor."

Handset still against her ear, Helena looked down at the seated black cat, now looking like a polished black glass statue, totally unmoving.

"You have more practical techniques at your command than I had expected," she said, wondering what exactly Kelvin was leading up to.

There was no way in Hades he could have made some significant advance in the field during the past few hours since Helena had visited him in Tumbleup Road and he had conjured up the living-obsidian cat and sent it back with her.

"That is right." There was some kind of edge to Kelvin's voice, but there was no way to work out exactly what it meant. "However, a fresh pair of eyes can often make a difference straight away."

A simple truism, but more: a sudden memory coalesced – of her using almost exactly those words in the thaumadynamics teaching laboratory years ago, to a young Kelvin Johannsson whose solo work already excelled, but whose collaborative project with two fellow then-novitiates was spiralling into difficulties, and he was the one to blame.

Under other circumstances, she might have laughed, but instead she felt a little sad, realising the incident must have lived in Kelvin's mind long after he had absorbed the actual lesson, while for her it had been a fleeting moment, one she would never have remembered later without this trigger from Kelvin.

She said: "Does that mean you have found something?"

"It does." Again, there was an edge to Kelvin's voice: worry with a hint of something else.

"And why have you not told me already what it is?"

"Because you're not going to like it, Professor."

There was a twitch of movement from the living-obsidian cat, its meaning indecipherable.

Oh, dear.

That was Helena's thought, hers alone, or maybe not: either way, it seemed apposite.

"I'm ready," she said. "Tell me."

"Alej Kandroknar is still alive."

Portals and reality vortices lived in her memory as absorbed experiences, things that she could handle even when other mages could not; but the way that her study seemed to whirl and jag back and forth and simply wobble, that was something different: a subjective measure of internal distress, of inability to cope with some part of the external world.

"Say that again."

"That confrontation when the seven mages died," said Kelvin from afar, "didn't play out the way you thought it did, Professor."

"There were after-incident reports and analyses and—"

"Not done by me and – respectfully, Professor – not done by you either, since you were a witness at the time, nothing more."

Blurring, now, the room, as the tears began to form: all that guilt, held for so very long across the decades.

More words came from the earpiece. "But you didn't fail, Professor," continued Kelvin. "It wasn't your fault."

All that guilt, those poor senior mages obliterated because her detection field failed to indicate the approach of that singleton wraith, the Draxoleth, so much more powerful and devious than she had ever imagined, destined to be the cause of her greatest failure ever.

"You… did… not… fail," added Kelvin.

"Of course I did."

"The Draxoleth didn't get past your detection field."

But she remembered everything: the dark open space of Hardhammer Heath, the black woods surrounding it; the figure of Kandroknar at the centre, and the seven mages closing in on him before reality exploded and everything went to Hades in the worst way possible.

"Kandroknar," she said, "didn't do all that by himself."

She did not need to explain what she meant by *all that*, not if he had read the accounts, and certainly not if he had read the pain in her eyes earlier when she recounted the happenings of that day.

"Of course he didn't," said Kelvin. "Without the Draxoleth, even Alej Kandroknar would've been taken down by Mordanto's finest enforcers."

"But—"

"The reason you never detected the Draxoleth's approach was that he was already there."

Helena gasped.

Then she realised Kelvin must have misunderstood something in the old reports.

"Only Kandroknar was there already," she said finally. "He was alone. I would swear to it. I *did* swear to it, during the hearings afterwards."

The memory of those times felt awful.

"Look at the cat."

Helena shook her head, but did as he requested.

It yawned and rolled over onto its back, lay there and wriggled as if inviting a belly-rub, then sat back up again, blinked, and reverted to statue-like stillness.

"I do not understand."

"Oh, Professor. The cat is a compactified-dimensions mentality, a minor wraithlet, bound to mesoscopic matter, okay?"

"I…"

And then she did understand, fully and totally.

It's not possible.

Yet it formed an explanation that accounted for everything – absolutely everything – that happened on that dreadful day, that worst of tragedies.

It can't be.

And yet…

"Kandroknar was no longer human by then." Now Kelvin's words sounded implacable. "He and the Draxoleth were combined into an aggregate, composite being already. They were *both* present, and more, since with a composite being—"

"The whole is greater than the sum of the parts." It was a truism within that field of study. "Yes. Of course."

"The Kandroknar-Draxoleth composite was waiting on the heath," said Kelvin, "with everything planned out well in advance. He – if you can call such a being *he* instead of *it* – intended to blow up the place from the very beginning, and make it look as if he went up in the explosion along with everyone else."

For a second or three, Helena felt unable to breathe as incredible tension took hold of her ribcage and paralysed her diaphragm; and then it was gone: the feeling had evaporated and she could breathe easily once more, perhaps more easily than at any time since that disaster decades before.

"You have worked out a lot of details," she said, "in such a short space of time."

"I know, Professor. But the thing is, once I questioned the initial assumption that the Draxoleth slipped through your detection field, everything else fell into place practically instantaneously."

"But how could you make that mental switch so fast?"

For a moment, the line hummed faintly, then Kelvin answered: "I didn't have to change any of my thinking."

"I do not understand."

"It happened a long time before you became head of Mordanto, but you see, I already knew that you couldn't have made a mistake, Professor."

Helena blinked hard.

Kelvin continued, "Since I knew deep down that your detection field would've been bug-free, all I had to do was work out what could have caused the explosion and all, and then it was totally obvious."

"I don't know what to say." Humbled by her own protégé, by his faith in her: that was how she felt.

Kelvin said nothing, no doubt understanding that she needed a few moments to process this revelation.

"I wonder if he went back to Zurinam," she said finally. "Or simply found some other part of the Federation to bury himself in."

Another silence, but this one felt different, then Kelvin said: "Professor, may I suggest a period of deep-trance reflection might be in order?"

Buried deep in her professional ethics and methodology was the concept of the student becoming the master, but her usual notion was of the new master teaching the next generation of students, not his own original teacher.

Yet right this moment, she felt on the brink of new insight, because of Kelvin.

"Tell me why you think that," she said.

"You needed to kick me up the backside," said Kelvin, "and out of my funk. I get that."

"Yes?"

"It's the timing, Professor. You brought up an old case today, and there might be no significance to the timing, but why exactly did it come to mind right now?"

She stared at her study, the bookcase with its furbats and all the rest, not really seeing any of it at all.

I woke up saying Kandroknar's name aloud.

But why today, after all these years? What had caused her to dream of him?

"There have been interesting manifestations of thaumic background radiation of late," she said slowly, "but with no particular relationship to that devil Kandroknar."

The business of Guardian Hellah and her sojourn in Crepuscula were entirely relevant here, and she would share the details with Kelvin if she had to, but for now this information ought to be kept as private as possible.

"Could Kandroknar's influence be suggested in any of this, Professor?"

"I… didn't think so."

But the subconscious mind is the greatest pattern-recognition device ever to exist: every first-year novitiate learned that as a matter of experiential fact as well as theory.

Kelvin could be right.

Of course he could be.

Resonances in the local thaumic background that I subconsciously recognised.

But the implications…

It would mean the Draxoleth-Kandroknar composite had hidden himself – itself – somewhere in Tristopolis for all that time… but it was possible.

No one was looking for Kandroknar.

Even mages are subject to preconceptions, to perception filtered by presuppositions, to undetectable bias.

Everyone had been so certain that Kandroknar was long dead.

"Come to Mordanto," she said suddenly.

"Of course," said Kelvin. "But may I ask why?"

She had wanted him to get out of his house and engaging with the world and so on – for his sake – but this was something more.

"I need you here," she said.

"Okay…"

"That intuition you just mentioned?" she said. "I'm feeling it right now, more strongly than I have ever felt it before."

"Uh-oh."

She almost laughed at the half-humorous, half-serious tone in his voice.

"Something bad is about to happen," she said.

It wasn't just that Kandroknar was alive. Something more was happening: some kind of build-up, or she would never have picked up on that resonance, however subliminally.

Something dreadful.

"Time to send out all the scanbats?" said Kelvin.

The municipal scanbats were requested by the police department but it needed a mage to read a scanbat's surveillance memories, which meant the eyries were right here in Mordanto and ultimately under Helena's control.

Those scanbats could perform more than visual surveillance, although that fact was not generally known.

"I'm going to deploy them all," she told Kelvin. "But I am not sure I need to."

"I don't understand."

Now that she was alerted, she could begin to parse her perceptions, to deconstruct sensations that originally arrived below the conscious level.

"I'm not sure we need to go looking for danger," she said into the handset.

"I think it might already be looking for us."

Kelvin's voice tightened: "You sense Mordanto is in danger?"

Helena looked up at the ceiling, which seemed to ripple even though in reality it remained unmoving.

Something is coming.

She swallowed, then said simply: "Yes."

A click sounded and then the simple buzz and sighing of a dead line sounded in the earpiece.

Alej Kandroknar.

It seemed impossible, after all this time.

And the Draxoleth.

Both deadly, and as a composite, even more powerful.

Some kind of reckoning was long overdue.

FORTY-THREE

Reality coalesced: dark and solid instead of blazing white light, a coolness in the air instead of the burning brilliance, and a soft quiet in which gentle sounds could be heard instead of a coruscating hiss as if she had been caged inside living lightning.

Mel was on her hands and knees, the stony ground was rough and hard and cold beneath her, and she let her head hang down just for a moment out of tiredness, but a smile was growing on her face all the same.

I've survived.

For some uncountable number of minutes or hours, some immeasurable duration of time, she'd thought the end could come at any moment, and would almost have been okay with that sudden extinction of everything, of her entire personal universe, were it not for the thought of leaving Finbar and Donal behind.

Coughing sounded beside her.

"Viktor," she said, remembering.

The detective had rolled himself to a sitting position on the ground, and he stared at her through the pale blue lenses of his glasses. "Mel. You appear intact. Feel okay?"

"Yeah," said Mel. "I do."

"Klaudius saved us."

"I suppose he did."

They were in one of the Caverns, presumably the same one they'd been inside when Klaudius snapped shield-cages of white blazing light into place around Viktor and Mel separately, and yet it appeared entirely different.

Serene, for one thing.

Drifting streamers of green airborne fluid lent the vast volume a sub-oceanic look, and three dark-orange shapes with trailing tendrils were also moving slowly through the air in the distance, far back in the extended

Cavern space, and if it weren't for the fact that the air remained breathable and entirely normal, it would've looked like a place where swimming was the best way to move.

Bluish-grey rocks predominated, while the weirdest thing was the illumination itself, because the dim light appeared diffuse, casting few shadows and those in different directions, with no obvious sources for the light.

"No major entities in sight," said Viktor. "Thank Thanatos."

An amused voice said: "Maybe you ought to be thanking me."

The Guardian was wearing the dark tunic and trousers he'd been in before, so much less flamboyant than past appearances. Maybe the flashiness was only for the times when he left this place, the Caverns.

"Klaudius." From her half-lying position on the ground, Mel looked up at him. "Thank you."

She got up to one knee then rose to standing.

Klaudius said, "You are very welcome, Mel."

His heptagonal irises of orange fire blazed a little more brightly than usual, and his pale skin looked damp with sweat, along with a certain lankness to his long blonde hair, like a young fit boxer who'd just worked through three or five hard sparring rounds and loved it, feeling ready for some more.

Pumped with temporary victory, perhaps.

"You've got the place under control," she managed to say.

The visceral fear his appearance induced in her remained, but she was controlling it better now.

"For a while," said Klaudius. "Sergeant Harman, you are unharmed, I take it?"

"Sure." Viktor stood up, hitched his high shoulders inside his leather coat, and resettled the Grausers in the twin shoulder holsters he wore. "My thanks, Guardian."

"You're still looking for Donal, presumably." The orange-fire irises seemed almost to revolve: some kind of illusion, for they did no such thing. "I have the more troublesome entities quietened down and in separate places for now, but I dare not leave the Caverns with you, I'm afraid."

Mel felt as if she wanted to cry – not a thing she did often – but partly that was just the effect of Klaudius's presence: that terrifying aura he projected, and her deep instinctual recognition of his incredible power and potential for swatting her and any other minor being out of existence like an insect.

"I understand," she said, unable to believe she was capitulating.

It wasn't that she wanted to give up on finding Donal, but the thought of pressing this overwhelming Guardian, insisting on further help from him, felt ridiculous, impossible.

I'll find another way.

There was nothing more she could do.

"I can put in a request for scanbat surveillance." There was a hopeless note in Viktor's voice. "There's a limit to the urgency I can mark it with, though."

Donal hadn't revealed a huge amount of procedural detail regarding his TPD career, but he had muttered about scanbats – along with the now-abandoned rooftop mirrors and lenses, no longer linked by festooned cables to Police HQ – being far less useful most of the time than people tended to imagine, and highly limited when it came to deterrence.

If Viktor had felt hugely confident in the scanbat approach, he would surely have put it into action straight away, instead of escorting Mel and Lamis down here.

"Oh, Death damn it," she said. "Guardian, we had Mage Lamis with us originally."

Klaudius raised an eyebrow, and frosty steam rose from his head and shoulders.

"Lamis, is it?"

Mel remembered that there'd been a confrontation between the two of them some time back, and although Klaudius hadn't been himself, Lamis had stood no chance whatsoever.

Heart pounding and sweating hard, Mel managed to say: "He was helping us."

Klaudius looked from left to right, but for some reason it seemed to mean more than a normal visual scan, as if he had ways of searching through all the giant Caverns – however many of them were here, however far they stretched down here, deep below ground – that depended on more than ordinary light.

"He's not here," said Klaudius, "but some activation resonance remains."

That made no sense to Mel, but Viktor said: "A booby trap, Guardian?"

Yet again, Viktor was a surprise, even though Mel knew in theory about his ThD and, according to Donal who'd learned it from task force colleagues, a longstanding reputation for reading highly advanced textbooks for fun.

"It looks that way," said Klaudius. "I'd say he's probably unharmed."

Viktor said nothing.

He didn't show his fear but he was surely feeling the same way as anyone else in a Guardian's presence – unless their name was Donal Riordan, which still made no sense at all, but never mind – and most likely he was mulling over Klaudius's use of the word *probably* and the general light-hearted tone of voice.

The orange fire in Klaudius's eyes intensified, then settled back down to a glimmer.

"Interesting," he added. "Some of those old vortex traps are a little overdue for replacement, I guess."

Mel opened her mouth, trying to ask for helpful details, but a croak came out, as if all the saliva in her throat had evaporated in an instant, desiccating her vocal cords.

Klaudius's narrow lips twitched in what might have been a sympathetic smile, but he turned to Viktor as he said: "The old 709th precinct possesses a labyrinth level in addition to the abandoned offices and other facilities. You might find a rather confused and grumpy mage down there, if you take a look."

"Lamis?" said Viktor.

"Indeed."

That was good, but Mel needed to find Donal, otherwise she wouldn't have come to this Death-damned place at all.

"I'm cold," said Klaudius, holding out his hand, which steamed the way an ice block might when taken into warmth.

"Um…" said Mel.

"So be careful with this." Klaudius reached inside his tunic and drew out a crystal on a neck chain, which he drew over his head, allowing him to offer the crystal and chain to Mel.

"Here." Viktor stepped forward with a blue-and-black cloth in hand that might have been a large handkerchief or a bandanna, pulled from his coat pocket. "Wrap it in this."

Mel took the cloth from him and held it out for Klaudius, who dropped the crystal onto the centre of the cloth, which Mel then bundled up and held by the knot, allowing it to dangle while its temperature normalised.

Klaudius adjusted his tunic, then looked at Mel and Viktor.

"The other crystal it's entangled with," he told them, "is currently hidden from me, but it ought to be with Donal. Unless he's lost it somehow."

"Oh," said Mel.

Again it was Viktor who seemed to grasp what was going on. "You think our Seek-and-Rescue seers will be able to run a trace?"

"Well, they might." Klaudius's mouth tightened, in disappointment or something else that Mel couldn't quite read. "They have the right kind of training, but this is a hard one. The thing is, I'm not sure the trace will work, so you need someone with more tricks up their sleeves than that."

Way off in the distance, a purple monstrosity of rotating tendrils studded with eyes and teeth and blade-like fins was floating along, causing the three smaller orange entities to flit away like frightened fish.

Klaudius wasn't lying when he said he daren't leave the Caverns for any length of time: a sense of background threat permeated everything, chilling Mel's skin, making it hard for her to breathe.

"If you mean Mordanto," said Viktor, "then I don't think we can just roll up at the gates and expect a welcome wagon, much less prod them into real effective action."

He knew Tristopolis far better than Mel ever would, but this matched her perceptions of the way the city worked: the mages held themselves aloof, most likely with good reason, while normal citizens liked it that way, because the things mages dealt with were matters best ignored if you wanted anything like a normal happy life.

Enough of this.

"I just want to find Donal," she said.

And go home with him to Finbar afterwards: that part didn't need saying.

"Which requires something to make the mages of Mordanto pay attention," said Klaudius.

Mel swallowed, mostly out of her continuing fear at being in the presence of a Guardian.

"A call from the Commissioner ought to do it," said Viktor. "Have you got something I can use to convince him?"

Phone calls, crystals, mages who lived in dark baroque towers: so many factors, so many ways to confuse running around busily with actually making progress.

None of this was good.

There has to be a quick way through this mess.

The problem was, Mel couldn't see it.

"I can't repurpose any talismans or authentication hex-crystals," said Klaudius, "but you could do with something that would make anyone take you seriously, the Commissioner or Professor Steele or anybody else in the know."

Grim lines deepened in Viktor's face, which puzzled Mel for a moment until she realised that whatever Klaudius came up with was likely to be dangerous and esoteric and altogether far too risky for ordinary human beings.

"I can go alone." Mel decided she had to speak up. "If you're talking about Mordanto, I can go there by myself to ask for help, if you give me something that will get their attention."

Otherwise she would be left standing outside the gates, ignored and unable to enter ancient premises that were protected and guarded in ways that someone like her would be incapable of imagining, much less defeating.

Klaudius was smiling at her.

Thanatos, he's frightening.

Even his approval scared her.

"That gives me an idea," he said.

Wonderful.

Mel braced herself for whatever was about to happen next.

FORTY-FOUR

Aggie swam through solid rock, far below the surface, like an oceanic creature in the cold-current depths, feeling her way forward via senses that had no human-language name as far as she knew, although with mages you never could tell what they picked up on.

I should have come here long before.

So many individuals nearby: a knowledgeable observer might think Cataclysm Reaches formed some kind of haven for wraithkind, given the sheer numbers that congregated here for social and dwelling purposes, for their own multi-level culture and subcultures: the kind of interactions that remained invisible to macro-flesh solids, plus the more visible wraith-humankind relationships.

They ranged from the everyday to the uncommon, from the business-like and official to the twisted and unethical and even downright sordid: all aspects of life existed here.

There were wraith dwelling-structures that to human eyes would appear like unremarkable hives, with small hollow cells containing the few macrodimensional objects their owners possessed, while the conjoining, parallel compactified-dimensional structure formed a blazing angular construct of rectilinear complexity and elegance surrounding the entire complex: an architectural glory shining in the equivalent of magnificent metallic hues no human had ever seen.

A few wraiths regarded her as she passed nearby, but no one broadcast animosity or even an untoward amount of interest: so far everything felt okay.

My lovely Donal.

She had carried the vortex endpoint with her as she travelled along the phone wires from Police HQ to the coffee shop where Donal had been ringing from. It had been like dragging an immense iron cage or similar, except that the resistance had not been mesoscopic or macroscopic inertia but a mixed-dimensional drag effect, a form of friction, and all the more painful for it.

It had hurt, but she needed young Donal out of the way and the vortex had offered a fast solution that should, in the end, leave Donal unharmed.

Not so young these days.

Humans were short-lived, that was the problem. It was hard growing so attached to them, when their time was so fleeting.

Still, he was always one of my favourites.

She hoped he was going to be okay, down there in the labyrinth below the 709th Precinct.

Brian is trustworthy in his own way.

Aggie had more than once turned a blind metaphorical eye to Brian Fixtovax's regulation-bending ways in the past: on occasion, she had even helped him smuggle goods in or out of Police HQ, always after making sure the goods in question were not going to cause a real problem for ordinary people of any kind.

It had amused her to help in those dodgy endeavours, all the while knowing she had a human ally ready for any occasion when she herself might need to act outside the normal constraints of TPD rules and wraith behaviour in the workplace.

After several human generations' worth of service to the TPD, she was accorded a considerable amount of leeway by the official powers that be, but from time to time that wasn't quite enough.

There hadn't been many occasions to make use of Brian in the past, but sending him to the 709th to check up on Donal Riordan – she had given Brian the instruction just before diving into the phone apparatus to see Donal, knowing already she was going to transmit Donal via vortex to the 709th's labyrinth – was decent payback for all the favours she'd done Brian before now.

Of course, it was Brian who earlier had warned her that Donal was investigating Talon's disappearance – the word came from Brian's cousin, the restaurant owner, who hadn't known the implications of the information he passed on – and the irony was, by sending Donal along the vortex, she was solving his investigation for him: Talon would still be there in the labyrinth, although whether he would survive his previous treatment, Aggie neither knew nor cared very much.

Talon's almost as bad as the Draxoleth.

Or more precisely, as she was beginning to suspect, the Draxoleth-Kandroknar composite: an unholy creature far different from her own reinvention as the aggregate of Xalia and Gertie, freewraiths both, who'd been through their own sort of trial and came out as the Aggie she was now.

Either the Draxoleth or the Draxoleth-Kandroknar composite had preyed for so very long on wraithkind: in vast swathes years ago, then quietly in the background so no one was likely to pick up on the odd disappearance here and there, followed by a recent resurgence in cases which Talon knew nothing of, but never mind.

Finding and torturing him had been deeply unpleasant, for all that he deserved it, but it confirmed who was responsible for the earlier cases: Talon's empire had been built on macroscopic blood and wraithkind agony, with Kandroknar at his right hand (and the Draxoleth in turn as Kandroknar's unseen right hand or more, something Talon himself barely understood).

More recent cases clearly had the same perpetrator or perpetrators, minus Talon.

I've got to stop them.

There was a shift in the solid medium through which Aggie swam.

Here it consisted of ancient bone, from a time that some among wraithkind remembered – the time of giants – and yet those few old-timer wraiths refused to share knowledge of that time, saying only that the suffering had been dreadful and could never be repeated, which meant all actual knowledge would die with them, the oldest wraiths of all.

I wish I could call on Hellah to help me.

The Guardian had proven sympathetic to Aggie's request regarding Talon's interrogation, and prior to that, Hellah had helped to maintain the vortex traps that led to the otherwise defunct 709th Precinct; but today Hellah was on a most important mission of her own, one that might – if successful – take months.

By now she would be sequestered on Crepuscula Island, which lay thousands of miles from here and straddled the Terminator Line: maybe the least of the strange factors dominating the nature of that island, according to tales shared by the few wraiths in the know.

So no immediate return for Hellah: that wasn't happening.

And no point in trying to enlist Klaudius's help: not only was he far less likely to be sympathetic to the cause of revenge for past atrocities regarding wraiths, he was right now the sole Guardian on duty in the Caverns deep below Police HQ, meaning he could not afford to leave even if he wanted to.

Aggie increased the speed of her flight through the solid ground.

Should I have suspected someone in this district all along?

Hellah had learned much from Talon – and passed it on to her, Aggie, back in Police HQ, just before Hellah's departure for Crepuscula – but Talon's association with Alej Kandroknar had finished years ago, ending in a way that made sense for them both.

At the time, those who knew anything at all had assumed that Kandroknar perished along with the team of enforcement mages sent to capture him.

More recently, with Talon under interrogation, most of what Hellah came back with was details of suffering wraiths back in the day, simply adding to the catalogue of atrocities that Aggie and a handful of other wraiths had already compiled – over the past five years in particular – but the nature of some of that torture had formed the first clue that led to a singleton being involved, not just a twisted mage from Zurinam.

Kandroknar had possessed a helper, or more.

A friendly security witch had helped the investigating wraiths access immigration archives – maintained by Bone Listeners, naturally – and some painstaking cross-referencing led Aggie and her friends to conclude that a singleton called the Draxoleth had entered the Federation around the same time as Alej Kandroknar.

Aggie remembered the mixed feelings in the group – its numbers varied between five and seventeen wraiths, including her, over time – as they grew excited before lapsing into doubt, a cycle repeated many times over, while they swirled around in a conference chamber formed of dull, insulating, compactified-dimensional para-matter that was safe from eavesdropping by others of their own kind.

Some of the victims had been made to serve a powerful master in unimaginable ways, coerced and subject to unbreakable commands, so Aggie and her friends trusted no one outside their circle: they couldn't afford to.

Now, flying on through solid ground, she replayed those conferences in her memory, but the chances of deducing something new were pretty much zero: she'd hammered at this for such a long time already.

Those official records regarding the Draxoleth entering the Federation were a long way from being conclusive – no one could know better than a freewraith like Aggie how easy it was to bypass human restrictions, even when witches and Bone Listeners and mages were involved – but there were other hints, from survivor tales among wounded wraiths whose stories had been catalogued, that a singleton wraith had been involved in controlling and torturing them.

And on feeding upon others: the number of wraiths who had simply perished was into the hundreds for sure, and might even be larger.

We can't fight a singleton.

Such wraiths differed from each other but invariably grew huge and possessed great power, and were hard to face unless a great mass of organised wraiths went up against them, but Aggie was practically on her own: she might be willing to fight, but her friends were far better at conducting sympathetic interviews with victims and compiling records for analysis than actual confrontation, much less all-out combat.

All signs were that the Draxoleth was powerful even for one of its ilk.

Aggie increased her speed even more, not knowing why she felt such a sense of urgency after years of investigation.

Donal. Why were you with the Abomination?

It went by the name of Martina, but that didn't matter.

When Aggie manifested out of the phone in the coffee shop, dragging the not-yet-visible vortex endpoint with her, she had been startled to recognise the white bipedal creature that had space-shifted instantaneously to take up position next to Donal Riordan.

Among the wraiths Aggie worked with on this mission for justice – part-time but consistently, starting seven years ago and intensifying after the first two years – the Martina thing was called the Abomination for good reason: it was a once-free spectre voluntarily bound to a quasi-golem macroscopic form, essentially a living mannequin.

It had appeared on three known occasions and most likely a handful more over the past five years, interfering when one or other of the investigating wraiths came close to following a solid lead.

Vicious encounters, all of them.

The Abomination preferred to wound rather than kill, judging by her actions, but that was the only good thing about her: the wounds that she inflicted brought delirium and madness as well as pain, while her very nature was an affront to every natural spectre and by extension to other compactified-dimensional denizens, meaning wraithkind in particular.

Disgusting.

Or perhaps Aggie shouldn't feel that way without knowing the full story, but there was a limit to how much empathy she could muster at times like this.

Her onward flight slowed.

Fewer wraiths inhabited the fossilised-bone surroundings here, so Aggie coasted to a near stop, drifting just a little inside the solid bone, opening up her perceptions, questing in every direction, part of her hoping she was right, the rest of her terrified of exactly that and hoping she was one hundred percent wrong, and that neither the Draxoleth nor Alej Kandroknar had ever been in Cataclysm Reaches or the neighbouring canyon-like feature called Cataclysm Chasm, where few sensible beings of any description cared to slither, fly or tread.

Back in the coffee shop, as Aggie had activated the vortex endpoint and directed it to swallow Donal – thereby transporting him directly to the labyrinth below the old 709th Precinct – the Martina Abomination had space-shifted away, straight to the corridor outside the coffee shop, clearly realising that a fight against Aggie wouldn't be as straightforward as her earlier confrontations, because Aggie was old and strong and knew how to fight, unlike the Abomination's previous victims.

Drifting now, Aggie let her senses spread out, alert for resonances of various kinds, sniffing out signs of wraiths under mental domination or being tortured or worse, but finding nothing, not yet.

I might be totally wrong.

There should have been time to talk to Donal in that coffee shop, to find out what he knew.

Aggie was almost certain that she'd sniffed singleton-wraith resonances upon him – a quasi-scent that shouldn't linger on a normal human being, even a resurrected man, but appeared to with Donal – plus a whiff of ethereal miasma, a phenomenon associated primarily with the Chasm in Tristopolis, and nowhere else nearby for hundreds of macroscopic miles – and these were strong hints, but an actual conversation would have been nice.

It had been the Abomination's presence, plus the need to control the vortex endpoint after dragging it all the way from Police HQ – few wraiths would understand the amount of effort and danger involved, and for sure no one else would – that had in effect panicked Aggie, making her act far more quickly in the coffee shop than she'd intended.

I could give up and go back to the 709th.

It was tempting.

Maybe I could say sorry and Donal and I could have a laugh together, just like old times.

Or maybe chance would be a fine thing.

Once Aggie had collapsed the vortex endpoint – the only quick way of making it safe – she had rotated most of her mass out of the macroscopic dimensions and flown through the coffee shop wall, barely processing the shocked human expressions at every table on the way, and out into the corridor, just in time to see the Martina Abomination space-shift out of sight once more.

It was clear the Abomination couldn't shift very far that way, but she could do it over and over again – how often, Aggie had no way of knowing – and that had been enough for the Abomination to disappear beyond Aggie's ability to follow, despite a swooping three-dimensional search pattern like an ever-expanding ovoid which perhaps should have been a sphere, but in any case failed to work.

After flying through halls and corridors filled with plenty of people but no white, shape-shifting, space-shifting living mannequin, Aggie had given up the search and began her current flight, following the clues picked up as scented resonances upon young Donal's form just before she stuffed him down the vortex to the 709th Precinct.

So here she was, drifting through solid giant bone, questing.

There's nothing here.

For over five years there had been all sorts of false clues and trails that led nowhere. She ought to be used to failure by now.

This is so hard.

She might be old and strong, but maybe she was *too* old, and if only she knew a younger, more powerful wraith to pass the mantle onto, she could have shifted most of the responsibility for hunting down the enemy to them.

Doesn't matter.

The other thing about growing old was learning to accept the world as it was, not the way you thought it should be, especially given the inevitable limitations of your own knowledge and expertise.

I'm here now.

Very quietly, letting herself grow silent inside, she spread out her senses even further.

Still nothing.

Like meditating, stray thoughts could be welcomed then allowed to disappear.

Nothing at all.

Solid bone, the ground all around, and she felt suspended in stillness the way a balaena-whale might float in place deep below the surface in an empty ocean, all alone.

Nothing…

So very peaceful, the—

Something.

Like a faint howl laced with the acid taste of great suffering, a distant resonance came to her attention.

Yes. That way.

She had it now.

I'm coming.

Aggie began to move in that direction, flying straight and true within the titanic stratum of ancient bone, feeling deadly purpose suffuse her being.

Hold on.

Moving faster.

Just hold on.

Wanting confrontation.

I'm coming.

Needing vengeance now.

FORTY-FIVE

Donal was out on the street with a fully loaded Magnus beneath his left armpit, a wallet with enough cash for a taxi fare to anywhere reasonable – not to mention an undeposited cheque for three thousand florins, courtesy of Susan Talon – and a burning desire to get to Police HQ and make his way somehow down to the Caverns.

In the past, the obvious lift-wraith to ask would have been Aggie, assuming he got inside HQ at all now that he was technically a civilian, but Aggie was the one who'd sent him to the labyrinth, so she was out.

What the Hades am I going to do in the Caverns?

He'd never even been there, but the answer was obvious: ask Hellah or Klaudius for help, since it was their domain after all, which disconcerted him because suddenly he didn't know why he was panicking on Mel's behalf.

Won't the Guardians be looking after her?

Lamis had said he hadn't seen a Guardian before he fell into a vortex trap, but that his falling into the trap would have triggered some kind of signal – or something of the sort – that Hellah and Klaudius would definitely have picked up on.

I need to know for sure, that's the thing.

So, Police HQ it was.

Hellah tortured Talon at some point.

Or simply terrified him enough by her presence that he spilled everything he knew, and this implied some sort of collusion between Hellah and Aggie, not to mention the other wraiths Talon had talked about – the ones who'd actually tortured Talon before Hellah turned up – all of which was puzzling but not truly worrying, because in the end Hellah and Aggie were on the side of righteousness.

They had to be.

Now, according to the rectangular indigo corner sign hanging almost overhead, this was 11507th Avenue, which meant it was going to take some time to get to Avenue of the Basilisks. A phalanx of purple taxis was caught up in what looked like gridlock, so he might be better off jogging a few blocks to find a clearer road or even the nearest Pneumetro station.

On the other hand, two black-and-grey phone booths stood across the street, both appearing empty, and that was the fastest way of all to get in touch with someone.

It was easy enough to thread his way among the stationary cars – their drivers looking annoyed or resigned or simply blank-faced – and to reach the far sidewalk, pull open a concertina door and slide into a booth.

He shovelled in coins and spun the cogs to a number he would probably remember for the rest of his life, and held the handset to his ear.

"Police HQ," came the answering voice. "Duty desk. How can I—"

"Hey, Eduardo. It's Donal Riordan."

A momentary pause, then: "Loot! You're okay!"

"Sure I am. You sound surprised."

"Your missus and Sergeant Harman and that mage, Mage Lamis, was worried about ya, is all." Eduardo might have been taking diction lessons from what he said before, but you wouldn't have known it from the way he sounded now.

"I'm worried about Mel," said Donal. "I know she went down to the Caverns. Is there any way to—"

"Hey, pal. I mean Loot. I mean Donal. She's okay. It's all… Well, she's sort of fine, really."

Outside the grimy booth, engines growled as the traffic started to move at last.

"I don't like that *sort of*, old friend."

"No Loot, see, she came back out and left along with Sergeant Harman, and she's walking just fine and all, so she's not injured or anything like that."

Street cops sometimes read out from their notes to describe a case or incident in a kind of strangled jargon, and occasionally sound that way when simply talking to a superior officer over coffee, but even at their most informal and laid back, they rarely actually babble; yet Eduardo sounded close to doing that right now.

"Slow down," said Donal. "Slow and easy, right?"

No beeps had sounded in the earpiece, but he shovelled in some extra coins just in case, not knowing how long this might take.

"She walked out under her own steam, like." Eduardo's voice deepened as he spoke more carefully. "Sergeant Harman was with her, walking beside her, kind of thing, but like keeping his distance."

"Okay…"

"On account of the glowing light thing around her, see."

Donal turned to look at the slow-moving traffic outside, not really focussing on it or anything else in the immediate vicinity: nothing apart from the words he heard.

"Tell me," he said.

"They headed down the steps and the deathwolves watched them, including FenSeven's son, you know? The doors stayed open so I watched them go all the way down to the motorbikes, right? The bikes was already waiting."

As a beat cop and then a detective, Donal had taken many a statement from a rambling witness, but Eduardo was a long-serving cop — his lower body being submerged inside and conjoined with the great granite block that served as the duty desk marked only the second half of his career — and he was usually more precise and concise than this.

"Which bikes?" asked Donal.

"Huh? Oh, the HRU, you know? Maybe thirteen, fifteen of the buggers."

Donal had never had much to do with the Helway Riders Unit, but Harald Hammersen had sometimes taken his Phantasm IV to the HRU training tracks, and once — at least once, to Donal's knowledge — Harald had taken Viktor with him.

Maybe Viktor had maintained contact with the riders, and been able to call in a favour or whatever.

"I rang down to the garage," added Eduardo without prompting. "Seems they're headed out to Mordanto, taking your Mel and Sergeant Harman with them. At least, that's what they told old Freddo before screeching off at high speed, like."

"Thanatos," muttered Donal.

But the main thing was, Mel was safe.

Nothing else matters.

Even if she was on her way to Mordanto.

Because she's still looking for me?

That seemed most likely — attempting to recruit mages to help her — but there could be other reasons he hadn't thought of.

"There was something you said," added Donal. "Something about Viktor keeping his distance from Mel. And a, what, shining light?"

"Er…"

"Eduardo. Tell me."

"Yeah, sure. I mean…" A kind of *hmmph* sound followed, along with something that was neither sigh nor moan but a little of both. "There's like circular sheets of light surrounding her."

"There's *what?* You mean surrounding Mel?"

"Um, yeah. Like two of them, I think, mainly. One kinda level with her waist, like a shiny ring of light but a few feet away from her body, kind of thing. And the other running like over her head and in front of her and behind, and disappearing into the ground underneath her. Flat circles, no, rings, like ribbons a few inches wide, but made of light."

"Around Mel," said Donal.

"Yeah. The rings move with her, you see. And there's other extra bits that appear and disappear, kind of jagged."

"Jagged."

"Like lightning, but the way a kid would draw it, or you'd see in a comic book."

It had been a long time since Donal looked at a comic book – and for now, Finbar remained far too young – but he got the point.

"She looks fine," added Eduardo. "I told you that, right? Like she was happy, almost, about the light rings or whatever they are."

"Bleeding Hades."

"That's what I thought, Loot. Don't ask me what's going on."

Donal rubbed his face and leaned against the booth, and thought.

"Heading for Mordanto," he said.

"Yep. What Freddo said."

"And Mel looked okay with these rings of light or whatever the Hades they are."

"Hundred percent, Loot."

Was Mel taking something to the mages? Something that would help them?

Or cause the mages to offer their help in return.

Maybe that was closer to the truth.

"Hey, Loot?"

"What is it?" said Donal.

"Got a whole load of struggling perps and some unhappy-looking officers coming up the steps. Looks like check-in time for the holding cells and seven or nine new guests."

Donal shook his head. "I'm sure they'll have a wonderful time. Thanks for your help."

"Hey, any time, Loot. I'm always here." Somehow, Eduardo never sounded glum when saying that.

"That's reassuring for the rest of us," Donal told him. "Hang loose, pal."

"You too, Loot."

Donal pressed the cradle to disconnect the line.

What the Hades is going on?

Mel going to Mordanto, okay. But surrounded by moving rings of light and escorted by a squadron of Helway Riders?

He lowered his hand, so the handset was down at his hip and the braided cord was stretched, and stared out at traffic that was starting to draw to a halt once more.

So much confusion.

Not thinking about traffic or urban infrastructure, not right now.

Lamis.

On the other side of the street, Lamis was the first to squeeze out of the nine-foot stone pedestal or miniature tower – whichever – then he turned to help first Talon and finally Brian through the gap made by the open black iron door, all of them looking worn out by the climb up from the catacombs below.

Talon.

Supposedly the object of Donal's current assignment, and that was something he could finalise in something like a professional manner.

"Someone will answer at any time," Susan Talon had said, back when she'd given him a phone number to memorise, along with the cheque for three thousand florins he had yet to deal with.

And later, the witch Rilena had said: "And the answering service can always reach me, pal."

There'd been a hint of playful flirting in those words, but she'd meant business, yet since saying goodbye to her and the muscular blue-skinned Balagron, Donal had managed without their help.

Not that things had exactly gone smoothly since that point, but never mind, because finding Konrad Talon was the whole mission as far as Susan Talon, Rilena and Balagron were concerned – not to mention Axelson, the Axe – and there was Talon Senior now, standing right there on the other side of the road, looking physically intact, more or less.

Traumatised for sure, but that was just tough: no huge amount of sympathy here. Talon was still a crime lord.

Or maybe an ex-crime lord, after all he'd been through, and perhaps that would work out better for everyone, although you couldn't tell: instability in the underworld was by its nature unpredictable, and there was always the possibility of innocents getting hurt.

Here we go.

Donal spun the cogs to the number young Susan had given him.

Five full rings sounded, before that young-old, girl-woman voice said: "Hello?"

"Riordan here. I've found your father."

"You've—"

Using his foot, Donal pushed open the concertina door of the phone booth and held it there, then used his free hand to point to Lamis, jabbed his finger in Talon's direction, and hooked his hand back in a beckoning motion.

Ignoring Brian over there, who looked like someone not wanting to attract any kind of attention at all, so fine: let him wander off by himself, if that's what he wanted.

Lamis said something to Talon, then tilted his head just as the traffic lights changed from blue to red, the *stop* signal, which surely couldn't mean that Lamis controlled the lights… or did it?

Mages.

Just when you think you know what they're capable of, out they come with some other surprise.

Lamis and Talon threaded their way among the cars, and as they neared the booth, Donal reached out for Talon's sleeve and handed him the phone.

"Talk to Susan," said Donal.

"To—Oh, Thanatos." And, into the handset: "Sweetie? Is that my girl?"

Something like a sob came from the earpiece, and Donal slid past Talon, moved him gently inside the booth, then let the concertina door pull shut, giving the man some privacy.

"Maybe we did some good, Mage." Donal glanced back inside the booth. "I like his daughter."

"Ah," said Lamis. "I missed that part, when you talked about the case back in Cataclysm Reaches. Talon might be shady but his daughter isn't, is that it?"

"About the size of it."

The traffic appeared to be moving freely now. Overhead, beneath the deep purple sky, a trio of scanbats slid through the air, in parallel with 11507th Avenue.

Three scanbats together?

Donal couldn't recall having seen such a formation before. Normally the things flew solo, and you could go many days without ever catching a glimpse.

"Something is happening," said Lamis, his deep voice hard to hear against the traffic sound, even for someone with a zombie's sensory acuity.

Like any Tristopolitan with an ounce of visual imagination, Donal could work out important directions by referencing a mental map of the city: he knew which way 11507th Avenue ran.

"They're heading for Mordanto," he said. "The scanbats."

Even as he said that, another two scanbats appeared, criss-crossing at oblique angles higher in the sky.

"Surveillance," said Lamis. "Those two are scanning downwards, flying in an observation pattern, while the first three are on their way back for analysis."

Not many people had witnessed that process: the way a scanbat would be lowered on a harness so its near-spherical "head" (more like a model of a giant moth's head than a bat's) approached a specialist mage's head, and continued to lower until both scanbat head and the mage's true head occupied the same space – some kind of quantal superposition or something – and when the harness eventually pulled the scanbat back up, the mage would be left with an eidetic visual memory of everything the scanbat had seen in its flight, from leaving the Mordanto eyrie to the moment of its return.

Donal had never been able to think about that without a queasy feeling in his stomach.

The things they get up to.

Whatever you might think about mages, no one could say they flinched at or backed away from unpleasant tasks. Nothing Donal had read or heard suggested a surveillance mage enjoyed the memory-merging process, not even a little bit.

"Maybe," said Donal, "the scanbats are the reason for the cars being on the move, after being stuck. Traffic control, getting rid of gridlock, all that."

Lamis shook his head.

Inside the booth, Talon was spinning the cogs to another number, making use of the money that Donal had put in the phone, but never mind: that cheque for three thousand florins remained in Donal's wallet right now, so you could call this a minor business expense, the kind that wasn't even worth writing down.

Far away down 11507th, a pillar of white fire shot up from the ground.

What the Hades?

A crack of sound: a percussive rip in the air.

One moment everything had been normal, then blazing whiteness tore upwards, bisecting the street view and the deep purple sky above.

And then it was gone.

Nothing.

Everything looked the way it always did, apart from the squeals of brakes as cars travelling towards Mordanto jerked to a halt, followed by the traffic coming this way, probably reacting to other cars stopping as much as the blaze that would have lit up their rear-view mirrors, for that one long moment.

Donal continued to stare, but nothing else untoward was happening.

"It took out the scanbats," said Lamis beside him.

"What?"

"The scanbats on their way to Mordanto. I felt the quantal scream of their immolation."

Donal stared into the blasted sockets where Lamis's eyes should have been. "I don't like the sound of that."

"You shouldn't."

Mel wouldn't have been anywhere nearby. She might be travelling to Mordanto, but she'd left a while back — *I should've asked Eduardo exactly when she left* — and her start point had been Avenue of the Basilisks, meaning she would approach Mordanto from a different direction without crossing 11507th at any part of her journey.

She was heading for one of the safest places in Tristopolis, surely.

"No one would ever attack Mordanto, would they?" Donal found himself asking. "It would be suicidal, even for a dark mage. I mean... Wouldn't it?"

The lines in Lamis's face seemed to deepen, the ruined eye sockets to grow darker like twin caves in a dangerous cliff, and his voice when he answered rumbled deeper than ever.

"A dark mage like Kandroknar might send others to die in his place."

That was a point well made, and it felt as if something had clawed Donal's stomach right out of him. "But he's just one mage, isn't he?"

Again, Lamis looked like the face of doom.

"I'm no longer sure of that," he said.

Behind Lamis, the phone booth door opened and Talon took a slow step out, blinking like someone waking up, rubbing his face, standing a little straighter than before.

"Help's on its way," he said. "I've organised a car."

Donal felt like calling him an idiot – surely he'd at least seen the flash of light – but maybe you had to have been looking in the right direction, and maybe Talon's cognitive state was irrelevant in any case.

Unless he could actually prove useful.

The traffic's still a mess.

He looked at Talon. No animosity showed in Talon's expression right now. Donal had sort of bullied him but Talon might regard that as a favour, all part of the process of freeing him from the labyrinth below the 709th Precinct.

"Your people," said Donal, "have a lot of fast transport, right?"

"My people? Of course we do."

"Couriers as well as heavy goods?"

"I don't... What are you getting at, Riordan?"

Donal pointed at the lines of mostly stalled traffic, with pockets of vehicles starting up then stopping shortly afterwards. "I don't think a car is going to make fast headway right now."

"Oh."

Standing behind Talon's shoulder, looming tall, Lamis gave a deep, lined smile, saying nothing.

"Motorbikes," said Donal, getting no reaction from Talon. "We need motorbikes."

Talon still looked nonplussed.

Donal looked at Lamis.

"I don't suppose," he added. "you're feeling stronger now."

The corner of Lamis's mouth twitched. "I might be. What are you thinking of?"

"Could you summon a bike for me?"

Lamis had worked with the TPD, in what had been essentially a cover role as the police commissioner's chauffeur, back when Commissioner Vilnar was the man in charge. Any chauffeur would have seen the kinds of motorcycle that cops rode, and not just the HRU.

Beyond that, most mages couldn't manifest portals, and most of those who could might manage a range of a yard or so, but Lamis at full strength was different.

"From Police HQ?" said Lamis.

"I was thinking closer to home. My home."

Hel Ave bisected 11507th Avenue at a forty-five degree angle no more than three miles from here.

"I might be able to create a narrow portal," said Lamis. "Enough for a summoning, maybe."

"Alright." Donal was glad he'd guessed right regarding the relationship between summonings and portals.

"But I'll need to sit down for a rest afterwards, most likely," said Lamis. "Maybe even pass out."

"I don't…" Donal was about to say that he didn't want Lamis to risk his health, but he couldn't complete the sentence.

Not with Mel potentially in a danger zone at Mordanto.

"I understand," said Lamis.

Donal swallowed, staring at the stop-start traffic without truly seeing it, vaguely aware of Brian shuffling around a corner on the other side of the street, and disappearing from sight.

Talon was back inside the phone booth, no longer relevant.

Donal's stomach roiled.

"If it's dangerous," he started to say, "don't—"

Silver fire sparked in the air between them.

"I'm already doing it," said Lamis.

He raised his hands and focussed.

Come on.

Desperation was growing stronger inside Donal, perhaps because he had to stand here, knowing that he could run as far as Mordanto but not fast enough, not if this threat was truly imminent.

Kandroknar.

Of course it had to be Alej Kandroknar behind all this. Fallen-cherub features, twinkling eyes, but a holder of immense power for sure.

You've been the real enemy all along.

Not Aggie, not Axelson, not Martina: they'd been involved in various ways, but they weren't the enemy.

Nor had some rival crime lord been making a move against Talon.

Donal hadn't played chess in years, but when he did back in the day, he'd always understood moves and tactics as branching sequences of logical steps, explicable but only with concentrated effort; yet what he felt right now was different, more a kind of intuitive reading of swirling, complex patterns, like comprehending the topography of a riverbed by staring at the turbulence and flow on a fast-moving surface.

Of course.

Kandroknar, that twisted mage, once the mighty fist behind Talon's rise to power – but actually much more than that – was the real threat for sure, even if Donal didn't yet know the threat's exact nature.

Things were coming to a head – that blast of white fire had been an overt declaration of something like war – due to things that might have been happening in the background over years, but those details could be picked apart later by others: all Donal wanted to do was help put an end to an imminent threat, any way he could.

From Lamis's expression – lined and sweating as he worked the silver fire – he was working hard.

The summoning took time and cost visible effort, and when it was done, Lamis sank down on the sidewalk and sat cross-legged, and slumped forward a little at the waist, almost like some homeless panhandler looking for change, except… No, the few people who noticed him also looked away fast, going on with their business, with an edge of fear they wouldn't have felt towards a beggar.

Clearly they recognised a mage when they saw one.

Come on…

Nine minutes passed, feeling like a lifetime.

Come—

And then, far down 11507th Ave, he saw it.

A black shape with a shining silver headlight, moving in the centre of the road, avoiding the cars and coming this way fast.

Very fast indeed.

At last.

Now he could get moving.

FORTY-SIX

With the black-scaled fuel tank vibrating beneath him almost against his chest, Donal rode low, squinting against the slipstream that battered his face, moving as one with the roaring Triumphant: zero delay in tilting with the bike as they wove in and out of stalled traffic.

One long section of 11507th Avenue formed a chicane – or near enough – because vehicles were pointing every which way due to the great blasted pit in the centre of the road up ahead.

This must be where the white pillar of fire had erupted from.

What the Hades could do that?

Never mind. It didn't matter.

Almost without thought, he and the Triumphant veered left, crossed diagonally over a corner sidewalk that was free of pedestrians – some were cowering in shop doorways – and then they were into a side street, hammering hard, down two blocks before screeching through a hard right turn onto 11503rd, back on the heading they required.

Heading for Mordanto.

No Triumphant could match the smart sentience of something like a Phantasm IV – the motorbike Harald Hammersen had ridden for longer than Donal had known him – but one thing Triumphants were known for, a hallmark of that Glian marque, was heart.

Courage, strength and loyalty: who could ask for anything more?

Thank you.

Donal felt grateful that the bike had come to him when summoned and was smart enough to find the way, and he-and-bike were beginning to merge now, as they had once before during a sheer hellride, becoming a single conjoined organism moving with thunderous power and speed.

Faster now.

There was a squad car up ahead and its lights began strobing black but if they wanted Donal to slow down and stop then tough: that wasn't going to happen, not today.

Faster still.

The squad car was behind them now.

Gone.

Donal-and-bike blasted through stop lights just before the cross-traffic started to really move, and hammered onwards, taking the centre of the road wherever they could, alert all the time for the slightest of obstacles, static or moving, because at this speed the slightest impact could prove catastrophic and they could not afford that, nor any delay at all.

Again, increasing speed.

Roaring thunder: Donal or the Triumphant or both, for they were no longer separate beings, not really.

Immense speed as they tore through junction after junction, until the distant giant skull of the Orb-Sinister Freeway came into view.

Two thousand feet high on the eastern edge of midtown, it looked small enough from here, but it meant they were nearing the point where all the avenues bent through a 33-degree angle, as if someone had decided the entire grid needed to be distorted just to keep people on their toes.

They were going to need a series of shifts to edge closer to the Mordanto grounds.

Slowing a little now, looking for a likely turn.

Here.

Tyres howling, they arced into an angled side street, and poured on the acceleration once more.

Yes.

Hammering along as fast as they could go.

The last part of the journey passed a familiar corner, because Donal-and-bike had made a stepwise diagonal detour to avoid more bunched-up traffic and, contrary to his original plan, ended up on Hollow Way Drive en route to Mordanto, accelerating hard once more.

As they whipped past that dark seven-sided tower on the corner – all ninety-one storeys: he remembered – it felt as if years had passed instead of hours since he'd entered the ground-floor diner and encountered the wild-talented, untrained witch called Gina, and called in Klaudius for help.

Too bad I can't do that now.

It must have been Aggie who whipped the call crystal away from him even as she forced him into the vortex and hurled him all the way to the subterranean labyrinth beneath the 709th Precinct without even saying sorry.

So Aggie's working with Hellah but behind Klaudius's back.

Slow traffic up ahead: no time for mulling over background information now.

Less than three blocks to go.

Bike-and-Donal leaped up to the sidewalk because a van had stalled at an angle in the centre of the road before them, and there were few pedestrians here because no one walked near Mordanto's outer walls unless they had to, and somebody shouted but he couldn't tell who and they were way behind him already, so never mind.

Last block, and it was time to squeeze the brakes.

Slow now.

The Triumphant's brakes howled as they decelerated, heading in the direction of the tall rearing gates.

Thanatos.

Stopped now, but for a second the world seemed to whirl past: the cessation of massive speed felt like a visceral, dizzying shock.

We're here.

No need for an instruction: the Triumphant extruded parking legs from its bone chassis, and settled into place, understanding that the not-quite-hellride was over.

"Thank you." Donal patted the black scales of the fuel tank. "You're the best."

Nothing untoward showed on the street, the tall ancient-looking walls stood as forbidding and unmoving as ever, and the tall black iron gates remained shut as usual. Only pale streetlight illuminated the wrought insignia that looked so familiar yet often felt threatening, as it did right now.

MORDANTO HOSPITAL

&

THAUMATURGICAL COLLEGE

chrd. 6397

Still sitting on the Triumphant's saddle, Donal stared up at that insignia, shook his head, and suddenly realised that he and the bike were lucky: hurtling here the way they had, they might easily have triggered Mordanto's inbuilt defences, meaning anything could have happened.

But it didn't.

He swung his leg back and dismounted.

"I'm a friend." It should have felt weird to talk to an inanimate gate, but this was Mordanto so you could make no assumptions, not really. "Professor Helena Steele knows me, as does Mage Kelvin."

He held back from mentioning Lamis's name. That might not do him any good, not here, which was a pity.

"I'm here," he continued, "because Mel Carson is possibly with you, along with Sergeant Viktor Harman of the TPD, and there's Guardian involvement plus a threat from a mage called Alej Kandroknar."

Sometimes a gate is just a gate. Maybe this was doing no good whatsoever.

"I think the threat is imminent. Plus Kandroknar is probably behind the destruction of at least three of your scanbats. They were flying above 11507th Avenue, headed in this direction, and white fire shot straight up out of the ground and destroyed them."

Still no reply, or any sign of life from the baroque mass of towers and battlement-topped buildings within the grounds.

"I'm Donal Riordan," he added finally.

This was getting nowhere.

Behind him, the Triumphant's engine continued to run, as steady as a purr but louder, ready for anything.

Blasted mages.

You could never tell what they were thinking, what their goals might be, or even what they really did behind the scenes. They existed in almost another reality, a kind of academia-plus-arcana that part of Donal wished he could fully comprehend while another part regretted understanding as much as he currently did.

Totally useless, these mages, and utterly—

A creak sounded.

"Hello?" Donal's voice sounded odd to himself.

The great gates pulled open, slowly and steadily, until the gap was a yard wide, and then they grew still once more.

Donal looked back at his black-scaled motorcycle. "I think you'd better stay here."

With a blink of its silver headlight, the bike powered its motor down: a diminishing rumble, then stillness.

Right. Mordanto.

He took a breath and walked through the gap between the gates.

After scrunching his way along knucklebone gravel halfway to the nearest pointed-arched doors, Donal stopped and looked back once more. The Triumphant looked okay, steady and still on its parking-legs, on the other side of the now-closed gates.

He hadn't heard them shut.

Typical.

Feeling chill and unable to tell if it was actually the air temperature dropping or just his own physiology – a zombie should know the difference, but this was Mordanto where the usual certainties failed to apply – he turned towards the doorway, but didn't take another step.

"Hello," he said instead.

A small welcome committee was standing in front of him: Mage Winona, with her pale blue shaven scalp and stony-looking face – no more friendly than before – and three other mages whose body language indicated they were her subordinates.

Not the same combat mages Donal had seen with Mage Winona earlier, and not as hard-looking, but whether that was good or bad or neutral, he had no way of knowing.

Behind the group, the doors remained shut, giving no indication as to how the four mages had appeared in front of the doorway.

Maybe they do this deliberately.

Or maybe freaking out ordinary people was beneath them.

"This seems to be my day," said Mage Winona, "for dealing with messed-up people who should've known better."

"You'd better not be talking about Mel," Donal told her.

Mage Winona blinked slowly.

Not used to people talking back, are you?

It was something to note tactically.

"Is she the one in the light cage?" she asked.

"Yeah." Donal let out a breath. "Apparently. From what I've heard. It's not like she normally walks around that way."

The corner of Mage Winona's mouth moved, then: "She caught our attention, in any case."

A mix of relief and fear filled Donal. Mel was here already, and that was great, except that *here* was Mordanto where all sorts of things might happen, and often did.

He wondered what had happened to the Helway Riders squadron, the ones who had supposedly escorted Mel and Viktor here, but there were more important matters to deal with first.

"Mel went to see Hellah and Klaudius," Donal found himself saying. "Maybe it's something the Guardians did to her, gave her, something like that."

Then he realised that Mage Winona would have a far better idea of the phenomenon's nature and origin than he himself could ever manage, especially since all he had to go on was Eduardo's description over the phone.

"Allegedly, Mr Riordan," said Mage Winona, "you yourself went missing in dire circumstances."

It was why Mel had gone to the Caverns below Police HQ in the first place: Mage Winona was right in that.

Donal kept his gaze on hers. "You wouldn't believe how dire, but I made it back."

"Then we'll release your – friend – from her bindings, and let you all go."

"She's my partner, call her my wife, but whatever you can do to help her," said Donal, "then thank you. I appreciate it more than you can know. But there's also something happening."

Mage Winona's features shut down. "Perhaps you should avoid involvement in things you can't possibly understand."

"I understand that your scanbats are being blasted out of the sky before they can return here to their eyries for processing." Donal hardened his voice deliberately. "And I know a dark mage called Alej Kandroknar is even more powerful than you people think, and that's present tense not past, because according to you lot he died years ago, taking a bunch of your best enforcers with him."

Again, the dark blink from Mage Winona.

When she didn't answer, Donal went on: "When I talked to him earlier today in Cataclysm Chasm, he had a twinkle in his eye and a sly sense of humour, almost entertaining, but the more I think back, the more I think he might be the most powerful mage I've ever met, present company included."

Again, Mage Winona did not speak.

"No offence," added Donal, emphasising the irony because this one could do with a verbal, emotional prod.

"Maybe I've misjudged you," she finally said in a neutral tone.

That judgement might be better or worse than before: she gave no clue either way.

"Touché," said Donal.

"Hmm."

Mage Winona looked up into the sky, which seemed no different from normal: unchanging deep purple – appearing a bit darker over Mordanto, but that too was usual – and devoid of movement, which perhaps was the problem.

"We've deployed our scanbats," she added.

"I know. I saw—"

"And I heard what you saw. The gates told me everything you said. What I mean is, we deployed *all* our scanbats. Every one of them."

"Oh."

"Exactly. We knew something was coming, or suspected it at least."

Suddenly, Donal felt out of place and useless.

"I don't want to get in your way," he said. "But I'd like to see Mel, if I can."

These people were gearing up for an emergency situation that he couldn't help with. Distracting them might be a bad thing for the city and everyone in it, Mel included.

Finbar.

Baby Finbar had a trained security witch to look after him, and Ingrid Johannsdóttir would defend him as if he were one of her own children – Donal knew that for sure, felt certainty in his bones – and normally that would be more than enough, but whatever was developing right now might be more than even she could handle.

The rearing citadel of Mordanto's buildings looked huge and foreboding, filled with power – which was exactly right: it truly was – and it might be the greatest defence possible against some dark arcane threat, but it might also be the target, therefore the worst place for a powerless mundane to be – actually two mundanes, him and Mel; three if you included Viktor.

"You'd better come inside," said Mage Winona, "and join your other half."

"Is that best?" Maybe it would be better for Mel to come out and they could leave on the Triumphant together.

For leave read flee: it would be a retreat, for sure. A flight from danger, the last thing he would have considered before turning into a family man.

And suddenly, the idea of running away turned one hundred percent abhorrent.

Mage Winona was starting to say something, but he overrode her with: "Mel's a fighter, and I'm… me. Whatever we can do to help, we'll do it."

That felt good, deep inside, as if his guts had been all twisted up before and were now settling into place, exactly as they should.

For the first time, Mage Winona smiled.

"You'll do, I think," she said, before turning to the other mages, adding: "You know what to do."

Without a word, the three stepped apart from each other and raised their hands in a series of gestures – conjuration mudras or some such thing – and the air grew even colder while another feeling grew, like the buildup of static with the approach of a storm, and it came as no surprise when a vertical ring of sapphire blue light manifested and began to whirl and brighten.

All three mages looked absorbed in concentration: a kind of mental focus as hard as anything a boxer might require in the ring or a sniper on the battlefield, drawing on every internal resource and generating a pitiless intent, the kind allowing nothing whatsoever to get in the way.

Donal got ready to dive through the portal.

"Now," said Mage Winona.

So Donal jumped.

Sapphire-blue light whirled all around, turbulent cold air washed over his skin, and for a moment he was falling forwards, face-and-chest-first, as if gravity had switched to a horizontal direction; and then reality crispened and darkened and he was through, landing on one foot then the other, absorbing the mild impact, his foot strike causing the tiniest of echoes, for he was inside a gloomy chamber.

No sign of Mel.

This ain't right.

Neither Mel nor Viktor, not young Mage Anderl or any other mage at all, appeared before him.

Instead, a porcelain-white figure stood there – just that solitary figure, no one else – in the centre of a stone chamber formed of grey blocks carved with odd angular runes; and Donal started to reach for his Magnus, but stopped himself.

The dark grey coat was gone, along with the headscarf and orange-tinted glasses, but it still wore the grey skirt suit and pale pink blouse. One detail regarding the feet: it wasn't clear whether those were actual shoes or a body-morph effect to make it look that way.

"What the Hades are you doing here?" he said.

It couldn't answer, of course, because its face was currently a blank convex surface, but the featureless head tilted to one side in a gesture that looked terribly human – suggesting a kind of amused disappointment – before it – she – put its/her hands on her hips.

Her.

Donal decided.

Her, not its.

Because there had been something there in her words, back when she had spoken to him, especially the first time, on the windy Hypoway station platform. Something that indicated she was more than some automaton, more even than a golem… and golems were in point of fact underestimated by almost everyone, as Donal had learned not so long ago.

"Martina," he went on. "Is this Mordanto?"

She nodded her featureless ovoid head.

You've subverted a mage portal.

Those three mages under Mage Winona's direction had been transporting him to somewhere else inside Mordanto – Mage Winona hadn't been entirely explicit, but he was almost certain of that – yet Martina had somehow redirected his passage so he'd ended up here, in some out-of-the-way cellar beneath one of the buildings, or so it seemed.

Clearly Martina had entered the grounds of Mordanto undetected. That in itself should have been impossible: you didn't need to be a mage to understand that much.

The thing was, Martina's nature remained unclear, but bypassing the ancient and powerful defences and messing around with other people's conjured portals… That couldn't be a natural ability, surely, nor even something she had trained to do.

She'd been given a tool or whatever, or been turned into one: that had to be the explanation.

"Is Kandroknar forcing you to do something?" asked Donal.

Martina let her arms hang straight down, and stood very still indeed.

Tiny spikes protruded from her face then, like fast-growing thorns, but only for three seconds, after which they sank back into the surface, rendering it blank and convex once more.

Then her woman features formed: elegant, heart-shaped, still pure porcelain-white like some carefully crafted mannequin, but capable of motion, of expression.

"You need to kill me," she said. "Please."

Zombie hearts don't stop with shock, which was just as well, because this was one Hades of a turn of events.

You have to be joking.

He felt totally out of his depth.

Kill you?

Out of his depth, and with zero idea of what was happening.

Not knowing what to do.

FORTY-SEVEN

Aggie could smell the stench of slaughter now, coming from up ahead as she flew through solid ground that was in fact ancient bone but huge, and that awful smell wasn't exactly airborne or even a true scent, but wraiths had never formulated alternative human-language words for their own private senses and there was no point in starting now.

Not floating molecules but their compactified-dimensional equivalent, capable of subtle resonances and delicate aesthetic combinations, evocative of times and places from memory, but not this, not now, not the overwhelming miasma of death and suffering she was flying into right this moment.

This was awful.

Wraiths don't invoke the name of Thanatos, even when everything goes to metaphorical Hades, and for the first time Aggie felt that was wrong, because she needed to cry out now for something greater than herself: no one could expect to face this kind of reality without at least imaginary support.

She flew on, not exactly gagging, but something very close: finding it unbearable but pressing on regardless.

Kandroknar.

Hardening her thoughts once more.

The Draxoleth.

Knowing she could not back down.

Or a composite, most unnatural.

So many dead wraiths, in the past and here and now, today, and all Aggie could think of was that this monster or monsters had to die: vengeance for the tortured and the dead.

You will pay.

She was a wraith alone, but that didn't matter.

Could not be allowed to matter.

Ten minutes later, she was trapped.

No!

Too late, as she passed chamber after chamber in a honeycomb dwelling complex set into a cliff-like side of the Chasm – a complex originally crafted for a community of sorts, refashioned into the headquarters or even palace of the Draxoleth and Kandroknar or the composite thing they had both become – in which wisps of translucent macroscopic matter were strewn, ribbons of torn ethereal offal, all that remained of what had been until today living, thinking wraiths.

Each had possessed a personal life, a world no less rich than Aggie's own, and the scale of all that suffering dwarfed even the atrocities she'd been logging for the past seven years; and all of it was dreadful and that was no excuse for letting her guard down, except she did just that and she was done for.

White bolts of something like lightning slammed through her.

Stop!

Slammed and continued to slam into her, pinning her in place in the centre of a gleaming marble-lined hallway, midway between floor and ceiling and the walls to either side, and maybe it wasn't a matter of having relaxed her defences after all, because how could she possibly have defended herself – even at her most alert – from something as fast and as powerful as this?

I'm dead.

Beams of burning white energy steadied now, piercing her: pure rods of energy at multiple angles, pinioning her in place: she was unable to fly in any direction or rotate any of her mass into or out of the compactified dimensions colloquially called crawlspace; and she would have given anything to be able to crawl away from here but too late: there'd been a defensive trap laid in place and she'd triggered it and that was that.

It hurts, so very much.

There were techniques for putting aside pain but this was pure agony and she could not deal with it, she just couldn't.

At least I'll die soon.

Agony until then, but at least the end of her life would end all suffering too.

She howled, in ways no human could hear but any wraith would pick up even from a distance, except there were no others of her kind around, not for miles, not now.

Perhaps some, the furthest from here, had been able to flee in time.

So many…

Just hours earlier, there had been many wraiths here in the complex and in surrounding parts of Cataclysm Chasm, maybe hundreds of them, but all of them had perished in the most dreadful way possible, nearly all in the past few hours, from what she could tell.

The entire complex had become a slaughterhouse, stinking with fear and evil and death.

So many dead.

If the Draxoleth or Draxoleth-Kandroknar composite had absorbed all those wraiths' energies in the way Aggie suspected it was able to, then this was an awful being, truly awful and stupendously powerful, and if only she'd done things differently there might have been a way to avoid whatever was happening now but thinking like that was no good, because here and now she was trapped and in agony, and all her reality was pain and nothing more.

And I'll be dead soon.

Except...

I could be dead already.

But she wasn't.

It must know I'm here.

There was no reading the mind or intent of a composite being that you couldn't call anything but evil, and maybe it wanted her to suffer for as long as possible, but if it was hungry for as much power as possible then wouldn't it want to suck everything out of her, and soon?

Maybe...

All the slaughter here could not go undetected, not even in Cataclysm Chasm. After all these years of quietly snatching wraiths who wouldn't be missed, many taken from within the compactified dimensions alone with no part of themselves in macroscopic space, the composite had radically changed tactics, which meant other things must have changed as well.

Maybe it's gone.

Fled from Tristopolis or about to bring down some kind of catastrophe, some openly violent action... or maybe both, if that was conceivable at all.

So I live.

Except not forever, in fact not for very long at all, not with these beams of energy running through her and bringing pain while sapping her energies until soon enough she would expire for sure, and the chances that anyone was going to stumble in and find her – someone capable of avoiding traps and freeing her – were as close to zero as you could get.

I need...

Everything already hurt as much as she could bear – no, more than she could bear – but she was going to have to make it even worse.

I need to pull myself free.

She shuddered and howled but there was no one to hear and it didn't matter anyhow because this had to be done: there was no other way.

Now!

Aggie pulled and twisted and pushed and flexed and the movements along with the pinioning bars of energy were ripping her apart and Thanatos – yes, by Thanatos – it hurt more than she could ever have imagined, and the more she moved the worse it got, and she screamed hard even though she didn't want to.

Hurts…

That could not be allowed to matter.

Ripping and tearing herself, she intensified her efforts to pull free.

Hurts so very much.

Agony filled her universe.

FORTY-EIGHT

Mel looked at Kelvin – Mage Kelvin, but for some reason his title seemed irrelevant – and he looked back at her, frowning with what looked like puzzlement.

"I don't understand," he said.

His scalp and cheeks looked freshly shaven, his robe – like a long, fastened tunic – was of dark blue and black embroidered fabric, looking rich and heavy and brand new or newly cleaned, and the whole impression he gave was one of formality and professionalism and something more: a kind of deep, settled determination.

A powerful mage in his prime.

Also, while talking earlier about Donal, he'd shown no sign of any lingering grudge, despite injuries sustained when helping Donal out some months back: perhaps he'd decided to let go of all that baggage, which was just as well.

Something's up.

They were in a book-lined study in one of Mordanto's towers, just Kelvin and Mel and, sitting on a couch carved from a giant black beetle carapace and upholstered with soft scarlet cushions, Viktor, his long legs crossed at the ankles, watching everything from behind his blue, round-lensed glasses, his expression giving nothing away: nothing at all.

Where the air had smelled faintly of incense and cats earlier on, an ozone tang rose up now, making Mel's nostrils dilate and causing her to blink.

"You said Donal was on his way." Mel kept her tone neutral, knowing she was out of her depth in this place.

"He should've been." Kelvin shook his head. "Give me a moment."

After looking up at the ceiling for a moment, he bowed his head and began to whisper, lips barely moving, like a penitent at prayer... except this penitent stopped as if listening to a reply, before murmuring words of his own once more, and he repeated the cycle several times.

There was a telephone formed of what looked like pure amber sitting on Kelvin's desk – she assumed this was his normal study, not a room he'd just commandeered – but mages were mages, so maybe there were other ways of holding a conversation.

It certainly looked that way right now.

Kelvin sniffed and blinked rapidly several times, as if disengaging from that unseen connection with another mage, then focussed and said: "Donal was on his way here via portal. One of my colleagues saw him enter the thing with her own eyes."

On the couch, Viktor uncrossed his ankles and tilted his head. "A portal intercept, Mage?"

Mel felt a twitch of a grin move the corner of her mouth, glad she had a non-mage ally who wasn't totally lost in this place.

"Yes." Kelvin's mouth tightened.

That didn't look good.

"What is it?" she asked.

"Donal was here," said Kelvin. "I mean outside the building but in the actual grounds. Within the outer walls of Mordanto."

"Reaping Thanatos." Viktor was sitting up straight now. "How could that happen?"

Mel felt very cold indeed.

Viktor never panics.

And he wasn't obviously doing so now, but there was more emotion in his voice than Mel had heard before.

"I don't know." Kelvin looked up at the ceiling once more, as if for inspiration, before returning his attention to Mel and Viktor. "But the outer shields are intact. No portal could pass through them."

"You mean the portal collapsed," said Viktor.

Now Mel was feeling sick as well as cold.

What happens if a portal drops with someone inside?

With a soft sound, Viktor was on his feet, long coat swirling, fingers twitching as if he wanted to rip his twin Grausers out from their shoulder holsters and begin blasting, while Mel struggled to understand what was happening.

"That's one possibility," said Kelvin slowly. "But I think it's something else."

"In this place," said Viktor. "Here inside Mordanto."

"I like it even less than you do, Sergeant, believe me."

Mel shrugged her shoulders and softened her knees, adding springiness to her stance as her fists tightened of their own accord. "Tell me."

Viktor stared at her from behind those blue lenses. "He means that the intercept happened here. Someone snagged Donal out of the portal, but whoever did it had to be inside Mordanto."

"And Donal must have stepped out into some other location in the vicinity." Kelvin gestured at the room around them. "Just not the actual place he should've arrived in."

It implied Donal was still alive, or should be.

That ozone smell had been the beginning of a portal exit forming, perhaps, but it wasn't the important detail here.

"You've got a traitor, then," said Mel. "One of your own."

Kelvin showed what looked like real pain as he shook his head. "I don't know what we've got."

Viktor said: "An intruder or a turncoat, Mage. What third possibility can there be?"

That was already one more option than Mel had thought of, and for a second she thought Kelvin was about to reel off several more, but that didn't happen.

"None," said Kelvin. "There's a binary choice about what kind of person is responsible, but either way it's a massive security breach and a major problem now."

Fine-sounding academic words, but this was Donal they were talking about, not some Death-damned problem in theoretical thaumadynamics or whatever the Hades mages wrote equations about and argued over in seminars and such.

She wanted to punch someone just as Viktor had looked ready to start shooting only a few seconds earlier, but the thing about fighting in the ring is you never, ever let your emotions get in the way of reading the situation and opponent and doing what you have to do in order to first of all survive, and second of all to win.

Breathe.

Control your breathing, control your stance, control your mind.

Again.

And control the situation.

Again.

Kelvin was at his desk. Still standing, he picked up the amber phone, turned the five golden internal-number cogs simultaneously with the fingers and thumb of one hand – a neat gesture of a kind you rarely saw – and said: "Kelvin here."

There was the faintest of pauses.

Then, "Immediately," he added. "Code scarlet, silent lockdown."

Another pause, even shorter.

"Agreed," continued Kelvin. "I'm authorising lethal force. Good luck."

His features looked as hard as Viktor's as he replaced the amber handset, then nodded.

"Shoot to kill?" said Mel.

Not liking any of this at all.

"Not bullets," said Kelvin. "But they will watch their backdrop and be careful of innocents in the foreground, just like Tristopolis's finest."

Viktor's mouth moved slightly: some kind of acknowledgment there.

"Combat mages," he said. "You're deploying combat mages."

"Of course I am. The situation clearly warrants it."

Donal was missing, but that wasn't what Kelvin was really getting at.

"When was the last time," said Viktor, "you deployed teams inside Mordanto itself?"

"Other than a drill?" said Kelvin. "It's been a lot of years, and the last time was a false alarm in any case."

"But you don't think it's a misunderstanding this time." Viktor made it sound like a statement, not a question.

Kelvin looked at Mel. "I think Donal's caught up in something real."

"Oh," said Mel.

"Very real indeed."

She'd been on the brink of reuniting with Donal, and now this.

I hate it all.

Things were worse than ever.

FORTY-NINE

Donal had drawn the Magnus but kept it pointed at the flagstones near his feet, holding it one-handed, while reminding himself that it was fully loaded but with no spare rounds for a reload, although none of that would matter if the danger proved arcane enough.

In the gloom of the cellar – the faint light came from glowmoths trapped in cages with tiny troughs filled with the silver-green lichen on which the moths subsisted: a good choice of illumination for a place infrequently visited – the white face and hands of Martina seemed almost to shimmer, while her grey skirt suit blended into the shadows.

"Why do you want me to kill you?" he asked.

"Because I can't kill myself," she said. "My master installed a behaviour-blocker hex knot inside me."

Not the clearest of explanations, but Donal got the gist, and he didn't like the word *master* at all. "So why would you want to kill yourself, if you could?"

"To stop me, of course."

"Stop you from doing what?"

"I—" Her mouth continued to work, but no more sounds came out.

After three seconds, she stopped trying, closed her mouth once more, and simply looked at him.

"Alright," said Donal. "I've got it. You can't tell me, any more than you can stop yourself from carrying out some task. Under compulsion, right?"

Martina didn't possess eyebrows, but a slender line over each eye on the porcelain-white surface suggested such things, and she raised one of those pseudo-eyebrows now.

"So I'm stating the obvious," added Donal. "But here's the thing. I like you, and I really don't want to kill you."

Now Martina blinked, and Donal had the impression that if she'd been capable of tears, she might at least be damp-eyed by now.

A question occurred to him. "Were you actually supposed to drag me out of that portal thing? Did Kandroknar want you to get me here?"

"No," she said. "I saw the opportunity, as it were."

So she was able to speak once more, therefore only certain topics were off limits.

More than that.

It wasn't just speech: it was actions.

That had to be the case. It seemed likely, the more Donal thought about it, that Kandroknar really wouldn't have wanted her to interrupt that portal journey and pull him, Donal, here into this cellar.

The implication seemed clear: Martina would try to act physically against her conditioning wherever she found a kind of loophole.

Good to know.

Now all he had to do was find a way to turn that insight into a tactical advantage.

"Can a mage, or a group of mages" – he formed the thought as he spoke – "prevent you from carrying out this action? Preferably without actually harming you."

Martina shook its – no, her – head.

"I don't suppose," Donal went on, "a freewraith could do something, could she? I know one who's pretty determined."

Not mentioning Aggie by name, or hinting that she was the one Martina had already seen in action earlier, when Aggie stuffed Donal into the vortex inside the coffee shop, which meant getting Aggie's help wouldn't exactly be an easy thing.

"No," said Martina.

Perhaps skirting the subject like this prevented her from being talkative but allowed short answers.

"Death damn it," said Donal. "If I still had my call crystal, we could get a Guardian here and everything would be okay."

Letting out your frustration is rarely useful, and Donal wasn't sure why he'd just done it.

"Oh," said Martina, and began to shiver.

The spikes popped in and out of view across her face, seven times in succession before blending back into the porcelain surface of her skin once more. Then she unbuttoned her skirt-suit jacket, shivered once, and began to undo her pale blouse.

"No," said Donal. "Don't do that."

He held back from grabbing her: keeping his distance seemed the thing to do, while none of this was playing out in a way that made any sense at all.

Her torso was ceramic-white and smooth, and she drew the blouse open only two inches, enough to reveal that she possessed no navel, which seemed consistent with her nature.

What happened next was completely unexpected.

No!

Martina hooked her hands and pulled them onto her belly – *into* her belly – as a vertical split formed and she drew both sides apart, revealing a five-inch-high cache inside her body, containing something that looked like a brown lump in the shadows here, but would appear a warm amber in brighter light.

The slender chain attached to it was scarcely visible.

"That's my call crystal," said Donal.

Or more precisely, the crystal that Klaudius had given him, and which Donal had already used once, obtaining Klaudius's help to get rid of the entity in that diner kitchen, the one summoned by the raw untrained talent of young Gina, who was presumably somewhere here in Mordanto now, maybe even close to this cellar.

"I can't let you take it," said Martina.

Donal hadn't moved.

Can I snatch it out of her?

He was fast by human standards, but Martina could shift through space at what looked like infinite speed, and he had no idea what would happen if she did that while his hand was inside her abdominal cavity.

Plus… It didn't seem right to do such a thing, even in dire circumstances.

"You took it off me in the coffee shop," he said.

"Yes."

"Alright." He assumed the shortness of her answer meant constraints were making themselves felt inside her once more. "Understood."

Not really, but it made some kind of sense: Kandroknar might well have ordered her to snatch the call crystal if she and Donal were about to be separated, although Kandroknar probably had more mundane possibilities in mind – like Donal going off by himself in a taxi or on foot – rather than a raging freewraith stuffing him into a vortex that acted much like a portal while being an awful lot less pleasant to experience.

"Can you activate it yourself?" he asked Martina, meaning the call crystal.

"I… don't think so."

Clearly, she hadn't considered even trying.

Then her head snapped up, then sideways, as if some invisible hands were trying to break her neck, but she blinked and continued to blink until her arms whipped straight out to either side, as if she were being crucified.

Her blouse hung open, and the open split in her abdomen still contained the crystal, but the air was beginning to shimmer all around her, vibrating with a sound like a buzz-saw, and something told Donal that if he tried to reach inside that volume of air then his hand would be ripped apart in all directions.

"I'm… sorry," said Martina.

She was shaking now herself, or maybe it was the air around her: as the sound grew and the vibrations intensified, it was hard to focus on Martina as everything blurred, more and more by the second, and she was either on tiptoe or rising off the floor and none of this made sense.

Thanatos.

Perhaps he should have tried to kill her when she said.

No.

Even if that had worked – and he doubted it, without knowing why – there had to be another way.

Has to be.

All he had to do was think fast and work out what to do and make it happen.

I need to stop this.

Whatever it was, whatever was going on, it formed some kind of attack on Mordanto, and due to a bizarre series of events, only he was in a position to do something about it, except what exactly he could do, well, that wasn't clear at all.

All these thoughts ran through him fast, and he didn't think he was frozen in panic, but he still wasn't making a move, and being a pure observer wasn't going to help anyone, not even himself, and for sure not Mel and everyone else in Mordanto.

He took a step forward but it was far too late.

"No! Please…" Martina's voice was a howl, piercing even the now-thunderous sound of the shaking air.

The temperature plunged: suddenly the air felt very cold indeed.

What the Hades?

Something bad was happening, and he'd done nothing to stop it.

"Damn it, damn it, damn it." He could scarcely hear his own words.

Left foot forward, he raised the Magnus in his right hand and used his left to steady the butt, and took aim as best he could.

"I'm sorry!" he yelled.

And pulled the trigger.

Thunder filled the cellar now, but not enough to submerge the flat percussive crack accompanying the shot.

Again.

Keeping his aim steady, knowing this might not work but also that he had to try, he squeezed the trigger once more.

Again.

He fired off a third shot.

I'm so sorry, Martina.

And kept on firing until he was done: no rounds in the Magnus.

While the blurred air continued to shake and roar and he tried to look past that barrier of pure vibration but it was hard, so very hard to make out what happening inside.

Martina?

Wondering if this was it, the end.

Mel...

Then the air split apart and all vibration ceased and Martina dropped forward, meaning something had changed, but whether that was good or bad, he couldn't tell.

"Martina?" In the sudden quiet, his voice sounded flat and weird.

He swallowed, lowering the Magnus.

No wounds.

His shots had been aimed to wound – shoulders and hips – which in a normal human would have been devastating, but no rounds had pierced the vibrations around her: even her clothing looked unmarked.

From her lowered position with one knee on the floor, Martina looked up at him.

"It's too late," she said.

Donal didn't want to ask, but knew he had to. "What's happening?"

For a second, it looked as if the behaviour-blocking hex was preventing her from speaking once more, but then she gave her answer.

"I'm sorry, but it's coming."

Donal shook his head. "What is?"

"The monster," she whispered.

The cellar looked as it had before, the walls in particular looked intact, and if it hadn't been for the memory of vibration and thunderous sound, he would have thought everything was normal here.

She's breached the defences.

He wasn't a mage, but he had military experience and all the rest, meaning he understood tactics and strategy, attack and defence, even if the modes and mechanisms lay far beyond his comprehension.

Breached them from the inside.

That made some kind of sense.

"Your space-shifting got you inside the grounds, and down into here," he said.

No doubt with all sorts of enhancements added by Kandroknar, carefully crafted over years of planning: nothing of this magnitude could happen on a whim, no matter how powerful the mage.

"I'm sorry," said Martina.

She knelt on the flagstones with her blouse open, the cavity still revealed, and her porcelain features showed a depth of sorrow beyond anything Donal would have guessed her capable of.

"Can you talk now?" He looked around, saw a dark door diagonally behind him to his left, then returned his attention to Martina. "Can you come with me to warn the mages here?"

Martina shook her head.

"Too late," she said.

But everything seemed normal once more.

"What's happening?" said Donal.

"I told you… It's coming."

"Yes, but—"

Then a vast crash sounded, and the cellar shook hard, and dust spilled from the ceiling, and Donal would have expected it to spill down earlier when the air vibrated around Martina but that was just one of those irrelevant thoughts that flit through the mind in times of crisis and he knew for sure that this was one of those critical times and the stakes were mortal now.

"It's here," she said.

"What is?"

"The end of everything."

Something massive pounded everything around them again.

No…

Hard enough to throw him off his feet.

FIFTY

It was time for the man known as Alej Kandroknar to transcend, although of course he had been more than just a man, more even than the most accomplished of mages, for a considerable number of glorious years already… but this was different.

This was more, joyfully so.

So much more.

Inside the hangar space – the outer doors were shut, as per orders, while his plane stood in place right here under the roof, loaded with valuables worth multiple fortunes by anybody's standards, with all its hatches open – he had room to expand his self, more or less unobserved.

Fleischmann was personally leading his team of operatives – mercenaries in suits and ties – and right now they were at the enclosed office cabin at the rear of the hanger, ushering Braunkin, the transport chief, inside.

I'm ready.

I know.

The power inside him felt tremendous: the energy of hundreds of wraiths like some howling furnace, boiling and roiling and threatening to explode.

Fleischmann, his expression shut down and revealing nothing, was the last to disappear inside the office cabin: his operatives and Braunkin were already in, and someone was pulling down the ivory-slat blinds, just as Kandroknar had ordered.

Anyone who peeked out would die: they understood that much without being told.

It's a good distance from here to Mordanto.

That does not matter.

Of course it didn't. His thought had been playful, not criticising.

Is it time?

Almost.

Soon enough they would be on their way. Only two-thirds of a mile away, in one of the dorm blocks at the edge of Tempelgard Airport, the pilot and crew were waiting for the phone call that would bring them here by car, already fully cleared, with the flight plan filed and all the rest.

Meanwhile the aircraft stood here like some symbol of freedom, its propellors ready to whir and claw a path up into and through the air above, promising so much: a new beginning.

Another new beginning: Tristopolis had been so amusing, so interesting, after his life in Zurinam; and now another adventure could begin in Illurium, a third phase of life, just as soon as he'd made his mark on this place, left the indigenous mages' prime establishment in ruins, and never mind if they failed to recognise who was responsible for their destruction, most delicious.

That part didn't matter, so long as they all died and their symbol of greatest power, Mordanto itself, died with them.

Then he felt it: an electric shudder passing through him, a signal pulse clearly received.

The Martina has carried out its task.

Yes. The route into Mordanto is clear.

Now he – they, it – could begin.

Time?

Yes.

He took in a breath and spread his arms, tilted his head back to regard the high hangar ceiling and then it all blurred as he felt the eruption inside him, like lava boiling out from torso and limbs and even from his mouth and eyes: such a massive explosion of energy, but one that just kept going, over and over, pouring out incandescent molten power, spreading through the air, roiling, shining, burning, until half the hangar space was filled with the incandescent energies surrounding him.

Neither singleton wraith nor man nor even a composite in the normal sense, not now: a boiling sea of energies spread in the air, rooted in his human-with-wraith body yet extended and growing, and all that energy could remain in this place like a whirlpool that could carry on like this for years but that was not the plan, not at all.

We need another.

But that wasn't the plan either.

What other?

No answering thought, just the continued build-up ready to explode for real.

We need another what?

But now the urgency was here, and neither part of him/it could formulate a verbal thought as everything rose up inside and this was it: the moment to cut loose.

Ah!

Ah!

Now.

Everything exploded outwards, a rushing channel, a river of destructive energy: a torrent that flowed down into the compactified dimensions where a clear signal channel lay, the quasi-plasma conduit manifested by the Martina thing, leading all the way from here to a cellar beneath the Mordanto complex, from which everything could erupt upwards in a fraction of a second.

Blowing all those towers and the mages inside them to Hades, and about time too.

A ravening tsunami of wraith energy flowed into the miles-long crawlspace conduit, heading for Mordanto, deadly in intent, unstoppable once it reached the other end.

Such a lethal flood, travelling fast.

Very fast indeed.

FIFTY-ONE

The room rocked and books spilled from the shelves and something made of glass fell onto the floor and smashed behind Mel as she stumbled but caught herself – years in the ring and all that, but never mind the self congratulation – and Kelvin somehow stayed upright, looking almost prim in his dark-blue robe with black embroidery, while Viktor caught hold of the black-carapace couch to steady himself.

"Attack?" said Viktor.

"I don't know," said Kelvin. "And that in itself is worrying, I have to say."

Mel patted herself, hand against her pocket, feeling the hardness inside, and cursed herself for not remembering the Death-damned thing earlier.

"Here," she said. "Try this. Maybe if you can find where Donal is, it'll help you with whatever's going on."

She pulled out the dark-blue bundle, the bandanna or handkerchief or whatever it was that Viktor had lent her earlier, and unwrapped the amber object inside, along with its slender silver chain.

"The call crystal." Viktor looked at Kelvin. "It came from the Guardian. Klaudius."

From at least nine feet away, Kelvin reached out his hand, and the amulet – call crystal – flew straight into his palm. Even with mages, that wasn't something you saw every day.

The crystal flared orange, then gold.

"I don't believe this." Kelvin's eyes widened.

"Sorry," said Mel. "I only just remembered the—"

"No, not that. The other crystal isn't in physical contact with Donal, but it is right here, inside Mordanto."

Mel shook her head, not understanding.

"That doesn't make any sense," she said.

Kelvin's voice deepened and hardened. "Neither does the breach in our security, nor does Donal getting snatched from inside a portal right here on the grounds, but both things happened and there's an intruder somewhere nearby and none of that can be coincidence."

Viktor said: "What can I do?"

Kelvin looked at him. "Get ready for quick transport."

That meant a portal, Mel felt sure.

But Kelvin was heading for his desk and the amber telephone once more. He picked up the handset, connected to the same number as before, and said: "I'm about to open a portal within the grounds. Track my exit, send a tac team to that location, and tell Professor Steele."

He waited less than a second for acknowledgment, then slammed the handset down and in the same motion whirled around, then raised his hands with those mudra gestures or whatever they were called and his lips moved slightly and the air felt suddenly electric as sapphire-blue incandescence appeared in the air before him.

The portal blazed strongly and opened fast.

"Ready?" Kelvin said to Viktor.

"I'm coming too," said Mel, as Viktor answered yes.

"Now," said Kelvin.

They didn't have to take a step: instead, the portal itself swung around Viktor then Mel then Kelvin himself and the world went crazy as the blazing blueness became a whirlpool sucking them down into a maelstrom of portal-transition energies or simply chaos because this was shocking and surely it couldn't be controlled by anyone, not this force of nature, but then everything went dark and Mel fell forward and she was on her hands and knees and the world made kind of sense once more.

Kelvin and Viktor were either side of her, both standing and she might have felt embarrassed about that but no, it didn't matter now. Cold flagstones beneath her, a shadowy interior and stone walls: she was in a large chilly cellar lit by glowmoth baskets, and she had no idea what she'd been expecting but this wasn't it.

A cellar, nothing more.

Then the most familiar voice of all came from behind her. "Mel! You're safe."

In a kind of magical transition that had nothing to do with mages and their conjurations but ordinary reality, she was on her feet and Donal was holding her and kissing her and everything was suddenly alright.

"Donal," was all she could say.

But things weren't alright, not really, so they had to disengage and work out how to face the current situation, once they'd worked out what it actually was.

A female figure with white ceramic skin or something was standing there and looking at them. Her blouse and jacket were open, but whatever had been going on between her and Donal, it wasn't what a state of undress would normally suggest, because there was a gaping cavity in the living statue's stomach with a call crystal nestled right inside.

The other crystal paired to the one that Klaudius had given Mel: it had to be.

"What the Hades?" Mel couldn't help her reaction.

"I'll tell you later," said Donal, his presence alone making everything feel right. "Martina here has been acting under compulsion, but I think that's over now, right?"

The statue nodded her head.

"Yes," she said, then turned to Kelvin. "My master is a composite of Alej Kandroknar and the Draxoleth, sir. The Draxoleth is a singleton wraith, if you know what that is."

Behind them, another blue portal opened, and a team of hard-faced mages clad in dark red combat gear stepped through three at a time – three trios in all – followed by a tall, ramrod-straight lady with white hair bound up with platinum wire, who stopped in place with a walking-cane in one hand and raised the other, at which the portal behind her collapsed and vanished.

Kelvin looked at her. "Professor, it's as we thought, and something massive is about to hit us, I'm sure."

There were nine combat mages in red, plus Kelvin and this lady of a certain age who had to be Professor Helena Steele, along with Donal and Mel herself, and Viktor – also the white statue, Martina – and this was a large cellar but they seemed to be filling the place.

Then the door to the cellar opened, and a young woman with lank black hair stepped inside, looking afraid and determined all at the same time.

She looked at Donal and said: "I sensed you here."

Helena Steele cocked her head to one side, eyebrow raised, appraising the new arrival, or so it seemed.

"Gina," said Donal. "It's not safe. You need to get away."

"I don't think it's safe anywhere, but... I belong here, all the same."

Mel felt her adrenalin rise, the way it did when an opponent upped their game and the time had come to do the same or face defeat.

Donal looked at Helena Steele.

"Where do we go?" he asked.

Mel had been about to ask the same thing.

Great minds.

She felt her mouth twitch but there was no time for actual joking.

Helena Steele answered: "There's no time to go anywhere, Donal Riordan."

"What does that mean?"

"We defend ourselves from here," she said. "Or else we die."

Such an elegant-looking lady, such a patrician voice, a cut-glass accent and utter precision in her words, not to mention the shining intelligence in her gaze, but the message was stark and hard and entirely suited to the grimness of their surroundings.

Mel tensed her fists because she had to.

But I can't stop this.

The fight was in the hands of mages now.

FIFTY-TWO

In the midst of imminent disaster, Helena felt an unexpected smile growing on her face, and thought maybe it was due to Kelvin as much as her own acceptance of what was about to happen.

Also, reality slowed, as a timescale of milliseconds stretched out into apparent minutes or more, allowing appreciation and reaction even when suddenness ruled from the viewpoint of any mundane observer, such as Donal Riordan or his partner Mel or that other detective, Detective Sergeant Harman.

Such a mundane environment, this humble cellar beneath the great edifice of ancient Mordanto, venerable and steeped in wisdom, the accumulated power of so many centuries of intellectual exploration: sometimes fearful, often fearless; sometimes tragically misguided, many times simply brilliant; and never, ever dull.

Yet the immediate surroundings mattered less and less as Helena expanded her awareness, because she was in the end the head of Mordanto, meaning all of its vast resources were under her command.

She raised her arms, still holding the cane one-handed but by its middle now, and closed her eyes in order that she might see more clearly.

So much glory.

Photons falling on her retinae in the cellar conveyed nothing of the true magnificence here, but her other senses revealed it all.

She could see, just not with her eyes: all nine main buildings and seventeen subsidiaries and ninety-three smaller subordinate structures, from the ordinary to the extraordinarily beautiful in either airy or the darkest ways: gothic towers with rows of decorative knots and statues and baroque ornamentation nearly all of which could come to life if danger threatened, which was why they were stirring now.

Likewise, the castellated roofs began to shimmer blackly as the battlements filled up with defensive hex ready to pour down upon intruders, and all the thousands of artefacts within the mages' private rooms and the research and teaching laboratories and all the rest were beginning to resonate with the buildup of defensive power.

So much power.

That was due to the people she perceived as sparks of blue light, most glorious, spread out in a three-dimensional pattern throughout the buildings, along with some nine-dimensional additions in one of the advanced research towers that operated almost as a law unto itself.

Almost but not quite, because every mage here shared the same deep loyalty at heart: to Mordanto first, and secondly to the city itself, to Tristopolis and all its ordinary citizens, even though it was impossible to think of them as anything but mundanes for the majority of the time.

Such vast magnificence ruled here.

Such glories of intellect, such wonder.

It was a privilege to study here and more so, so much greater, to lead this place and all the brilliant minds within it, and perhaps it was fitting that the greatest danger should come like this, via a part of reality – of the greater reality most mundanes barely glimpsed or wondered about – that she herself was deemed an expert in: the study of singleton wraiths and their greater capabilities.

That confluence of technical speciality and professional leadership meant this was indeed her moment.

All my life has been a preparation for this, here and now.

It was such a blissful realisation that she felt herself smiling back in her tiny physical body even as her projected locus of consciousness expanded to take in all of Mordanto: every last part of it.

Like a chilly rivulet, she sensed the conduit that the intruder – the poor spectre-mannequin binding, compelled to carry out this sneak penetration by the true nemesis, the Draxoleth-Kandroknar composite – had laid down from within the cellar.

That conduit pierced the inner and outer shields and arrowed off in the direction of Tempelgard Airport, which might or might not be significant in itself.

Why there?

She sent her senses questing outwards, out beyond the boundaries of her institution, her home, paralleling the conduit all the way through the city, driving her awareness forward at speed until…

No!

Her focus, her locus of awareness stopped moving.

Impossible.

A vast torrent, a great tsunami wave of wraith-derived energies was coming towards her, plunging towards Mordanto, and she'd been expecting some tremendously powerful attack but not as vast as this.

The power here roared and shook and felt entirely overwhelming.

Hades.

She flung herself back towards Mordanto, trying not to panic, reached a point halfway between the onrushing wavefront of disaster and the safety of her home institution, and then she stopped and whirled once more: metaphorically turning to face the oncoming danger.

Coming so fast.

It was hard, but she sent a fragment of her projected volition, just a part of it, back along the thread connecting her mental awareness to her body in the cellar, and caused her body to speak aloud, for the sake of Kelvin first and secondarily everyone else who remained physically in that cellar.

"The attack is huge." It was impossible to tell what tone of voice her physical self was uttering, since most of her attention had to remain here, in this remote projected locus of consciousness.

She added: "I need all mages with me. I cannot face this one alone. Kelvin, please start the linkup now."

Like a spreading net of sapphire blue light, she could sense Kelvin and the nine combat mages and, almost impossibly, the new arrival who was not even a neophyte, combining to form the centre of that net, then starting to link up with every other mage inside Mordanto: a fast-expanding network of arcs and nodes where each node was a brilliant mind, a fellow mage.

They were all her fellows, her peers, from the newest arrival and junior neophytes to the most experienced and advanced of adepts.

Each arc within that network, each link, was a resonant mental channel of the deepest kind, so rarely employed but part of everybody's training from the earliest of their days as mages.

Such power and beauty: it would be wonderful to capture it as a painting or a symphony so that mundanes might taste at least a hint of the marvels that Mordanto mages were capable of seeing and creating and, at their best, manipulating for the greater good.

Irrelevant.

Fractions of a second were passing like handfuls of minutes, and she could be proud of the rapidity with which her people were reacting, but the enemy would be here soon enough.

Two thousand and ninety-seven mages linked minds into a single star-configuration network within those towers and buildings, with fewer than twenty unable to join because of being trapped inside sundered hyperdimensional pockets of reality or similar temporary predicaments.

The network formed in truly record time as if everyone had been galvanised by the magnitude of the onrushing danger.

That seemed in fact to be the case: the whole network resonated with fear in addition to power and courage – less a contradiction than an indication that every mage did their level best to retain their humanity no matter how arcane their interests.

Kelvin sat at the topological centre of that net, and he created the most powerful imaginable ultra-high-capacity link to her, Helena Steele, granting her full control via himself as proxy.

Thank you.

This was the most incredible gift of her entire life.

She needed to dismiss thoughts of Orin, her sort-of-late husband, and her children – poor dead Laura, poor distant Victoria-turned-Vixen – because her personal memories didn't matter here, as destruction felt imminent and that great wave of evil was closer now.

Travelling even faster than she'd imagined.

Soon now, very soon, the moment of confrontation would be upon her and all the mages of Mordanto combined: call it one form of composite against another.

And the world would get to see which type was greater after all.

I'm ready.

A great roar of encouragement came along that link, every one of those two thousand and ninety-seven mages cheering her along, even though each of them was likely to perish in the blowback blast along the network links if she lost the fight out here, halfway between Tempelgard and Mordanto.

Then again, if she failed to stop it here, the greater attack tsunami would simply carry on rushing along its conduit and erupt inside Mordanto so everyone would perish anyhow.

All those ancient baroque and gothic towers and buildings would be blown apart to shards and dust and that could *not* be allowed to happen, not so long as she, Professor Helena Steele, head of Mordanto, remained alive.

Get ready everyone.

She felt their conjoined determination rise, and in that moment, formed a realisation first and then a thought but there was no time to send it back and distribute it along the network because a narrow beam of wraith-derived energies struck her projected locus and she should have thought of it earlier, should have expected this.

The Draxoleth-Kandroknar tsunami had transmitted an attack vanguard of its own.

An even faster moving projection ahead of the main onrushing mass.

Helena yelled as she threw up shield after crumbling shield and the great enemy lance of energy was powerful and hard but she kept on blocking and finally one shield held and then another and then the narrow attacking beam dropped out of existence, defeated.

Defeated but with an edge of triumph, because the enemy had learned Mordanto's capabilities and it was not, in the end, dismayed.

It is even more powerful than I thought.

She could have kept that realisation private but chose not to, because all of her mages might die here and they deserved to know that they were into their final seconds of existence in all probability, unless she could raise her game even more than she previously considered possible.

Now, after all this time, after so many years and her beginning to transition into what she had begun to think of as a period of gracefully controlled decline.

But while part of her awareness was considering all this, another part had been analysing the taste of that advance contact with the enemy, and the results of that analysis were academically thrilling and tactically startling.

Unbelievable.

If it hadn't been for Guardian Hellah and her voyage to Crepuscula Isle, the idea might never have occurred to her, or at least not so quickly, not in time.

She was something like ninety-seven percent certain that she understood what the Draxoleth portion of the Draxoleth-Kandroknar composite was up to.

An imminent split.

The composite's overall objective might be revenge, but the portion that remained a singleton wraith wanted something more: to split, to form another.

To procreate.

"It's budding," she told her fellow mages, forming the words purely mentally, faster than normal thought. "The composite is attempting to spawn another singleton wraith while remaining a composite, which wouldn't normally be possible but right now it has so much more power that it can manage a spawning and an overwhelming attack on us all at the same time."

She had tasted the diverging strains within that moment of onslaught, and again, it was sheer luck that she, with her particular background, was the person at the forefront of Mordanto's defence right now.

Sometimes *luck* is another word for chains of inevitable causality too intricate to unravel and understand.

Again, she realised that all of this was proceeding on a scale of nineths of ninetieths of seconds, not minutes on end, meaning the mundanes back in the cellar with Kelvin would have had time only to blink since the moment the mage network began to form.

Even for her, time was running out, but there was an important thing she needed to say, because of the second realisation that had seeped up inside her.

"Fellow mages, it had been my privilege and my honour to serve you as head of Mordanto. My designated successor is Kelvin Johannsson, and I hope the Senatus Collegiorum ratifies his position unanimously. Good luck to us all."

And then it hit.

Dear Thanatos.

A vast torrent of malevolent energies, like a tsunami wave a thousand feet high, fell upon her.

It's so—

Fell and overwhelmed her.

FIFTY-THREE

In the cellar, Kelvin's eyes were blazing a bright sapphire blue that should surely have blinded him, while the nine red-clad combat mages and even young Gina were doing the same, and everyone else seemed frozen but Donal wanted to speak.

Instead, he simply thought: *They're fighting back.*

All of that signified little compared to Helena Steele: her old-lady form was now sheathed in blazing light that hovered between blue and blinding white, so it was impossible to look on her: he had to avert his eyes.

He simply had to.

Kelvin turned to look at Donal, although how a mage's eyes could shine forth brilliance while also receiving light and processing information was impossible for Donal to understand.

How are you seeing this?

It was a thought originating in Kelvin's mind, not Donal's.

I don't know. Nothing like this – whatever this was – had happened before, ever. *What's going on?*

The answering thought from Kelvin was grim: *We're losing.*

Perhaps it had been inevitable.

The enemy was hugely powerful, and they'd known that all along.

Mel…

Donal started to turn to look at her, though she and Viktor and Martina continued to stand quite still, but stopped as another thought from Kelvin resonated, strong and surprised and somehow – by some synaesthetic overtone – flavoured like tears.

Dear Thanatos, she's fighting back.

Helena? Donal's answering thought was immediate.

Kelvin's mouth tightened as his words sounded in Donal's awareness.

She's driving a wedge back.

Donal shook his head. *What does that mean?*

This conversation wasn't just proceeding without actual speech: it was happening many times faster than normal vocalisation or even normal thought.

I'm not… certain. Kelvin's thought seemed almost to stutter.

It was an interesting admission for a mage to make, particularly this one.

Tell me, Kelvin.

Again Kelvin's expression changed, though the blazing blue light from his eyes made it hard to decipher that expression exactly.

She's… No. It's not possible.

Donal would have sighed, if he were still a redblood and this conversation were verbal instead of mental, and proceeding at everyday speed.

What is it, Mage?

The blue light from those eyes shone even brighter.

She's trying to split the composite apart.

It sort of made sense, but Donal needed more than that.

Split how?

Then Kelvin answered in a way that anyone could understand.

She's trying to split the Draxoleth from Kandroknar, to cut the composite asunder.

Now Donal understood the words, but that was all.

None of this seemed possible.

Helena? Donal tried to look at her, at Professor Helena Steele, but the light surrounding her was incandescent, forcing him to squeeze his eyes shut.

I think… A pause, then Kelvin's thought continued. *Thanatos, I think she's doing it.*

Now white nova light, centred on Helena, flared up.

Blazing.

Incandescent.

Filling the cellar.

Looking bright enough to fill the world.

FIFTY-FOUR

They met: the Helena-led network of over two thousand mages versus the composite formed of a singleton wraith – currently attempting to bud or spawn a new singleton – plus a mage steeped in the darkest arcana of distant Zurinam.

The wraith bud could never become a duplicate of the original, for the whole point of singletons was that each new individual formed a species unto itself due to radical mutation; and as for the mage, in Zurinam individuals of power walked different paths to those of Mordanto and the other institutions of the Federation and nearby lands.

So many mysteries regarding the deepest nature of the Draxoleth-Kandroknar composite.

But now: confrontation, nothing more.

They clashed, energy-tsunami versus network of minds.

Great powers, smashing together in macroscopic and compactified space, all at once: a cataclysmic explosion-versus-explosion, blazing with colours beyond anything humanity might imagine.

At the deepest level there was unimaginable complexity here, nanoscopic hex configurations – attack spells and coherent matrices of quantally-directed reality waves – building up fractal, near-infinite structures morphing dynamically nine billion times per second, in both the mages' and the composites' attack fronts: an uncountable number of miniature battles raging, but from all that complexity a single emergent property arose: sheer power versus sheer power.

Strength against strength.

Might against might.

Violent intent versus violent intent.

The Draxoleth had fed on vast amounts of power, was drunk with it, while Helena went into the fight with a different kind of knowledge. She had every intention of stopping the Draxoleth's attack – any notion of Alej Kandroknar seemed trivial at this stage, almost irrelevant – with every weapon at her disposal.

And one of those was guile.

Now.

She twisted and formulated and solved equations in ninetieths of a second and cast, with the powers flooding through to her from all of Mordanto's mages, a shearing plane of hex whose leading edge was a razor edged with fractally turbulent frequencies.

It sliced through oncoming resonances with a kind of warrior beauty, and the Draxoleth or its composite tried to bat the razor edge aside, suddenly understanding Helena-plus-network's intention.

But the singleton wraith – or wraiths: the bud was starting to form already – reacted a ninetieth of a second too late and that was that.

Its yell would have toppled buildings had it been composed of ordinary sound, while Helena's soundless shout was one of triumph.

Yes!

She wielded her power – her and all of Mordanto's power – like a throwing axe, one that cut over and over with deadly intent all the time it spun through the air.

Flinging it forward, back along the incoming line of attack.

Done it.

It was riven, that torrent of energy: shearing longitudinally all the way back to its origin in Tempelgard, splitting the ethereal root from its macroscopic body, its human host, the mage known as Alej Kandroknar.

Now it was pure wraith, the enemy.

Split from its human body, after so many years of living conjoined.

I hope that hurts.

But the Draxoleth remained a singleton of vast, titanic power, more angry than ever.

No...

Smashing down upon her.

Raging.

No!

Wanting nothing more than vengeance and the end of Helena Steele.

And all of Mordanto next.

FIFTY-FIVE

Helena held her disembodied position, her projected remote locus of consciousness, the spearpoint of Mordanto's defence, while energies raged and battered her.

She held.

Held on for even longer than she had thought possible.

I must.

Her physical form remained in the cellar beneath her beloved Mordanto, but all of her energy and focus was centred in her remote locus of attention, her transmitted mind in a more than metaphorical sense.

Here, she could act as a conduit for all of Mordanto's combined might against the ongoing onslaught from the Draxoleth and its budding spawn, but she could not last forever.

When she fell, the enemy's advance upon Mordanto would be very fast indeed.

Kelvin.

Such a find, her protégé.

All of the mages were projecting their power through Kelvin as their hub, and him to her, Helena, in turn.

I am so very proud of you.

But even Kelvin would not be able to react fast enough once she fell: to reconfigure the Mordanto defences and continue the fight against the incoming wrath of the Draxoleth.

Not when the Draxoleth was filled with new power gained from consuming so many helpless wraiths… No, not even Kelvin could manage that.

Not even if Helena's brother Lamis were here to help him, and things had not worked out that way – so many wrong turns – but never mind that now.

Life happens the way it happens.

So this is it.

So magnificent, the power and intellect of all the mages she was privileged to serve.

Such truly meaningful years.

Absolutely wonderful.

Then she formed her final instruction.

Her last command, and it had to be obeyed.

"Everything through me. Now. Every ounce of energy you've got."

The words *get* and *got* were seen as vulgar in her schooldays, the lazy person's verb, and it was ironic that *got* should be her final word ever, the last of her life, but so it was.

That was that, and this was it: the end.

She felt the sorrow of Kelvin along with the blast of transmitted friendly power rising up inside her.

Thank you.

In her remote locus, effectively her true self, the power expanded in an instant, a growing cloud of fire.

Thank you all so much.

Huge and burning, filled with might.

Thank y—

Her universe blew apart.

And the last thing she knew was this…

I'm dying, but not alone.

She was done for, but so was the Draxoleth, screaming as it died, along with its budding spawn that never had a chance to be born, but that was just too bad.

Taking the enemy with her into dissolution: into nothingness.

And that was that.

Done.

The end of everything that once was Helena Steele.

FIFTY-SIX

In the cellar, the blazing whiteness surrounding the form of Helena Steele suddenly winked out of existence and the walking-cane she'd been holding was dropping to the floor while Helena herself was toppling and Donal reacted faster than thought.

She was in his arms before her head could hit the stone floor.

The cane clattered as it struck a flagstone and lay there.

"Oh, no," said Donal.

It didn't take a zombie's sensory acuity to recognise a corpse.

She felt so light in his arms.

Then Mel and Viktor were moving, and Donal looked up to see what they were up to and it was much as he had done: all nine of the combat mages and the young woman, Gina, were slumping to the floor, their eyes no longer shining with blue light, but they weren't dropping like bundles of sticks, like marionettes whose strings had been severed: some kind of muscle tension remained.

A good sign: unconsciousness doesn't look like death, and these mages were collapsing in something akin to a faint, which wouldn't help if the enemy fell upon Mordanto in the next few seconds.

Clearly, they could no longer defend anyone.

Some fell before Mel or Viktor could reach them, but others were caught in time to at least control their slump to the flagstones.

All around, the shadows seemed to lift from the chamber, as if something had caused the glowmoths to shine more brightly than normal. A faint herbal scent accompanied that brightening.

It didn't make sense to Donal, but then today had been insane pretty much from the start.

Martina said: "My conduit is empty."

That sounded like some sort of wisecrack or off-colour joke, but no one was in a laughing mood, and Kelvin said: "It's gone. The Draxoleth is dead."

Donal had scarcely realised that Kelvin was still standing.

"You're sure?" Donal spoke while still holding Helena, or the thing that once was Helena Steele, in his arms.

He lowered her body to the floor, carefully, and then stood up.

Kelvin's face appeared lined, his shaven scalp shiny with sweat, and his dark blue robe with the black embroidery looked rumpled, but his stance remained upright.

Ramrod-straight, the way Helena Steele had always stood in life.

No blue light shining in Kelvin's eyes now: they were back to something like normal, albeit with a sorrowful strength that was new and possibly permanent.

"She detonated her remote self," said Kelvin. "That's as near as I can explain it."

Both he and the absent Lamis could lapse into technical jargon at any time, but this seemed clear, and Donal almost wished it wasn't, that he didn't understand the manner of Helena's voluntary death.

Helena, mother to Laura, also dead.

"Mordanto is safe," said Donal.

"Yes."

So she had won, this strong, courageous old lady, sacrificing herself for the sake of the people she nominally commanded but in the end served, giving up everything she had.

"Single-handed," said Donal.

"Well, no." Kelvin paused, then: "She became a channel for all of us, for all of our power. I mean everyone in Mordanto."

"That's a lot of mages."

"Two thousand and ninety-seven, my friend."

Donal let out a long breath, almost as if he were a redblood once more. Things had been fraught between him and Kelvin for a while; now it looked as if all that were behind them.

"So they're dead," said Donal. "Kandroknar and this wraith that possessed him or whatever."

Martina had said something about a singleton wraith, whatever that was.

Now, Martina shook her head, but it was Kelvin who answered: "Professor Steele severed the composite apart. She defeated the wraith, but the mage Kandroknar would not have been affected by the… let's call it an explosion. The final detonation."

Donal felt his own expression harden into stone. "Where is he then, old Kandroknar?"

Mel looked up from the mages she'd been helping. "Unfinished business, my love?"

"Yeah."

"Then do it."

"Right."

No doubt: Mel was the woman for him.

Kelvin said: "I can't manage a portal to his location."

It occurred to Donal that maybe most of the mages in Mordanto had collapsed in exhaustion or whatever – perhaps some had even died, for they weren't all combat mages – after transmitting all their energies to Helena in what Kelvin had called a final detonation.

Maybe it was a tour de force of some kind that Kelvin was still able to stand and talk more or less normally.

Not just that: he was walking up to Martina, his expression turning gentle, and lowering his voice to match.

"I beg your pardon," he told her. "I would like to transmit a portion of matter along your conduit."

"Sir?" Her tone sounded small, subdued, yet somehow less fraught than ever before.

Kelvin pointed to the still-gaping cavity in her abdomen, and the amber call crystal that remained in place inside her.

"I want to send that crystal to the other end," he said.

"Oh."

"Do you mind?"

"I…"

"Once it's done, I can collapse the conduit. Take it away from you forever."

"Sir, please. I would like that very much."

"It may hurt, but not for long."

Martina shook her head. "That truly doesn't matter."

"Then brace yourself, my dear."

Kelvin formed conjuration mudras, one hand above the other, and the air cracked and smelled suddenly of ozone as blue light blazed inside her abdomen.

At that, Martina flung her head back, mouth open as if yelling but entirely in silence, and then she tipped her head forward as the light inside her went out.

The cavity in her abdomen was empty now.

"It's gone," said Martina. "The conduit… Thank you, sir."

"You're welcome," said Kelvin. "And you don't need to call me sir all the time."

"I… Yes."

"Good. Thank you for allowing that."

Viktor was on his feet, watching, and Mel also stood up. The combat mages were all arranged on the floor in what looked like sleeping positions, safe enough for now. The young woman, Gina, had tears on her cheeks but her eyes remained shut.

Kelvin stood in front of Donal, with a call crystal in his hand.

"Sleight of hand?" said Donal.

"This isn't the crystal that was inside her." Kelvin nodded towards Martina. "This is the counterpart crystal, the one Klaudius wore. Your Mel brought it here, which is how we found you and Martina."

Mel grinned. "I did good, didn't I?"

"You helped to save us all," said Kelvin, and looked at Martina once more. "As did you. If you'd kept the crystal sealed up inside you, I'd never have been able to sense it."

"Well done," Donal told Martina, then looked at Mel. "And I'm proud of you, like you wouldn't believe."

Sapphire sparks brightened inside the amber crystal that Kelvin was holding. "You've used trackers and homing crystals before?"

"Sure," said Donal.

"This one will lead you to its mate, the crystal it's paired to."

Donal looked at Martina, who nodded. Her abdominal cavity was sealing up, which looked kind of interesting, but Donal returned his attention to Kelvin.

Accepting the crystal, Donal said: "You think that's where Kandroknar is? With the other crystal?"

"Yes," said Kelvin. "But I also know it's somewhere around Tempelgard Airport, which means Kandroknar might not remain in that vicinity for long."

"Catching a plane, after all this? You have to be kidding."

Nevertheless, Donal looped the chain over his head, letting the crystal rest against his tie: not exactly a fashionable look, but this wasn't the time to care about trivia.

"Kandroknar can't carry on living a quiet life hidden in Tristopolis," said Kelvin. "Not after everything he's done today."

"Ah."

"I can't portal you all the way to Tempelgard," said Kelvin. "Not after everything we… Well, never mind. But I can get you to the outer gates, where I gather you have transport waiting."

Donal felt a smile growing on his face. The Triumphant, faithful and loyal, was standing where he'd left it, by the sound of things.

"It's still quite a distance to Tempelgard," he said.

Then he felt stupid, since that was exactly the reason Kelvin couldn't transport him there directly via portal.

"Maybe I can do something about that," said Kelvin, before looking at Viktor. "Sorry, Sergeant Harman. I can only manage one person through the portal."

Viktor nodded, face hard.

"I've run out of ammo." At some point Donal had reholstered the empty Magnus beneath his left armpit. "But if Kandroknar's as wiped out as you are, Mage Kelvin, then maybe it won't matter."

There was a slick sound as Viktor shrugged his way out of his long leather coat and let it drop to the flagstones. Then he wriggled out of his elaborate shoulder harness and held it out, with both holstered Grauser machine pistols dangling, offering them to Donal.

"You're kidding," said Donal.

"Take them. Make good use of them."

Donal nodded. "I will."

He grabbed hold of the harness in his left fist: no time to put the thing on, not now.

"Ready?" said Kelvin.

"I am." Donal looked at Mel, and she looked back. "For anything."

"That I can believe," said Kelvin.

He raised both hands.

And the sapphire fire came, blazing blue, surrounding Donal.

Enveloping him.

Kandroknar.

Falling through a maelstrom of shining blue, and it had happened a few times before but you could never get used to this: never, ever.

I'm coming for you.

Then he fell out onto knucklebone gravel that scrunched beneath him as he straightened up, the twin holstered Grausers dangling from his left fist.

Good.

He was inside the great black iron gates, but they stood wide open, and his black-scaled Triumphant was there, already rumbling into life, silver headlight shining.

Outside, on the otherwise empty road, a triangular formation of grey bone motorcycles swept into view, each grey-clad rider with a bone helmet like a horizontal teardrop pointed at the rear, while each bike glowed with three slitted green headlights, and three narrow barrels pointed forward like lances: machine guns loaded with hex-impregnated spell-piercing rounds.

Helway Riders.

Fifteen of them in all.

This was going to be interesting.

Time to get Kandroknar.

Now.

FIFTY-SEVEN

This time it truly was a hellride, roaring ahead, right through the crowded streets of Tristopolis, which should have been impossible but things were very different today.

Donal-and-Triumphant thundered forward with a trio of Helway Riders ahead of them like an arrowhead, while two others rode as outliers and the rest followed like the shaft of an arrow as near as Donal, crouched over the black-scaled fuel tank, could tell.

No time for looking back at this speed.

Slipstream battered his face and he didn't care at all.

Come on.

Traffic was at a standstill – cars and vans all unmoving, on the cross-streets as well as the route they were thundering along – and Donal had no idea how Kelvin had managed this but it wasn't happening by accident: traffic signals shone red in all directions at every intersection.

Watch out.

An idiot pedestrian – no, a driver who'd decided to get out of his car and investigate – fell back with a yell as one of the Helway Riders nearly hit him or perhaps actually struck the idiot but not in a way that affected the Rider so right now that seemed entirely okay.

The Triumphant was all heart: matching speed with superior bikes like these, pushing very hard indeed.

Faster now.

Another oddity: over every third intersection or so, a scanbat hung in place, hovering some seven yards above the roadway, far lower than usual, which looked almost as strange as the fact that it was just hanging there instead of smoothly moving through the air.

Call it a signal to the populace that something odd was going on and the authorities were involved.

Meaning: get out of the Helway Riders' way.

We're making amazing time.

If Kandroknar had been possessed by – no, conjoined with, whatever that really meant – some vastly powerful kind of wraith for many years, then maybe being split from the wraith formed a kind of trauma, one that would knock him to the floor and need time to recover from; but you couldn't count on that.

A fleeting thought: maybe without the wraith, Kandroknar's personality would change, and he might even be a nice guy.

Is that possible?

It didn't seem likely.

Donal leaned even further forward, chest towards the fuel tank, the crystal hanging from his neck and the Grausers' harness wrapped around the back of his neck, not fastened properly, but one Grauser hung beneath each armpit and they weren't going anywhere.

He kept his eyes squinted almost shut against the slipstream – he really should have had goggles but this wasn't a time for checking every box and getting every detail right – and reminded himself that he was a PI by law and previously a police officer, and no longer in the Army, not for a long time now.

Shoot to kill wasn't in his job description.

Engage with and destroy the enemy.

Once upon a time, yes: back in his Army days, that actually *had* described his professional responsibilities.

Faster.

The bikes ahead were accelerating more and the Triumphant was suffering – Triumphant-and-Donal were hurting together but giving it all they had – and they couldn't keep this up for very long but that wouldn't matter because suddenly, shockingly, they were into clear countryside with darkness to left and right.

Field-like areas surrounded the outer boundaries of the great cleared stretch where Tempelgard Airport stood.

Soon, now.

Faster again, and it shouldn't have been possible but Donal-and-Triumphant were keeping up as the Helway Riders roared through the outer entrances: the bone barriers were pointing straight up like fingers, while security personnel were using aimed shotguns to keep the ordinary car drivers unmoving.

Then they were wheeling onto a vast area of tarmac which led to runways and terminal buildings and hangars everywhere, and the Helway Riders ahead moved to either side and slowed down a fraction.

Donal-and-Triumphant were in the lead now.

Amazing.

Whether it was the motorcycle or the resurrected human who felt filled with pride at leading a formation of Helway Riders, that was hard to tell.

Triumphant-and-Donal took the lead position, keeping a straight heading as they roared across damp tarmac – condensation rather than quicksilver rain – and the crystal hung forward from around Donal's neck and so far the blue sparks remained centred.

He still had the Grausers: they hadn't slipped off.

For another minute they roared on, Helway Riders and Triumphant-and-Donal, then the blue sparks in the crystal shifted to the left and that was the signal: Kandroknar, or at least the location where the attack conduit to Mordanto had started from, had to be in one of those stark buildings, over in that direction.

Hangars, all of them, still a long way away.

Donal-and-Triumphant arced into a wide screeching turn and all fifteen of the Helway Riders followed, then straightened up and roared onwards, shifting very fast, serious as vengeance.

Tempelgard, dark and spread out, occupied a vast amount of land, and they were still some two-thirds of a mile from the hangar complex when suddenly the Helway Riders dropped out of Donal's peripheral vision and he glanced to either side but they'd fallen right back, so he slowed the Triumphant – it felt almost sickening to decelerate – and he came to a stomach-churning halt, turning the bike so he could more easily look back.

All fifteen Helway Riders bikes were stationary, and their formerly green headlights had gone dark: three shadowed slits at the front of each.

Some kind of hex defence.

The lead rider was waving to Donal, and the signal could have meant anything but that didn't matter, because he knew what he had to do.

Time to get Kandroknar.

He patted the black-scaled fuel tank.

"See?" he said. "All their finery, hex gadgets and souped-up sentience and all, and you're stronger and better than they are, in the end."

At least not vulnerable to hex shields aimed at tactical law enforcement vehicles.

The Triumphant purred and rumbled beneath Donal, the vibration transmitted through his upper legs into his entire body.

Kandroknar might have laid down other automated hex defences – in the military, layered defences had been standard for any fortified position, and a mage like Kandroknar would have his own understanding of tactical advantage – but there was no choice in terms of what to do next.

If Kandroknar had a plane ready – and with the wealth he almost certainly possessed, he could afford to own a bunch of private aircraft, never mind chartering just one – then time might be running out, so only a direct head-on approach was available now.

Plus, when the Helway Riders rode through that hex shield or whatever, triggering the defence that powered down their motorbikes, that defence activation might be something Kandroknar could sense, meaning he knew the authorities were almost upon him.

If he really did intend to fly away from here, he'd be speeding up his final preparations, assuming he wasn't already up in the air and gone.

Only one way to find out.

Donal gunned the engine and the Triumphant roared forward.

Accelerating hard, and the blue spark in the crystal shifted slightly.

Third from the left.

He had it now: the exact hangar that Kandroknar had been in when the attack on Mordanto began, and with luck Kandroknar remained inside.

Be there.

It was almost a prayer.

Just be there, Kandroknar, in that hangar.

Roaring onwards.

Fast across the tarmac.

Come on.

Almost there.

The hangar doors had finished sliding open and a plane was pointed at the opening but the propellors weren't moving yet and that was all Donal needed: he and the Triumphant took a curving trajectory into the hangar interior, the screech loud and echoing as he squeezed the bone brake handle and the Triumphant locked down and stinking blue smoke rose from its tyres as it turned sideways into a controlled skid and stopped.

Without needing a command, it snapped its bone parking legs out, allowing Donal to roll off into a standing position, and the crystal sparked brightly because its companion was nearby but that didn't matter now.

Donal tugged hard enough to snap the chain and tossed the crystal to the floor.

The aircraft's nose was raised, its undercarriage beneath the wings being higher than the single wheel beneath the tail, giving it an air of wanting to be off, even with the propellor vanes standing still. There was an open hatch midway along the fuselage, leading to what might have been a cargo hold, and a set of steps had been rolled into place for access.

Kandroknar stood at the foot of the steps.

Perhaps he'd been about to climb up, but with Donal here, his attention was all in this direction, his quizzical smile and grey goatee beard and gentle, twinkling eyes and raised eyebrows all forming a kind of warm welcome on the surface; but the very fact of Kandroknar's appearing relaxed in the present circumstances told a very different story indeed.

Donal strode forward very fast, the dangling Grausers banging against his arms but irrelevant for now.

"My dear chap," said Kandroknar. "How delightful to—"

An electric tinge had been growing in the air, some mage thing that the welcoming words were supposed to distract attention from, but Donal's left fist snapped out almost of its own accord exactly as his left foot stepped forward, an automatic speedy jab, and the follow-up was immediate.

Donal dropped his weight and the straight right's power came all the way from his toes and through the core and horizontally forward into Kandroknar's chest, aiming for the heart, and the mage's eyes widened with shock as he dropped onto his back and lay there, looking up at the hangar ceiling but most likely seeing nothing much at all.

Conscious, but processing only the sudden massive impact that had rocked him.

A door banged open at the rear of the hangar – some kind of office cabin there – and a wide-shouldered man in suit and tie came out with a pistol held high and squeezed the trigger and a shot banged out.

Donal moved to the left and grabbed one of the Grausers and pulled it out of its holster as he went to one knee and fired back: rapid fire and it was hard to control the thing and the first few shots went wide but then blood flowered from two places on the shooter's left leg and the guy dropped, but he wasn't alone.

Three more men sprinted out of the cabin, all of them opening fire as they came out, but Donal was rolling sideways and he fired three more bursts and then a long one, and it was too bad the enemy were using simple automatics because Grausers might be hard to aim but their firepower was something else again, giving Donal the advantage, except that it was too easy to shoot off all your rounds at once.

A click sounded from the Grauser and—

Empty.

—percussive cracks overlaid each other like massive thunder as the enemy fired, all at the same time, and they were good, highly trained—

Watch out.

—but so was Donal and fear accelerated his dodging movement and then he had the second Grauser free of the harness and he pulled the trigger desperately and the first of the enemy toppled back and Donal cut the legs out from another and finally a head shot dropped the third.

There had been four in total, but the wide-shouldered man was chest-down and struggling to crawl across the floor because his weapon had been thrown clear, and his grasping hand almost had the weapon when Donal's rising kick took him in the temple and knocked him back.

A civilised person would stop there but these guys were trained and deadly so Donal followed up by stamping with his other foot directly onto this guy's head and that was it: the enemy was out of it.

All four gunmen were down.

In the hangar space the gunshots had crashed loud enough to deafen temporarily, but a scrape sounded now and Donal whirled, aiming the Grauser at the doorway of the office cabin, but the man who stumbled out had his hands raised and he was shaking and soaked with sweat.

Entirely consumed with fear.

"I'm… My name is Braunkin." His voice trembled. "I'm just in charge of transport. I don't—"

Suddenly, the Grauser in Donal's hand felt hot, burning hot, and all he could do was fling it aside to clatter on the floor, and he felt himself snarling like an animal, but this Braunkin guy wasn't responsible: his eyes had widened, looking past Donal, and then he turned and bolted, heading for a small side exit door.

Donal hadn't even noticed it before.

"Tsk, tsk." The voice sounded amused.

Donal turned, weaponless, to face Kandroknar.

This is bad.

The mage, Alej Kandroknar, was standing upright once more, looking quite recovered, and in his twinkling eyes a kind of polished blackness shimmered and somehow sparkled, which could only mean his mage defences were fully up and no third-of-a-florin gumshoe armed with only fists was going to get near him now.

I've had it.

Maybe it had always been going to end this way.

Perhaps I can keep him talking.

The Helway Riders would be trying to restart their stalled motorbikes or else running this way on foot – maybe some of them were running and the others were working on the bikes – and they were capable specialist cops with all sorts of tactical training so maybe they would stand a better chance than Donal by himself.

Or maybe not: a black glow was beginning to grow around Kandroknar, similar to the projected blackness that squad car strobes emitted, but deeper in quality – somehow – and utterly cold.

Even in this hangar space, Donal could feel this new chill on his face.

"I have wealth, and I will recover nicely." Inside the shimmering blackness, Kandroknar gave another of his whimsical smiles. "Far from here, of course, dear boy."

"Someone will hunt you down," said Donal.

Kandroknar chuckled, as if delighted.

"Mayhap," he said. "Such a nice old word, that. *Mayhap.* It may happen, and if so, I will destroy my pursuers, with great gusto and pleasure, I assure you."

Donal was going to die listening to this facile idiot bandying words.

I'm not just going to stand here.

Even a mage couldn't understand how fast a trained man can move, especially in the most extreme of circumstances, and Donal went for it now, covering a good seventeen feet with one sliding lunging step, closing the distance very fast indeed, with his fist beginning to—

No.

—stop in mid-air as his body froze and his feet were glued to the floor—

I'm done for.

—or seemed to be and the blackness intensified around Kandroknar, and more than that: it rose up above him like a wave about to crash down upon Donal, meaning this was it, the end at last, and there was only time—

Mel. Finbar.

—to think of his family before he died—

I'm sorry.

—and the shimmering blackness fell towards him and there was nothing he could do except let it happen but then another kind of glimmer filled the air between him and the falling blackness, and this was a different kind of thing indeed.

A wraith, rippling with what might have been ethereal wounds, but strong and angry nonetheless.

Having fun all by yourself, dearest Donal?

The paralysis fell away, and Donal felt himself grinning.

"Aggie, you old dear. I'm so very glad to see you."

Blackness and wraith seemed to roil, to wrestle with each other.

Of course you are. While I'm holding the void-hex back, perhaps you'd care to do something about this little squirt? I mean Kandroknar.

The mage's hands were raised and he was swaying from side to side, clearly struggling.

"Got it," said Donal.

This time when he punched, he aimed for the throat.

Yes.

Hooked low to the liver and a low right to the spleen and the blackness disappeared and Kandroknar was tipping forward so Donal helped his head downwards at the same time as whipping his right knee upwards into the face and the impact was nicely hard.

Still, he rammed a downward hook into the back of Kandroknar's neck just to make sure.

The mage smashed face-first onto the hard floor.

That's got to hurt. When he wakes up.

Donal was breathing hard, despite his zombiehood, all attention on Kandroknar because you never could tell with mages, especially one like this.

That was when three grey-clad Helway Riders came running in, handguns at the ready, and they took in the situation very fast, and two kept their weapons aimed on the face-down Kandroknar while the other fastened hex-laden cuffs around Kandroknar's wrists, at the small of his back.

The lock runes shone silver when the cuffs clicked shut.

A minute later, twelve Helway Riders came screeching in on their bikes, along with three riderless motorbikes who came over to their owners before stopping.

Aggie billowed in mid-air, some seven feet above the ground.

I was trapped in Cataclysm Chasm, but suddenly all the hex just vanished.

Donal looked up at her. "That'll be the mages at Mordanto. They took out the wraith that Kandroknar was combined with, or something."

You mean the Draxoleth.

"Yeah, that's the one."

Aggie continued to hover there.

I'm surprised the mages defeated it. Even Mordanto mages.

"It cost them," said Donal. "It cost them a lot."

Ah.

The Helway Riders took up position all around the hangar, some checking the office cabin and going up inside the parked aircraft, which was filled with cargo but turned out to be entirely uncrewed.

Shortly after that, a bemused flight crew disembarked from an airport car just outside the hangar, just as what seemed like dozens of emergency vehicles converged on the same spot, coming from all over Tempelgard Airport.

Black lights strobed all over the place, like some kind of mad celebration party, but no one was cheering or laughing.

No one truly relaxed until a van full of federal spellbinders turned up, their eyes unreadable behind the usual tactical shades, ready to take Kandroknar into the kind of custody nobody – not even the most powerful of mages from Surinam (or Zurinam, whichever) – could dream of escaping from.

So we've done it.

Donal grinned up at Aggie. "I guess we have."

Then he walked over to the Triumphant, and patted it and gave the fuel tank a hug, while several of the Helway Riders came over to add their congratulations, to human and motorbike alike.

Finally, they were done.

Time to go home, via Mordanto. Aggie was already sinking down into the solid ground, disappearing, no doubt intending to make her way at a leisurely speed to Avenue of the Basilisks.

"You up to carrying a pillion passenger?" he asked the Triumphant.

It purred.

Do you understand I'm talking about Mel?

He thought perhaps it did.

Some people can go through their entire lives being underestimated by the people around them. Perhaps that applied to motorcycles too.

"Time to go," he said.

And swung his leg over the saddle.

The parking-legs retracted.

"Later," he told the Helway Riders nearby.

They exchanged fingertip salutes.

A lot of people were going to want to talk to him for a long time, all with after-action reports they needed to fill in, but that was their bureaucratic problem, not his.

Donal and Triumphant headed slowly for the hangar exit.

No need to rush.

Not now.

FIFTY-EIGHT

When the limo turned up at the corner of 11507th and Krankway, it came exactly as Talon had ordered: with Rilena at the wheel, and the muscular Balagron next to her. It had taken a while, since the traffic had jammed up again, even more than before, and it took an age before everything started moving once more.

The tall mage, Lamis, with the ruined eyes sort of like Rilena's, stood on the corner next to Talon, keeping watch, giving every indication he was on Talon's side, so okay: he might prove useful again.

What was it with mages and witches and their eyes, though?

Also, as per instructions, two more cars followed the approaching limo, one with Axe – Talon's ever-dependable lieutenant – sitting in the rear, the other filled with armed street soldiers.

Not that Axelson wasn't formidable in his own right, should anything nasty occur.

I'm probably safe for now.

But that wasn't the same as one hundred percent certainty, hence the extra protection. For one thing, one of the other organisations might have decided to make a move on him, if they'd picked up some hint that he was experiencing trouble.

Huh. Trouble.

If only they knew the torture he'd been through… but that didn't matter, did it?

Susan. Dear Susan.

He needed to get home to his girl, his daughter who'd put that Donal Riordan on his tail, and while Riordan was some kind of wise guy, he could certainly handle himself. Talon might never have made it out of that Death-damned labyrinth if it hadn't been for the guy, so okay: that was that.

Whatever Susan had promised Riordan, Talon might even add a bonus on top.

Here we go.

The limo stopped at the kerb, with the other two cars halting where they were, blocking traffic.

Nobody honked their horns, either because they understood what kind of people used limos that rode low on their wheels due to the weight of the armour, or because they took one look at Lamis beside Talon and understood that patience was in order here.

Still, the street looked normal, the usual canyon of buildings beneath a deep purple sky, traffic fumes, pedestrians going in and out of shops: just another day in the city for the ordinary citizens.

Schmucks, the lot of them, but who cared?

Rilena cracked her door open, about to get out and hold the rear door open for Talon to climb inside, but he waved her back and opened the rear door himself.

"Perhaps," said Mage Lamis, "I should accompany you."

Talon looked into the scarred, ruined pits where a normal person would have eyes. "Yeah, maybe you should."

Riordan wasn't around, but this Mage Lamis seemed to be friends with Riordan. It would be good if there were somebody able to tell Riordan how this all worked out in the end.

Talon climbed into the back, and slid across so Lamis could join him.

Soon enough, they were on the move, with Rilena driving carefully, and Balagron sitting silently beside her, which was vastly different from his normal talkative self.

Maybe he knows what's about to happen.

You had to expect a certain amount of camaraderie between people who worked together for a long time: maybe that was it. Or maybe it was just Mage Lamis being here, because you don't ever discuss business in front of outsiders, and Balagron knew that as well as anybody.

Look at the width of that neck, the mass of those shoulders. The shaven blue scalp just added to the appearance of muscle mass. Maybe Balagron should be the one to—

No.

There had been a time when Talon had carried out all his violence in person, and even now, those who worked for him needed the occasional reminder that his power didn't just reside in his ability to give orders that had to be obeyed: he was still a force to be reckoned with, simply as a physical man.

All that pain…

No. Forget that.

Forget the wraith tendrils entering him, slithering inside, bringing so much—

Stop. It's done.

Beating someone to death with his fists would help to deal with the memory of torture, just as his whole career had formed a way to forget the horrors of his childhood, so forget that, forget it all.

Focus on the beetlewax smell of the polished pterahide upholstery, the luxury of the limo that was the least of the rewards he had earned for himself over the years, always working hard.

Always.

The last few miles passed almost in a pleasant trance, until the car turned into a yawning entrance and dipped, slowing as it descended the shadow-shrouded ramp, and tyres squealed softly as the two escort cars followed them in their descent.

Two levels below ground, they came out into the parking garage that could hold hundreds of cars but contained only a handful, all of them his. The pillars looked as if they belonged in a temple, and their classiness was one of the reasons he'd chosen this building in the first place.

The knot-and-blade pattern carved into them was archaic but could have served nicely as his personal emblem, if he needed such a thing.

"Here we are," he said, as Rilena stopped the limo. "Home sweet home. Everybody out."

A minute later, they were standing in the middle of a lane in the near-deserted parking garage, the whole place warmly lit by flamewraiths, having halted halfway through walking to the exit doors.

Because Talon had told them to do just that.

Everyone stood silent.

Waiting for me.

That was good.

All of them not knowing what to expect next.

Rilena stood between Balagron on the one side – his earring with the miniature sprites inside glowed a brighter green than usual, or maybe it just looked that way because of how the shadows fell here – and Axelson, the Axe, on the other.

Axe's lumpy face looked like stone, the deathblossom in his lapel looked fresh, and his polished skull cufflinks looked spiffy as ever. He looked like someone who'd done his level best to keep the organisation running in his boss's absence... or like someone trying to convey that impression now.

I'll take a careful look before deciding.

You got information from a variety of sources, asked a bunch of different folk, and you could kind of triangulate on the truth. For now, give Axe the benefit of the doubt.

Nobody shoulda been able to snatch me.

That had been obvious from the start.

The street soldiers and Mage Lamis stood off to the right. For a second, Talon considered asking the mage to leave, but no, Mage Lamis wouldn't interfere if he knew what was good for him.

"You." Talon pointed to the nearest soldier. "Your weapon. Give it to me."

"Sure, boss."

It was an Illurian model, a Gladius of some kind and nothing Talon would have carried himself, but no matter: he took the automatic off the guy, racked the slide, and brought the gun up.

The street soldier back away, swallowing.

Fear is good.

Then Talon swivelled, aiming the automatic straight between the traitor's eyes… or where her eyes would have been if they hadn't got burned out years ago, somehow.

The witch never did give him the whole story.

"Rilena," he said. "I'm going to kill you here, but I'm going to tell Susan you just resigned and left, because I know she likes you."

Rilena's mouth opened, but she had nothing to say.

"I really don't like traitors," added Talon. "I'm going to enjoy—"

His hand was empty.

What the Hades?

From his right came the sound of someone clearing his throat. Mage Lamis was there, holding the automatic by its barrel, and shaking his head.

In his deep voice, Mage Lamis said: "It was not the witch who betrayed you, Talon."

Anger rose up inside, but Talon forced it back down.

How do you know, Mage?

But the answer was in the question: this was a mage, simple as that.

"Someone did," he said.

Mage Lamis pointed with his free hand. "That one."

Talon followed the gesture.

"Balagron. You?"

The big man swallowed. "I don't… know."

Balagron looked guilty but confused.

You're going to die.

Then the green-glowing earrings glowed brighter and brighter, and Balagron stumbled but Rilena moved fast, both hands snaking out, snatching the earrings from his earlobes before tossing them aside to the foot of a carved pillar, where they continued to burn with emerald flames.

"Ensorcelled," said Mage Lamis. "A very obscure kind of wraith technique, one that not even a talented witch like Rilena here could detect. But Mr Balagron wasn't the wraiths' real target."

"I bought those earrings in a shop," said Balagron. "It was just an ordinary shop."

Blood dripped from his torn earlobes, but he didn't seem to notice.

"You were being observed, I should think," said Mage Lamis. "Someone took great care to have those sprites set up the way they were. They eavesdropped on you, in effect."

Wraiths.

All those tendrils…

A door crashed open, and there she was, framed in light: his Susan, her cowl and carapace and six arms and everything just perfect.

"Daddy?" she said.

Then everything froze into a tableau, and Talon could not even move his eyes, but words that were not sound rumbled in his head, and he knew they came from Lamis, the mage.

Retire, and take care of your daughter.

It could almost have been his own thought, but he knew for sure it wasn't.

Do that, and you will live.

Still, Talon couldn't turn his neck or blink or do anything at all, and no one else was moving either. Were they paralysed, or was this simply happening in some kind of accelerated time?

Maybe it didn't matter either way.

You have a choice, Talon.

There were always choices, yes. And there was Susan, his perfect girl – so different, so unique, but perfectly herself – who needed her father, even if he didn't deserve to be needed by her.

Choose the right path, or die. Here and now.

Sapphire blue blazed from somewhere on the right, and then the paralysis or stasis was removed and everyone was in motion once more and he himself could move.

"Oh, Daddy," said Susan.

Rilena and Balagron and Axe and the street soldiers were all looking at him, waiting to see what he would do. No sign of Mage Lamis, though: he was simply gone.

Maybe that was no surprise.

Time for me to choose.

Except, no: he'd already chosen, and that was why Mage Lamis had disappeared.

Tears blurred Talon's eyes, even though Axe and his street soldiers were watching, which meant things could never be the same again. Command presence, once lost, can never be regained; but that no longer mattered.

Sobbing, Konrad Talon ran towards his daughter.

FIFTY-NINE

It was late, well into the hours when most people slept, and Ingrid and Mel were both wide awake having drunk too much coffee and helebore tea, sitting on the couch in the modest apartment living-room, in what had once been the temple presbytery.

Donal, from his favourite armchair, smiled.

Finbar was asleep, and a faint aura of protective hex glowed over his cot which they'd moved in here from the bedroom, and everything felt good.

"You've had one Hades of a day," said Ingrid finally. "But I need to love you and leave you, meaning it's time for me to go home."

"Or you could stay here," Donal told her. "The couch is comfy."

"And I can use it," said Mel. "You can have the bed, Ingrid."

Resurrected humans don't sleep, so Donal didn't feature in these calculations.

"I prefer my own bed," said Ingrid, "but thanks for the offer."

She rose and leaned from side to side, stretching her back.

"I'll take a stroll to the phone box on the corner," said Donal, "and ring for a taxi."

But Ingrid tapped the bulbous ring she wore on her right hand, with its violet-and-white knuckle-sized orb held in a claw-shaped setting. "No need. I've already called for one. It's about a minute away."

"Bleeding Hades." Donal shook his head. "Whatever next?"

Mel laughed as she stood up from the couch. "Come on, Ingrid. We'll see you out."

They checked on baby Finbar, but of course he was safe. Donal led the way out to the greater space of the boxing gym, barely lit at this hour, spacious and shadowed, with the heavy bags hanging there, the sparring ring waiting to be used, all of it comforting.

His home.

As Mel and Ingrid continued to the back door, chatting away, Donal stopped at one of the bags, remembering the frosty hand-shaped imprint that Klaudius had left on it only yesterday, although it felt like the distant past.

"Thanatos," he said.

Mel and Ingrid stopped and looked back at him.

"What is it?" said Mel.

Donal blew out a breath. "All the things we got up to, there's still some unfinished business, because Klaudius asked me to do him a favour."

"You're kidding," said Mel. "He didn't say anything to me about that, down in the Caverns."

"Because you were having such a long carefree chat."

"Well, yeah. Meaning no. It really wasn't a chatty kind of situation."

Donal looked at the heavy leather bag once more.

"It's about Hellah," he said, not sure about sharing this but feeling he had to, all the same.

"Hellah?" said Ingrid.

Her tone of voice was hard to read, but there was some kind of respect in there as well as fear, and it was an ongoing sadness in Donal's life that everyone else was scared of his friends, the Guardians.

"Yeah, she—" Donal stopped.

A fizzing sounded in the air, and silver sparks were coming from a location about level with his chest, maybe seven feet away.

"Everyone stand back." Ingrid was raising her hands. "I'm going to… No."

She lowered her hands once more.

"What is it?" said Mel.

"I think Donal should be careful what he says," said Ingrid. "Although talking about a Guardian doesn't usually cause one to appear, just like that."

"What?" said Mel.

But for some reason, Donal didn't feel surprised at all as the silver sparks grew and widened until they framed a fizzing opening about a yard in diameter, hanging there disembodied, and inside it a scene appeared.

A smell of sulphur wafted out as well.

And in the foreground, a smiling face, her skin the exact shade of red of freshly spilled blood, her eyes filled with the heptagonal orange fires that were her irises, and she was looking great.

"Hellah." Donal smiled at her.

Dark blue flames and drifting streamers of white formed the background, but he couldn't make out any details.

"Hey, Donal. I need you to pass on a message to my brother, okay?"

"Sure," he told her. "You know I will."

"I'm on Crepuscula, which means I'll be away for a while. He'll know what that means."

"Huh," said Donal. "Crepuscula. Is that some sort of medication?"

"Only you would come up with that."

"Sounds like a laxative to me."

In the silver sparkling frame, Hellah laughed. "There might be something in my tummy, at least the way you'd explain the facts of life to a child. It's too soon to be sure, so I shouldn't say anything, but I've got a feeling, you know?"

There were gasps from Mel and Ingrid, possibly as much from the fact that Hellah was sharing this news with Donal as much as the news itself.

"Hey," said Donal. "That's brilliant."

"Thanks, my friend. It's also not quite the same as you and Mel producing Finbar, you know?"

Donal glanced at Mel, then looked through the silver sparking frame into Hellah's burning orange eyes. "I'm sure it's only details."

Hellah, pregnant. What wonderful news.

"Maybe." Hellah smiled inside the silvery portal-like frame. "The head of Mordanto is going to be in charge of childcare."

That made Donal pause.

"Um, listen," he said. "There's been a few things happening in—"

Somewhere behind Hellah, a column of white and blue flames shot up, and a strange kind of warbling filled the air.

"Sorry," said Hellah. "Got to go. Bye."

She blew him a kiss.

Then the frame winked out of existence.

"—Mordanto," finished Donal.

Silence reigned in the shadowed gym for the best part of a minute. Finally, a soft knock sounded on the end door.

"My taxi," said Ingrid.

"Yeah," said Donal.

Mel gave Ingrid a hug. "Thank you again for guarding Finbar."

"Any time."

Ingrid went to the door, opened it, said something to the waiting driver, then looked back at Mel and Donal. "You know what? Since meeting you two, my life has been anything but boring."

"Uh-huh," said Donal. "Do you mean that in a good way or a bad way?"

"Of course," said Ingrid.

She smiled and left, closing the door behind her.

"That told you," said Mel.

"Yeah."

Donal took hold of her, and kissed her.

"You okay?" he said.

"Of course. You going to check on the Triumphant yet again?"

Donal looked in the direction of the corridor where the bike was standing, now draped with what had been an embroidered tablecloth. "Probably."

"Do that. Finbar and I will be waiting for you."

Mel headed for the ex-presbytery living-room.

All around, the empty gym went back to being its usual self, comforting in a way Donal could never have put into words.

Ingrid's right. No boredom around here.

Then he grinned at nobody and nothing at all.

This was his life.

And everything was fine.

ABOUT THE AUTHOR

John Meaney writes thrillers, science fiction and fantasy. He has won the IPPY Award and been a finalist for the Locus Award, and for the BSFA Award multiple times. He has several series in progress.

His contemporary cyber thriller series features spec-ops cyber specialist Case and his fierce partner Kat, operating in the interzone between physical action and digital tech.

On The Brink is the first in a new series set in the 1950s and featuring schoolteacher-turned-spy Paul Reynolds.

Near-future thrillers feature Josh Cumberland, an ex-special forces cyber specialist driven by family tragedy, in a near-future Britain wracked by climate change, a legalized knife culture and political corruption.

The Donal Riordan novels feature a detective in the city of Tristopolis, where the sky is perpetually dark purple, and the bones of the dead are fuel for the reactor piles.

The seven Pilots novels include the epic Ragnarok trilogy, which begins with alien influences on humans at the dawn of the Viking era, covers the birth of the digital age at Bletchley Park, and concludes with a galaxy-spanning conflict, a million years from now.

Outside the world of writing, Meaney is a lifelong martial artist, a computer consultant with degrees from the Open University and Oxford, and a trained hypnotist.

Visit John at www.johnmeaney.com for the latest news.